THE INTERN

THE INTERN

Michele Campbell

ST. MARTIN'S PRESS
NEW YORK

First published in the United States by St. Martin's Press, an imprint of St. Martin's Publishing Group

THE INTERN. Copyright © 2023 by Michele Rebecca Martinez Campbell. All rights reserved. Printed in the United States of America. For information, address St. Martin's Publishing Group, 120 Broadway, New York, NY 10271.

ISBN 9781250274977

For Will

Part One

Madison

1

....

She loved the way her professor moved. The swish of auburn hair. The grace of her gestures. The nervous energy as she paced behind the podium. Madison had admired Kathryn Conroy since she'd heard her speak at a high school career day years before. A thousand times, she'd imagined herself following in Conroy's footsteps. Having a career like hers. Starting out as a crusading prosecutor, taking on the mob, the drug cartels. Holding press conferences, appearing on TV, looking amazing doing it. Then getting appointed to the bench, presiding over high-profile cases, writing opinions that were read across the land. Becoming so renowned that she'd be invited back to teach, with students hanging spellbound on her every word the way she did with Conroy now. Such a future was within the realm of possibility for Madison. She was one of the stars of her year. Top grades. Law review. A summer clerkship at one of the most prestigious law firms in Boston. On top of that, the special sparkle that came from her looks, her way with words, her confidence in the face of a challenge. Call it charisma, whatever—she had it. Coming out of Harvard Law, her opportunities were limitless.

Correction. *Should be* limitless. But there was a crack in the perfect facade, which came from her past. The fault lines were threatening everything she'd built. She worried that . . .

"*Miss Rivera.*"

Shit. She'd tuned out for a split second, and now Conroy was staring at her from the lectern with a finger on the seating chart. She had no idea what the question was. There was nothing for it but to admit that and brazen it out.

"I apologize, Professor, but could you repeat the question?" she said, sitting up straight, her voice ringing out across the staggered rows of the classroom.

People turned to take notice when Madison spoke, just as they did with Conroy. If she flubbed now, it would be with all eyes on her, including those of the professor she idolized. Judge Conroy crooked a delicate eyebrow, making a note before replying. That was class participation points lost, but she was positive she could recoup them once she knew the question.

"How did the Gates case change the search warrant process?"

Madison could answer that. She could answer anything, really. It wasn't just talent, but hard, slogging work. She did the reading every night, briefed the cases, wrote out answers to every possible question. She met the judge's eyes like they were equals and launched into a detailed reply. From there, the class devolved into a Madison-and-Conroy show. They parried hypotheticals back and forth, refined the principle, even made a couple of nerdy law jokes. By the time the judge glanced at her watch and called time, she'd redeemed herself in Conroy's eyes and cemented her position as the whiz kid who never missed. Classmates on either side high-fived her as they got up to leave.

Now the race was on for face time with Conroy. Madison was in the middle of a row, locked in as her classmates took their time shutting their laptops, putting on coats, gathering their things. *Frustrating.* She wanted to capitalize on her ace performance by doing a little networking. Thanking Conroy for the great class, asking a few follow-ups. That was just smart. Maybe she could parlay today's exchange in class to an invitation to office hours, even coffee. She got on the end of the line, rehearsing in her mind what she'd say, feeling more nervous than she should. Since the beginning of the semester, she'd been meaning to bring up the fact that they'd attended the same high school, that she'd heard Conroy speak years before, that it had influenced her path. She just couldn't figure out how to drop that into a conversation around the lectern without seeming gushy. It was so personal.

The minutes ticked by as the students ahead of her monopolized the judge's attention, just as she'd monopolized it in class. This was Harvard Law, and fair was fair. You had to fight for every inch of turf. The prof for the next class showed up and everybody scattered. Judge Conroy was pulling on her plaid trench coat, about to depart. Then she looked at Madison and smiled.

"Miss Rivera. Wait a minute. I hope I didn't embarrass you, cold-calling you before."

"Not at all. You have to keep us on our toes, right?"

"Exactly. And you recovered admirably. I was impressed."

Madison blushed. "Thank you."

The judge hesitated, then seemed to decide something.

"I don't know if this would fit your schedule, but I just had an internship position open up in my chambers unexpectedly. Normally, you have to apply a year in advance, but I need someone right away. I'd like you to apply."

"For an internship—with *you*?"

"Yes. Are you interested?"

Of course she was. An internship with Conroy would be a dream come true, not to mention a gold star on her résumé. And Madison adored gold stars. The timing *was* tricky, though. What were the chances that, if she went through an application process right now, Conroy would find out about her younger brother's legal troubles? That would be embarrassing. And definitely something she'd prefer Conroy not know about her.

The pause as she considered the question lasted longer than she'd intended.

"Well," Conroy prompted. "Yes or no?"

The opportunity was just too good to pass up.

"I'm flattered to be asked, Judge Conroy. I would *love* to apply."

"Good. Get in touch with my chambers, and they'll give you the specifics. I look forward to interviewing you."

As Conroy walked out the door, Madison's phone buzzed in her pocket, and her smile faded. There were several missed calls from her mother. And one text. More bad news, it read.

2

....

She was gathering her things when Ty Evans came up to her. They'd been the power couple of their year until she broke things off last spring. He was a former Stanford tight end, handsome and charismatic, reigning moot court champ, on the short list for law review president. A job she wanted for herself and planned to get. Trouble was, everything Ty did, Madison did, too, just as well if not better. And that didn't make for a smooth relationship. Harvard Law was the sort of place where people would knock down their grandmother to get ahead. Was it any wonder that competition broke them up?

She shoved the phone in her coat pocket so he wouldn't see her mother's text, forcing a smile.

"Sucking up to the prof, I see," he teased.

"Jealous much, Ty?"

"What do I have to be jealous of? She loves me best."

"Right. Who doesn't?"

He laughed. "You know it. What were you two talking about just now?"

"A follow-up about the Gates case."

She didn't want news getting out about the internship, especially not to Ty. He'd apply, and out of the entire second-year class, he was her biggest competition.

"Huh. It looked like more than that."

Madison shrugged, dropping the subject. Ty blocked for her as they fought the tide of remaining students flooding through the doors for the next class. Crossing the atrium, he started talking about the latest political battle on law review, but she could barely pay attention. Her hand was sweaty in her pocket, clutching her phone. She had to get rid of him and call Mom, to find out the latest in the saga of her troubled younger brother, Danny. A week earlier, Danny got swept up in a narcotics dragnet, arrested along with a dozen hard-core drug dealers from the old neighborhood, even though, as far as Madison knew, he wasn't involved in anything remotely like that. Danny was now in federal custody awaiting trial. Nobody at school knew about it, not even Ty. *Especially* not Ty. He was a decent enough human being beneath his bravado that, if he found out she had family problems, he'd start asking questions that she didn't want to answer. And probably end up getting the truth out of her, which she couldn't afford. Appearances mattered too much here. You kept your game face on at all times. She didn't want people finding out about Danny until she had a better handle on things.

"Pit stop," she said, nodding toward the restrooms.

"I can wait. You want to grab a coffee or something?"

"Can't. I have stuff to do."

"All right. But hey, come out tomorrow? It's my birthday. I'd love to see you."

"Right. Chloe told me. I'll be there."

"She told you. Good. I'm glad," he said.

From his tone, she could tell that inviting her had been a bone of contention. Chloe was Ty's new girlfriend, and she kept a close eye on his interactions with Madison.

Ty left. Madison looked for a quiet place to make her call. But the atrium was buzzing with students coming and going. She caught snippets of conversation. Grades. Exams. Recruiting. Weekend plans. Mere days ago, her life had been that simple, that carefree. But the past, her family, her background always reared their ugly heads. They just wouldn't let her go.

She made her way outside to the law quad. New England fall was winding down. There were still patches of vivid color in the trees, but you could smell winter in the sharp, cold wind. The forecast was for heavy rain later, which would suit her mood. She found a sheltered spot in the lee of the building and placed the call with shaking fingers. Her mother picked up on the first ring.

"Maddy, thank God. Where were you?"

"In class. What's wrong?"

"Danny pled guilty."

"How can that be? He swore to you he was innocent."

"He still says that, and I believe him. I know it in my heart."

"Why plead guilty if you're not?"

"They made him."

"*Who* made him?"

"I don't know. He won't say. It was, like, a thirty-second phone call from the jail, then he said he had to go and hung up. Maddy, he sounded scared."

"Honestly, that doesn't make sense. I studied criminal law, Mom. There are supposed to be *negotiations* for a plea. He was just arrested, what, a week ago? It's too fast."

"I thought so too."

"What does his lawyer say?"

"I don't know, and I don't care. I don't trust that guy. He's the one who forced Danny to take the plea."

"Forced him how?"

"What do you think? He threatened him."

"That sounds like an excuse. Did Danny say that or is he—"

"Is he what? Making it up? You don't believe your brother?"

"Don't make this about me and him, okay? I'm just trying to understand the facts."

"The facts are, this lawyer shows up in court. We didn't hire him. And then he starts telling Danny what to do."

"You not hiring him is not unusual. The court appoints lawyers for defendants who can't afford them."

"That's not what happened. Something's off, I'm telling you. He's this old guy with dandruff who looks like he hits the bottle."

"That doesn't mean he's not qualified."

"Why are you taking the lawyer's side? If you'd been in court, you'd understand what I'm talking about."

"I already apologized for not being there. I told you, by the time I got your call that Danny had been arrested—"

"Right. I know how busy you are."

The edge in her tone got Madison's back up.

"I wasn't *too busy* to come to my brother's arraignment. My phone was off. If I knew, I would have dropped everything and—"

"Maddy, I don't want to fight."

"Then say you understand that I had my phone off. I can't keep it on all the time on the off chance Danny gets arrested for drugs."

Most people get to assume that won't happen to their brother, she thought, but held her tongue. Danny had a long and checkered history for someone who was only twenty-one years old. Her mother didn't understand how detrimental this was to Madison's own plans, her future. How draining it was worrying about him all the time. But you couldn't choose your family, and she loved him no matter what. He was her brother, after all.

"I don't blame you, Maddy. Really."

"I hope not. But thank you for saying that."

"It's a question of what we do now. We're a family. Families stick together in tough times."

Too bad that had not always been the case in her family. Their past was fraught, and never far enough from their present. Madison sighed, wishing things could be different. But they weren't. She needed to suck it up and deal with reality.

"Tell me how I can help, Mom. You want me to call the lawyer and find out what happened?"

"No, I told you. That lawyer's trouble. We need to go see your brother."

"You mean visit him in prison?"

"Yes. Something's wrong. I need to look him in the eye and get the truth."

Would visiting get her name on a list? Her relationship to an indicted drug dealer could come out just as she applied for an internship with a federal judge. But what choice did she have? Danny was her brother, and he needed her right now, inconvenient as that was.

"Fine, I'll go with you. I can do it Saturday."

"*No.* Tomorrow morning, first thing."

The prison was far away. It would be a long drive there, a long wait to get in, a long drive back. She'd miss her morning class, with finals coming up. Argh, what else was new? Danny's problems had been screwing up her life since she was a kid.

"*Please*," Mom said. "He's in serious trouble this time, and I don't know how to help him. I work in a nursing home. You're a student at Harvard Law. I need your help."

"Of course, Mom. Just tell me what time. I'll be waiting outside my dorm."

3

....

It was still dark out with freezing rain when the old Toyota pulled up in front of the dorm the next morning. Madison got in and pecked Mom on the cheek. She'd been up late reading for class, working on a moot court brief, and—most exciting—applying to the judicial internship in Conroy's chambers. Her eyes were tired and scratchy, but her mother looked more exhausted than she felt. And older than she had just weeks ago, with new threads of silver in her hair and deep purple shadows under her eyes.

Danny's fault, as usual.

"I got you a coffee," Mom said.

There was a Dunkin' sitting in the cup holder.

"Thanks."

Madison took a sip and put it back down. Light and cloyingly sweet, the way she liked it when she was a kid. Her dad died when she was thirteen and Danny ten. Mom was frozen in that moment and still treated them like she did back then. Which meant indulging and enabling Danny. And expecting Madison to drop everything to take care of her little brother.

"Can you find this place in Google? The goddamn thing won't talk."

The facility where Danny was being held was all the way in Rhode Island, in some crappy little town just over the Mass. border. Madison took her mother's phone and typed the name into Google Maps.

"Take Mem Drive, get on 90, and then I'll tell you from there. It's saying an hour and twenty-six minutes with the traffic."

"Jeez, we'll be the last ones in line," Mom said.

The drive was harrowing on the slick roads in her mother's little car, with its broken heater and smell of gasoline. The parking lot near the prison was full by the time they arrived. Her mother circled, looking for a spot, face tight with anxiety. They left their handbags in the trunk and locked it. You weren't allowed to bring anything into the facility except your ID and a single car key—not your phone, not an extra Tampax, not even a stick of chewing gum. The hulking concrete prison loomed over the street, surrounded by a tall metal fence topped with coils of deadly looking barbed wire. As her gaze traveled up the grim facade, Madison felt sick. No matter how mad she was at Danny, he was still her goofball kid brother, a string bean with big ears and an infectious laugh. Young and foolish, but never mean; certainly not evil. And not beyond redemption. No matter what he'd done—and if she was honest with herself, there was some chance the charges were true—she couldn't stand to think of him locked up in this god-awful place.

The line of visitors stretched down the block, around the corner, huddled in winter coats, some of them holding newspapers over their heads because you couldn't bring in an umbrella. It took them forty-five minutes to make it to the entrance, by which point Madison's boots were saturated, and her puffer jacket and jeans soaked. The lobby looked like something out of a gulag. Harsh lighting, cinder block walls, scuffed linoleum floors streaked with muddy water. The smell of wet clothing was everywhere. The buckles on Madison's boots set off the metal detector, and a female CO patted her down roughly before waving her on to the next CO, who was checking IDs.

"Yolanda and Madison Rivera. Here to see Daniel Rivera. My son," Mom said, handing over their driver's licenses.

She recited Danny's inmate number from memory. The corrections officer checked the number in the computer, and waved them through to the visiting room. The cavernous space was filled with screaming babies and sobbing girlfriends. Guards stationed at intervals along the wall scanned the crowd, alert for any physical contact or other violation of the rules. Madison and her mother sat down at a table to wait. Every few minutes, an air horn would blow, followed by the sound of a lock disengaging with a heavy clank of metal. An inmate would then shuffle in, chains rattling, clutching a manila folder in his manacled hands, escorted by a CO.

About ten minutes later, that inmate was Danny, and she had to stifle a cry of dismay. He walked toward them stiffly, like he was in pain. The guard uncuffed him, and her mother threw her arms around him. He towered over her, coltish and lanky, just a kid embarrassed by his mother's emotional embrace. The other inmates could see from the way Yolanda's shoulders shook that she was sobbing.

"That's enough, ma'am," the corrections officer said. "You need to limit physical contact, or the visit will be terminated."

Mom stepped away, wiping her eyes with the back of her hand, too overcome to speak. Madison had a lump in her throat and tears in her eyes. She blinked them back as the three of them sat down, waiting until the guard moved away to voice her concern.

"You're walking funny," she said, keeping her voice low. "Are you hurt?"

Danny shook his head, tears in his eyes, too. They were all struggling to get their emotions in check enough to talk. It occurred to her that this was the worst thing that had happened to her family other than her father's death.

"Don't worry," Danny said. "I'm just happy to see you. I was surprised when they called me for a visit. Are you sure it's okay for you, Mom? Maybe it's too much."

Yolanda wiped her eyes and sat up straighter, shaking her head.

"I'll be okay, son. We came to ask you why you pleaded guilty when you're innocent. We don't understand. Tell us what's going on."

His face clouded over. "Ah, Ma, look, if that's why you're here—"

"I'm here because I love you," she said, her voice cracking. "And I need to understand what's happening."

The tears in Danny's eyes spilled over. As he wiped them with a shaking hand, Madison had a sudden vision of him crying in her arms as a small child. Just like then, she wanted to make things better for him. But it wasn't always within her power to do.

"I don't want you guys mixed up in this," he said.

"We are mixed up in it, whether you like it or not," Mom said.

"Like Mom said, we want to understand," Madison said. "Why plead guilty if you're innocent? At least there should've been negotiations. They should offer you a plea to a lesser charge. Isn't that how it usually works?"

Danny looked around nervously, making a shushing gesture with his hand. "I can't talk about this. Not here."

"Why not?" their mother said under her breath. "Did somebody hurt you? Threaten you?"

"Mom, leave it alone. It's too late. What's done is done."

"That's not true," Madison said. "If something illegal happened, you can challenge your guilty plea."

"Listen to your sister. She's a law student, she knows."

Madison nodded. "I could give better advice if I knew the specifics. Do you have a copy of the plea agreement?"

"The lawyer wouldn't give me one."

She narrowed her eyes skeptically. "He's supposed to give you copies of everything."

"Jesus, Maddy, they tell you something in school, and you just swallow it. You don't have a clue what goes on in the real world."

This was why she'd missed a whole day of classes—so Danny could tell her she didn't know what she was talking about? She tried not to let get him to her, but Mom was crying again. All the gray in her hair was from him.

"This isn't about me," she said. "Look what you're doing to Mom. You claim you're innocent. You pled guilty because you were forced, so now she's worried that somebody's hurting you. Just tell the truth. We'll still love you."

"You want me to say I sold drugs? Because that's what you think, right? That I'm lying?" He leaned toward her, eyes flashing, lowering his voice. "I *am* innocent. I haven't touched drugs in two years, and that's to use. I never, ever, ever sold them. Not once in my entire pathetic, fucking life. Adrian, though. That's a different story."

Adrian was Danny's best friend from high school, and he was bad news.

"I should've known it was him," Yolanda said, shaking her head and cursing in Spanish under her breath.

"Don't get down on Adrian. He was trying to help me out. You know how I want to open my own garage, right?"

After a number of false starts, Danny had found something he was passionate about and good at. He completed the automotive program at a local community college and got what seemed like a great job at a local garage. But he didn't get along with the boss and had started talking about opening his own shop. The problem was, he didn't have the cash.

"I found the perfect location. It's all set up—tools, jacks, lifts, everything. That type of opportunity won't come around again. Between the lease of the property and buying the equipment outright, I needed twenty-five grand."

"Why didn't you come to your family for help, son?" Yolanda said.

"With you paying so much rent now, Mom? Madison up to her ears in debt for law school, and Aunt Nilda about to retire? I'm not gonna burden any of you. Adrian's my oldest friend. I knew he was making bank, so I asked him. He said he's overextended and can't personally float me. But his boss, this guy Ricky Peña, was looking for legitimate investment opportunities."

"This Ricky. He's a drug dealer?" Mom said.

"Yeah, but I would have nothing to do with that. He's looking to go legit and invest in legal businesses."

"Invest *drug* money," Madison said.

"Money is money. And beggars can't be choosers. You think a bank is gonna give me a loan, with no collateral?"

"They might. Did you try?"

"There's no point. I'm a nobody. I don't have a Harvard degree like you. To me, this was my big chance, so I went to meet Ricky at this bar he owns. That was my first mistake. Ricky sells out of that place. Right when we started talking, he took a phone call, then he stood up. I heard him tell the bartender, 'It's a go.' Then he says he's going to the john and disappears. The bartender comes out from behind the bar, drops a duffel bag on the table in front of me, and *he* disappears. I'm thinking maybe this is the cash up front for the investment, so I pick up the bag. I'm about to open it and look inside when the DEA busts in. They arrest everyone in sight, including *me*. This bag is in my hands. It turns out to have heroin in it, and now it has my fingerprints, too."

"But they weren't your drugs," Yolanda said. "So that's not your fault. You need to tell somebody what's going on. Someone who can do something about it."

Danny wrung his hands, his face gray.

"There's no one to tell. The cops are on the take. Ricky pays protection, and that phone call he got—it was a tip-off. I'm ninety-nine percent sure that it came from the detective running the case. What am I gonna do, go to that detective and say I'm innocent? He'll kill me—like, *literally* kill me."

"You have to tell your lawyer," Madison said.

"My lawyer is in on it, too. Him and the dirty cop are working together. These guys are as bad as Ricky. Worse."

"They can't make you plead guilty if you're innocent," Madison said.

Danny looked at her like she had two heads.

"Did you hear anything I just said? They can. They did. The night before I went to court, some guys cornered me in the bathroom and beat the crap out of me. They said to keep my mouth shut 'tomorrow.' I'm like, *What's tomorrow?* And they said, *You'll see. Do what you're told, or next time we won't be so gentle.* I go back to my bunk, bleeding, in pain. I'm afraid to go to the infirmary. I got no one to turn to. No friends inside, no allies. I go to the pay phone and try calling Adrian, who got away clean, the asshole. He changed his number. All I know is, if I tell the guards, those guys who beat me'll come back, and this time I'll be dead. So, I keep my mouth shut. I go to sleep, and next thing I know, the CO's shaking me awake. They put me in the van to court, where that lawyer meets me. He tells me the case is overwhelming and my only hope is to plead guilty and throw myself on the mercy of the judge. He gives me a paper to sign. It says the drugs are mine, and

I'm looking at ten years. And I'm like, *No.* He goes, *Danny, if you do this, I can ask the judge to go easy. But if you resist, she'll think you have no remorse. You'll be locked up for life. And your friends will think you shafted them. I know these people. They don't play, and they know where your mother lives.*"

Madison went cold. "Your own lawyer threatened you? And threatened Mom? That really happened?"

"Yes, it happened. You think I'm making it up?"

"No. I—I'm just shocked."

"Yeah, because you live in a fantasy world where everything is pretty."

"Did the prosecutor object?"

"He wasn't there when the lawyer railroaded me. Nobody was."

"Did you ask to speak to him?"

"To the *prosecutor*? So they think I'm a snitch? That'll get me killed for real."

"What about the judge in the case?"

"What about her? In court, she asked for the evidence. And the prosecutor just said I was in possession of the bag, and my prints were on it. Which was true. As far as the judge is concerned, that's the end of it."

"Did you say the drugs weren't yours?"

"I would've had to say it in open court in front of the lawyer and the dirty cop. Besides, it's pointless. My lawyer goes way back with this judge. Has her in his pocket. He bragged about it. So, she's dirty, too."

"That can't be true. It's *federal* court. That's like— How can I explain? The national court, the top, the most elite. The judges are highly educated, honest. Things like that don't happen there."

"Well, they did."

"What's the judge's name?" Madison asked.

Danny shook his head. "Maddy, look, I appreciate that you

came to visit. But I don't want you in the middle of this. I was in the wrong place at the wrong time, and now I'm screwed. I need to keep my mouth shut, or things will get worse."

"You can't just give up," Madison said. "At least let me look into it for you. Find out if there are previous complaints against the judge, or your lawyer. Whether it would make sense for me to try to talk to them, or—"

Danny put his hands in his hair, pulling at it anxiously.

"Are you listening to a word I say? The judge is tight with the dirty lawyer. They're in on it together. If you talk to either one of them, you'll get me killed. Is that what you want?"

All the blood drained from their mother's face. "Of course she doesn't."

"Then stay out of it. Not just for my sake. For Mom's. I told you, they know where she lives. Ma, the guys who beat me up, they said your address. I can live with the consequences for me. But not for you. I couldn't handle that."

Tears stood out in their mother's eyes. "Son, I'll take that risk. You're what matters."

"No. I'm not letting you." Danny turned to Madison, grabbing her hands. "*You* promise me, Maddy. For Mom's sake, say you won't talk to *anyone*. Not the judge. Nobody. Say it."

"I promise I won't talk to anyone without clearing it with you first. Just tell me the judge's name, so I can do the research."

From the corner of her eye, she saw guards rushing toward their table. Danny looked up in alarm.

"No physical contact," one of the guards yelled. "Hands in the air."

Danny threw his hands up. The guards yanked him to his feet and kicked his legs apart. One of them patted him down.

"What did she give you?"

"Nothing, that's my sister. We were just—"

"He's clean," the guard said, shaking his head.

"This visit is terminated," the other one said, pulling a pair of handcuffs from his belt.

Madison sought his eyes urgently. "Danny? The name?"

"Remember, you *promised*," he tossed over his shoulder as they led him away. "It's Conroy, Kathryn Conroy."

4

....

They drove in stunned silence, both upset by the visit. They were nearly back to Boston before her mother spoke.

"You're going to talk to the judge, right?"

"Mom, he said not to. He made me promise."

"He doesn't know what's good for him."

Madison shook her head. "It would be a mistake."

"Don't listen to him. This is too important."

"I can't even believe what he's saying is true. This is crazy, but I *know* her."

"You know the judge?"

"Yeah. She's teaching at the law school. I'm taking her class."

Mom gripped the steering wheel, turning to Madison with burning eyes. "Danny's judge is your teacher?"

A car honked.

"*Mom.* Watch out."

Yolanda looked back at the road. "But that's wonderful. That makes it easy."

"You're wrong. It makes it really complicated."

She couldn't just walk up to Professor—*Judge*—Conroy and

start questioning her about a pending case, involving a family member, no less. It would be so inappropriate that the judge wouldn't only refuse to talk to her. She'd throw Madison's internship application in the trash. That would accomplish zero for her brother while screwing up her chance at something she really wanted for herself. But try explaining that to Mom, who knew nothing about the legal system and even less about getting ahead in this world. She'd just assume Madison was being selfish. Which, okay, maybe there was an element of that. The situation was just impossible.

"Why complicated? Tell your teacher Danny is innocent. She'll listen to you. You're her student. She *knows* you."

"She'll think I'm trying to sway her judgment in a case."

"People help their families. Everybody does it. She'll understand."

"Not in this situation. Not with a judge, not when she's my teacher, not when the charge is *drugs*."

"Oh, I see what's going on. You think your brother is guilty. That he's lying. You're ashamed."

"What *I* think doesn't matter. Judges rule based on evidence. Danny said it himself. He went to a known drug spot to meet with a dealer, and his fingerprints are on that bag. I can't change that. The judge won't ignore it just because she knows me from class."

"Madison, he's your *brother*. You have to help him."

"I *want* to. It breaks my heart seeing him in jail. But try to understand. Judge Conroy is not my friend. She's a professor up at the front of a big classroom. She hardly knows me, and she wouldn't take it lightly if I tried to influence her."

That was basically true. Yesterday was her longest conversation to date with Judge Conroy. Mom expected her to work miracles, but Madison had no pull. The fact that the judge liked her answers in class, or invited her to apply for an internship, meant nothing in terms of how she'd handle Danny's case. And once Conroy learned that Madison's brother was charged with heroin trafficking in her own courtroom, her feelings about Madison would surely change. It probably wouldn't affect her grade in the class. But she'd be a lot less likely to hire Madison as an intern. Come to think of it, was it even worth going through with the interview? Maybe she should withdraw her application. Or tell the judge about Danny herself, so it didn't look like she was hiding something. But what if she got dinged because of Danny? Ugh, it felt so unfair. She *wanted* that internship.

At a minimum, she had to make her mother understand that she absolutely could not, and would not, under any circumstances, try to influence Judge Conroy's ruling on Danny's case.

"Well?" her mother said.

Mom would never understand. She had to fall back on her promise not to say anything.

"I promised him I wouldn't say anything. He's afraid of retaliation. I won't second-guess him. It's too dangerous."

"So you're just going back to your life like this is not your problem?"

She turned on her mother with the anger of a lot of years.

"I've been dealing with Danny's problems since I was a kid. I did *more* than my fair share of taking care of him, and you know it."

Tears glittered in Mom's eyes. "After Dad died, I wasn't myself. I had to send you kids away. Danny suffered, more than any of us."

"I suffered, too. But that doesn't seem to count for you."

"You're the strong one. That's why we rely on you. You can do things that your brother and I can't. I'm asking for your help here, love. Please."

"I *want* to help. But you need to understand, I can't just walk up to a federal judge and talk to her about a case. Judges aren't allowed to discuss those things outside of court. If someone approaches them, it's like they're trying to influence the judge. It would be seen as improper. I could get in trouble. Is that what you want?"

"No," her mother said. "Of course not."

She sighed, looking out the window. Silence fell. Her mother wiped away tears. The sound of her sniffling tugged at Madison's heart.

"There are some things I *can* do," she said after a moment. "Get information. Do research. Come up with a plan. Danny doesn't seem to have the most basic documents from his case, like the plea agreement. I'll get the documents and try to figure out the next step. Get him a better lawyer. Appeal. I don't know, but there have to be options, things we can do without trying to influence the judge."

"Yes. More information. And a plan. That would help."

They exited the highway. Not long after, her mother pulled up to the gates of Harvard Yard, turning on the blinkers.

"Jump out. There's no stopping here, and I have to get to work," she said, her jaw tight.

"Are you mad at me? You look mad."

"I'm angry at the situation, Madison, not at you. I know you'll do everything in your power to help your brother. *Right*?"

Madison's chest tightened, but she nodded.

"Yes. Talk soon, okay?"

She blew a kiss goodbye and hopped out into damp, diesel-scented air. Passing through the gates of Harvard Yard was like entering a secret garden. The rain had stopped. The paths were carpeted with wet leaves that gave off a smoky smell. Madison inhaled the fragrance, breathing deep, consciously putting space between herself and her family troubles. All she wanted was to be just another student heading to class with her Starbucks and her backpack. No secrets, nothing to be ashamed of. No worries but studying and law review. The same as anybody else.

But she wasn't.

Securities Reg had already started. The prof glanced up as Madison slunk in the door at the top of the classroom. Eyes on her feet, she hurried down the tiered rows to her assigned seat. The room was classic Harvard Law—beamed ceilings, ornate light fixtures, the smell of dust and history. She whispered apologies to the students on either side as she set up her laptop. Chloe, Ty's girlfriend, sat to her right, a fluke of the seating chart. Not enemies by any means, they weren't friends, either. Chloe graciously angled her computer so Madison could read her notes. The topic was insider trading, something Madison would normally find fascinating. Apparently, her famous powers of concentration could be shaken after all, though it took something as awful as seeing her little brother locked up in prison. She caught only snippets of the lecture, typing random phrases into her notes without comprehending their meaning, as her mind wandered, visions of Danny dancing before her eyes.

Danny in the playground at ten years old, bleeding from a cut lip after a fight. The other kid, bleeding worse. Danny outside the principal's office, suspended again. Madison getting called out of class to take him home when they couldn't reach Mom. *I know your father passed,* the principal said, talking to her like she was Danny's mother, though she was only thirteen. *But this can't continue. I have other students to think of.* Getting home, finding Mom dead asleep on the couch, dirty dishes piled in the sink, a stack of bills on the table. Shaking her mother awake. *You didn't go to work?* She was just so tired, she said, pulling a blanket over her head.

That was the night Madison gave in and called Aunt Nilda. Not only because Danny kept acting out. They'd had nothing but peanut-butter sandwiches to eat for a week, and the utility bill said

"Final Notice." Nilda was Mom's younger sister. No kids of her own, a high-paying job as a nurse in a big hospital, a two-bedroom condo in Brooklyn that she owned. She adored her niece and nephew, which was why Madison hesitated to call. Nilda would step in and take charge. Madison was afraid things would change, when they'd changed enough already.

She was right.

Mom was severely depressed, Nilda said. She needed help. Medical care. A break. The kids would live with Nilda in Brooklyn while Mom got better. *For how long?* Madison asked. Well, they'd have to wait and see.

She remembered sitting with Danny on the Greyhound bus, distraught at leaving her home, her friends, her *mother*. Taking it out on him. *This is all your fault.* He looked so devastated that she gave him the chocolate bar she'd bought with her last money. That first night, he trashed their room in Aunt Nilda's condo, and Uncle Hector came in with the belt. It was a bad start. Hector was Nilda's fiancé, a beat cop who believed that discipline kept kids off the street. That approach didn't work on Danny. He needed love.

Madison thrived at Nilda's from the start. She liked sitting down to dinner every night, saying grace and *please* and *thank you*. But Danny just squirmed and refused to make eye contact. Nilda took them to museums, concerts. Danny was so bored that he fought going, and eventually Nilda left him alone. Her apartment was tastefully decorated, with rugs, plants, books on the shelves. Madison loved it. Danny couldn't stand the level of neatness required. Granted, she was a thirteen-year-old girl, and he was a ten-year-old boy. But it was also just a bad fit. She loved structure. He hated rules. He fell in with the troublemakers at school and was in the principal's office constantly, just like back home. Nilda wanted to put them in Catholic school to get Danny away from the bad influences, but Hector objected to the expense. *It's my money. You don't decide,* she said, which started an argument that never seemed to end.

The more Hector and Nilda fought over Danny, the more Madison threw herself into school. She'd been placed in the gifted class. She became the extra-credit queen, volunteering for every club, making friends with the smart kids. They weren't just a bunch of wallflowers, either, but artsy, verbal, political, unusually mature for eighth graders. New York did that—gave you an edge, made you grow up fast. Hanging out with them, Madison got interested in her Puerto Rican heritage for the first time. She perfected her Spanish slang, read the news, read history. Six months in, she was happy in New York, when Danny got caught smoking weed in the park. He was only eleven but tall for his age and hanging out with older kids. Hector went in to talk to him, and somehow, it turned into a blowout. Hector gave Danny a black eye, which was not okay. Nilda kicked Hector out, but it was too late to salvage the situation. Mom insisted they come back to Boston. *That* was too soon. She wasn't back on her feet, which meant Danny couldn't get on his.

The more things changed . . . Her brother had seemed so much better lately, until the arrest exploded their lives. That scene in the visiting room today, when he was led away in cuffs. She couldn't get his face out of her mind. The fear in his eyes.

She was afraid he'd die there.

Class ended. Chloe was closing up her laptop. Her screensaver was a selfie with the Supreme Court justice who'd been her dad's best friend in law school. *Tell me you're a legacy admit without telling me you're a legacy admit.* She wrapped a voluminous cashmere scarf around her neck and fluffed her perfectly highlighted blond hair. The girl had game, Madison had to admit, as much as she envied Chloe's head start in life.

"See you at the party tonight?" Chloe said.

She felt suddenly exhausted from pretending that nothing was wrong. She wasn't sure she could keep up the charade through an entire birthday party.

"I may not be able to make it."

The spark of triumph in Chloe's eyes annoyed her. Things were just too easy for that girl; and on top of it, she gets the guy? A guy whom Madison admittedly let go, but even so.

"Though I did promise Ty. So on second thought, yes—I'll be there."

And she flashed Chloe a smile.

———

Around seven thirty, Madison pushed her way into the pizza place in Harvard Square that was a big law-student hangout. It was shoulder to shoulder at the bar, every table full, and *loud*. She took a deep breath, inhaling brick oven and beer, and put on her game face. Ty was visible, head and shoulders above the crowd, surrounded by people. So handsome, smooth operator, golden boy. Some people still refused to believe that she was the one who broke up with him. Misogyny at work, since the two of them were obvious equals.

As she made her way over, Chloe's blond head popped into view at his right. Her eyes grew wary as Ty leaned down to shout into Madison's ear.

"We're waiting for a table to open up. Can I get you a drink?"

She was tempted to let him, but why antagonize Chloe? Things were tenuous enough at the moment that she shouldn't go making enemies.

"I'll get it myself. You want anything?"

He shook his head. Madison fought her way to the bar. She

was motioning for the bartender's attention when a guy from Trial Advocacy class tapped her on the shoulder. They were shooting the breeze a few minutes later when Ty turned up beside her, his perfect smile lighting up the bar.

"What? You don't have a drink yet?"

"Ah, I decided not to. It's a school night."

"But it's my birthday."

"I'll catch you later," the other guy said, glancing at Ty as he slunk away.

Ty had a funny habit of coming between her and anybody she showed interest in. If it wasn't his birthday, she'd have called him on it. He ordered her a Manhattan, and one for himself. An obvious play—that had been their celebration drink when they were together. She crossed her arms and raised an eyebrow. But his next sentence wiped their relationship issues from her mind.

"I hear you're applying to the internship in Judge Conroy's chambers. That true?"

"Who told you that?"

"Remember Sean Chen? Buddy of mine, graduated last year? He's clerking for her this year."

"Sean is Judge Conroy's law clerk?"

"That's right."

"And he told you I applied for the internship? Why is that any of your business?"

"He thought we were still going out."

"Even if we were, he shouldn't be blabbing like that."

"He was just making conversation. You know this place is a fishbowl. Nobody can keep a secret."

"Why do you care if I apply? Unless you want the job for yourself?"

She'd felt so flattered when Judge Conroy invited her to apply.

Well, maybe she wasn't the only one the judge asked. Ty would be formidable competition.

"I'm not applying. I hear it's a rough place to work, so I decided against it. I'm simply passing along that information. There's a cloud around Conroy. I thought you should know, so you could reconsider if it's a good use of your time."

She looked at him in surprise, remembering that Danny claimed Judge Conroy was in on fixing his case. She didn't believe that for a minute. Then again, it had been burned into her mind from way back that Danny was unreliable, and Kathryn Conroy walked on water. Conroy was one of the most noted alums of Madison's prestigious Catholic high school. Years after she left, the nuns sang her praises. Conroy was why Madison first got interested in becoming a lawyer. She couldn't be corrupt. No way.

But then, what was Ty talking about?

"What kind of cloud?" she asked.

"I'm not sure. I've just heard rumblings."

"*Rumblings*. Seriously? If you know something, spill it, or else don't badmouth people."

"I'm just worried you're overly impressed with her. You hang on her words in class like she's this fountain of wisdom."

"She's a renowned federal judge. An amazing teacher. So yeah, I'm impressed. Nothing you said changes my mind."

"It's not a good place to work, that's all." He started ticking off the problems on his fingers. "They're strict with deadlines. It's a heavy case load. They want a lot of hours. And the last intern left on bad terms. They actually fired her. Imagine that happening to you."

"You just described every judicial internship that exists."

"Who fires an *intern*?"

"Maybe she did a poor job. I'm not worried. I plan to kick ass."

Earlier, Madison had been thinking of withdrawing her application because of the complication with Danny. Count on Ty to rile up her killer instinct. His opposition made her want the internship even more.

"The last intern probably thought that, too."

"You know what I wonder, Ty? I wonder if you're planning to apply for the position, and you don't want the competition."

"I said I'm not."

"Can you blame me if I'm skeptical? Everything's a move with you."

That had been a problem between them. He had a bad habit of fighting dirty when it came to getting ahead, like a lot of people at Harvard. He also came from a gilded background. Maybe not as much as Chloe, but his father was a prominent African American surgeon, his mother a high school principal, and they had a high profile in their hometown. Someone like Ty could never understand where Madison was coming from or some of the things she had to do to get ahead. He'd never struggled.

"Look who's talking," he said.

"You still don't get me, do you?"

"I could say the same."

The drinks came. She took out her wallet, but he waved it away.

"I'm paying," she insisted, handing over her debit card. "Happy birthday, this is your present."

"What about the crazy stuff in her past? Assassination attempts? Violence? Did you know her husband was murdered?"

"Yeah, I know all about her."

Madison had Judge Conroy's résumé practically memorized. Top of the class from Harvard Law. A prestigious clerkship. Ten years in the U.S. Attorney's Office where she prosecuted high-profile cases before getting appointed to the bench as one of the youngest federal judges in the country. It was true that the judge had faced down terrible tragedy, but she carried on. How could you not admire that?

"Right, she went to your high school. I remember you saying that. No wonder you stick up for her. It's the old girls' network, huh?"

"No, I just don't like to hear a good woman slandered."

"*Slander?* That's harsh."

"Her husband was murdered, and you're implying it was her fault."

"I'm concerned that the murder had to do with her cases. Not that she killed him or anything."

"I thought it was random. But even if it was because of her work, the way she soldiered on, doing what she believed in, just makes me admire her more. So, sorry. I'm still your competition."

He snorted. "You're impossible. Just remember, I tried to warn you."

She pushed both cocktails toward him. "Chloe's giving us the stink eye. Here, tell her I bought her a drink. I have to work on the internship application anyway, so I'm gonna split. Enjoy your party. Happy birthday."

And she planted a kiss on his cheek.

Ty always managed to get under her skin. On the walk back to the dorm, she couldn't stop his warning from rattling around in her head. She had to bone up on the judge to prepare for the interview tomorrow anyway. Why not look up her husband's death? It had happened after Madison left Catholic Prep, during her freshman year of college when she was busy and distracted. She'd followed the story in the news because of her interest in the judge. But maybe she'd missed something.

Sitting cross-legged on her bed with her laptop open, she googled "Judge Conroy husband murder," and it came right up. Matthew Latham, age thirty-eight, a teacher at St. Alfred's Country

Day School, had been gunned down "execution style" while un-loading groceries in front of the home he shared with his wife, Judge Kathryn Conroy, in Wellesley, Massachusetts. A neighbor heard three shots, looked out the window, and saw a dark-colored SUV speed away, but didn't get the plate number. There was no description of the shooter. The investigators looked for links to the judge's cases. But they never found the killer, so the motive was pure speculation. That was five years ago. The murder was still unsolved.

Still. Execution style. At their house. That didn't seem random. It was chilling.

5

....

Walking into the soaring lobby of the federal courthouse the next afternoon made Madison's heart race. There were lawyers everywhere, male and female, all ages and races, united mainly by the soberness of their attire and their urgency as they hurried to court. Clients of every description filled the hallways, as well as law clerks, cops, security guards, a television crew setting up to film with a reporter whose face she knew from the nightly news. As far as Madison was concerned, this was the center of the universe. Where she belonged. Her destiny.

She passed through a metal detector and took the elevator to Judge Conroy's chambers, where she was buzzed into a tastefully decorated reception area with spectacular views over the harbor to the skyline. The receptionist told her to take a seat. The judge was stuck in court, and it might be a while. *Court.* The very word thrilled her. She'd never been in a real courtroom before, only the mock trial room at school, and correcting that oversight was just one reason that she wanted this internship so badly. Losing the chance because of Danny's legal problems would be a terrible blow. And yet, last night, she'd nearly decided to withdraw the application. Lying awake in the dark, she struggled—apply or don't apply, tell or keep quiet? If she didn't say anything, would Judge Conroy find out on her own that Danny was her brother? Hard to say. Rivera was a common enough last name. Maybe the connection would escape notice if Madison didn't bring it up herself. What harm would it do to keep quiet, as long as she didn't try to influence Danny's case? The temptation to say nothing was powerful. And yet, after hours of mental struggle in the dark, she came down on the side that it just wouldn't be right to withhold the information. Madison was an honest person. She knew in her heart that she should come clean about Danny, so the judge could have all the facts when she made the hiring decision. Who knows, maybe she'd be impressed with Madison's honesty and hire her anyway.

She decided to go ahead with the interview but tell Judge Conroy about Danny. It was the right thing to do.

When morning came, though, reality hit, and her resolution faltered. She got dressed and took the T into Boston, in a panic over how to broach the delicate subject. At what point in the interview should she mention it? What exactly should she say? She rehearsed scenarios in her head, but they never went well. As she took her seat in the waiting area, she was feeling shaky and unprepared. Not because of her credentials. Those, she was confident of. But because of the Danny problem.

A young man and woman were already seated, both wearing conservative dark suits. She didn't recognize either of them. She murmured a greeting.

"You're here for the internship?" she asked, and they nodded.

No sign of Ty? Was it possible he hadn't applied?

"Do you know if there are other applicants, or is it just us?" she asked.

They shrugged, not meeting her eyes. A tense silence fell.

They were each other's competition, after all. Madison sized them up, running through the calculations in her mind. They weren't Harvard Law, or she would recognize them. BU, then? Or BC, Northeastern, Suffolk? There were many good law schools in the city, but none with Harvard's cachet. It was just a fact. Harvard hooked you up. Judge Conroy—an alum—hired exclusively Harvard grads as her law clerks, like Ty's friend Sean. That said, the judge wouldn't hire someone based on their Harvard pedigree alone. They had to have the grades, the credentials, and the personality to ace the interview. Fresh off law-firm recruiting season, Madison knew she could do it all. Her interview pitch had been honed on a dozen corporate law partners. She went over it now, in her head. *Top grades, law review, internship at the legal clinic last summer, hands-on experience, a people person, organized, a hard worker, rose from humble roots, yada yada yada.* It worked before. She had the offers to prove it, the pick of the top Boston firms. Besides, Judge Conroy knew her and had personally invited her to apply. This internship should be hers for the taking. And it would have been, if not for Danny.

Ugh. She wished she could just ignore the problem. But she had to tell the truth. It was the right thing to do. Integrity mattered. Judge Conroy would expect nothing less.

As if Madison's thoughts had conjured her, the judge swept through the reception area in a swoosh of black robes, trailed by two young law clerks and an older woman with gray hair. The group disappeared through a door at the opposite end of the reception area without so much as glancing at the applicants. Judge Conroy wore business attire to teach. Madison had never seen her in robes before. *Impressive.* The vision lingered, along with the fragrance of the judge's perfume, a velvety whisper of rose petals that she recognized from the classroom and breathed in now. How amazing to be part of Kathryn Conroy's team, sitting in the courtroom during trial, coming back to the office to talk through the thorny legal issues. The judge asking her opinion, praising her legal analysis. Yet it could all slip through her fingers if she revealed the truth about Danny.

Beyond the tall windows, the sun set over the harbor. The receptionist was young, round, and pale, named Kelsey Kowalski, according to the plate on her desk. Kelsey looked at her watch, launching a jaw-cracking yawn. She lifted the telephone and spoke in a low tone.

"They'll be out for you any minute," she then said.

Then she put on her coat and walked out the door. The three candidates exchanged glances and settled in to wait, scrolling on their phones to avoid talking. Contrary to Kelsey's assurances, it was forty minutes before the door to the inner sanctum opened and the law clerks emerged. Madison recognized them both— HLS grads from last year. The Black woman had been high up on law review when Madison was a first-year. The other was Sean Chen, Ty's friend. He stopped short, looking at the applicants, and picked out Madison right away.

"*Madison*. I'm Sean. Tyler Evans told me all about you. Welcome," he said, sticking out his hand.

They shook.

"Thanks, Ty mentioned you, too. Great to meet you," she said.

"Tell him sorry I missed his party. We've just been real busy around here. Uh, Nancy's gonna call you guys in one by one," he said, directing the last remark to the group.

As Sean left, the other two cast resentful looks Madison's way. The assumption was she had a leg up because of her connections. Maybe so, as far as the Harvard network went, but when it came to her brother, the opposite was true.

The gray-haired woman came up to them with a clipboard in her hand.

"I'm Nancy, Judge Conroy's case manager, and I'm in charge of this application process. I'll collect your transcripts and writing samples now, please."

The case manager handled the judge's docket, filing papers, scheduling court appearances, that sort of thing. Nancy looked the part of paper pusher, small and neat with a bland expression, dressed in slacks, a sweater, and loafers, with hot-pink readers hanging from a chain around her neck. They handed over their transcripts and writing samples. She went through the pages, shuffling them, sticking Post-its in places, then clipping them to her board.

"The judge will see you in alphabetical order by last name. Joshua Ackerman?"

The male candidate sprang up and followed Nancy into the judge's office.

"What's your name?" Madison asked the woman.

"I'm Priya Patel."

"Madison Rivera. Nice to meet you. I guess you're next."

Joshua came and went. Priya was called. The interview blocks seemed to be about half an hour but felt longer to her as she sat there obsessing over what to say about Danny's case. By the time Nancy called her, the sun had long since set, and Madison was starving on top of being mentally exhausted. She walked toward Judge Conroy's office feeling lightheaded, shaky, and unusually anxious. Yes, she gave great interviews, but this time she was at a distinct disadvantage.

Goddamn it, Danny. Why do you always have to screw things up?

Then Nancy shut the door behind her, and she was alone with Judge Conroy.

She paused on the threshold, struck by the beauty of the scene. The skyline shimmering beyond the windows, and the judge, looking like an ice queen, all frosty blue eyes and pale skin, in a white silk blouse with diamonds glittering in her ears. For a second, Madison felt shy. Then the judge came out from behind her desk, a welcoming smile transforming her face. And Madison remembered that she was born for moments like these. She'd find the right words. She always did.

"*Madison*. I'm so glad you decided to apply. Come in, come in."

"Thank you, Professor—or, I mean, *Your Honor*. I'm thrilled to be here. I was so flattered when you asked me to apply."

"'Your Honor' is for the courtroom. Call me Judge; it's less formal. Come, let's sit over here."

She led Madison to a cozy seating area with a sofa and armchair, and a coffee table with a perfect vase of white roses. Sinking into a corner of the sofa, Judge Conroy leaned back with a happy sigh, looking like she was ready to kick off her high heels. (She didn't.) They were lovely, Manolo Blahniks, if Madison was not mistaken.

"It's been a long day," the judge confided. "A very dull trial, and now these interviews. I'm ready for a nap."

Close up, the judge did look tired, with makeup caking in the delicate lines on her face and a tinge of sadness in her eyes. Or was she imagining that? The details of her husband's death, fresh in Madison's mind, cast her in a tragic light. From what she'd read in her search last night, Judge Conroy's husband had been a wonderful human being and a dreamboat to look at. She'd never remarried. Of course, five years wasn't that long a time to stay single after a loss like that. To the judge, it must feel like yesterday.

Wanting to cheer her up, Madison decided to hold off on mentioning Danny for the moment. She put on a perky smile.

"I'll try not to be boring with my answers," she said, perching on the edge of the armchair.

"I didn't mean to imply that I expect to be bored. To the contrary. I've been looking forward to our chat. I enjoy your participation in class. You're well-prepared and always have an opinion. I can tell you're passionate about the Fourth Amendment, and it makes me feel the extra hours I'm putting in are worthwhile."

"Oh, they are. I absolutely adore your class. We all do. You know what Harvard Law is like. So many of the profs are ivory-tower types. All theory, with no understanding of the real world. You tell it like it is, and that's invaluable to me."

The judge actually blushed at the compliment. "Thank you. I love teaching. But not everybody here is excited that I'm doing it. Nancy is unhappy about my absence from court. We're falling behind on opinions, and she hates that. It's a point of pride with her to have the fastest docket in the courthouse. Which is why we're moving to fill this internship quickly, to maintain staffing levels, to churn out opinions faster."

Madison was tempted to ask what had happened to the last intern. Was she really fired, and if so, why? Judge Conroy seemed relaxed and open enough that she might answer. Better to keep quiet, though. Sensitive questions were best reserved for *after* getting the job. Although not when it came to Danny. That, she had decided to disclose up front. Yet here she was, dragging her feet. Maybe she should just get it over with.

"Judge, I should probably mention—"

Judge Conroy held up a finger. "Hold on, let me review your CV," she said, perusing the application.

Madison folded her hands in her lap. Taking a deep breath, she looked around the room. The office was large and beautifully decorated in shades of blue and gray, with soft lighting and silk drapes to soften the angular, modern lines of the architecture. In addition to the imposing desk and the seating area where they were, there was a conference table with chairs, and bookshelves lined with leather volumes. The one thing missing was any clue to the personal life of the woman who occupied it. The law partners with whom Madison had interviewed boasted credenzas covered in family photos, walls hung with diplomas, side tables brimming with their kids' art. There was an explanation, of course. Her husband had been murdered. She had no children. There was no kid art to hang, no family photos. Even a wedding photo would be too painful.

The judge looked up, and Madison imagined she saw shadows in her eyes.

"Your credentials are impressive, but I need you to understand, this position is extremely demanding. You'll be working for the law clerks, doing legal research and writing memos summarizing the results. The research you do will be directly used in drafting judicial opinions. The workload is intense. Do you think you can handle it?"

Madison had been asked that question on repeat during recruiting season. Her mind stuck on the Danny problem, she rattled off her standard reply. *High honors in legal research class. Law review. Moot court.* Judge Conroy nodded like she was paying attention, but her eyes glazed.

"I have to say, that sounded rehearsed," the judge commented.

Madison's cheeks flamed. She was distracted and screwing up.

"Sorry. I've been interviewing a lot."

Conroy tossed the application aside. "Let's get away from scripted answers. Tell me what's *not* on your CV."

What did that mean? Did she think Madison was hiding something? Was it possible that she knew about Danny?

"What I'm getting at," the judge said, sensing Madison's consternation, "is, what's your background? Who influenced you? What made you want to be a lawyer?" the judge said.

"*Oh.* Okay. Well, *you* influenced me, to be honest."

"I'm not looking for flattery. Dig deeper. Something from your past."

"That is from my past. I went to Catholic Prep, like you did. I saw you speak at Career Day when I was fourteen years old. From that moment, I knew I wanted to be a lawyer."

The judge's mouth fell open. "I remember giving that talk. They asked me because they thought I'd set an example. I can't believe you were there. Are you serious?"

"Absolutely. It was a tough time in my life, and school was my refuge. Hearing you speak was so exciting. I imagined myself in the courtroom, just like you. It gave me a goal to work toward. It meant a lot."

Madison had wanted to tell her about their connection for the longest time. Now, the personal details came spilling out. Dad's death, Mom's breakdown, being sent to live at Aunt Nilda's. The judge listened intently.

"My aunt supported my education," she said. "She wanted me to go to private school, because I was academically gifted, and my mom was—well, she was going through a lot. My aunt was the one who helped me apply to Catholic Prep and get a scholarship, though it didn't cover the whole tuition. I always worked outside school. But it was worth it. That place changed my life. I did Model UN. Debate. Student government. I branched out, took risks, tried new things."

"Fantastic. Give me an example of that."

"Well, for instance, I always loved to swim, but I never thought of myself as an athlete. I was encouraged to join the swim team. Turned out, I was pretty good. My year, the team went to the finals. Between the academics, the clubs, sports, and the excellent college counseling, I got into Harvard for undergrad. But I never forgot hearing you speak. From the beginning of college, I was aiming for law school."

"I went to Harvard undergrad, too. Were you a Gov major?"

"Social Studies."

"No kidding. Same. We went to the same schools, had the same major. And the personal journey really resonates, too. Madison, I can't tell you how much this sounds like my own story."

"Really?"

"Word for word. I'm from Southie, from a modest background, too. And I had hardships growing up."

She never would've guessed. South Boston had gentrified a lot recently, but its history was as a tough, working-class neighborhood, mainly Irish, at least in the old days.

"I'm surprised. I would've thought your ancestors came over on the *Mayflower*."

"I get that a lot. Whether it's how I look, or the way I talk. And you, your heritage?"

"Puerto Rican from East Boston, though my mom recently moved to Revere. Rents are higher there, but the neighborhood is better. I'm glad for her. She has a good job now and is finally back on her feet. Things were tough after my dad passed."

"I know just how that is. My mother wasn't well, either. She had leukemia when I was a kid, and eventually passed away."

"I'm *so* sorry."

"Thank you. I get the sense you understand the loneliness of it. The responsibility. Were you an only child, too?"

"Yes."

What the hell? In the heat of the moment, the lie just fell out of her mouth. She was supposed to come clean about Danny. Instead she got caught up in their conversation and claimed he didn't exist. Why? To seem more like the judge? She was an idiot. Now it was out there. She had to take it back. But how? The judge was leaning forward, her face aglow with emotion, going on about how alike they were.

"I *knew* it. You remind me so much of myself, Madison. I even had someone in my life—a family friend, but I called him Uncle—

who supported my education when my mother couldn't. Like you said, it wasn't her fault. She was just ill, like your mom. Without Catholic Prep, I wouldn't be where I am today. It made all the difference. The structure. The resources. Forget about Harvard. It's our shared high school experience that convinces me you're the right person for this job. And to think my Career Day talk all those years ago influenced you to become a lawyer. And brought us here, to this moment. That's very meaningful to me. I want you on my team, Madison. You're hired."

Crap.

Instead of being thrilled, she felt trapped by her stupid mistake. It was too late to correct the record now. What could she do—say she forgot she had a brother? How would that look? The judge would start to wonder. She'd probably get suspicious and investigate. She'd find out about the drug case and think that Madison concealed it intentionally. Madison would look dishonest—exactly what she'd been trying to avoid.

Oh, God. She'd screwed up royally.

Maybe she should turn down the job.

But no, that would look bizarre, too, declining a position she'd just applied for after acing the interview. It wasn't credible to say she'd had another offer. Nobody would believe that. Besides, after their conversation, she didn't want to say no. She felt closer to Judge Conroy than ever before. The judge saw Madison as a younger version of herself. She could become an important mentor. They might even be friends one day. Was she really going to turn down this incredible opportunity because of Danny? That would be too unfair.

Of course, she'd have to tell eventually. She *would* tell. This just wasn't the right moment.

The judge stood up and stuck her hand out for shaking. It was hanging there, becoming more awkward by the second.

"Thank you, I'm thrilled to accept," Madison said, and shook her hand warmly.

"I'm so glad. We need you to start right away. See Nancy on the way out. She'll give you the employment forms to complete. I'm so looking forward to working with you. Welcome aboard."

"Thank you, Judge. I won't let you down."

The veteran of many practice interviews and numerous real ones, Madison recited those parting words automatically. But as she walked from the office, her smile faded. The truth was, she'd already let Judge Conroy down, and not in a small way. She lied to her face about having a brother. And not just any brother—a drug defendant in the judge's own court. Not only did she feel terrible about it, but once the judge found out, the consequences could be severe.

They'd fired the last intern. What would they do to her?

....

6

Nancy, the case manager, sat behind the receptionist's desk.

"She offered you the position, didn't she?" she asked, eyeing Madison narrowly as she exited the judge's office.

"How did you know?"

"She likes the Harvard kids, and you were the only Harvard kid."

Gee, thanks. This lady was not warm and fuzzy, that was for sure.

"Take a seat, there's paperwork," Nancy said, coming over to the waiting area, a folder in her hands.

They sat side by side on the sofa. Settling her glasses on her nose, Nancy spread the forms across the coffee table.

"Here we go: employment form and NDA. They're *quite* detailed. Would you like to sit there and read all the fine print? Or I can just walk you through."

Nancy glanced at her watch impatiently, making clear what the right answer was. A good lawyer read documents before signing. But Madison was afraid to annoy her.

"I'd appreciate that," she said.

"Starting with the NDA—that's a *non-disclosure agreement*," she said, enunciating like she thought Madison was incapable of understanding.

"I'm familiar with those from contracts class."

"Forget everything you think you know. This NDA goes well beyond what you're used to, because Judge Conroy has unique security concerns. You can't discuss anything about this internship with outsiders. And absolutely nothing about the judge. Not what she says or does, who she meets with, what she wears, the papers you see on her desk. Her friends, her pets, her home address. It's all confidential. That may seem extreme, but it's for her security."

"I understand."

Nancy flipped the form to the signature page. Madison took a deep breath and signed on the dotted line.

"Now, the employment form. We use this with our law clerks. It asks for a lot of specific information that you may not have on hand at the moment. Names, addresses, phone numbers, and so on. Of past employers, references, roommates, housemates, family members. Basically, everyone you know."

Family members. Shit. She would have to put down Danny's name, then. Well, of course she would—she'd been planning to tell the judge about him anyway, to clear up the misunderstanding. She just didn't want to do it on a personnel form, with no context. This was too big a deal. She'd pretended to be an only child, with no siblings. It would look like she lied. Well, because she *did* lie. To a federal judge, a woman she admired and felt a meaningful connection to. The judge felt it, too. She'd surely feel betrayed. This required an explanation, and an apology. She needed to go back in there and clear things up. Now.

She got to her feet.

"Where do you think you're going?" Nancy said.

"There's something I need to tell Judge Conroy."

"The interview's over. Sit down."

"But—"

"I *said* sit down."

Nancy spoke softly, but with an edge to her tone that couldn't be ignored. Madison obeyed.

"If you want to succeed in this office, Miss Rivera, you need to understand something from the start. The judge is a very busy woman with an extremely important job. We're here to support her, not distract her. If you have questions, or concerns of any kind, you come to me, or ask the law clerks. You do not, under any circumstances, approach the judge. Is that clear?"

"But when we talked in the interview—"

"She can be quite *warm*," Nancy said dismissively, like that was a character flaw. "It creates a misimpression."

"A misimpression. Exactly. You see—"

"*No.* You need to understand, you're here to do legal research under the supervision of the law clerks. Your contact with Judge Conroy will be limited to observing her in court. You're not to knock on her office door or try to initiate small talk or get face time. I know you Harvard kids are hot to network. But if you want to succeed here, keep your head down. Complete your assignments in a timely fashion. And *never* bother the judge. Are we clear?"

"Yes."

"Good. Now, where was I? Oh, yes. The form. Take it home. Fill it out, sign the bottom. You're affirming the truth of your responses under penalty of perjury—"

"Perjury?"

Her mouth went dry. There it was—possible *criminal* charges if she didn't write Danny's name down. Yet no way to speak to Judge Conroy in advance to clear up the misunderstanding. This was a freaking disaster, and she didn't know who she was madder at—Danny or herself. She swallowed hard, hoping that the panic didn't show on her face.

"Is that a problem?" Nancy said, giving her a sharp look.

"No, of course not."

But Nancy was eyeing her suspiciously.

"Just so you know, I go over these things with a fine-tooth comb. Any misrepresentations or inaccuracies *will* be reported to your law school dean, as well as referred to the FBI for investigation."

"I assure you, that won't be necessary," Madison said, as an anxious pulse beat in her throat.

"I hope not. Bring it back tomorrow when you start the job."

After coming to terms on the hours Madison would work, they said good night. Nancy saw her out, shutting the chambers door firmly behind her.

Back in her dorm room, she scarfed down a Kind bar as she studied the specific wording of the question about family members. It was airtight, asking for the names, addresses, and Social Security numbers of mother, father, spouse, children, and *siblings*. For each, it asked you to fill in place of birth, immigration status, place of employment—and whether they'd been convicted of a crime. There was no way to avoid mentioning Danny, or his drug case, other than to lie, which obviously she wasn't going to do. Lying to the judge during the interview had been a stupid mistake made in the heat of the moment. It was not intentional. And she didn't plan to repeat it. That would be insane when the form had to be filled out in writing and signed under penalty of perjury, and Nancy had put her on notice that she'd be vetting it carefully.

Madison read through the form again, looking for a place to explain why she hadn't brought up Danny in the interview. But there was no way to expound on your answers. No box saying "other" or "additional information," only specific questions with limited space to respond. That was just as well. This problem was too big to fix with a couple of sentences on a form. If she wanted to salvage her working relationship with Conroy, she needed to speak to her personally. It was the only way. Nancy had made it clear that wouldn't be happening in the office. She'd have to approach Judge Conroy after class, at the law school. But Conroy only taught once a week. Madison wouldn't see her at the law school for days.

The form was due tomorrow.

She slept poorly that night. The next morning, she sleepwalked through her classes with the case manager's voice echoing in her head. *Perjury perjury perjury.* At noon, she walked up to the door of the judge's chambers with the employment form still uncompleted in her backpack. She was all about her career and new horizons, and normally, onboarding at a judicial internship would have been a thrill. Instead, she felt like she was taking her life in her hands, and not in a good way.

Kelsey, the receptionist, buzzed her in. She was sitting at her desk, eating a burrito.

"Everyone's in court. You sit in the law clerks' office. That way."

She waved toward the back hall.

"Thanks."

"Oh, wait. Employment form? Nancy said to collect it from you."

Madison caught her breath. She'd been nursing a small spark of hope that they would forget, though of course they hadn't.

"I'm still tracking down some addresses. Can I give it to you later?"

Kelsey's eyebrows shot up to her hairline.

"Nancy hates when things are late. It's your funeral."

Kelsey turned back to her burrito. Madison found her way to the law clerks' office with a sour taste in her throat. But the office was everything she'd imagined. Large and bright, with a great view of the city, yet messy and wonderfully lived in. Scuffed government-issue furniture, shelves of law books, and old metal filing cabinets that held the wisdom of the ages. It was a dream. There were three desks—two of them clearly occupied, covered in books and papers, coffee mugs, half-drunk bottles of water. The third desk was crammed in a corner, its surface clear except for a desktop computer and a folder with her name on it. She threw off her coat and sat down eagerly, opening it to find her first assignment, a jurisdictional issue she recognized from first-year Civil Procedure. She was officially a judicial intern, and it was going to be great. The Danny problem receded from her mind in her eagerness to get started.

There were footsteps in the hall. A moment later, the two law clerks spilled through the doorway, laughing. Imani was tall and stylish, with braids that skimmed her shoulders. Sean wore his hair in a man-bun and had on a Hawaiian-print tie with his business suit. The courtroom was the last refuge of formal business attire, and Madison was here for it, wearing a skirt and blazer herself. She got to her feet with a smile. They were her supervisors, but she expected they'd become friends.

"Here's the fresh blood. Hard at work already, I see," Sean said.

Imani gave Madison an appraising look. "Have we met?"

"You probably don't remember, but I was one of the peons on law review last year, when you were in charge."

Recognition dawned in her eyes. "Oh, I do remember. You're the girl who was dating Ty Evans."

Madison laughed in astonishment. "*That's* how you remember me?"

"Hell, yeah. Ty's like king of the law school."

"No. I'm the queen, and he was my consort."

"Was? You let that boy slip away?"

"Yep. He's with Chloe Kessler now."

"Humph, I know her. Legacy admit," Imani scoffed.

"Imani, give it a rest," Sean chided. "You'll drive Madison away, and we can't afford to lose another intern." He turned to Madison. "Please forgive my co-clerk. She can be quite opinionated, but she has a heart of gold."

"Oh, we want to keep you. Ty's not the only thing I remember about you. You were a good little researcher if I recall."

They joked around a minute longer. Madison felt comfortable enough to ask the awkward question.

"Hey, I hope you don't mind my asking, but what happened to the last intern? Is it true she was fired? I'm trying to figure out what *not* to do."

Sean threw an anxious glance over his shoulder at the hallway.

"I'm not sure we should get into that," he said.

Imani gave him an impatient look, lowering her voice to a near whisper.

"C'mon, Sean. We have to give her a heads-up, if only out of self-interest. I've got a pile of research I need done."

"All right, but can we talk somewhere else? I'd feel more comfortable."

"She should come to lunch with us," Imani said.

Sean nodded. "We usually go to the salad place. Come along, and we'll give you some survival tips."

Survival tips? That didn't sound good.

"Great," she said.

In the reception area, Kelsey's desk was empty. The door to Judge Conroy's office stood open, and Madison could hear her voice, low and calm, talking to someone. She craned her neck toward the door, hoping to catch a glimpse of the judge.

Imani noticed the direction of her gaze.

"The judge doesn't eat lunch with us except for special occasions like birthdays and so on."

"Though you will get to sit in on court regularly, so you can observe her there. It's just, when it comes to the judge, interns are expected to be seen and not heard," Sean said.

"Oh, yeah, I got an earful from Nancy—"

Imani looked horrified, drawing a finger across her throat just as Nancy's flinty voice rang out from the judge's office. They quickly left chambers.

"Sorry," Madison said once they were outside.

"Oh, no worries as far as we're concerned," Imani said. "But watch your back with Nancy. That woman has nooo sense of humor."

Outside, it was raining again, with a bitter wind coming from the north. They ran across the street and ducked into an office building that had a takeout salad place. Lunch out wasn't in her budget, but sometimes you just had to network. She looked forward to the day she was a real lawyer, when money would not be an issue. They got their salads and found a table under a glass atrium streaked with rain, making small talk about the usual subjects as they ate. Which classes Madison was taking, gossip about people they knew in common at the law school, that sort of thing.

"It's amazing that you're taking a class from the judge," Sean said. "What's she like as a teacher?"

"Very charismatic. Really organized. Lots of inside scoop on the justice system. It's amazing. I'm lucky to have the chance."

"I suppose you got a leg up in getting the internship, since you knew her from school."

"It definitely helped. Although I can't say I *know* her. It's hard to get a word with her after class, and she doesn't do office hours as much as some of the other professors."

"Well, she's got her plate full here. The truth is, we don't get much face time with her either. It's not the sort of chambers where the judge socializes with the law clerks."

"Yeah, Nancy made that clear."

"She's pretty possessive of the judge," Imani said.

"*Protective* is a better way to put it," Sean said.

Once the food was gone, Imani pushed aside her miso bowl and looked Madison in the eye.

"About your question from before," she said, "we do want to give you a heads-up. But anything we say about chambers culture is absolute cone of silence. Agreed?"

"Of course. I know all about the confidentiality requirement. I had to sign that crazy NDA."

Imani and Sean exchanged glances.

"Huh, that's weird. I never heard of them making interns sign that before," Imani said.

"It must be post-Olivia syndrome," Sean said, and Imani nodded.

"Olivia?"

"Your predecessor. And yes, to answer your question, she was let go."

"Which Olivia? There are at least three in my year."

"She wasn't from Harvard."

"Really? I thought Judge Conroy only hired from Harvard."

"We thought so, too. But I'm pretty sure she said she went to BC Law. Imani thinks it was BU."

"And yes, it's weird that we don't know, and that we had different impressions of which school she was from," Imani said. "That's bizarre, in fact. We don't know what she did to get fired, but we think it had to do with misrepresenting herself. Which is a significant security violation, as well as an ethical issue. Obviously, you're not misrepresenting yourself, Madison. So, in that sense, you have nothing to worry about."

Shit. Little do they know.

"On the other hand, we wanted to warn you, because ever since the Olivia fiasco, Nancy has gotten very strict. Which, look, we get it. She takes any threat to the judge's safety seriously," Sean said.

"The intern threatened the judge's safety?"

"Not that we know of specifically. But obviously anyone who'd lie about their identity raises security flags, don't you think?"

And if they lied about their brother being a defendant in a drug case? Even worse.

"I guess. Though, if it was a matter of padding her résumé to try to get the job, maybe that's not really a security threat, per se?"

Madison's palms were sweaty, and her heart hammered inside her chest. Could they tell she was hiding something? Though she hadn't lied on the background form *yet*, if only because she hadn't finished filling the damn thing out.

"Maybe, but you can't be too careful. At least, Judge Conroy can't. I don't know if you're aware, but she was targeted before," Imani said.

"Are you talking about what happened to her husband? What I saw online says his murder is unsolved."

"They never were able to verify a connection to her cases," Sean said. "And she never speaks of him. We assume it was connected because of how security conscious she is. Anyway, it was years ago. I don't want you to worry about working here. I mean, security-wise."

"I'm not worried."

"Good. We don't want to scare you. Just to explain why Nancy made you sign an NDA. She wants to protect the judge."

She should ask them about the background form. Maybe they'd have an idea for how she could delay completing it. If she could just put off submitting it until next week, she could speak to the judge in person after class and explain about Danny.

"Oh, I understand. By the way, that's not the only form she wants me to fill out. There's this crazy employment form that could take me days to finish. Is there any way around that?"

The clerks looked at her with blank expressions.

"Employment form?" Sean said.

"You don't mean the FBI background-check form?" Imani asked.

"Yes, I think that's it. Nancy did mention the FBI," Madison said, her stomach tightening. *FBI. Jeez.*

"That's strange. Interns never had to fill that out before," Imani said.

"Wait a minute, that confirms our theory of why Olivia was fired," Sean said. "Why else would Nancy make an intern fill out that FBI background-check form? The last intern must've lied on her résumé, right?"

"We knew that."

"No we didn't. Not for sure."

"Whatever. I feel for you, Madison. That form takes hours," Imani said.

"And Nancy wants it back right away. I don't have all those details at my fingertips. Can I get an extension somehow?"

"She wants it in one day?"

"Yes."

"That's nuts. What do you think, Sean? What should she do?"

He frowned. "On the one hand, completing that form overnight is not realistic. On the other, Nancy is a stickler for deadlines. She'll have a cow. And believe me, she can make your life unpleasant."

"What if Madison hands the form in with the answers she knows, and anything she doesn't know, she leaves blank and says she's working on it?"

"Good idea," Sean said, nodding.

"The FBI won't mind?" Madison asked.

"Oh, the FBI has nothing to do with this. It's just for Nancy's benefit."

"I don't understand."

"They're not actually going to run an official background check on you. It's too resource intensive for a job that doesn't handle classified information."

"Are you sure? I would hate to submit something incomplete to the FBI."

"Positive. Nancy made me and Imani fill out the same form. *We* were never checked by the FBI, and we're salaried government employees. She just likes to have the information on file for her own peace of mind."

"Is that normal, for a case manager to ask so many personal questions?"

"It *is* kind of odd now that you mention it," Imani said, crooking an eyebrow. "Nancy pretends it's some official process, when it's not. It's just *her*."

"Yeah, because she's the one who handles hiring paperwork," Sean said. "Naturally, being Nancy, she uses the most ridiculous, burdensome form in the world. You'd expect nothing less. But there's nothing weird about it."

"I guess."

"Anyway, Madison, you have no choice. Suck it up and fill out the form, just like we did. If you're pressed for time, do what Imani said. Hand it in with some blanks. Stick a Post-it on it saying you're waiting for more information. But don't delay. If there's anything that sets her off, it's missing a deadline. Speaking of, we should get back," he said, checking his watch.

They bussed their table.

Madison took the law clerks' advice, handing the form to Kelsey right after lunch with a yellow Post-it on the front that said

"Incomplete, awaiting information." She even left it unsigned for extra CYA. The plan was: drag her feet for long enough to speak to the judge after class next week and explain that stupid omission about Danny. Then she'd circle back and complete the form. At least in the meantime, there would be no perjury, nothing to blow up her life or destroy her future.

She *hoped*.

....

7

Madison spent that afternoon settling into her internship duties under Imani's watchful eye. It was borderline disturbing how eager the law clerks were to have her avoid the mistakes of the mysterious Olivia. She did her best to put Olivia out of her mind, and Danny, too. There was so much to learn, like Judge Conroy's preferred format for legal memoranda, how to access the online research databases, how to prepare a binder of cases for the judge to consult on the bench. Hours passed in a blur of excitement and a constant buzz of stress. Imani set her up with a login ID and gave her a lecture about computer security. She wasn't to use her work computer for personal purposes, which obviously meant she couldn't research Danny's case. Not that she would have, though it was kind of a shame, given that she now had full online access to all of Judge Conroy's case files. All she'd have to do was type in Danny's name. She resisted the temptation. After all, she'd just dodged a bullet with the employment form. How stupid would it be to turn around and get fired for unauthorized accessing of files? *No, just no.*

Madison put her head down and made quick progress on the first research assignment. The judge was old-fashioned. She still liked her information on paper. Madison printed the most important case precedents off Westlaw, highlighted the holdings in yellow, three-hole-punched them and put them in a binder for the judge, just like Imani showed her. Then she got to work on a memo summarizing the key points. Shortly after five, Sean returned from court. He and Imani were both mired in work, behind on draft opinions. All three of them sat at their desks in silence for the next couple of hours, the only sounds the clacking of keyboards and occasional sighs.

At seven, Sean got up, stretched, and yawned.

"I think I'll head out."

Imani raised an eyebrow. "Hot date?"

"Yeah, with my sofa and a carton of noodles."

Imani started gathering her things. "It *is* Friday night, and it's been a long week. We should go home. You too, Madison."

"I'm close to done with this memo, and I really want to finish. Is it okay if I stay another hour? That way you'll have the memo on your desk first thing Monday morning."

The clerks exchanged glances.

"It *would* be good to get it to Judge Conroy," Imani said.

"If we leave her alone, and there's a problem, we'll get blamed for not supervising. And we're not supposed to give out the code to the door."

"She's an intern. It's not like we're giving it to DoorDash."

"I know. But just—*Olivia*."

"Who freaked out after Olivia? Nancy. Who's breathing down our necks to speed up draft opinions? Nancy. She can't have it both ways. Madison's just trying to help out."

"True." He sighed. "Okay, Madison, we'll give you the access code, but you can't let anyone into chambers, understand? Whether you know them or not, no matter what they say. You're not authorized to admit people."

"I know that. I would never."

"When you leave, turn off the lights, enter the code in the keypad on the door to the reception room, then you have sixty seconds to exit."

"By the way," Imani said, "once you have the code, you can get into the building after hours through the employee entrance. Just FYI if you need to work this weekend to get the memo done by Monday. Have a good night."

The clerks left. Madison kept working. Her phone buzzed intermittently, but she knew it was Mom, wanting to talk about Danny. This wasn't the time or place. Only after she finished the memo and emailed it to Imani did she check her messages. There were numerous missed calls and two voicemails from Mom. She listened to the older one first.

"Hey, honey, give me a call. It's important. I need to know if you talked to that judge and what you found out about Danny's case. Love you."

She never said she'd speak to Judge Conroy. In fact, she said she wouldn't. The most she promised was to get a copy of the plea agreement or other documents, so they could make a plan. Which, granted, she hadn't done yet, but it had not been long, and she'd been busy.

The tone of the second voicemail upset her.

"Madison, I left you a message before. Please call me back. I need to know what you found out. Tomorrow's Saturday. I'm going to visiting hours. I want you to come with me. We need a game plan for how we're getting him out of jail. I'm counting on you. Don't let me down."

A game plan for getting Danny out of jail? That was asking for the moon. No way could she deliver. She couldn't even get the documents from his case before visiting hours tomorrow because the Clerk's Office had closed at five and wouldn't reopen until Monday morning. Of course, she could just pull them up on this computer she was sitting in front of right now. Danny's case was in there. It would be easy enough to find his plea agreement, print it, and bring it to the visit.

She wouldn't be hurting anybody.

Except herself.

She'd been explicitly told not to use the work computer for personal purposes. Not only that—if she got caught, they'd figure out that Danny was her brother. That she'd lied to the judge in the interview. And didn't write his name on the form. It wouldn't matter that she never signed the damn thing, or if she put a Post-it on it. She'd be fired faster than you could say *Olivia*.

Why should she risk that for him?

She could hear her mother's voice. *Because he's your brother*.

But what if she got caught?

If. She might not. She probably wouldn't. How would they find out?

Mom expected her to help Danny. He needed her legal expertise, which she couldn't deliver without looking at the case file.

Ugh.

Heaving a sigh, she got up to take a reconnaissance stroll. The lights were on in the break room. She flipped them off. In the reception area, they were also on, though Kelsey had left hours ago. The door to Judge Conroy's office was closed, a bar of light visible beneath it. Did that mean the judge was still here, or just that she wasn't good about conserving electricity? No way to know. There was no sign of Nancy, whose office Madison had been told was way on the other side of the floor, next to the courtroom. Though she wouldn't put it past Nancy to stay late just to spring a surprise inspection.

If she accessed the files, she'd have to be very, very careful.

She could handle that. Just keep her ears open for footsteps. It was a long hallway. Nobody could sneak up on her unless she got sloppy and let them. And she wasn't sloppy.

It was just a few documents that were publicly available anyway.

Back at her desk, she tilted the computer screen away from the door and typed Danny's case number into the database. Pages and pages of documents loaded, putting a scare into her. *What?* How guilty was Danny to have so many court filings? Oh, wait a minute . . . Thank God. It turned out that case number wasn't just for Danny's case, but for all sixteen men charged in that conspiracy to sell heroin. The lead defendant was a guy named Ricky Peña. She remembered Danny mentioning him. Ricky was who he met with about bankrolling the auto body shop. He was a major drug kingpin, the boss of the organization, which meant that the case was named after him—*United States v. Peña.* He was also, according to an indictment that had the word "FUGITIVE" stamped next to his name in bright red letters, long gone. So Peña got away. As did most of the other named defendants. Danny said that. They all ran. Her hapless brother was one of the few who got caught, and he was the innocent one.

She found an affidavit summarizing all the evidence in the case. It had been sworn out by a Detective Charles Wallace on the night of Danny's arrest.

Wallace. He must be the dirty cop who Danny had talked about.

The affidavit went on for fifteen pages about Peña and his crew. It gave detailed descriptions of surveillances, meetings with informants, hand-to-hand sales of heroin. Wallace had the goods on the lot of them. Too bad most of them escaped justice. Of the three who'd actually been apprehended, one was Danny, who was barely mentioned. She found one paltry sentence about him on the very last page of the fifteen-page affidavit.

Upon entering the premises, Det. Wallace observed defendant DANNY RIVERA with a black duffel bag, which was subsequently opened, searched, and found to contain one hundred bundles of heroin of the brand 'Rocket' commonly sold by the Peña organization and indicated by a stamp of a rocket ship printed on the plastic bag in red.

In the visiting room, Danny had told her that he was in the bar, talking to Ricky, when the phone call came in from Wallace, and everybody ran. Everybody except him, because he didn't know any better. He got left holding the bag—literally.

Jesus. Was he telling the truth?

He claimed he was framed. Up until that moment, if she was honest with herself, she'd had her doubts. But there it was in black and white, just like he said.

Mom needed to see this affidavit. It backed Danny up a hundred percent. Of course, Mom had believed him from the beginning. It was only Madison who'd doubted him.

Doubted *her own brother.*

What was wrong with her?

Damn, she owed him. She ought to help him straighten out this mess, even if it was risky.

She sent the affidavit to the printer, then searched for a copy of Danny's plea agreement. She read it with fists clenched and head buzzing with rage. Danny had signed away his rights, including the right to challenge the plea, and pleaded guilty to the whole freaking conspiracy. Everything the Peña crew did. All the heroin those lowlifes sold. All the shootings and murders. He wasn't there for any of it, but he agreed to pay the price. How was that possible? They had no evidence on him. The case was so weak. Madison hadn't graduated from law school yet, but even she knew better than to let a client take a plea this unfair.

How could Danny's lawyer have let this happen?

Her brother had told her the answer. The lawyer was in on it.

As much as it shook her faith in the justice system, she had to admit that was the only explanation that made sense.

She sent the plea agreement to print, then started researching the lawyer, Raymond F. Logue. He was an old-timer, admitted to the bar in 1972. The Massachusetts Bar Association website showed a long history of disciplinary complaints, for everything from misappropriation of funds to conflict of interest to failure to maintain malpractice insurance. He'd been fined multiple times, referred for continuing education, and suspended twice. But never disbarred.

How was *that* possible? This man should *not* be practicing law. Did he have friends in high places? She heard Danny's voice in her head. *My lawyer goes way back with this judge. Has her in his pocket.*

Danny had been telling the truth about everything else. But Judge Conroy being in league with a dirty lawyer was a bridge too far. That, she would never believe.

A shadow fell across the carpet. Somebody stood in the doorway behind her. She caught the scent of rose perfume.

"Madison. You're here late," the judge said.

8

....

Judge Conroy picked up the pages off the printer. Madison forced a smile, but her heart had stopped beating for a second. The judge handed her the pages without so much as glancing at them, and she placed them face down on her desk. She wasn't out of the woods yet. The computer screen was tilted away from the door. If the judge took a step to the left, she'd see the research into Logue, the dirty lawyer she was supposedly in league with, according to Danny. Not that Madison believed that. She didn't. Not for a second.

"Shame on the law clerks, leaving the new intern to man the fort—on a Friday night, no less," the judge said.

She stood beside Imani's chair, her hand lingering on its back, looking impossibly glamorous in a navy sweater dress, a long strand of pearls, and sky-high heels that must pinch at the end of a long day. If she decided to sit, she'd have a bird's-eye view of the screen.

"They told me to go home. But I wanted to finish up my assignment so you'd get it first thing Monday."

To her own surprise, Madison's voice came out calm and steady.

She had to hand it to herself: she was smooth in a crisis. Moving her hand to the mouse, she clicked, and the list of Raymond Logue's disciplinary complaints vanished. Not a moment too soon. The judge sank into the chair with a sigh and kicked off her shoes, looking right at that screen.

"You wrote a whole research memo on your first day. I'd say that calls for a reward. Have you eaten?"

She was confused by the question.

"Have I— Oh. Yes. The clerks took me to lunch."

"It is after eight o'clock. I was asking about dinner."

The judge's question made her realize she was famished, and her stomach let out an audible rumble. The judge laughed.

"That answers that. I'm heading out to get a bite. Join me."

"You want me to, to come to dinner?" she stammered.

"Yes, was I not clear?"

So much for the idea that the judge only socialized with her staff on special occasions. Maybe she liked Madison more than the law clerks. They did have that special connection because of high school. Too bad she had to ruin it. This was her chance to speak to the judge alone. To admit she'd—what? Fudged? Omitted? Forgotten to mention Danny? One way or the other, she would spit it out.

"I'd love to join you. I, um, just need to finish up a few things—if that's all right."

She couldn't leave without covering her tracks. Getting caught researching Danny's case would make her transgression a thousand times worse.

"I can wait. Do you like sushi? There's a little place in my neighborhood. I could go on Resy and see if they have a table."

"That would be awesome. *Thank you.*"

"I'll be in my office. Come get me when you're done."

She watched in amazement as the judge picked up her shoes,

walking away in stocking feet. Not only hadn't she been caught, but she'd been invited to dinner? Hanging with Kathryn Conroy. She felt *chosen*. But she couldn't let herself get distracted, or she'd blow it. Nancy would come in, find a document with Danny's name on it, and Madison would be toast. Clicking around the computer screen, she searched for minimized documents, carefully closing each one before exiting the database and logging off. She stashed Danny's documents in her backpack and headed to the bathroom.

After a long, stressful day, her makeup had melted, giving her a shiny look. She freshened it, slicked on some red lipstick, brushed her hair till it shone, and twisted it into a quick bun to look dressier. If only her clothes were better. She wore what she could afford. H&M, Uniqlo, Zara, whatever she found on the sale racks marked down to nothing. Her outfit was office appropriate; that wasn't the issue. But she looked like a poor student playing dress-up. Which she was. Someday soon, she'd be a lawyer with a lawyer's paycheck—and oh, the clothes she'd buy. Maybe then she would look the part of the friend of the renowned judge dining on fancy sushi. Until then, well, *fake it till you make it*, right?

Walking up to the judge's door, she took a deep breath and knocked.

"Come in."

Judge Conroy had on a plaid trench coat—Burberry, Madison thought—with the collar turned up to frame her face, and had swapped out heels for a pair of chic weatherproof boots.

"Ready?"

Madison nodded, stepping aside and holding the door open, but the judge shook her head.

"We'll go out the back," she said.

Madison hadn't known there *was* a back. What she'd thought was a closet door opened into a brightly lit, windowless hallway. She followed the judge to an elevator that operated with a biometric sensor. The judge pulled off a black leather glove and pressed her fingers against the screen, and the doors slid open with a high-tech swoosh.

"This is the secure elevator. Reserved for judges. The doors are bulletproof."

Madison nodded, impressed. As they got in, she felt like she was stepping into another life, one of privilege, but also danger. It was thrilling, though maybe it shouldn't be. Judges had these protections for a reason. Litigants got angry. They protested, nonviolently the vast majority of the time, but sometimes—well, just because the murder of the judge's husband remained unsolved didn't mean it wasn't retaliation.

The elevator deposited them in a dim, echoing underground garage, freezing cold and smelling of gasoline. Bulbous security cameras bristled from the corners of tall concrete posts. The judge walked quickly, shoulders tense, boots ringing on the hard floor, looking around like she expected an assailant to leap out at any moment. They came to a white SUV. Before getting in, the judge looked in the back seat. Checking for intruders, perhaps? They got in. Anxiety came off the judge in waves. It was unnerving.

"Do you drive, Madison?" she asked, backing out of the spot.

"Occasionally. I have a license but no car."

The judge nodded, as if weighing the answer. Madison wasn't sure whether she'd passed or failed that one.

They drove up a ramp to a metal gate. A tone sounded and the gate lifted, putting them out on a rain-slicked street. Tree branches and street signs swayed in the wind. They stopped at a traffic light and watched a pedestrian struggle to hold on to his umbrella.

"Thanks for coming out with me. I didn't want to be alone tonight."

The words sounded like they came from the heart, and Madison shot a surprised glance the judge's way. In the light from on-coming cars, her face looked white and strained.

"Is something wrong?"

The judge shook her head, clamping her lips tight, eyes on the road. Madison wondered if she was thinking about her husband. The clerks said they never spoke of him in chambers. But talking was good for the soul, for healing. The swish of wipers and drumbeat of rain on the roof created a sense of intimacy. Maybe the judge would open up to her. Though she was known to be very private, and Madison didn't want to pry. Besides, once she came clean about Danny, the judge might not trust her with personal confidences. That thought was so awful, she wanted to cry. Maybe she should put off mentioning him until later in the dinner.

"Thank you for asking me to dinner," she said to fill the silence. "I'd probably have forgotten to eat otherwise."

"Oh, I remember what it was like, being a law student. Every second spoken for. Classes, extracurriculars. And I imagine you have a big social life. Friends, a boyfriend perhaps?"

"Not at the moment. I dated Ty Evans last year, but we split. We were too competitive to make it as a couple."

"Hah, I can totally see that. He's with Chloe now, right?"

"Yes. How did you know?"

"Her dad's a friend from my prosecutor days. For what it's worth, Doug Kessler really likes Ty."

"Well, charming parents is the sort of thing Ty excels at."

The judge's mouth quirked into a half smile. It came as no surprise that she knew Chloe's dad, a big-name partner in the firm where Madison would work next summer. Douglas Kessler was the kind of lawyer that Judge Conroy probably actually hung out with, as opposed to that lowlife Raymond Logue, who seemed like he got paid with suitcases full of cash. Danny was telling the truth about some things. Madison saw that now. But he was wrong about Judge Conroy being corrupt. She knew it in her heart. Besides, he had no evidence.

They pulled into an open parking spot and dashed through the rain to the restaurant. At the hostess station, the judge once again seemed jumpy.

"A table in the back, facing the door, please," she said, and Madison shot her a glance.

Coming from someone else, that would sound melodramatic, like the person thought they were in a gangster film. But given the judge's history, there could be reason for concern. As they followed the hostess through the bar, Madison found herself looking over her own shoulder. What she saw was heads turning as they passed, people checking out Judge Conroy. Was she known outside the legal community? Or just a beautiful woman, impeccably turned out on a stormy night, like the raindrops left her alone?

The hostess seated them at the far edge of the softly lit bar area, at a small marble-topped table. Music played in the background, mingling with the low buzz of conversation. Judge Conroy shrugged out of her plaid coat, smiling.

"It's so nice being here with you. I really feel that we connect."

Madison lit up. "Me too."

But when they loaded the menu on their phones, she got a shock. Damn, she couldn't afford this place.

"I'm thinking an omakase platter to share, and a bottle of sake. How's that sound?" Judge Conroy asked.

Her brow scrunched. "Well, it's just . . . I bought lunch out, and I—"

"Oh, my treat, of course."

"Are you sure?"

"Madison, I'm not a million years old. I remember what it felt like to be a broke law student."

"Then, thank you. I'm very grateful."

"Thank *you* for accompanying me. I know women are supposed to be cool eating alone in fancy restaurants, but I always feel conspicuous. It's nice to have a companion."

They ordered, then got to chatting. The trial happening in the judge's courtroom. How one of the jurors kept falling asleep. The lawyer who appeared to have a flirtation going with her young associate. And so on. It was fun. So much fun that she didn't want to spoil it.

The waitress brought the sake on a tray with two miniscule cobalt-blue glasses. The judge poured with a ceremonious flourish and then threw hers back like a shot.

"Cheers," she said, her cheeks pinkening.

Madison followed suit and gasped, tears coming to her eyes. She'd been expecting a hot, oily drink. But it was ice cold, fruity, as bracing as gin, and went immediately to her head.

The judge laughed. "Powerful stuff, huh?"

She nodded, choking.

Judge Conroy poured her another, and she downed it. They were tiny glasses after all, and it was Friday night. Being out with the judge, she didn't want to seem like a lightweight or a prude. After the third glass, her head was spinning. If Judge Conroy had kept up with her, it didn't show. Other than two spots of color burning in her pale cheeks, the judge seemed completely unaffected.

The sushi platter arrived and was the most beautiful thing she'd ever seen, the pieces expertly arranged, colorful as jewels in a velvet case. The room shimmered and swayed through her alcohol haze, the conversation flowing like the sake. It was a mind meld. They were kindred spirits who'd gone to the same high school, college, and law school (albeit twenty years apart). They talked about their favorite teachers. About the cliques at Catholic Prep, and where they fit into them—or didn't. The judge claimed to have been a late bloomer socially, awkward as a teen, which Madison couldn't believe, looking at the woman now. Was she really more popular in high school than Kathryn Conroy had been? That somehow led to a discussion of how men treated women in law school, and in the legal profession, and if that differed depending on whether the women were perceived as attractive, the underlying assumption being that they both fell into that category. Then on to how to dress for success. What clothes they liked. What books they read. *Bliss.* She imagined her friends wandering in and seeing them together. Not just any friends. Ty and Chloe in particular, because if she tried to tell them about this, they'd say, *Pics or it didn't happen.* Well, it *was* happening—a heart-to-heart over delicious sushi with the woman she idolized. And the best talk she'd had with anyone in ages.

The sushi was gone. The judge ordered a piece of chocolate fondant cake for them to share, though didn't touch it. She was busy showing off photos of her cat. With ink-black fur and seafoam eyes, the cat looked like a witch's familiar.

"She's *gorgeous.*"

"Matthew gave her to me when she was a tiny kitten. You should've seen her when she was little, so precious. I wish I had those photos on here."

"Matthew? That's your husband?"

A sudden sheen of tears appeared in the judge's eyes. *Shit, what was I thinking?* She'd upset the judge, who put her phone away.

"Let's get the check," she said.

She signaled for the waitress, and Madison's stomach went hollow. This magical evening would end on a sour note because she'd said a stupid thing.

"I'm *so* sorry, Judge. I shouldn't've—"

"No, it's no problem. It's just late."

"I screwed up."

"Madison, it's fine."

"I want you to know," she said, desperate, "it's been an absolute dream having dinner with you. And if you ever want to talk again, I'm here. I'm a good listener, really. Very discreet. I would never share a confidence. You might not believe that, the way I blab on, but it's true."

"Thank you," she said absently.

The judge had broken off eye contact during Madison's outburst. She was looking toward the door, probably desperate for the waitress to come and free her from the crazy stalker girl. She waved again, and the waitress dropped off the check. Judge Conroy glanced at it, then tucked a credit card into the folder. Madison reached for her bag, but the judge shook her head.

"You don't have to," Madison said.

"Relax. I'm not mad."

"You're not? Because I feel like I pried. I know we're not actual friends, that I just work for you. I should know better than to ask personal questions."

"We *are* friends. I consider us friends."

"You do?"

"With all we have in common? After our great talk tonight? Of course. But don't go telling people at the office. It'll cause jealousy."

"I won't, promise."

"And look, I'm the one who brought up Matthew, so I can hardly blame you for asking. He *was* my husband. I lost him, and that's why it's difficult to talk about him."

"I understand."

"I know. You're a good friend."

The judge squeezed her hand with a smile so sad that it made her heart hurt.

"Judge, if there's ever anything I can do to help you out, anything at all, you can count on me. Just ask."

"Actually, there *is* something. I have a favor to ask. I know we're just getting to know each other. But this was such a great conversation that I sense I can trust you. Come to my house now. We'll have a glass of wine, and I'll explain."

9

....

The sake headache that set in on the way to the judge's house didn't stop Madison from appreciating the Back Bay. It was the most beautiful neighborhood in America on any night. But to-night, shimmering with rain, it was utter romance. Ornate town houses, flickering gas lanterns, towering trees wrapped in fairy lights. She held her breath and imagined living here. *Someday.* In the meantime, she was a guest of the woman in the driver's seat, who was as dazzling as the neighborhood.

"We're about to get to my street," the judge said, her voice tight with anxiety. "This might sound strange, but would you mind ducking down?"

"Would I— What?"

"Lean over so you're not visible? I hope you don't think I'm paranoid. I just don't like people seeing who comes and goes from my house. Nosy neighbors, strangers walking by. You never know."

The judge had exhibited an outsize anxiety all night, though you could hardly blame her. The poor woman's husband had been gunned down in their driveway five years earlier. This was

a different house in a different location, but she obviously wasn't
over the trauma.

"Sure, no problem."

Madison doubled over in the passenger seat. The street was icy,
and the car skidded slightly on the turn. Good thing the judge
was sober. Madison couldn't've passed a Breathalyzer to save her
life. Feeling dizzy, she braced herself against the door. From the
little she could see bent over, they were driving down a narrow,
dimly lit alley with high walls on both sides. Pulling up next to
some trash cans, the judge switched off the engine, and they got
out of the car.

Judge Conroy tapped a code into a keypad, and a metal gate
slid open. Madison followed her into a long, narrow courtyard,
as the gate closed behind them. The courtyard was surrounded
on three sides by high walls, and on the fourth by the towering,
four-story town house. She saw a gas grill covered by a tarp, a few
bedraggled planters, and no other furniture. It must look cheer-
ier in better weather. At the back door, Judge Conroy unlocked
three separate locks with the sureness of long practice. The burglar
alarm was already beeping by the time they stepped into the foyer.
The judge typed a code into a keypad on the wall, and it stopped.

"You have a lot of security," Madison said.

They hung up their coats and took off their shoes. The judge
went around turning on lights. They were in a stark, modern
kitchen, with a giant island, sleek cabinets, an enormous stainless
steel Sub-Zero with matching wine tower. She took out a bottle
of red and set about opening it. There were tall, graceful windows,
though the shades were drawn. It was open plan, presumably the
result of an extravagant renovation to what looked like a century-
old house. You could see all the way through the dining and living
rooms to the front door, a distance of at least fifty feet.

"*Wow*. This place is gorgeous."

"Thank you."

She handed Madison a glass. They clinked.

"Cheers. Let's sit."

They walked toward the living area, the judge calling out for the cat. Madison gazed in wonder at the twelve-foot ceilings, magnificent staircase, parquet floors, fireplace with marble mantel, moldings, chandeliers, elegant furniture. The walls were glossy white, hung with bold, colorful art. All on the most expensive street in Boston. Judge Conroy must have family money. But wait, no—she claimed to be from South Boston, daughter of a single mom. Her husband had the money, then. Whatever. It was magnificent. Fit for a queen. *This* queen.

A black cat came bounding down the stairs. Judge Conroy knelt and scooped her up, kissing the top of her head, apologizing for being away all day.

"She's so pretty," Madison said.

"She's my baby."

They sat side by side on the sofa, with Lucy purring in the judge's lap. The judge picked up a clicker and switched on the gas fireplace. As the flames danced, the cat stared at Madison with arresting, sea-green eyes. To be polite, Madison sipped the wine, but she'd had enough to drink. *Too* much. Her head hurt, and at moments, she heard herself slurring her words. Not to mention that she'd lost track of exactly why she was here.

"Did you say you needed a favor or something?" she asked.

"Yes. It has to do with Lucy."

Madison reached out to pet the cat, who yowled, an unmistakable warning.

"Hmm, I'm not sure she likes me."

"She takes a while to warm up to new people. As do I, normally. Yet after our conversation tonight, I sense that I can trust you, Madison. Which is why I asked you here. Would you be able to watch my house this weekend and take care of Lucy? I have to go out of town for work, and my normal pet sitter isn't available. I hate to leave her alone."

"You want me to stay here?" Madison said after a moment.

"Yes."

"For how long?"

"Until tomorrow night, or Sunday morning at the latest. I won't be any longer than that. And of course, I'd pay you. What do you think? Could you help me out?"

She had a ton of schoolwork. Finals started in less than two weeks. But her laptop was in her backpack, sitting on the bench in the back hall where they'd come in, giving her access to all the assignments. Actually, being in this house with no distractions would be ideal for studying.

But wait, wasn't there something—

Oh. Mom. Danny. Shit.

Whether from the alcohol or the thrill of having dinner with the woman she admired, her problems had slipped to the back of her mind. She just blanked. Yet those documents from Danny's case were sitting in her backpack. She was supposed to go with Mom to visit him in the morning and come up with a game plan. And—*oh, God*, she still needed to tell the judge about that whole mess.

"You look concerned," Judge Conroy said. "I can show you the rest of the place. It's very nice."

"Oh, I have no doubt."

"Come, let me give you a tour," the judge said, getting up.

The cat trotted ahead of them as they ascended the grand staircase. Trailing her fingers along the polished mahogany banister, Madison looked up four floors to a skylight far above. A cold rain beat on it now, but on a sunny day, it would fill the house with light. The entire second story turned out to be a single, ultra-luxurious master suite. Madison *ooh*ed and *aah*ed at the elegantly appointed

bedroom, with an alcove for a canopy bed, a separate seating area
with its own fireplace and large bay window facing the street—
curtains drawn, though. Gawping, she compared it mentally to
her dorm room, with its dingy wall-to-wall carpet and grimy old
furniture, so narrow that when she pulled the desk chair out, it
bumped into the bed. Quite the contrast. They walked through a
door into a fabulous dressing area, with racks of clothes arranged
by color, shelves for handbags, cubbies full of expensive shoes,
and a vanity table with a makeup mirror. Just beyond, Madison
could see a spa-like master bath with marble floors and a glittering
chandelier.

"Now, you're probably thinking, *How can I stay the weekend
when I didn't bring clothes?* I can answer that. Look."

Judge Conroy took Madison's arm and drew her to a full-length
mirror.

"Have you noticed that you and I are the same size?" she said.

The observation was odd enough to raise the hackles on Madison's neck. But it was also true. She thought of the judge as taller,
more willowy, certainly more graceful than she'd ever be. But in
stocking feet, they were the same height and strikingly similar in
shape. Their coloring was different, that was all—Madison dark
where the judge was fair. The fairest of them all, with the most
beautiful clothes. The thought of having the run of this closet was
tantalizing. Yet strange.

She met the judge's eyes in the mirror.

"You'd let me wear your *clothes?*"

"Only what you'd need for the weekend. Loungewear, T-shirts,
jeans, that sort of thing. Because otherwise you'd need to go back
to Cambridge now to get your things, and unfortunately I really
need to get going."

Madison rubbed her eyes. Her mind felt foggy. Was she understanding correctly?

"You're leaving *now*?"

"In the next fifteen minutes if I'm going to make the last flight to DC. I know it's a lot to ask."

"Where would I sleep?"

"There's an au pair suite upstairs that's just darling, with a clawfoot tub and a brass bed with a down comforter. I just need to turn on the heat up there, and you'll be very comfortable. I'll give you my Instacart login. You can order from Whole Foods, Eataly, whatever you like, and just work all weekend, like a retreat. Doesn't that sound good?"

Should she really be staying here? What with the drug case, Danny, the blank spot on that employment form?

"I—um, unfortunately, I have obligations, so—"

"I'm sure you do, Madison, and I know it's last minute. But you'd be very well-compensated. How does a thousand dollars for the weekend sound?"

It sounded fantastic, but still.

The judge checked her watch, then placed a hand urgently on Madison's arm.

"Please. Say yes. Really, I'd be in your debt."

That decided it.

"*Yes*," she said.

More than the money, or the beautiful house, or the Instacart from fancy food purveyors, Madison wanted Judge Conroy to owe her a favor. That was the way out of her predicament. She'd be the perfect pet sitter, and Judge Conroy would be grateful. Then, when Madison told her about Danny, she'd be less likely to fire her. Or inform the dean. Or refer her for prosecution.

Hopefully.

10

....

Judge Conroy slipped out the back door and melted into the darkness. The cat had gone into hiding. Madison refreshed her food and water bowls, scooped out the litter box, and called her name repeatedly, to no avail.

A headache hammered behind her eyes like an icepick. In search of Tylenol, she rummaged through the pantry cabinet. Just a dusty box of crackers, a jar of cornichons, some expired olive oil, and several cans of tuna fish. Was there any real food in this house? She peeked inside the refrigerator. The vast, gleaming expanse was empty except for a container of almond milk, some sriracha, and an open bottle of Perrier, which had gone flat. As she spilled it into the sink, she heard a thump and froze.

Lucy?

But the cat was nowhere in sight. A gust of wind, maybe? The house settling? It was enough to remind her that she was alone here and ought to arm the security system. The judge said to do that. On her way out the door, she had numerous security instructions, way more than she did about the cat. Keep the blinds drawn. Don't answer the door or the landline. Keep the security system armed at all times. Madison took frantic notes as the judge spouted off the alarm codes. There was a code for the doors, another for windows, a third to bypass the interior motion sensors. They had to be inputted in a precise sequence. If you screwed up, something as simple as the cat walking around the house could trigger the alarm. That would result in a call to the judge's phone and an alert to the police. Things had to go well this weekend. She couldn't let that happen.

Squinting at the notes on her phone, she tapped a long series of numbers into the keypad in the back hall. As the word "Armed" flashed in red letters, she breathed out. Crisis avoided.

Next, she texted her mother, apologizing that she couldn't make it to the jail tomorrow.

I got the court documents like we discussed and will be following up leads tomorrow. I'm sorry I doubted Danny. I realize now that he's telling the truth. Call after the visit and tell me how it went. Love you!

Now, where was that cat?

She stood at the bottom of the grand staircase. A glow of light from the judge's bedroom spilled onto the landing.

"*Luuucy?* Are you up there?"

Clutching her phone, she ascended, unnerved by every creak of the treads, looking up at the darkness above. Where were the light switches? And what was that noise? There it was again, a knocking sound, coming from the judge's bedroom. The door stood ajar.

"Lucy? Is that you, kitty?"

Her voice came out high and thin. Her heart was palpitating. She hesitated to go in. That was the judge's private space. It was like a luxury hotel in there. Thick drapes, plush carpets, soft lighting, a bed piled high with silk pillows. But she had to find Lucy, and make sure the noise was nothing bad.

She stepped into the room. A black streak shot past her, out the door.

Jesus.

Faint and dizzy, she bent over to catch her breath. She needed to lie down. Her head throbbed, and she was starting to shiver. Her work clothes had never dried completely from when she ran through the rain to the restaurant. The judge said to borrow something to wear—pajamas, jeans, whatever she needed for the weekend. Even with permission, that seemed too familiar, almost like trespassing. She felt weird even being in this room. But she couldn't sleep in these clothes.

In the dressing room, she found a drawerful of pajamas. A silky black pair with white piping fit perfectly. She normally slept in old T-shirts and sweats. Imagine dressing so glamorously every hour of every day. It would change you, at least in other people's eyes. She grabbed a bottle of Tylenol from the medicine chest and hurried out, pulling the door closed behind her. Her phone's flashlight cast weird shadows as she went upstairs. The fourth-floor landing was narrow and bare of furniture—servants' quarters, with a ceiling so low that she could jump up and touch the skylight if she tried. In the attic bedroom, she turned on the light, startled by the sight of a haggard, dark-haired woman. But it was herself, reflected in a mirror over a chest of drawers. The room had been shut up for a long time. It smelled musty. Judge Conroy had forgotten to turn on the heat. It was freezing in there. She found the thermostat and cranked up the heat. After a couple of minutes, the ancient radiator began to hiss. The room had an old-fashioned charm, with sloping ceilings, a braided rug on the scuffed wood floor, and a brass bed tucked under the eaves. A door at the far end led to a little bathroom with a pedestal sink and clawfoot tub. She washed her face, took two Tylenol, and went to sit on the edge of the bed. The down comforter felt thick and cozy. She lay down and pulled it up to her chin, resting her eyes while the room warmed up.

———

In her dream, she was running down a dark street at night, chased by cop cars. Sirens blared. She opened her eyes.

The siren was real.

She bolted upright, hitting her head on the sloped ceiling. *Ugh.* She'd been so careful with the codes, but somehow, the cat had triggered the alarm. She staggered from bed. The sake hadn't worn off yet. She wanted to throw up and then stand under a hot shower. But she had to turn that alarm off ASAP. She grabbed her phone and stumbled down the stairs. She'd left the first-floor lights on when she went upstairs earlier. She saw a second keypad beside the front door, closer than the one in the back hall. Vibrating with adrenaline, she found the code on her phone and punched it in.

Silence. She heaved a sigh.

The next second, a pounding on the door shattered the calm.

"Kathy, open up!"

Who the hell was that? A man's voice. There was no peephole to look through, and the shades were drawn. Judge Conroy had said not to let anyone into the house, under any circumstances, and to use the video monitor to check before opening the door for deliveries. *Video monitor.* Madison located the button, pressed it, and a screen came to life, in black and white. She saw a man in his forties, pale, wearing a dark windbreaker. He jerked his head up, looking into the camera.

"So, you *are* in there. Open the door."

She stepped back, staring at him, heart pounding. Her phone started buzzing in her hand.

It was the judge.

"Hello?" she whispered.

"Do *not* let him in."

"How did you know?"

"I got an alert on my phone."

An alert that said there was a man at the door? She must be able to see the video feed remotely.

"He's angry. What do I say?" she said, keeping her voice low.

"I'll say it. Put your phone on speaker, hold it up to the monitor, and push Audio. He needs to think it's me talking, like I'm there in person."

"Got it. Hold on . . . Okay, go."

The judge's voice flowed from Madison's phone through the security system out to the man on the front steps.

"It's the middle of the night, Charlie. What do you want?"

His face settled into a scowl. "Your alarm went off. I came to investigate."

"You just happened to be in the neighborhood? What a coincidence."

"I was driving by."

The judge's sigh was audible over the airwaves. "Uh-huh. Well, there's no reason to be concerned. It was the cat. She triggered the alarm again."

"Why don't I come in and verify that? Just to be safe."

"It's fine. Go home."

"If I don't check, I'll worry about you. It'll interfere with my sleep."

"You're interfering with *my* sleep. Good night, Charlie."

Madison let up on the Audio button. The man glared at the camera, fists clenched. The wind gusted, blowing open his jacket, and she saw a holster under his arm. *He has a gun*. Taking a step closer to the door, he rattled the doorknob.

She whispered urgently into the phone, "Judge, he has a gun, and he's trying the door."

"Put the phone back. I'll tell him not to."

"Is the door strong enough to keep him out?"

"Put the phone back, Madison."

Her hand shook as she held it up.

"Get away from the door, Charlie, or I'm calling the *real* police," the judge said.

"Explain something to me. A friend of mine saw your name on the manifest for a flight to DC tonight."

"That's obviously a mistake. I'm right here."

"He's a reliable source."

"Some lowlife who you pay? Please."

"Open the door."

"*No*. I know what you did. You tried to get in. Well, I'm sick of it. Get the fuck away from me. And if you try that again, I'm serious, I *will* call nine-one-one, and you can explain to your superiors. As if you don't have enough complaints on file. Now, I'm going to sleep."

The call dropped. Madison was rooted to the floor, staring at the doorknob, afraid to move for fear that he'd hear her. Slowly, she backed away.

Her phone buzzed with a text.

Are the blinds drawn?

Yes you said leave them down, she replied.

The request hadn't seemed that strange at the time. In retrospect, it was ominous.

Good, keep them that way. Now reset the alarm.

Hold on.

Hands clumsy with nerves, she had to try twice to get it right.

Done.

OK turn off all lights and go back upstairs. And stay back from the windows. I don't want him seeing your shadow or he'll know it's not me.

What would he do if he figured that out—shoot her through the window?

Who the fuck *was* this guy?

Trembling, she went around making sure the lights were off. In the darkened kitchen, she heard a noise and froze. Something brushed against her leg. She stifled a cry, then heard a meow. *Lucy.*

"Hey, girl, you scared me. C'mere," she whispered, voice shaking.

Scooping up the wriggling cat, she crept up the stairs. At the top, without warning, the cat clawed her arm and jumped, bolting into the darkness.

"*Ow.* Not nice."

She hurried up to the attic room where she'd been sleeping, dousing the light and creeping over to the dormered window. Tugging the blinds aside, she peered down. From this angle, the front steps were obscured by the jutting facade. He was probably still down there, biding his time, planning to make another attempt to get inside. He'd tried to break in. That was what triggered the alarm. Not Madison getting the code wrong. Not the cat on a midnight prowl. It was him, the man at the door. If he tried once, he could try again. She either needed to leave this crazy house or call the cops. But how could she leave when he was down there? He would see her come out. She should call the cops, then. But she should give Judge Conroy a heads-up before bringing the police to her home.

She dialed the judge's phone.

Judge Conroy picked up on the first ring.

"I'm worried he's still out there," Madison said breathlessly.

"Can you see him?"

"No, I just feel it."

"Did you turn off the lights?"

"Yes."

"Where are you?"

"Up in the au pair room. I'm going to call nine-one-one."

"*No.* Madison, it's not necessary. I'm sure he's gone."

"What if he isn't? He had a gun. I saw the holster."

"Don't worry. He was giving me a hard time, but I read him the riot act. You heard."

"What if he doesn't listen?"

"He will. Trust me, I know him."

Her mouth fell open. Until that moment, she'd been too preoccupied to focus on the nature of the judge's relationship with the man at the door, but there it was. They were close. He'd called her Kathy. And she'd called him—

Charlie.

Wait a minute. The gun, the windbreaker. The reference to "real police." She knew suddenly who he was, who he had to be. And it made her sick to her stomach.

"He's a cop, isn't he?" she said. *The cop from my brother's case.*

"It doesn't matter."

"I'm in your house, alone, and an armed man comes to the door? It matters to me."

"I can't get into it. It's personal. But I promise, he doesn't want anything from you."

"Is he your boyfriend?"

"*No.*"

"Then what?"

"It's complicated. Look, I'm sorry for the confusion. I'll pay extra for the hardship, okay?"

"This is not about money. I agreed to take care of your cat. A man trying to break in—it's more than I signed up for. I don't feel safe."

"That's understandable. But you're completely fine. Just stay inside, and when you order in food, check the camera to make sure that—"

"If I'm safe, why check the camera?"

"That's just a smart thing to do in a city. I'm getting another call, and I need to take it. Okay? Get some rest."

The call dropped.

Madison snorted. Another call. *Right.* The judge didn't want to answer questions, that was all. A cop tried to break into her house. Someone she knew well, who seemed to be tracking her whereabouts. Their entire interaction had an air of impending violence. Yet the judge instructed her not to call 911, because it was *personal.* Was he a jealous ex-boyfriend?

A cop named Charlie. *Charles.*

Madison sat down cross-legged on the floor with her phone flashlight and flipped through the documents from Danny's case, just to be sure she was remembering correctly. Yes. There it was, the very first line in the affidavit: "Detective Charles E. Wallace affirms and says . . ."

Coincidence? Maybe, maybe not. She should try to figure out if he was the same guy.

She opened her laptop and googled the name "Charles Wallace" together with "Boston PD." Several stories popped up, all from the *Globe*. One of them looked familiar. "Case Closed in Drive-By Shooting." She'd read that just the other night, after Ty's party, while researching the judge's husband's murder. Studying the accompanying photo and its caption, her stomach sank as she realized it was definitely him. The man at the door just now was pictured in a group photo of the team investigating Matthew

Latham's murder. It was *all* him. The man at the door, the lead investigator in the judge's husband's murder, and the detective on Danny's case. One and the same. *Detective Charles Wallace.* She couldn't wrap her head around it. The woman she'd admired since high school, and connected with so powerfully tonight, was mixed up with a dirty cop who'd failed to solve the murder of her own husband.

Danny claimed the judge was in on the corruption. *My lawyer goes way back with this judge. Has her in his pocket. She's dirty, too.* Madison had refused to believe that. What if it was true? She needed to finish the research on that lawyer that the judge had interrupted earlier tonight. She already knew that Logue had numerous disciplinary complaints and had been suspended from the bar, then reinstated. Now, she looked into his cases—at least, what she could find on Google. There was an avalanche of results. Over forty years, he'd represented literally hundreds of mobsters, extortionists, murderers, drug dealers. She went cross-eyed reading the old news articles, yet learned little about his relationship to Judge Conroy. She'd been the judge on some cases where Logue was the defense lawyer, and—going back years—the prosecutor on others. Knowing that didn't tell Madison much. She needed court records, but couldn't access them from here.

There were a number of hits on "Logue" and "Wallace" together, though most of those were about the wrong Wallace—a detective named *Edward* Wallace who'd been murdered in the '80s, gunned down execution style in his own driveway. Mob retaliation, they said. Case never solved.

Interesting coincidence. Gunned down in his driveway, just like the judge's husband.

Researching Detective Edward Wallace, she was shocked to learn from his obituary that he was Charles Wallace's father. That had to mean something—but what? She couldn't think straight.

Her back ached. Her vision was blurry. It was starting to get light outside, with a faint glow showing around the edges of the blinds. She needed caffeine.

Downstairs, she tracked down a bag of espresso, zapping the almond milk to make a halfway decent latte, which she took over to the sofa. The shelves on either side of the fireplace looked straight out of a shelter magazine, white vases and coffee-table books and framed stock photos with no people in them. This house was as sterile as the judge's office. That seemed odd. Normal people had photos, scrapbooks, souvenirs. A pile of junk mail. Why didn't the judge? Was she just a neat freak, or did she keep her personal things hidden for some reason?

A thought occurred to her, and she didn't like it. What if this whole thing was a setup from the start? As in, the judge knew that Wallace would come looking for her, so she asked Madison to stay to act as a sort of decoy. That wasn't a spur-of-the-moment decision like it seemed. But premeditated. She had scrubbed her home of personal mementos because she had something to hide. *No.* Too paranoid.

Yet the thought nagged at her.

It was wrong to pry, to rummage through Judge Conroy's personal effects trying to ferret out her secrets. That would be an abuse of the trust the judge had placed in her. Unless, of course, that trust was itself a ruse. She couldn't stop thinking about Wallace at the door. His anger, his borderline violence. The judge had been looking over her shoulder all through dinner. She knew Wallace would come for her, which meant she intentionally put Madison in a dangerous situation. And what about Danny? How much danger was he in because of these people?

She flicked open the photos on her phone and looked at pictures of her brother. He'd been trying to get his act together when the world turned on him. It was terrible judgment to go to that bar. But one mistake shouldn't be a death sentence. His freedom, his very life, hung in the balance. She couldn't afford to ignore the voice in her head telling her that something was rotten in Judge Conroy's world. She had to investigate. It was the right thing to do.

She got up and walked around the living room, not exactly sure what she was looking for. A blinking red light up near the ceiling caught her eye. It was one of those motion sensors, but suddenly she thought, *That could be a camera*. She shouldn't do anything suspicious within range of its creepy red eye. She put her coffee cup in the sink and headed up the stairs, pausing outside the judge's bedroom. There was another motion sensor on the landing. It was probably nothing, but she could manufacture an alibi, just in case.

"Lucy? Are you in there, girl?" she called, for the benefit of whoever might be listening, before she ventured inside.

In the master suite, she checked for motion sensors. There were none in there, so she was free to search. She went through the nightstands, the desk, the antique armoire, the decorative chest. Strikeout. Under the bed. The luxurious dressing room. The bathroom cabinets. Nothing unusual. She felt bad doing it and thought she ought to stop. But first, she googled "where to hide evidence" to make sure she hadn't overlooked anything. *Inside the water tank of the toilet*, it said. That seemed far-fetched; but just to be sure, she put her phone down and set about lifting off the lid. Lucy ran in and jumped up on the toilet seat, staring accusingly.

"I'm doing this for my peace of mind," Madison told her.

She lifted it up. There was a plastic bag taped to the underside, full of cash.

Fuck.

She sat down on the edge of the tub and put her head between her knees. Did it have to mean something bad? Maybe the judge just didn't trust banks.

She had to keep looking.

It took another hour of searching to find the two photo albums, hidden in an old suitcase at the back of a closet. The first one was white satin with a tulle bow on the front. A wedding album. Not the sort of thing your average person would squirrel away, but then again, the judge's husband had been murdered. Maybe her wedding photos were too painful to look at? Though there was one on her bedside table.

She sat on the dusty floor, turning pages. The photos were sharp and bright, like they'd been taken yesterday. The judge, exquisite in a white silk gown with flowers in her hair. Her husband tall and gorgeous. Both of them looking blissfully happy, with no inkling of the tragedy to come. But it was a photo from the dance floor that made her stop and gasp. Judge Conroy, dancing with *Raymond Logue* on her wedding day. The dirty lawyer. That was him, she was certain. Burly, red-faced, thinning white hair. She'd seen his photo online, and besides, this man matched her mother's description of Danny's lawyer to a T.

She went through every crowd scene and found Logue in several more. He wasn't just someone Judge Conroy knew from work, then. He was a friend. A close enough friend to invite to her wedding. That seemed suspicious in itself. Guilt by association was a thing for a reason.

The second album was yellowed with age, full of childhood and school photos of the judge. Wow, she wasn't kidding. She *had* been awkward as a kid. The pictures weren't relevant to Madison's investigation, however. She shouldn't indulge her base curiosity.

As she went to put the album back in the suitcase, several photos fell out from between the pages. *Shit.* They'd been loose in there. If she didn't put them back in the right order, Judge Conroy might figure out she'd snooped. She gathered them up, kicking herself for not being more careful.

And there was Raymond Logue.

A younger version of him. But definitely him, his arm draped in fatherly fashion around a very young Kathryn Conroy. She couldn't've been more than fourteen or fifteen in the photo. And if Madison needed proof of that, she recognized the school gymnasium where they stood and the school uniform that Kathryn wore.

That was Catholic Prep.

Judge Conroy and the dirty lawyer went back. *Way* back. Who was he to her? And who was Charlie Wallace? Those men framed her brother, and the judge was close to both of them. Madison had admired the judge for as long as she could remember. But how well did she know her? And who was Kathryn Conroy, really? Not who she pretended to be.

Part Two

Kathryn

11

....

Thirty years before

The house was a dump, a rickety saltbox that smelled of seaweed and mildew. But she adored it. The rough planks of the floor, the sloping roof that leaked in the rain. And most of all, the sugary-sand beach two blocks away that sloped down to the lacy waves of the Atlantic. Her mother would warn her to stay away from the water, but then she'd disappear inside with Eddie and lock the door, leaving Kathy unsupervised. Kathy would grab her metal pail and shovel and hurry to that magic spot where the sand met the water met the sky. Plopping down, she'd dig moats and watch them fill. Build drip castles and let the waves smash them. In the tide pools, she'd find treasures. Sand dollars and starfish and mussels with iridescent purple shells, alive and spitting water. Tiny crabs that scuttled as the gulls cawed overhead. The sun would scald her shoulders. The sand fleas would bite, but she would've stayed forever if they let her.

Her earliest memories were of Eddie's house in Gloucester. *Uncle* Eddie was what her mother made her call him, though she knew in her heart that he was really her father. She understood that much. What she didn't understand was why she couldn't call him that. Her mother's name was Sylvia, and Kathy called her Mom. Why couldn't she call Eddie Father or Dad, or Pop, like Charlie did? Though she didn't know Charlie at first. But she always knew that beach shack, from as far back as she could remember.

At the end of the long summer days, her mother would come shouting for her, and they'd go back to the house for supper. A plastic bag full of bloody fish on ice would be sweating in the sink. Bluefish, swordfish, cod—whatever was cheap and fresh. Eddie would pour charcoal into the rusty old barbeque and douse it with lighter fluid. She loved the acrid smell as the flames whooshed up into the sky. They'd eat the catch slathered with tartar sauce, with canned corn on the side, or fries from the bag in the icebox. The battered table in the corner only sat two. Eddie and Sylvia would linger there, drinking and smoking, while Kathy ate on the moldy sofa in front of the TV, watching *Brady Bunch* reruns. It was the only time she didn't wish her life looked like the Brady kids' lives, because she had something they didn't. She had the beach.

But it didn't belong to her. As time went on, they were invited less often. Kathy spent the sweltering summer days drawing hop-scotch squares on the sidewalk or playing kickball in the street with neighborhood kids. As she got older, and the kids got rougher, she'd stay inside with the fan on, eating ice pops and reading. She loved books. They kept her company. Eddie still came by occasionally to pick up Sylvia for a night on the town, but for the most part, he ignored Kathy. It might have been different if she were a boy, instead of a pale, freckled girl child, painfully thin, with reddish hair too much like his own. In some ways, it was a relief, because he scared her. His bulk, his height, his booming voice, the edge of violence in his eyes. Plus, she hated him for taking her mother away. The second the makeup bag came out, she'd whine.

Sitting on the edge of the tub, watching Sylvia curl her eyelashes or slick on lip gloss, her stomach hurt imagining the moment when she'd go. By the time the doorbell rang, Kathy was begging and sobbing. Sylvia would say, *You want him seeing you like that, with snot dripping out your nose? You won't get a present.* But what present did she ever get? If she was lucky, a pack of Twizzlers, or those candy dots on paper. Usually nothing. It was a trick to get her to behave. "Uncle" Eddie would chuck her under the chin, and they'd hurry out the door, leaving Kathy to fall asleep on the sofa with the lights on and the TV blaring.

Why couldn't it be different? Eddie didn't behave like the dads on TV, not even as good as the Russo kids' father across the hall. Mr. Russo worked for the sanitation department. He yelled and screamed, but he laughed, too, and on Sundays, he wasn't above tossing a ball on the sidewalk before supper. And what suppers they must have in that apartment. She could smell the roasts and the red sauce. When she complained, Sylvia would say, *Make some mac and cheese if you're so hungry. I'll have some while you're at it.* Sylvia was too busy painting her nails or reading her magazines to take care of a kid. In her daydreams, Kathy had real parents. A mom who cooked for *her*, instead of the other way around. A dad who wasn't Eddie, or even Mr. Russo, but Mike Brady—rich and handsome and kind. Sylvia turned men's heads. Who was to say that Mike Brady wouldn't fall for her? The quicker that happened, the sooner Kathy could have that pink bedroom in the suburbs, and the quarrelsome, adorable brothers and sisters.

But her luck was rotten, and it stayed that way.

Through Kathy's childhood, Sylvia worked answering phones in the office of Eddie's friend, Uncle Ray. Uncle Ray wasn't her uncle either. Not by blood. But at least he acted like an uncle should. He stopped by their apartment frequently, bringing *real* gifts. Flowers or perfume or elaborate boxes of chocolates, Barbies or crayons or ribbons for Kathy's hair. As she got older, records and books, and even one time at Christmas, a brand-new Walkman that ended up getting stolen in the schoolyard. Kathy eagerly awaited Uncle Ray's visits, and not only for the swag. He'd ask what she was reading or how school was going. He'd notice she was alive. Sylvia, on the other hand, dreaded Ray's visits. She'd fix him a drink and make polite conversation, but the whole time she was gritting her teeth, storing up insults and complaints that she'd let loose the second he left. His pudgy fingers, his dandruff, his shiny suits. *He grosses me out,* she'd say, or, *When's he gonna realize he's not getting any, the lech?* But she never told him to buzz off, and she kept on working for him, because the pay was good. And besides, Ray cared, and that had to count for something.

Uncle Ray was the only one, other than Kathy, who noticed when Sylvia grew thin and pale. When she got unexplained bruises or strange spots on her skin that the makeup couldn't hide. He told her to go to the doctor, that's what the health insurance was there for, and she should think about her daughter. But she didn't listen. She started suffering from chills and fever on the regular.

On a cold, wet day in December, just after Kathy's eleventh birthday, Sylvia called in sick to work. Kathy begged to stay home with her, but Sylvia wouldn't hear of it.

"You need to be in school."

"I want to stay home with you, Ma, please."

"I said no."

"*Pleease.*"

"Stop hovering. You're driving me up the goddamn wall. Now go. You'll be late."

Her eyes welled. "Mommy, I'm scared. Why are you always sick?"

"Don't be such a drama queen. It's a touch of the flu, that's all. Get out of my hair and you can have McDonald's for supper, okay?"

She went. But that day in school, she was catatonic, filled with terrible visions of what she'd find when she got home.

They came true.

There would always be before and after that moment. She walked up to the door, put her key in the lock, and her heart was pounding. She opened it, and the apartment was dim, but not dark. She could see crimson splotches on the carpet and smell the gamy odor. Sylvia's foot peeked out from the kitchen. Following the trail of blood, Kathy advanced like a sleepwalker until she found her mother, sprawled, pale and lifeless on the floor.

A scream rose in her throat.

The next thing she remembered, she was pounding on the Russos' door, yelling and sobbing.

"They killed my mother! They killed her. Help!"

Two cops arrived, a man and a woman. They made Kathy wait in the hall while they checked the apartment. Mrs. Russo cracked her door, staring out, but she didn't invite her inside. A few minutes later, the female cop beckoned Kathy back to the apartment.

"What made you say somebody hurt her?" she asked. "Did you see something?"

Kathy was crying so hard that no words came out. The cop rubbed her shoulder.

"Hon, your mom's not dead. We don't know what happened, but she's not stabbed or shot or anything. And there's no sign that anyone broke in. Her pulse is weak. She mighta threw up blood. Is she sick?"

Kathy nodded.

The place looked like a crime scene, but it wasn't. The cops called the paramedics, who arrived within minutes and conducted an examination. It turned out Sylvia had a massive nosebleed and fainted. They would take her to the hospital.

As they loaded her onto the stretcher, her eyes fluttered open, and she looked right at Kathy.

"Was it you who called the ambulance?" she said.

She shook her head, not wanting to admit it was her. Technically, the cops had called. She waited for her mother to get mad, to yell, or cluck her tongue in annoyance, because usually Sylvia hated asking for help. She hated fuss. But this time was different. She held out her hand. Kathy squeezed it, shocked at how cold it was.

"Don't worry, babe, I'll be fine," her mother said. "You know I would never leave you alone."

But that was a lie. Sylvia left her alone all the time, and they both knew it. She turned her face away as they wheeled her mother out the door.

The minute she was gone, the cops asked Kathy who to call. Would her grandparents come stay with her, or could they take her to them? There were no grandparents. Then who? An aunt or uncle? That jogged her brain, and she thought of someone, relieved to have an answer so she didn't seem unwanted and alone.

They could call Uncle Ray.

He came immediately. They went to the hospital together, and over the next few days, he got things sorted. Sylvia had leukemia. It was fairly advanced, and her prognosis was not great. If there was hope, it would be found at the Mayo Clinic in Minnesota. The health insurance would cover most of the treatment, and whatever it didn't, Uncle Ray would cover out of his own pocket. He'd accompany Sylvia on the airplane, because somebody had to, and that was no job for a kid. He would stay out there for a while to get Sylvia settled, which begged the question: What would happen to Kathy while they were gone? She could still smell the hospital waiting room where they had that conversation. The sharpness of disinfectant, the damp odor of carpet muddy from the rain. Uncle Ray looked at her under the harsh fluorescent light with pity in his eyes.

"I'm gonna talk to you like you're a grown-up, okay, Kathy? You have to be brave."

She was terrified, but she wanted him to think well of her, so she raised her chin and nodded.

"I reached out to your grandparents."

She stared at him, sick to her stomach.

"You know who I mean, right? Your mom's folks?"

"I never met them. They don't like me."

"That's not true. They had a falling-out with your mom."

"Because of *me*."

"No. It was about your mother's lifestyle. Her behavior. You have no responsibility for that. You're just a kid. Your grandma understands that. She told me to say that she would help you out if she could. Unfortunately, she's not able to right now."

"Right."

"I'm serious. You shouldn't take it personally. After they moved to Florida, your grandad had a stroke. He went into a nursing home, and your grandma's fallen on hard times. Unfortunately, where that leaves us is, well . . ."

He cleared his throat.

"You, uh, you know Eddie's your dad, right?"

Her face went hot with shame. Of course she knew. That didn't mean she wanted to talk about it.

"Him and me, we're like brothers. Grew up next door to each other, had each other's backs all through school. And we work together to this day. I know he acts like a tough guy. That's from being on the job, all the pressure and whatnot. Some rough people he's involved with. But trust me, there's a good heart underneath.

He knows Sylvia's in the hospital, and he's broken up about it. He really cares for her. And he cares for you, even if he's not one to show it. Bottom line, I think the best thing to do is to talk to him. He'll come through in the end. I believe that."

But he didn't sound so sure. She stared at the rug. It was gray and pink, in a diamond pattern, breathtakingly ugly, stained, and frayed.

"I'm going to ask him to let you stay there until your mom comes home. He'll do it if he can, but there is one complication."

She looked up and caught his apologetic shrug.

"His wife."

12

....

Eddie lived in Danvers, though it was against the rules of his job. He listed Uncle Ray's office in Boston as his official home address to satisfy the city. She learned that later. As they pulled into the driveway of a modest ranch-style house, she had no idea what awaited. She didn't even know it was Eddie's house, just that he was bringing her somewhere until Sylvia got better. The house looked bedraggled in the rain, sad and hollow, like Kathy felt. Her worldly possessions were in a cardboard box in the back seat. Everything she owned—clothing, school supplies, her sketchbook and pencils, her books and lip gloss and curling iron.

Eddie carried the box into a beige-carpeted living room, set it down on the coffee table, and told her to wait. There was a suite of matching furniture, upholstered in gold brocade and fitted with tight plastic covers. The plastic made a squeaking sound when she sat. Eddie disappeared down a small hallway, calling his wife's name. After a moment, fast footsteps approached. A small, neat woman with short hair, clad in slacks and a sweater, stared daggers at her.

"Jesus friggin' Christ," she muttered, and turned away.

Kathy's stomach clenched. That woman knew who she was to Eddie without being told, and she wasn't happy about it. She was going to kick Kathy out on the street. Where could she go? Foster care was the next stop. There was a foster kid at school. Kids made fun of him for wearing the same clothes every day, but it was his eyes that Kathy noticed. *Haunted*.

In the next room, Mrs. Wallace was shouting at Eddie. Kathy put her hands over her ears, trying to block it all out. But she couldn't block the smell of the place, a combination of cleaning fluid and yesterday's cabbage that got into her throat and eyes and hair.

Her hair.

"She has *red hair*!" Mrs. Wallace screamed.

"It's brown."

"It's red in the light."

"Am I the only redhead in Boston, for Chrissake?"

"How stupid do you think I am? That's *her* kid. Admit it."

"Who?"

"You know exactly who I mean. Sylvia, that shanty Irish tramp."

How dare she? *Keep my mother's name out of your ugly mouth*, Kathy wanted to shout. But she couldn't say a word. This woman had power over her—whether she was safe and housed and fed. Biting her lip, she clenched her hands in her lap.

"That ended years ago," Eddie said.

"Then who's that sitting on my couch? Be a man and admit what you did, Eddie. That's your bastard out there."

"The mouth on you."

"You bring your bastard into this house and expect me to act like a lady about it? Get *the fuck* out."

"All right, all right. She's Sylvia's kid. There, I said it. Happy now?"

But he hadn't said the thing that mattered most. He hadn't claimed her as his own. He never did. She could hardly expect it now, in front of his witch of a wife. Still, it stung.

Mrs. Wallace had noticed.

"Your kid. She's *your* kid. Say *that*."

"Why do you dwell? What good does that do?"

"Jesus Christ, I'm sick of your bullshit."

"What's past is past. I got nothing going on with Sylvia any-more. Haven't for years. She works for Ray as a receptionist. He came crying to me, saying she's sick with leukemia, can I take the kid while her mother gets treatment."

She hated Eddie then, not for herself, but for her poor mother, who'd wasted her life on him, ungrateful monster.

"If Ray's so concerned, let him take her. She's not *my* problem."

"He can't. He's at the Mayo Clinic with Sylvia."

"The Mayo Clinic? Wait a minute. How long are you asking for the girl to stay?"

"Just while Ray gets Sylvia settled. Then he's coming back, and he'll take the kid. I'll make sure of it."

"Till he gets her settled? What's that mean?"

"A few days, that's all. The kid's quiet. She'll be no trouble."

"And what if the mother doesn't come back? What then?"

The way she talked about Sylvia dying, in a voice so cold, so matter-of-fact—Kathy wanted *her* dead. She closed her eyes and prayed. *Please, God, strike down that evil witch.* But nothing happened. They were still talking in there, and Kathy had to hope they'd let her stay.

"She's not gonna die, I promise," Eddie said.

That was the first hopeful thing she'd heard. She grabbed on to his words, whispering them like an incantation as she fidgeted on the plastic-covered sofa. *She's not gonna die, she's not gonna die, she's not gonna die.*

"*No,*" Mrs. Wallace said loudly.

"What do you mean, no? Don't tell me no."

"It's too much to ask. I don't want her in my house."

"*Your* house? This is not your fucking house. *I* pay the mortgage. *I* pay for your car, your clothes, your food. *I* support your mother and your deadbeat brother. You know what that means? What I say goes. And I say, make her up a bed in the sewing room. Feed her. And send her to school with Charlie in the morning. It's a few days. You can handle it."

"Charlie! Did you think about him for one second? About your *legitimate* son? What am I supposed to tell him?"

"Whatever you want. Say she's a long-lost cousin. I don't care."

"How dare you put her above this family! Goddamn it, Eddie. *You motherfu*—"

There was a crash, followed by the tinkling of broken glass, a scream, and several loud thumps. Mrs. Wallace let out a wail. Stomach in knots, Kathy cowered on the sofa, pulling a hard, shiny cushion over her head to block out the yelling and crying. It went on for a while, but eventually things got quiet. She sat up, hearing muffled sobs and Eddie talking in a soothing tone. She couldn't make out the words, but the pitch was conciliatory. Did the wife win the argument? She didn't want to stay in this creepy house that smelled of cabbage with a crazy lady who hated her guts and a man—*her father*—who from the sound of it just hit his wife. But the other option was foster care. They fed you dog food there, beat you with belts. And worse.

A key turned in the front-door lock. A kid entered, taller than her, his red hair dark from the rain. This must be Charlie, the *legitimate* son. She sat up straight and pulled her hand across her face, wiping away the tears that had leaked. Kids already called her names. She didn't need him to see her shaking and go telling everyone she wet her pants or something.

Catching sight of her finally, he stopped short.

"Who are you? What's going on?" he said.

"Your parents are fighting."

"No shit, Sherlock. They always fight. I asked who you are."

"I'm Kathy. Who are you?"

He took off his coat and hung it on a hook near the door, looking at her through narrowed eyes.

"Charlie. What are you doing here?"

"I don't have anywhere else to go."

"What are you, like homeless?"

"No. My mom is sick."

He nodded, not unsympathetically. "Okay, but why did they bring you to *my* house? Your folks know my folks or something?"

She should claim to be that long-lost cousin, or there'd be hell to pay with Mrs. Wallace. The lie was on the tip of her tongue. But that ugly word rang in her ears—*bastard*—making her hot with rage. Screw that lady; it would serve her right to tell her precious son the truth. She itched to rock the boat, even if she tipped it over.

"No. It's because I'm your sister."

His face went slack. "*What?*"

"They brought me here because Eddie is my dad. Last time I checked, that makes me your sister."

His eyes registered shock, then resistance, then the fear that she was telling the truth. The kid knew his father well enough to wonder, at least.

"If he's your dad, then who's your mom? Not *my* mom?"

"No, you wouldn't know her. Her name's Sylvia."

He stared at her open-mouthed.

"You do know her?" Kathy asked.

"I met a Sylvia one time, with my pops. At a Red Sox game. Really pretty, blond hair, red dress?"

Sylvia had made quite the impression, apparently.

"That's her."

"You don't look like her."

She shrugged, but underneath the bravado, she felt gut-punched. Her mom had gone to a Red Sox game with Eddie's kid and didn't invite her. And now she might die, so they'd never go to Fenway together. It wasn't fair.

Kathy wasn't the only one upset. Charlie sat down beside her hard enough to rock the couch. There was an ugly flush under his eyes, and his chin was trembling.

"Oh, are you gonna *cry*?"

She needed to take her pain out on someone, but the taunt didn't have the intended effect. He sniffed hard, squared his shoulders, and turned on her.

"Girls cry. I'm not a *girl*. I'm just pissed because I wanted a brother, and I got *you*. Wait, you are a girl, right?" he said, casting a snide glance at her flat chest.

"Yeah. No shit, Sherlock."

That wrung a grudging smile out of him.

"You have a crooked tooth on top, like me," she said, pointing to her own.

"So what?"

"And we both have reddish hair."

"I don't give a crap about that shit. What I care about is, do you play video games?"

"*Tetris* with my friend sometimes."

"*Tetris* is for dorks. I play *Super Mario*. I got a Nintendo for my birthday."

"Nintendos are cool."

"You never played Nintendo in your life."

"Maybe not, but you could show me."

"You'd mess it up."

"I'm careful. Tell me what to do, and I'll listen."

"Humph," he said, but she saw that he was warming to the idea.

"I promise."

"Okay, but if you break it, you pay for a new one."

Like she could afford that. He led her down the narrow hallway where Eddie and Mrs. Wallace had disappeared earlier. There were three closed doors. As he reached for one, another flew open, and Mrs. Wallace stepped out. There was an angry red handprint across her left cheek and a glint of murder in her eye.

"I thought I heard your voice, young man. What do you think you're doing?"

"We're gonna play *Super Mario*."

"Not in your room you're not. No girls in there."

"You think I'm gonna do it with my *sister*? Gross."

Mrs. Wallace's small, colorless eyes flicked to Kathy.

"*What* did you say to him?" she said, her voice quiet as death.

Telling Charlie the truth had felt good in the moment, but she would pay for it for sure. With her short hair and plain features, Mrs. Wallace had the persnickety air of a mean schoolteacher, but Kathy could see that she was far more dangerous.

Eddie emerged from the bedroom.

"Hey, son, so you met your—"

"—my *sister*. I know, she told me. We're gonna play Nintendo until supper."

"Fine by me."

Eddie got the last word, if only because he didn't hesitate to use his fists. Charlie opened the door to his room, shooting a triumphant glance at his mother. There was rage in her eyes as they settled on Kathy. She prayed in her mind, *Please, God, make my mother better. I can't stay here with this crazy lady.* But she knew better than to hold out hope. God didn't like her, and her prayers were rarely answered.

13

....

She shifted on her feet, perspiration trickling down her back. The hand-me-down black dress was scratchy and way too hot for the weather. The priest droned on. Everything he said was a lie, and everybody in the cemetery knew it. *Pillar of the community. Respected in the neighborhood. Public servant.* Really? Then why was Eddie's casket closed? She'd heard the whispers, seen the story in the paper. He crossed the wrong people and paid with a bullet to the back of the head. *Family man.* Right. When the priest said that, a few mourners cast pointed glances in Kathy's direction. She quaked at the thought that Mrs. Wallace would see them. But no, thank God, she was way up in the front, narrow shoulders tossed back in a prideful way, her face like stone. She didn't look sad so much as pissed off that her life was disrupted. The only person crying out of the whole crowd was Charlie—surprising, given how he talked about his father when his parents' backs were turned.

Kathy stood off to one side with Uncle Ray, who'd insisted that she come. *Your dad would've wanted you there*, he claimed. Like Eddie gave a crap about her. But Ray even went to bat with Mrs.

Wallace to allow Kathy to attend, and for some reason, she gave in. Probably to force Kathy to stand in the stifling heat while people gave her dirty looks and whispered slander about her. Eddie did her no favors by taking her into his home, then leaving her at the mercy of his sadistic wife, who punished her endlessly for the crime of being born. Kathy got the back of Mrs. Wallace's hand on the regular, the burnt ends of whatever the family was having for supper, slimy cold cuts in a baggie for her school lunch. If she dared complain, she got called a shanty Irish slut on a good day. On a bad day, she got the belt. She lost weight. She lost hair. She lost what little spark she'd had. Became a pale ghost girl riding the school bus, sitting unnoticed in the back of an unfamiliar class-room. Eddie didn't stand up for her through any of it. Not once.

Bad as things had been, they'd be worse now that he was gone.

The service ended. Uncle Ray left her side, going up to the casket with the family to throw down a handful of dirt. Was he crying, or was that sweat running down his face? Both, she decided, with a rush of fondness. He wasn't much, a beer belly sticking out from a rumpled suit jacket and a pink scalp showing through graying hair. But Kathy loved him anyway. Ray had a good heart and did his best to help her. If his best wasn't enough, well, at least he tried. Nobody else did. He was the only family she had until Sylvia came back. *If* she came back.

Kathy worried about that, day and night. Ray always claimed that the treatments were working, that it wouldn't be much longer. If that was true, why had months gone by without a single phone call from her mother? She worried Ray was lying, that Sylvia was already dead. Or worse, that she had gotten better but didn't want the bother of a child. She was back in their apartment, moving on with her life. And Kathy was doomed to live with the Wallaces forever. It was her worst fear, and it took such a grip on her imagination that she became convinced of it. To the point that, a while ago, before Eddie died, she went back to the old apartment, certain she'd find her mother there and determined to confront her.

Eddie kept his wallet on his bedside table. One morning while the grown-ups ate breakfast, Kathy slipped into their bedroom and lifted ten bucks. At lunchtime, she walked out of school, using the money for a bus to the mall and another into Boston. It was February, gray and bitter cold. She waited on the street outside their building, stamping her feet to keep them from going numb, until a lady came along with a key. Following her inside, she breathed in the familiar smell, dust and paint and last night's dinner, and thought her heart would explode from the longing. At the door of her apartment, she leaned on the buzzer, her vision clouded with tears.

The woman who answered was old, and possibly Jamaican, judging by her looks and accent.

"What can I do for you, child?"

"I'm looking for my mother."

"Your mother?"

"Sylvia Conroy. She lives here."

"Oh. Wait one minute. I have something for you."

The woman shut the door. Kathy waited in suspended animation, holding her breath, unable to imagine what it was. A letter? A gift? Or, pray God, Sylvia herself?

The woman returned.

"Here," she said, thrusting a pile of mail into Kathy's hands. "If you find her, tell her to change the address with the post office. I'm tired of getting all this nonsense."

The mail was all junk.

That night, Eddie beat her with a belt for stealing and ditching class. His arm was stronger than his wife's, and Kathy hurt for days. He let Mrs. Wallace change the lock on the sewing room door so they could lock Kathy in at night. That's what Eddie did for his daughter. Was it any wonder she didn't cry at his funeral?

The wake was at the house, with an open bar. Kathy was put to work unwrapping casseroles. When she was done, she went to look for Ray, thinking they could have a talk about what happened next. But he'd gotten to the whiskey. Slumped on the sofa, his face the angry red of a sunburn, he was muttering to some guy in a patrolman's uniform and barely acknowledged Kathy. She decided to wait. But an hour later when she went to the bathroom, she discovered him passed out in Charlie's room, snoring like a foghorn, with vomit stains on his shirt.

That was Ray.

The air-conditioning couldn't keep up with the heat, and the living room was stuffy with cigarette smoke. Charlie was in the front yard tossing a football with some neighborhood kids. She heard yelling and the occasional burst of laughter and thought, *Anything's better than here*. She was opening the screen door to join Charlie when Mrs. Wallace grabbed her by the wrist.

"No you don't. Get in that kitchen and start cleaning up," she whispered viciously.

She was doomed. Her only option was going to be running away, and runaways wound up as hookers in cheap motels. Was that her fate?

Kathy was scraping food into the garbage when she heard raised voices from the living room.

A tingle raised the hair on her skull. *Is that— Could it be?*

"You should be in the grave instead of him. Get out of this house."

"Give me my daughter and I'll be gone. You'll never see either of us again."

The aluminum pan slipped from her hands, clattering to the floor. She ran to the living room. Ray must've slept it off, because he was in between the women, trying to keep them from tearing each other apart. Sylvia caught sight of Kathy and screamed.

The next few minutes passed in a blur. Sobbing in her mother's arms. Throwing her meager possessions into a trash bag as Mrs. Wallace watched with gimlet eyes to make sure she didn't steal. Then she was out in the hot sun, avoiding Charlie's eyes as they ran for the taxi idling at the curb. When the door slammed shut and the cab pulled away, Kathy stared out the back window, cackling like a crazy person at her narrow escape.

"Let me see you," Sylvia said, grabbing her, holding her away, looking her up and down with a horrified expression. "You look like hell, kid."

"So do you."

It was true. She was skeletal, wearing a turban that made her look like an old lady.

"I had cancer. What's your excuse? Didn't they feed you in that house?"

"Not really. Why didn't you ever call?" Kathy said, tears leaking from her eyes.

"Babe, I did call. I called over and over, but that bitch always hung up on me."

Figures. To the end of her days, she'd hate Mrs. Wallace with every bone in her body. Hell, she'd kill her if she ever got the chance, a knife between the shoulder blades, like that evil woman deserved.

"I even wrote to you a few times, care of Ray. And you know how I hate to write letters. Why didn't you write back?" Sylvia said.

"I never got them."

"Didn't Ray visit to check up on you?"

"Once in a while he'd come over, but he didn't bring any letters."

"Jesus, that jackass."

"It doesn't matter. Everything is okay now that you're home, Mommy."

"It does matter, and things are *not* okay. We got no place to live. I have no job. Everything depends on Ray. He gave me his keys and said we can stay at his place tonight. And I can work for him again, but he doesn't know it's gonna be a while till I can manage a full day in the office. The point is, it's a problem if Ray's not reliable. We're depending on him to live, and he better come through."

"Oh, he'll come through, all right. Not for me. He'll do it for you."

They stayed with Ray for months, until Sylvia saved enough for a deposit on a dingy one-bedroom in Dorchester, where Kathy slept on the foldout sofa. When the time came to move, Ray begged them not to. They could stay forever as far as he was concerned. He considered the three of them a family, he said. But Sylvia heard it just as him wanting her in his bed. She wasn't the type to care for a man because he treated her well. Just the opposite, in fact, judging by Eddie, and the guy she took up with next—Marty, who owned a restaurant in Scituate that he managed with his wife. Marty dumped Sylvia, as did the guy after him. Ray, ever hopeful, was always there to pick up the pieces.

Kathy feared the day he gave up on them.

Beginning when they were staying at his house, Ray took an interest in her education. It started one night when she asked Sylvia to quiz her for a history test, and Sylvia couldn't be bothered. But Ray happily stepped in, asking the sample questions, critiquing her answers. The next day when she brought home a hundred on the test, he was tickled. After that, he promised to pay ten bucks for every A on her report card. When she made straight A's that term, he actually paid up. Sixty bucks—she bought clothes with it. Maybe that was a normal thing for a parent to do, but nobody had ever done it for Kathy. Ray Logue made her into a serious student. It wasn't because she wanted money. She just couldn't stand the thought of disappointing him.

The way he started paying for her education, though, was a bit more complicated.

One afternoon in eighth grade, she had a hall pass to go to the bathroom. She was walking down an empty hallway when a kid came running, folding up a knife. He slowed down, making eye contact and putting a finger to his lips. *Mikey Bruno.* He was bad news. She froze. But around the corner, someone was screaming. She found Mikey's victim writhing on the floor, covered in blood, and ran for the nurse. That kid ended up losing an eye. The cops wanted to interview her. But Ray wouldn't allow it. *We don't snitch,* he said, *and besides, I know that kid's father. You don't want to mess with him.* Kathy was upset. It was wrong to stay silent. But Ray insisted it was too dangerous, and ultimately she was persuaded. Something good came of it in the end. He decided her school wasn't a good fit. A smart kid like Kathy was wasting her time in that dump, he said. He helped her fill out the application for Catholic Prep and agreed to pay her tuition, a promise he kept even after they moved out, and despite the fact that Sylvia continued to rebuff his advances. Maybe Kathy should've questioned his motives. She just thought he cared.

He *did* care. He couldn't've faked that for so many years, with the effort he put in, the way he showed up for her. Encouraging her interest in history and English, hiring a tutor for math, which was her weakness. He even found a college consultant who told her which extracurricular activities to pursue if she wanted to get into an Ivy. An Ivy. *Her?* Ray was a BC man, college and law school. She wouldn't've dared to dream beyond what he'd done himself, but he dreamed for her. Kathy was smarter than him, he said. And the truth was, her grades were perfect. There were few distractions. Boys scared her. She wasn't one of the popular kids and didn't run in the fast crowd. She was the treasurer on student council, sang in the chorus, and volunteered as a Big Sister. The teachers who wrote her letters of recommendation talked up how remarkable she was, as the child of a single mom who'd dropped out of high school and been ill throughout Kathy's childhood. She didn't feel remarkable. But the combination of her accomplishments and her life story was enough to get her into Harvard.

On the day of her college graduation, Kathy was sweating beneath her cap and gown, hung over from partying the night before. Freshman year, she'd discovered drinking and never looked back. She collected her diploma and went hunting for Sylvia in the massive crowd. It was Ray she spotted, big and bulky, coming toward her, waving and beaming with pride, her delicate mother on his arm. And her heart swelled.

He'd booked them a table at Union Oyster House to celebrate. The place was jammed that day, a line out the door of the old brick building with its mullioned windows. Ray pushed his way into the paneled dining room and claimed the prime booth set aside for him, which had a gilded sconce and an oil painting of that same room a hundred years ago. A regular for decades, he knew everybody in the place, and the waiters were falling over themselves to bring them champagne, oysters on the half shell, a seafood platter to share.

"This is my goddaughter, Kathy. Just graduated Harvard, magna cum laude. Isn't she amazing?" he said to anyone who'd listen.

Ray wasn't actually her godfather. She had no godparents. Having been born out of wedlock, she was refused christening. But she loved him for claiming her like that, the way Eddie never had. For once, she was a normal girl, with a regular family who feted her on graduation day. Like a Brady kid.

She thanked him for lunch with tears in her eyes.

"Not just for lunch. Say thank you for this, too," Sylvia said, picking up the tube that contained Kathy's diploma and waving it at her.

Kathy threw her arms around his neck. "Thank you, Uncle Ray."

"Aw, well. You're a very deserving girl, Kathy. It makes me proud to help you out."

"I can never repay you for what you've done for me."

"Oh, I don't know about that. Have you thought about your future? I got to tell you, you'd make one hell of a lawyer. You got the brains, the excellent record. The looks. Who would've thought that skinny kid with the pigtails would turn out as pretty as her mother?"

Ray was not a big believer in credit cards. He threw down a wad of cash, and they got up to leave. On the street, Kathy said she had to go pack up her dorm room and move out. The plan was, work for a few months, save enough for a plane ticket and Eurail pass, then bum around Europe for a while and figure out her life. She had a few leads on waitressing jobs.

"What do you want with waitressing?" Ray said, waving his hand dismissively. "It's a dirty business. Your clothes smell, men grab your ass. Come work for me in the office, with your mom. There's plenty of projects that could use attention. I'll pay you ten bucks an hour. You'll save enough for your vacation in no time."

By then, she understood that Ray's law practice was not a hundred percent above board. You couldn't be Eddie Wallace's best friend and closest associate without bending the rules occasionally. But she didn't see how that would affect her if all she was doing was secretarial work. And the offer of easy desk work at a good wage was hard to turn down.

"Really? Are you sure?"

"Of course. I'd love to have you. Just come in with your mom on Monday, and we'll put you to work."

"That would be great."

"I'm warning you, though, I'm gonna keep bugging you about law school. You know I got no kids of my own to follow in my footsteps. I consider you like my own. I'll pay whatever financial aid doesn't cover, just like with college."

She smiled and pecked him on the cheek. "Wow, thank you, that's a beautiful offer. And very generous. I'll definitely keep it in mind."

"I'm serious. Think about it. You could graduate debt-free," he said.

Kathy didn't know it at the time, but some debts went beyond money. Her debt to Uncle Ray would be like that.

14

....

Five years later

In the first year that she was a prosecutor, the debt came due.

It had been a long day of listening to wiretap tapes in a windowless room. Ten hours straight of the bug in the barbershop where Salvatore Fiamma planned his hits. But the tapes were useless. Locker-room talk, sports teams, the manicotti they had for dinner last night. When those guys had something incriminating to say, they took a walk around the block. Kathryn could've told her boss, *You'll never catch them. They're too smart for you and way too vicious.* She knew that, from Ray. But she was a junior prosecutor, only six months on the job. And her connection to defense attorney Raymond Logue was not something to brag about. On the contrary, it was something to hide.

She walked down the long hallway toward her boss's office to give her report, hesitating on the threshold. BRADLEY MCCARTHY, CHIEF, ORGANIZED CRIME, the nameplate read. She was afraid to go in, or more accurately, ashamed. Despite not having done much to compromise herself yet, she'd done enough. Ray ambushed her on her mother's birthday, at a celebratory dinner in the North End, over a plate of lasagna. He waited until Sylvia went to the ladies' room to lean in and say he needed a favor. *A small thing, nothing really. Have I ever asked you for anything before?* It was only information, he said. She wanted to say no. But it was Ray, and she owed him so much. She made a deal with herself. She'd pass him information, just not enough to compromise herself too badly, or harm anyone else.

She knocked and pushed open the door. Brad was on the phone. He covered the receiver with his hand.

"Anything?" he mouthed.

She shook her head. He motioned for her to sit.

"Yes you are, yes you are. Daddy's good girl. . . . Hon? Hon, are you there? Yeah, someone just walked in. . . . By ten at the latest. . . . I promise, I'll work from home this weekend so you can have a break. . . . Kiss the kids for me. Love you."

Brad hung up and scowled at her. "Really? All those tapes, and *nothing?*"

Kathryn shrugged. "I got a good recipe for manicotti out of it."

He laughed. She crossed her legs, which were famous around the office. Brad was a devoted family man, but he looked.

"What's your take?" he said. "Did the bug get blown somehow? A leak?"

Well, yes, and the leaker was sitting right in front of him. She felt sick. And yet she told herself that there were other ways besides a wiretap to make a case. They'd get Fiamma eventually, and she would help them. She would even things out in the end.

"I don't think so. They're just careful."

"It costs an arm and a leg to monitor. I'm starting to think we should take it down."

"Your call."

"It's a tough one. A lot of high-value targets come into that barbershop. Half the syndicate. I keep thinking they'll slip up eventually, but . . ." He shook his head. "There's another way we could go. With our new star witness, I'm thinking we take a direct run at Old Man Fiamma."

"You're talking about Mad Tony? Will he agree to that?"

"He has to. Did you draft the plea agreement?"

"I put it in your inbox this morning. You didn't see it?"

She stood up and started shuffling through the overflowing pile on his desk.

"Here."

She handed him a sheaf of papers in a brown paper wrapper, stamped "CONFIDENTIAL" in large block letters. It was the plea agreement for Anthony "Mad Tony" Capito, a capo in the Fiamma crime family who had the potential to bring down the biggest mobsters in New England.

"Sorry, I must've missed it. This day has been insane," Brad said, running his hands through his thinning hair.

There was a stain on his tie. He looked worn out. She felt sorry for him, how little time he had with his family.

"How did the debriefing go?" Kathryn asked.

Ray told her she needed to be in the room when they proffered Mad Tony, but every deputy chief and supervisory special agent in Boston had already called dibs. Kathryn was too junior, and her request was denied. The truth was, she was relieved. The less she knew, the less they could force her to reveal.

"I was just about to head over to Villa Carlotta to meet up with the task force guys. You want to join? I'll fill you in on the way."

She raised an eyebrow. "Villa Carlotta? Really?"

"What, just because it's a red sauce joint, you think it's mobbed up?"

"Is that place mobbed up? *Definitely*."

He laughed, not realizing how serious she was. "You should come along. If you can get in good with the task force, you'll be set with cases for the rest of your career. Relationships matter in our line of work."

Kathryn knew what kind of *relationships* those FBI hotshots wanted with her.

"Thanks, another time. I have work to catch up on."

They said good night.

Back in her office, she closed the door and laid her head on the desk, feeling drained. After a moment, she noticed a buzzing sound coming from the locked lower drawer. The secure flip phone was hidden at the back, behind her handbag and makeup kit, her extra sneakers and box of tampons. She didn't know what scared her more—answering or not answering.

Her heart pounded as she opened the phone. "Hello?"

"I need an update."

She hunched over, shielding the phone as she whispered, her eyes on the door.

"What are you doing, Charlie? You know not to call me at work."

"I'm supposed to know you're still at work?"

"Assume I always am. I'm hanging up."

"No. Wait."

She'd warned Ray that bringing Charlie into this would be a disaster. He didn't understand boundaries. When it came to Kathy, that problem was magnified a hundredfold.

I'd love to work with you myself, Ray had said. *But you need a handler, and it can't be me. Our connection is too well-established after all these years. It would look bad, be dangerous. You can trust Charlie. He's family, but nobody knows that.*

I don't trust *him. I haven't seen him since high school. And he was never nice to me.*

Kathy, the guy loves you like crazy.

Love? That's not what I'd call it. He used to purposely walk in on me in the bathroom when I lived there. My own half brother.

I'm telling you, he's very protective whenever your name comes up. There's not a lot of choices for a handler. You won't do better than him.

A handler. She should have known from Ray's use of that term that they had more in store for her than a little information here or there. They wanted a full-blown spy. And now Charlie was calling, demanding that she comply.

"Go talk to McCarthy," he said. "Bat your eyelashes, ask about his plans."

"I can't. Brad's on his way to dinner with the task force guys."

"Really? Where?"

That part, she could give up without guilt. The second the feds walked in the door at Villa Carlotta, someone would spill.

"They're going to Villa Carlotta," she said.

"No kidding. Did he leave yet? Maybe you can tag along."

"I have work to do."

"Stop dragging your feet, Kathy. People are beginning to notice. What kind of car does he drive?"

"Who?"

"McCarthy."

"Why do you want to know?"

"To be honest, some people don't trust you to give accurate information. I've been told to check the intelligence before passing it along."

"Who are these people you keep talking about who don't trust me?"

"Guys above my head. You're better off not knowing names. Look, I don't like it either. I got better things to do, but they're gonna want me to drive by the restaurant to make sure he's really there."

"Fine. He drives a blue Volvo with a Red Sox sticker on the

back," she said. But the second the words left her mouth, she regretted telling. "You're sure this is just to check my information? Nobody's going to get hurt?" she said nervously.

"What, kill a prosecutor? You think I'm nuts?"

That rang true. The mob whacking an informant like Mad Tony was par for the course. But going after law enforcement was considered beyond the pale. It brought down too much heat. Even cops were off the table unless they were dirty, like Eddie, because then nobody cared. But a prosecutor as highly regarded and honest as Brad McCarthy would be considered untouchable.

Still. This was Charlie.

"You're *sure*?"

"Will you stop? I would never do anything like that, and if I did, I certainly wouldn't mix you up in it. Now, go have a nice dinner and don't worry. I'll call tomorrow to see what you heard. That's all. Nothing more. Promise."

That was fine. She'd go to the dinner, pretend that she tried and came up empty. He wouldn't know any different.

They hung up. She threw on her coat and managed to catch Brad at the elevator.

At Villa Carlotta, Kathryn ordered their famous chicken parm but couldn't eat it because she was so nervous. She drank like a fish, though. It was nearly eleven when dinner broke up. She was sweating Chianti, her head full of cotton wool. Those task force guys could talk your ear off. She'd learned a few tidbits that she could pass along without guilt. Things that wouldn't get anyone hurt or compromise the case. They divvied the tab down to the last cent. In government work, there were no expense accounts.

"You need a ride?" Brad asked Kathryn as they got up from the table.

"I'll take her, boss. It's out of your way."

The guy who'd spoken up was Morelli, one of the few Boston

PD guys on a task force full of FBI agents. The feds didn't trust him, which made Kathryn wonder.

"How do you know where I live?" Brad asked, narrowing his eyes.

"Family man, I figure you must be in the burbs. I'm right here in town." Morelli put his hand on Kathryn's arm insistently. "C'mon, I got you covered, Kathy. My car's down the street."

Kathy? Nobody in the prosecutor's office called her that. Was he one of *them?*

She shouldn't be seen leaving with him.

"No thank you, Detective. I'd prefer to take a cab."

"Suit yourself," he muttered, and walked out.

"Woohoo, she shut him down," one of the FBI guys said.

"I'd prefer a cab to your ugly mug, Detective," another guy said in a high-pitched falsetto.

There was guffawing. Brad shushed them. They walked out of the restaurant in a big, noisy group, lingering for a few last jokes. It was cool and crisp outside after the stuffy restaurant. She took some deep breaths. The agents went their separate ways, but Brad was still hanging around. She couldn't look him in the eye, she felt so guilty.

"Hey, I apologize for the guys. They can be crass sometimes, but they don't mean anything by it," he said.

"Don't worry about me. I can handle myself."

He nodded. "Okay. Good. Get home safe."

"Thanks. See you tomorrow."

The North End late on a Tuesday night was quiet as the grave. There were no cabs in sight. No people either. Brad crossed the street, his wingtips ringing against the pavement. The blue Volvo with the Red Sox sticker also had those stick figures pasted on its rear windshield. A dad, a mom, two little boys, and a baby girl.

As she watched him take his key from his pocket, something nagged at her. Charlie claimed he needed the make of the car in order to drive by and confirm that Brad was at the restaurant. But Morelli had been there, too. Why not just ask him and confirm Kathy's information without the bother of a drive-by? Maybe she was wrong about Morelli. Maybe he didn't work for Charlie after all. Though he'd been strangely aggressive about giving her a ride. *Why do that, unless . . .*

He wanted to stop her from getting in that car.

A sick feeling swept over her.

No.

She ran toward the Volvo, waving her arms, screaming.

"Brad!"

The car exploded into a fireball that lit the night. Shop windows blew out with a whoosh and a tinkle of falling glass. A rain of debris fell from the sky, some of it wet and red. Kathryn screamed till her throat was raw, sinking to the ground, feeling the heat of the fire on her face. When the cops arrived, they found her prostrate on the sidewalk, sobbing uncontrollably, her hair and her clothes flecked with the blood of a man who had never been anything but kind to her.

Later that night, Ray came knocking on her door. She knew why he was there. The FBI planned to interview her first thing in the morning. Ray was going to deliver the same message he had years before, when she witnessed that knifing in the hallway at school. This time, her answer had to be different.

Her voice shook as she confronted him.

"Charlie lied to me. He promised no one would get hurt. Brad was a good man. I can't do this anymore."

Ray patted her shoulder consolingly.

"I'm very sorry about what happened. I'll ask him to back off for a while. Give you some time to compose yourself."

"Not for *a while*. Permanently."

"Honey, I'm afraid that's just not possible."

"Well, it has to be. You tell him, or whoever pulls his strings, either I'm out or we have a problem. I'll tell the FBI he's involved."

Ray looked alarmed. "Don't get crazy on me now."

"I mean it. I just *can't* anymore, Uncle Ray. It's over, even if that means testifying."

His jaw jutted stubbornly, and his face flushed red, the very picture of getting his Irish up.

"Well, I hate to do this," he said, taking something small and silver from his coat pocket.

She recoiled.

"Jeez, it's just a tape recorder," he said. "You think I could ever hurt you? Not that I can say the same for some of my associates. Sit down. I'll get you some water."

He led her to the sofa, bringing her a glass. As she drank, he held up the tape recorder.

"You're a grown-up now, Kathy. I need you to listen to this, and then I'm going to be very frank with you. We have to stop pretending that things aren't what they are. For your own sake."

He pressed Play. It was her voice on the tape, the words spliced together for maximum culpability.

> "Brad's on his way to dinner with the task force guys. . . .
> They're going to Villa Carlotta. . . . He drives a blue
> Volvo with a Red Sox sticker on the back."

She looked at Ray in shock. He just shrugged, like, *What did you expect?* All those years. All that tuition money. She believed he truly thought of her as a daughter. But that wasn't his only motive.

"If it was up to me," he said, "I'd let you walk away, but the people above my head will never do that. You're too valuable an asset. You need to accept that, or the consequences will be severe. I'm sorry, Kathy, that's just the world we live in. You belong to them now."

15

....

Present day

When Kathryn told people that teaching at Harvard Law was an escape for her, she meant it more literally than they would ever know. She was desperate to make a run for it. But there were eyes on her at all times. At home. At the office. Every place in between. The best-laid escape plans would fail if you were being watched. She'd learned that from hard experience, having tried to run before. It was a disaster, the worst thing that happened to her in her entire cursed life. Because they were watching. They found out. They retaliated. She lost Matthew and would have ended her own life if not for—well, there were other people she loved, who gave her reason to live. People who needed her protection. This time when she ran, she was determined to make it, for their sakes. But achieving that would require something that she lacked. *Privacy*. She needed a private space in order to make the complicated arrangements necessary to disappear without a trace. A place where her captors couldn't follow her. A place they wouldn't object to, where they would allow her to spend time.

The academic dean at Harvard Law was an old friend from law review days. He'd been begging her for years to teach a course. Working as an adjunct professor wouldn't normally have been an attractive proposition for Kathryn. It was a lot of work for pittance pay, and she had no need to burnish her résumé by hyping her connection to Harvard. But it did come with one important perk—office space. There were four shared offices set aside for adjuncts that could be reserved on a rotating basis, for any day on which you taught a class or held office hours. During the period that the office was reserved, it was yours exclusively. It had a door that locked with a key, a desktop computer with internet access, and a landline telephone. Private space. Above reproach. Enhancing her reputation served their interests. She went to Ray with the idea. He approved it right away. And not a moment too soon. Her problems weren't just getting worse—they were converging.

On the day that Kathryn invited Madison Rivera to apply for the internship in her chambers, two bad things happened. First, she got a phone call with terrible news, though it was not unexpected. It came in from an unidentified number whose caller ID was blocked, just as she'd instructed.

Sylvia sounded even weaker than the last time they'd talked.

"I'm worried about you, Mom," she said. "You don't sound good."

"I beat it before. I'll beat it again."

"You need help. A home health aide. Or a nanny. Or both."

"That's a terrible idea, and you know it."

"I'd vet them carefully."

"No strangers, Kathy. It's not worth the risk."

"What happens if you collapse? Your platelet levels—"

"Don't you dare use that doctor's report against me."

"I'm not using anything against you. I'm just worried about you. About *her*."

"If it makes you feel better, I'll talk to my neighbor Denise.

She's good people. I trust her in a pinch. You spend your energy getting out, understand? I want to see you again while I'm still aboveground."

The knock on the office door made her jump. Instinctively, she knew it was more bad news.

"Sorry, I have to go," she whispered, and hung up. "Come in!"

Her throat went dry when she saw who it was. Andrew Martin had been a hotshot prosecutor in Boston, with that killer combination of Ken-doll looks and naked ambition. Juries loved him. He was assigned to all the big cases. But then a few months ago, he surprised everyone by transferring to the Public Integrity Section in Washington, DOJ's equivalent of Internal Affairs. Not long after, Ray received a tip that Martin had joined a new DOJ investigation into law enforcement corruption in Boston. They were adding prosecutors and agents at a rapid clip, looking into everything. They were even planning to reopen the cold-case murder of Brad McCarthy. Ray dropped in for a visit, supposedly to reassure her, but she knew better. He was getting his ducks in a row. *It'll be all right*, he'd said with a warning look, *as long as nobody talks*.

And now Andrew Martin was at the door. Thank God it was here and not in chambers, where there were spies. But he probably knew that.

"Judge Conroy, I hope I'm not interrupting. Andrew Martin from the Department of Justice."

"Yes, I know who you are. What are you doing on campus? Teaching, already, so early in your career?" she said, though she knew he wasn't.

He placed a hand on the back of the guest chair. "No, I'm actually here to see you, Your Honor. May I sit down? This won't take long."

"Okay, but could you—"

She didn't have to finish the sentence. He understood the

danger. Nodding, he closed the door, then drew the chair close to her desk and kept his voice low.

"I'm here because I'm working on an investigation of an influence-peddling scheme by prominent individuals in law enforcement. We have reason to believe that you might have pertinent information."

"*Me?*"

"Yes."

She swallowed visibly. How much did they know?

"Anything is possible," she said. "I've worked in the justice system for over fifteen years. I know literally hundreds of law enforcement officers. I'd like to help, but you'll have to be more specific. Who exactly are you investigating?"

"Unfortunately, I can't disclose that right now."

"Then I don't see how I can comment."

"I'm not asking you to say anything here, or now. It's not secure. I think you know that. I'd like to invite you to DC for an interview. We can discuss specifics then. I work with Brooke Lee, who was just appointed the new head of Public Integrity at Main Justice. She would very much like the opportunity to sit down with you."

The blood drained from Kathryn's face. So the rumors were true. Brooke Lee, all five feet and a hundred pounds of her, had been considered the toughest organized crime prosecutor in the United States. She could've gone anywhere from there. Partner in a lucrative law firm. Professor. Judge, like Kathryn. Instead, she took on the single most thankless task in law enforcement—prosecuting your own. And she would be damn good at it.

"You're asking me to fly to DC for an interview, with no explanation of why or what it's about? You've got nerve, Mr. Martin."

"I'm simply extending an invitation, which of course you're free to decline. I wanted to extend it personally, and to let you know that we're prepared to take every precaution for your safety. We'd do this discreetly, bring you in at night or on a weekend, through a back entrance. Anything you need to feel comfortable."

"What would make me comfortable is basic transparency. And a modicum of respect. I'm a federal judge. I expect you to share information."

"No disrespect intended, Your Honor. I'm sure you understand, this is highly confidential. I've said all I can for the moment, until you agree to sit down with us under terms of confidentiality. I hope you'll accept the invitation."

"And if I decline?"

"We'll build our case without you. Did I mention that racketeering charges are in play? In a case of this magnitude, other witnesses are sure to step forward to fill in the blanks, and that won't be to your benefit."

Racketeering. Other witnesses. Not to your benefit.

She recognized that threat. She'd used it herself back in the day, many times. Looking a mobster or a kingpin in the eye and trying to flip him on his associates, she'd tell him: *Be smart, these are serious charges, do yourself a favor and come in before anybody else does.* Because the first rat in the door gets the sweetheart deal.

Would she be the first rat?

"Think it over," Martin said, pulling a business card from his wallet. "Call me any time, day or night, and we'll make the interview happen at your convenience. Thank you for your time, Your Honor. Have a good day."

She watched him go in stunned silence, her mind racing. This was a complication she had not foreseen. Could the timing be any worse? She was waiting for documents that were complicated to obtain. The money piece was not yet in place. Nor the medical care for one of the people who'd be escaping with her. The physical logistics of disappearing all three of them at once were already daunting, given how closely she was watched. Now add to the list of watchers Andrew Martin, Brooke Lee, and their FBI cohorts. It felt impossible. She needed more than simply a private office. She needed help. Allies. People who would do her bidding, who'd be discreet. People she could trust. And they didn't exist.

Spots danced before her eyes. She couldn't breathe. Her phone was buzzing. If she answered the phone now, she wouldn't be able to speak. She sent the call to voicemail with eyes brimming. If she got arrested by the feds, the people who relied on her would be all alone in this world, vulnerable, ruined. Possibly dead. *Not again.*

She had to teach in ten minutes, and she was in no kind of shape. Blotting the tears with a Kleenex before they smudged her mascara, she talked herself down off the ledge. Be logical. *Think.* She'd been a prosecutor for years. She knew how to analyze a case. One thing seemed clear—they didn't have the evidence to arrest her yet. If they did, that knock on her door would've been the FBI with handcuffs, not Andrew Martin with an invitation to chat. For a sheltered girl like Kathryn, the shock of a jail cell would loosen her tongue faster than anything. The prosecutors knew that. The second they had proof of her involvement, they'd pounce. Which meant they didn't have it *yet.* She had a window. There was still time to change her fate. But not much time, and she couldn't do it alone.

Who would help her?

———

Teaching law would have been an ego rush if Kathryn had enjoyed being the center of attention. But power was wasted on her. Like the litigants in her courtroom, the students listened raptly to every word she said. Their eyes followed her around the classroom. The whole hero-worship thing made her queasy, because she knew something they didn't. She was a sham.

After class, when they descended, vying for her favor, it wasn't gratifying. All she felt was crowded and ashamed. She wasn't cut out to be anybody's idol. Too much pressure. But as she stood there talking about the Fourth Amendment, Andrew Martin's visit preyed on her mind. She should go to Washington and hear what they had to say. Maybe the feds could help her get away. But if she tried to travel, she'd be discovered in a minute. She needed an ally. Actually, what she needed was a decoy. Someone to divert attention while she met with the enemy. A woman would be best. Here was a classroom full of students who admired her, albeit some more than others. Among them, surely, she could find a willing accomplice, or if not, a dupe. As terrible as she'd feel recruiting an unsuspecting young law student into the disaster that was her life, she didn't have much choice. Or rather, she had one choice. Who would she rather have suffer? The people she loved most in the world, or a virtual stranger?

She could use the open internship position as bait.

The last student in line was always vying for Kathryn's attention. She was bright, wildly ambitious, and about Kathryn's height. Put a plaid coat and a red wig on her, and it just might work. If that seemed a bit cloak-and-dagger, even silly, well—she was desperate. Anyway, this girl would jump at the prospect of an internship, and not ask too many questions. She knew that in her gut.

She put on her brightest smile.

"Miss Rivera. Wait a minute."

16

....

At 8:00 A.M. on Saturday, when Andrew Martin ushered Kathryn into the conference room at Main Justice and shut the door, she was already screwed. She'd only just closed her eyes in her hotel bed last night when the alarm was triggered back home, feeding to the app on her phone. She watched Charlie pounding on the front door of the town house from hundreds of miles away, the bottom falling out of her stomach. The little ploy with the intern wouldn't be enough to save her. Turned out he had a guy at the airport who'd told him about her flight the second she booked the ticket. How could she think he'd be fooled by an impostor brought in to make the house look occupied? The charade with holding the phone up was laughable. He'd be waiting for her when she got back to Boston. And as terrifying as that was, it was the least of her problems.

Kathryn trembled with fatigue as she reached out to shake Brooke Lee's hand. She'd anticipated that they'd put on a show of strength, that she would find a busy war room full of FBI agents, with boxes of evidence piled to the ceiling. But the room was sterile as a lab, and it was just the three of them. The quiet was unsettling—because it was smart. They weren't giving anything away.

Kathryn had dressed up in honor of the solemn occasion. A suit, pumps, pearls—the uniform of the female lawyer of her generation. But the two prosecutors were business casual, underlining the difference in their ages. Martin in khakis and a fleece vest like a tech entrepreneur who'd just sold his start-up. Brooke could have been an Instagram influencer: in trendy jeans and white sneakers, a cute blazer and red lip her nods to formality. The youngbloods of DOJ had her outclassed and outsmarted. They were ready to eat her alive. She wanted to give up now and save them the trouble. But she couldn't. There were people who depended on her.

Kathryn sat down on one side of the table, the two prosecutors on the other.

"It's good to finally meet in person, Your Honor," Brooke said.

Finally? Her stomach lurched. They'd been working on this investigation for some time, then. Or they wanted her to believe that.

"Yes, well, thank you for coming in on a weekend. That made it easier."

"We know you have a busy schedule. And this way, it's more discreet," Martin said.

"And thank *you* for coming in voluntarily, so we didn't have to issue a subpoena," Brooke said.

Another lurch. Subpoenaing a sitting federal judge was a huge deal, requiring approval up the entire chain of command at DOJ. It almost never happened. If they'd actually been prepared to subpoena her, it meant they had the goods on her already. Enough evidence to pass muster with a committee. Unless Brooke was bluffing.

God, let her be bluffing.

"Of course," she said, putting on a serene smile. "I have nothing to hide."

She had plenty to hide and had been hiding it for a very long time. But the clock was ticking on the Kathryn Conroy charade. The honorable judge, a pillar of the bar, was a figment, nothing more. These two did their homework. They knew that. The laptops sitting in front of them on the table would be full of documents and spreadsheets and phone records pointing to her complicity in crimes going back decades. She might be here for reasons of her own. But she couldn't forget that speaking to them was an extremely dangerous play.

"Before we begin, could I have a cup of coffee, please?" she said.

The request was just a delaying tactic to let her catch her breath. She didn't need more caffeine. Having guzzled three cups at breakfast, she had the shakes already.

Martin left to get the coffee. Brooke folded her hands in her lap and gazed at Kathryn with an unreadable expression. It was unnerving enough that she buckled under the pressure and broke off eye contact. There was a strange buzzing in her ears, a pressure behind her eyes. The silence built until he returned a few minutes later, bearing a cheap Styrofoam cup. She took a gulp of the bitter brew and gagged.

"Too hot?" he said.

"No, it's fine. Thank you."

"My hope, Your Honor," Lee began, "is that this will be a collegial discussion where we ask some foundational questions and lay the basis for a productive working relationship going forward as we continue our investigation."

"I hope that, too. In terms of collegiality, it would help if you explained why I'm here."

"Yes, of course. You see, we're looking into some disturbing allegations of corruption among our own."

"Oh? In Boston?"

"Yes. An influence-peddling scheme going back decades. Wide-ranging. Involving numerous highly placed individuals in law enforcement and the judicial system."

"*Numerous?* How many targets are we talking about, exactly?"

The answer to that question mattered a lot, and not only because she was trying to figure out what they knew. For her entire career, Kathryn had been controlled by a very few people. They were the only ones she saw. From her perspective, they *were* the conspiracy. When terrible things happened—and they had—it was those people she blamed. What if that wasn't true? What if there were others, invisible and cruel, who were calling the shots? For all these years, her hatred would have been misdirected.

"We were hoping you could tell us," Brooke said.

Kathryn scoffed. "This guessing game again? We're getting nowhere."

"If you want us to get more specific, we'd need to sign an agreement first."

"A nondisclosure?"

"No. A plea agreement. Have you considered retaining counsel?"

The room went dark. Brooke's words seemed to echo. A plea deal meant charges. For Brooke to come out and say that, things had gone further than Kathryn had imagined. Her timetable would need to shift. She would have to run sooner—if that was even possible.

"Judge Conroy, are you all right?" Martin said.

She had to pull herself together, or this was going to be a fucking rout. She had to find her anger. Turn on them like a cornered dog and go on the attack.

"Of course I'm not all right," she said, squaring her shoulders, lifting her jaw. "I am *shocked* that you raise the question of counsel only now, when you had plenty of opportunity to speak sooner. You lured me here under false pretenses, leading me to believe this would be a friendly discussion, and that I was merely a witness."

"I did no such thing."

"Well, your colleague certainly did. Mr. Martin said I'd be speaking with you as a potential witness, not as a target of your investigation. Lawyers are for targets. So, are you telling me I'm a target?"

Martin's jaw was set. A bright red flush spread up Brooke Lee's neck. She'd succeeded in rattling them. Brooke was opening her mouth to answer, but Kathryn wouldn't cede the ground.

"If I *am* a target, you'd damn well better say so right now, or you'll be perpetrating a fraud, and I'd be within my rights to seek disciplinary action against you, both within DOJ and with the bar association."

That was an aggressive play, but a necessary one. Brooke would now be forced to tell her whether she was officially a target. In order for a federal judge to be designated the target of an investigation, committees had to be convened, evidence reviewed, votes taken. Knowing whether that had happened yet would reveal how much time she had. She'd know if it was a matter of months or weeks until they moved against her. Or days.

Or, God forbid, they'd arrest her before she left this room.

"I'm sorry, but I'm not in a position to disclose that at the present time," Brooke said.

"What exactly does that mean? Are you saying that my status is still under review?"

"I'm not at liberty to answer."

"Ms. Lee, if you decline to advise me that I'm a target, and it's later revealed that I was—that I *am*, as we sit here—not only would this interview be thrown out as improper, but any investigative leads derived from it would be suppressible as fruit of the poisonous tree."

"I'm not sure that's right."

"*I* am."

They stared each other down, and this time Brooke was the first to flinch.

"I'm not prepared to advise you of your status today. If that's a problem, we can adjourn this interview and reconvene at a later date. If you're a target at that time, I would notify you in advance of the need to obtain an attorney."

Aha. Kathryn gave a tight smile. That answer suggested that she had not been officially designated a target. *Yet.* They brought her in to shake the tree. To get a read on her. Would she stonewall, or would she cooperate? They would eventually dangle the poisoned apple of cooperation, whispering in her ear once they had her on the ropes. She knew all the things they would say, because she'd said them herself, to targets, in her day. *We have the goods on you. We brought you here to prove there's no way out. Your only hope is to join us. Free yourself. Turn on them before they turn on you. Take your revenge.*

Brooke Lee would offer her full immunity and WITSEC in a heartbeat. All she had to do was fold. It would be tempting if not for the fact that she'd seen this dance play out in a hundred other cases. She knew how it would end. A tidy little house somewhere in a warm climate. A new name, plastic surgery, some hair dye. A mindless job eight hours a day to help her forget the dead she'd left behind. If she was lucky, she'd get to enjoy it for a year or two before a stranger walked up and put a bullet in her brain. No, cooperation was a false god. She'd disappear, all right, but on her own terms. Protect only herself and the ones she loved. Before she left this room, she would get as much information as possible. And tell no one, because you'd better believe they were waiting to see who she contacted once she hit the street.

"Given that you have no attorney present, I'd like to state for the record that you are free to leave at any time, and to refuse to answer any question that's posed," Lee said.

"And *I'd* like to state that, while I came here fully prepared to cooperate and answer questions, your duplicity has forced me to rethink that. I'll stay to hear what you have to say. As for answering questions, that's off the table, at least until I understand the scope of your investigation."

Brooke looked taken aback. *Shot yourself in the foot, didn't you?*

"Okay, um. Let's start with your FBI background check."

"That's ancient history."

"I'm not referring to the process you went through twenty years ago to become a prosecutor. It would be understandable if you don't remember that. But the more recent one, the background check to become a federal judge."

"That's still, what, eight years ago? But sure. Whatever. Go ahead," she said, crossing her arms, putting on a long-suffering expression.

"Do you recall speaking with Special Agent Justin Greco for your judicial background check?"

Greco. So, that's where this started. Had he developed a conscience? Been arrested? *Flipped?* Greco could do some serious damage. They'd be going over every security clearance he'd ever worked on, not just Kathryn's. And there were some big fish in that sea.

"Justin— Who?"

"Special Agent Justin Greco? He was in charge of your background check. You met with him on several occasions."

Lee took a manila folder from a briefcase and shuffled through the contents. Kathryn wanted to rip it from her hands and see what the hell was in there. Eventually, Lee withdrew a photograph and placed it before Kathryn on the shiny conference table. Her heart skipped a beat. It was a surveillance photo, in living color but somewhat blurry, taken from some distance away, of Greco walking with a second man. She recognized Greco by his bulk and his shaved head. She recognized the second man from—well, her entire life. It was Charlie.

How much did they know? Was it possible to distance herself?

"Do you recognize these individuals?"

"Is that Greco?" she said, pointing to the bald man.

"So you recognize the gentleman with the shaved head as Justin Greco?"

"Not really. It's just process of elimination, because I do recognize the other man, who's *not* Greco. That's Detective Wallace from the Boston PD."

"Yes. How well do you know Wallace?"

"I worked cases with him when I was a prosecutor. Occasionally, he appears in my courtroom on cases for which I'm the assigned judge."

"*That's* how you know Charlie Wallace? From *cases*?" Lee said, raising her eyebrows.

It wouldn't do to show emotion. Her strategy was working so far. Shrug nonchalantly, say nothing. Let them come to her with more information.

Brooke Lee went thumbing through her folder again.

"Take a look at this photo and tell me if you recognize anyone."

Pinpricks of tiny stars swamped her field of vision. *Eddie's funeral.* The past went through her like wind, and she was standing in that cemetery in her mind. The nineties. The women with their big hair and shoulder pads. The men in suspenders, shirts with contrasting collars like something out of Wall Street, though plenty of mobsters dressed like that to this day. And that explained why they had this old photo. The FBI had been taking surveillance pictures that day, hoping the mob would show up to pay their respects. They'd been his clients, after all. In her head, she could still see the people flipping off the guys with cameras who stood on the periphery of the cemetery. Hear their voices. *Shame, for shame. Fucking vultures.* It was all for naught. The mob was who whacked Eddie—for not listening, for being a pain in their ass. There wasn't a wiseguy in sight at that funeral, only their lackey Ray Logue standing beside Kathy, his arm around her shoulders. And *Mrs. Wallace*, that witch, kind of a mobster in her own right, stone-faced in the front row with Charlie by her side. She didn't look grief-stricken, because she wasn't capable of love. Kathy's cheek still burned from being slapped by her. Her mouth was full of spit. God, she hated that woman. Every night, she went down on her knees and prayed the bitch would just drop dead. But no. The good died young, the wicked flourished. And Mrs. Wallace was still in her life.

Her time would come.

"This appears to be a funeral," Kathryn said, her voice steady.

"Who is, who are"—Lee leaned over, tracing a finger across the second row of mourners to the far side of the graveyard, until she came to a middle-aged man and a young girl, standing side by side—"those two people?" she asked.

Kathryn made a show of putting on her reading glasses and squinting at the photo.

"Is that you, Judge Conroy?"

"Hmm, that does look like me. Yes, I think that's me."

"What was your relationship to the man whose funeral this was?"

"I can't answer that unless you tell me whose funeral it is."

"Lieutenant Edward Wallace of the Boston PD? Also known

as Fast Eddie or Eddie the Shark. A cop with a gambling addiction who was known to be an enforcer for the Boston mafia."

"I'm sorry, I don't recall who that was."

"We believe you do," Lee said.

"Don't tell me what I remember from my own childhood."

"If you don't know Eddie Wallace, then why are you at his funeral?" Martin put in.

"It was common in my neighborhood to attend funerals. Also, christenings, confirmations, weddings, and so on. The Irish Catholic community in South Boston is very tight. You're expected to show your face, even if you're not that close to the family."

"Who is the man standing beside you?"

"I'm not sure."

"Did you know a Raymond Logue?"

"I know a Raymond Logue now. He's a criminal defense attorney."

"Did you know him when you were a child?"

"Are you saying that's him next to me? The man in the photo is so much younger. Thinner. More hair. I can't be sure."

"That is him. How did you know Ray Logue?"

"My mother at one time worked in his office as a receptionist."

"Your mother was Sylvia Conroy."

"Yes."

"And she passed away?"

She paused, marshaling her best poker face for the lie.

"Yes, a couple of years ago, of leukemia."

"Mr. Logue was a friend of hers?"

"I wouldn't say friends. He was her employer."

"And is that her in the photo in the row behind you? The woman in dark sunglasses?"

"Um."

Kathryn looked. *Was* it? Sylvia had returned to her life that same day, so many years ago, but she had not attended Eddie's funeral as far as Kathryn knew. She held up the photo to the light. The woman in dark glasses didn't look like Sylvia at all. It was somebody else.

"No."

"*No?*"

"Definitely not. I know my own mother, and that's not her."

"Oh. Hmm. But— Okay. Did your mother have a relationship with Eddie Wallace?" Lee said, regrouping, coming back in for the attack.

"A *relationship*? You mean, a romantic one?"

"Yes."

"Ms. Lee, my mother was a lady. She did not speak to her daughter about her private affairs."

"Maybe you saw them together? Or he came to your house? I can show you a photo of Eddie—"

"*Don't*. Really, I mean it. This is a highly improper line of questioning, and it needs to end. I'd heard good reports of your professionalism, Ms. Lee, but apparently they were mistaken."

The color heightened in Brooke Lee's cheeks. "I'm not trying to imply—"

"Yes, you are. You're asking about my mother's sex life. How am I supposed to take a question like that? Is it because she was a single mother?"

"No. I—"

"Would you expect to come into my courtroom, Ms. Lee, and have me ask about *your* mother's sex life?"

"I did not mean to offend you, Your Honor."

"Well, you succeeded. My mother was very dear to me. I miss her every day. I resent your suggestion that she was some dirty cop's paramour."

"I apologize. I'll just note for the record that you're claiming to be unaware of your mother's relationship with Eddie Wallace."

"*Claiming?* Are you suggesting that I'm lying? You need to put that photo away and apologize, or else I'm leaving."

"I do apologize for any offense given. And I will put it away. In a minute. But first. If you could tell me, who is *that*?"

Lee jabbed a finger at the image of a tall, sullen, redheaded boy standing next to Mrs. Wallace.

"I have no idea."

"Is that Detective Wallace?"

"This is a funeral I attended as a child, that I have no memory of. But *you* seem to know an awful lot about it, Ms. Lee. So why don't you tell me?"

"Fine, I'll lay the cards on the table. Our investigation of former Special Agent Greco led us to revisit the security clearances that he performed. Yours was red-flagged. Something very important was left out of your clearance, and it raises troubling questions."

Lee drilled her with an angry gaze. Kathryn felt the floor shifting. *They know.*

"Eddie Wallace was a dirty cop who was murdered in a gangland-style shooting. We have evidence that he was also your biological father, which would make Detective Wallace your half brother."

"This is intolerable. You should be ashamed of yourselves. Not to mention that you're completely wrong. My father was a businessman, not some dirty cop with a gambling addiction."

She leaped to her feet and gathered her things, every movement tight with rage. It wasn't entirely an act. She'd been trapped since she was just a kid. And the people in this room, instead of helping her, were sitting in judgment. As if they would have been braver or stronger than she'd been when push came to shove.

Screw them. Fuck them all.

"Judge, please. Wait," Martin said, alarmed now that he realized his advantage had been squandered.

"I'm an Article Three Judge with lifetime tenure. How dare you insult me this way. Your supervisors will be hearing from me. This meeting is over."

She stomped out of the conference room, expecting them to run after her to try to change her mind. Part of her wanted them to do exactly that. But hurrying to the elevator, she glanced over her shoulder and saw that no one was there. Just ghosts from the past who refused to die.

17

....

After walking out on the feds, Kathryn went straight to the airport and caught the afternoon flight back to Boston. She'd left Brooke Lee and Andrew Martin with the impression that she would never flip, and she regretted it already. Striking a plea deal was sort of like romance. Playing hard to get could be an effective tactic, but only if you didn't take it too far. She was afraid she'd pissed them off, when she might need them someday. Someday very soon, in fact, given how desperately she needed to get away.

On final approach, she watched the landmarks of Boston come into focus. The rain had stopped. The sun was setting. The Citgo sign flashed red, and the Bunker Hill Bridge was lit up like some prehistoric bird about to take flight into the purple sky. Most people seeing those sights would experience the warm glow of homecoming. She just felt the walls closing in. In Central Parking, she dragged her roller bag for miles, looking over her shoulder and listening with every ounce of concentration for the sound of footsteps behind her. She'd forgotten where she parked, apart from a vague recollection of facing out into open air, with a long walk to the nearest exit. Her car looked like a thousand others.

A recent-model, mid-priced, white SUV with no identifying stickers or decorations. A popular car in a popular color, chosen for its ability to fade into the background and frustrate anyone who might try to follow her. Yet another worthless precaution undertaken to give her the illusion of control. Stupid ploys wouldn't save her when they tracked her with advanced technology and the complicity of the people closest to her. Hell, with her own consent. Her worst enemy was herself.

She spotted a car that could be hers in a spot that looked vaguely familiar, held up the key fob, and pressed. The lights blinked and the doors unlocked with a soft beep. She couldn't wait to be home with a glass of red wine and Lucy purring in her lap. Then she remembered—the intern was there. That would take some smoothing over if she didn't want her ploy to turn into a fiasco. The girl wasn't stupid. She'd already started asking questions. The whole thing was a mistake. It would've been smarter to just tell Charlie that she was going to DC. He didn't believe her stupid ruse anyway.

As she opened the rear hatch, a wisp of cigarette smoke reached her nostrils, and she froze. She'd imagined it happening a million times, just like this. In the dark recesses of a parking garage. Someone stepping up from behind. A loud pop, then blackness.

"Kathy, what a surprise," Charlie said, appearing from behind a pillar. "Funny, for someone who stayed home all weekend, you turn up right when the flight from DC is letting out. Here, let me get that for you."

Her heart clutched as he snatched the key fob from her hand and heaved her suitcase into the trunk. She had a gun in her handbag. She ran through the pros and cons of killing him then and there. Pro: she hated his guts. Con: he was her brother. Pro: she'd be getting rid of him before he could murder her. Con: there were cameras watching, and he wasn't worth spending the rest of her life in prison.

"Get in. I'll drive you home."

"I can drive myself, thank you."

"Don't make me ask twice."

It would feel so good to splatter his brains across the windshield. As much as she wanted to, her hands were shaking. The power dynamics formed so many years ago were hard to overcome, and Charlie had always scared her. The violence was just beneath the surface, ready to rear its head at a moment's notice. He got that from his father *and* his mother. Kathryn's mind raced as they exited the garage. He knew she'd been to DC, obviously, and that she'd lied about it. She could admit that she'd met with the feds. Or make up a different reason for her trip and risk getting caught in another lie.

"Before we get into what you did on your little vacation," he said, "tell me something. Who's that staying at the town house? And before you open your mouth, I'm warning you. I know the answer. Fuckin' lie to me, and they'll find you floating in the river."

He gave her a look that made her blood run cold. She took the measure of her surroundings. They were in a no-man's-land of parking lots, diners, and chain hotels, with no street life. There was nowhere to go, and no point in running. Her best move was to turn and face him down, like a mailman chased by dogs. Charlie was feral. He sniffed out weakness but cowered at a show of strength.

"You're blowing smoke, Charlie. You'd never hurt me. I'm too valuable."

"Maybe that was true once. Not anymore. Now I view you as a security risk."

She folded her arms and squared her shoulders. "*You're* the security risk. You want to know why I was in DC? I was cleaning up your mess."

"What are you talking about?"

"The feds ambushed me and dragged me down to Main Justice, where Brooke Lee raked me over the coals. Were you aware that she's now running the Public Integrity unit? No? I didn't think so. You know what else you don't know? Justin Greco flipped."

The car swerved. So, she was right, then. They were in the dark about Greco. She could use that to her advantage.

"*Greco?* You serious?"

"Uh-huh. Now everyone he background-checked is at risk. Not just me. God knows how many others. I guarantee, Brooke Lee's bringing in every single one and confronting them. Somebody will flip. If they haven't already. Doug Kessler, for one."

In the headlights from an oncoming car, he went a paler shade of white.

"Jesus, you think Lord Fuckleroy is snitching?"

That was his nickname for Doug back in the day, when they all worked together, and Doug and Kathryn were having that affair. Charlie had always been weirdly jealous of her romantic relationships. It bordered on the perverted. She wondered sometimes if his preoccupation with her played a role in what happened to Matthew. The thought was upsetting enough that she had to push it from her mind to focus on the matter at hand. Doug was a threat. Likely to flip. He had too much to lose, and he was constitutionally incapable of putting anyone ahead of himself. He was probably already talking. And that was bad for her because her life right now was a race against the clock.

"I don't know whether he talked. I would if I were him," she said.

"We need to find out. He was inside on the McCarthy thing."

"Tell me about it. Too bad the feds aren't sharing their witness list."

The reflection of raindrops from the windshield made dark spots on his face. They looked like bullet holes.

"You said you'd flip if you were Kessler. What if you were you?" he said.

"You're asking if I snitched? Don't be an idiot. I went in to find out what they know, that's all. And yes, I put someone in my house as a decoy, because I knew you'd try to stop me. Face it, you're a blunt instrument, Charlie. Strategy is not your strong suit."

"Enough with the insults. What did you find out?"

"They were cagey. But it seems like they've been at this for a while. I have a bad feeling."

"Jesus. And you had to choose this moment to bring a stranger into the house?"

"Who cares? She's just some intern who thinks she's pet-sitting."

"Wrong. This girl is a plant, like Olivia was."

She turned to him, jaw dropping. "What are you talking about?"

"Madison Rivera is an informant. Or *something*. I don't know yet."

"Impossible. She's a student from my class who applied for an internship. I recruited *her*, she didn't come to me. If you have reason to believe she works for the feds, you need to tell me."

"I have a reason. She's the sister of Danny Rivera, the patsy in the Peña case."

"Who?"

"*Danny Rivera*. Skinny doofus, took the weight for Ricky and his crew? He just pled out last week. He's snitching to the feds, I'm convinced. That's your intern's brother."

"You're mistaken. Rivera is a common last name. Madison is an only child. She told me so."

"She lied to you. I can prove it."

They stopped at a light. He thrust a file at her.

"What's this?"

"After what happened with Olivia, we thought it would be smart to vet your new intern. She filled out a background check form. I was tasked with verifying the information."

"So you and Nancy cooked this up behind my back?"

"You should thank us. The girl's prior address jumped out at me. I'm thinking, *Where do I know that from?* Turns out, it was from booking her lowlife brother. I pulled their birth certificates to make sure. The proof is there, Kathy."

Kathryn squinted at the papers in the dimness of the car. The documents did indeed appear to show that Madison had a brother name Daniel.

She lied.

"How do you know this Daniel Rivera is the same one from the Peña case?"

"Look at the booking form. Same DOB and same Social as the Daniel Rivera on that birth certificate, who has the same parents as this girl who works for you. It's all there in black and white."

Oh, God. Her stomach hurt. Until that moment, Kathryn hadn't realized how much she was depending on Madison to be her ally. She'd even started to feel an emotional connection. But if these documents were to be believed, the girl had played her. Lied to her face.

If the documents were real. They could be forgeries.

Think about it. Charlie knew that Madison was staying at the house, that Kathryn had used her as a decoy. He would view her as a threat if for no other reason than that she'd helped Kathryn fool him. She didn't know Madison well enough to be certain that she was trustworthy. But she knew Charlie. He'd been a liar and a bully since childhood. You couldn't take anything he said at face value. She'd be a fool to discard Madison on his say-so. She should do her own investigation and make her own decision.

"You've got a mole. I want you to fire her right away," he said.

"Don't tell me how to run my chambers."

He laughed. Kathryn didn't run her own chambers, and they both knew it. But what Charlie didn't know was that she'd reached her limit. She was planning to get out, and fast. She needed help to do it. She couldn't afford to follow his instructions, at least not until she knew if he was telling her the truth.

"You just admitted you don't know if she's an informant," Kathryn said. "There are other reasons she might lie. Maybe her brother put her up to it, and it has nothing to do with the feds. Maybe she just wanted the job, and it's a coincidence that he's a drug dealer. Let's figure out why she's there and what she wants before we let her go. It's valuable intelligence."

He pulled into the alleyway behind the town house, face flushed with pique that she was talking back. He'd been in charge since they were kids. As far as he was concerned, he was the boss of her forever.

He waved toward the courtyard, where light spilled from the house.

"She's in there right now. You have no idea what she's doing. She could be going through your things."

"She's not."

"You don't know that. Kathy, I'm telling you, this kid is a threat. The longer you keep her around, the greater the risk. She needs to be eliminated quickly. Either you do it, or I will. And *I* won't be nice."

Part Three

Madison

18

....

A few hours earlier

Something thumped against Madison's chest. She gasped, opening her eyes to Lucy walking over her body. The cat turned a pirouette and settled at her feet.

"Good morning to you, too."

It didn't look like morning, though. When she finally went to sleep, the sun was fully up. Watery light now slanted through the dormer windows at the angle of late afternoon. She rubbed her temples, groaning as she sat up. Grabbing her phone off the bedside table, she saw it was after two, and there were five missed calls from Mom, the last one just minutes ago. Her phone had been on silent.

She tapped the number. Mom answered immediately. It sounded like she was crying.

"What's wrong? Are you okay?"

The reply was garbled.

"Slow down. I can't understand."

Her mother crying hit Madison in the gut. Suddenly, she was

thirteen again, standing outside her parents' bedroom while her father died inside.

"Mom, what happened? Tell me!"

"He's—he's *gone*."

She went cold.

"Gone? Danny is *dead*? He's *dead*?"

She started to hyperventilate.

"I don't know. But he's not *there*."

"Where? What are you saying?"

"I went to the jail. They didn't know where he was. They couldn't find him in the system. They said he might've got moved, but they didn't know. How could they not know?"

Rage flashed. "Ma! Jesus Christ, why would you scare me like that? I thought he was dead."

Her mother struggled to get the crying under control.

"He might be dead. He could be dead," Yolanda said between sobs.

"Don't say that unless you know it's true. You'll give yourself a heart attack."

"Why won't you—you don't—take this seriously."

"Mom. They moved him to another prison. That's all."

"The guard said if he got moved, there'd be a transfer order. There's nothing. *Nothing*. He's missing from the computer, like he never existed."

"It's a mistake. They don't lose inmates. He's got to be somewhere."

"You don't know. You're just saying that."

"You don't know, either. Calm down, *please*. I'm telling you, a prison is a bureaucracy. They move people around. It can take time for the files to catch up. That has to be what happened."

"He said they were gonna kill him, and now he's *goone*."

She wailed like her heart was broken, and Madison couldn't

bear it. She made soothing noises into the phone, fighting tears of her own. What if her mother was right, and something had really happened? It would be her fault for not believing Danny sooner and doing more to help. Mom would think so, too. She'd never forgive her. She had to find Danny and help him fight the case. Enough worrying about the repercussions for herself. The repercussions of doing nothing were a hell of a lot worse, for all of them.

Her mother's sobs were wearing themselves out.

"Ma, listen. If he was dead, they'd tell us. They might lie, say he got killed in a fight or something. But they wouldn't claim not to know. This transfer thing has the ring of truth. I'm telling you. Mom? Stop crying, *please*. He's alive. I'll prove it. I'll find him."

"How, Madison? How you gonna find him when the guards don't know anything, and that lawyer won't lift a finger to help us?"

"Did you ask him?"

"The lawyer? Why would I bother calling that—crook?"

"You're right. He *is* a crook. I researched him. He's got a long history of disciplinary complaints. The detective in the case is dirty, too. *Wallace*. I don't like the looks of him from what I see. Was he in court? Did you meet him?"

"No. But Danny says he's the devil."

She shivered thinking about him pounding on the door last night, only a piece of wood between them.

"Whatever happened to Danny, those two know about it. I'm going to call Logue and see what he says."

"He won't tell you a thing. He'll just make trouble. When are you gonna call that judge, Madison? She could really help."

Or *hurt*. She thought about the plastic bag full of cash taped inside the tank of the toilet in the master bath. When it came to Judge Conroy, the only thing she knew for sure was that she didn't know enough.

"It's complicated. I think there's some chance that Danny is right, that the judge is on the take. I don't want to approach her until I know. Where are you now?"

"I just got home, but I can't sit still. I'm climbing the walls. I have to do something."

"Like what?"

"I don't know. Talk to Danny's friends, or—"

"*No.* Absolutely not. It's dangerous. Mom, please. I need you to lie low, take care of yourself. Eat something. Get some rest. Let *me* deal with this. I can't help Danny if I'm worried about you. Understand?"

"All right. But you promise you'll find him?"

"I'll do everything in my power."

"Madison."

"I *will* find him. Yes. I promise."

They hung up. Wind gusted, sluicing rain against the windows. She collapsed back onto the pillows, crushed by this day before she'd even gotten out of bed. Would she be able to make good on that promise? She had no idea. She did know that talking to the judge about Danny at this point would be a mistake.

Lucy licked her paws, eyeing her with indifference as she snuggled down into the blankets.

"Fine, stay in bed. Some of us don't have that luxury."

Downstairs, she made another latte and choked down a few stale crackers. She was starving, and there was nothing in the house to eat but Purina or tuna fish. Opening a can of the latter, she gagged from the smell. But somebody liked it. Lucy came bounding into the kitchen, leaped up on a chair, and sprang over to the countertop, swatting Madison's hand away with a yowl.

"It's yours. No need to hurt me."

Her phone dinged with a text from the judge saying she'd be home by dinnertime. *Great.* Just what she needed. After everything that had happened overnight, the thought of facing Kathryn Conroy made her queasy. She didn't trust the judge anymore. She might actually be afraid of her. Yet there was a chance that Conroy knew Danny's whereabouts or was involved in his disappearance. Madison had to find a way to wring it out of her.

She sat down at the island and ordered groceries on Instacart. When that was done, she started looking for her brother in the most obvious place, because she wanted to cover the bases. The Bureau of Prisons website had an inmate locator that would tell you where someone was housed. All you had to do was enter the inmate's name or registry number. She tried his name, holding her breath for the few seconds it took for the search to load, in the hope that it would spit out a result and prove his "disappearance" was a mistake or misunderstanding, that he wasn't lost but simply in transit from one prison to another. But the screen said Inmate Not Found. She tried his registry number, date of birth, different spellings. The results were the same. It appeared that the guards had been right. Danny wasn't in the registry. From what she could tell, that shouldn't happen. An inmate who'd been remanded to custody and assigned a BOP registry number should always be findable by the locator. If they were released or in transit, it would say so. But her brother wasn't listed at all.

The doorbell rang, and she jumped. The judge wouldn't be back for several hours. Could it be Wallace? She held her breath as she flipped on the video monitor. It showed a woman in a Red Sox cap holding grocery bags. She relaxed. *Instacart, that's all.* Madison stood all the way to one side as she opened the door, so she wouldn't be visible from the street. He could be out there watching.

She poured more coffee, ate some bread and cheese with honey. Fortified, she looked up Raymond Logue's office number. He had a bare-bones website, just contact information and a headshot showing the red-faced old boozehound with crossed arms and a belligerent expression, under the heading "Let Ray Logue Fight For You." *Yeah, right.*

She took a deep breath and called the phone number. He picked up on the first ring.

"Hello?"

"Mr. Logue?"

"Who's this?"

"I'm calling because the BOP has been unable to locate a client of yours, and I was hoping you could help me. His name is Danny Rivera."

Long pause. The mention of Danny's name had obviously put him on his guard.

"Uh, look, it's Saturday, lady, and I don't have my files."

He sounded like the photo looked, the phlegmy voice matching the watery eyes, a townie accent, *hostile.*

"Are you saying you don't remember Danny? You were in court for his guilty plea just last week."

"Call my office Monday and somebody'll help you."

"This *is* your office. I called the number on your website. I need help now."

"Look, Rivera pled out. It's not even my case anymore."

"That's not true. He hasn't been sentenced yet. Until he is, and appeals are exhausted, you're still counsel of record."

Another long pause.

"What exactly is your relationship to this inmate?" he asked, suspicion in his tone.

"I'm a family member."

"Funny, because I met that kid's mother, and you're not her. I could tell the minute you opened your mouth. Who *are* you?"

It was Madison's turn to fall silent. She couldn't pretend to be her mother, but if she gave her own name, he might look into her background, which could lead to him outing her to Judge Conroy.

"Yeah, right, I thought so," Logue said. "I have two words for you, Olivia. Fuck. Off."

He hung up.

Olivia? The intern? What the *hell*?

She asked Danny's lawyer to help locate him, and not only did he stonewall, but he accused her of being Judge Conroy's former intern. Why would Logue know about that intern or assume she was the person calling to inquire about Danny? That only made sense if there was a link between Danny's disappearance and Judge Conroy's chambers.

Madison had better double down and do what it took to get information from the judge. Judge Conroy was the key to this puzzle.

....

19

Around six, Madison heard a noise at the back door. She'd been cooking dinner in the fabulous kitchen, with its stainless-steel range, pot filler, separate prep sink in the marble island, and expensive cookware. She put the spoon down, listening nervously to the sound of a key in the lock. Lucy sidled past her, heading for the back door, and she relaxed. That was no intruder. The judge was home.

The alarm started to beep. Madison rushed to enter the code, putting on a smile for the judge.

"Welcome home, Judge. Let me get that bag. Here, I'll trade you."

Picking up the cat and thrusting her into the judge's arms, she stepped outside to grab the suitcase. The rain had stopped, but an evil mist lingered near the ground, its chill getting in her bones. As she turned away, a motion in her peripheral vision caught her eye. There was a man in the alley. The gate slid closed, obscuring him from view, but she'd seen enough to know him. *Wallace.*

She grabbed the suitcase and rushed inside, locking the door behind her.

"Judge, there's a man in the alley. I think it's him."

Judge Conroy was stroking the cat and murmuring endearments. She peeked out through a crack in the blinds.

"Where? I don't see anyone."

"Well, now the gate's closed. But he was there, watching."

Setting Lucy down, the judge took off her coat, then touched Madison's arm with a reassuring smile.

"It was just a neighbor, putting out the trash. I can tell you're still on edge from last night. Don't worry, that was nothing. A misunderstanding between friends."

So that's how it was going to be. Wallace was out there, and the judge knew it. She would've seen him, possibly spoken to him. She was presumably covering for him. And lying to Madison about it, which didn't bode well for this endeavor. The whole point of the dinner was to ply her with food and wine and get her talking. It had always been a long shot to think a few well-timed questions would unearth her secrets. With Wallace lurking outside, it began to seem downright dangerous.

"It smells divine in here. What are you cooking?" the judge said.

She'd been sautéing shallots for fettucine with a lemon cream sauce, a dish she'd perfected. She picked up the wooden spoon and gave them a stir.

"Just making us some dinner. I figured you'd be too tired to cook after your travel day."

"Hah, my idea of cooking is opening DoorDash. You'll spoil me, Madison."

Judge Conroy looked around appreciatively. The house gleamed, fragrant with lemon furniture polish. The fireplace was lit. The sound system played jazz at the perfect volume. A bottle of chardonnay sat chilling in an ice bucket on the island. She'd laid her trap well. Who knows, it still might work. She had to try, for Danny.

"Dinner will be ready in ten minutes."

"I'll go change, then. Right after I open that wine. God, I need a drink."

She looked it, her face white and strained, deep purple shadows under her eyes. Madison squelched a rush of empathy. The judge was her quarry. Not her friend.

"Here. Let me."

She plucked the wine from the cooler, opened it with a flourish and poured two glasses. They clinked.

"Was your trip okay? You seem stressed."

"Oh, yes, fine. Hey, those joggers are adorable on you. You should keep them."

Madison wore sweatpants and a T-shirt from the judge's closet. They were the simplest things she'd found and yet the height of luxury, the sweatpants of pale blue cashmere, the T-shirt from a high-end brand. Keeping them would put her in the judge's debt.

"You're too generous. I can't accept."

"No, I insist. And that reminds me."

Taking out her wallet, she counted a thousand dollars cash onto the island like a blackjack dealer throwing cards. Then looked at it, frowned, and added five hundred more. Madison remembered that plastic bag of cash, hidden in the judge's bathroom. Was this dirty money? It was certainly an exorbitant amount for twenty-four hours of pet-sitting. She recognized a bribe when she saw one.

"That's more than we agreed."

"I know, but the weekend turned out to be more *eventful* than we agreed. I said I would make it up to you, and I mean it. I'm compensating you for your trouble and showing appreciation for your discretion."

"You don't need to buy my silence."

Judge Conroy was taken aback by her directness.

"It's not like that. To come home to Lucy being in a good mood, dinner, a clean house—that's worth a lot to me. I appreciate you, Madison. I was trying to show it, that's all. Keep the money. Now, if you'll excuse me, I'm going to change."

She took her wine with her as she pulled the suitcase toward the stairs, the cat prancing alongside and threatening to get under her feet. Madison left the money sitting on the island for the moment, uneasy. As many uses as she had for it, she knew she ought to refuse it, as well as the cashmere pants. Really, she should leave this house and not look back, never speak to the judge again outside class, quit the internship. But she couldn't. Danny was missing, and the judge knew something, or at least she was tight with people who did. To find out more, Madison had to get her to stop stonewalling and start confiding. She'd be better able to do that if she seemed like someone whose silence could be bought.

She tucked the money in her backpack and went to set the table.

Ten minutes later, the judge was back, in flowy pants, a cashmere sweater, velvet slippers, her hair loose around her shoulders. She set her empty wineglass on the island, and Madison rushed to fill it. She needed Judge Conroy to believe that she was still the adoring student, the acolyte, whose discretion could be counted on. She felt a pang of loss that it was no longer true. Whether the judge was a victim or a villain, she wasn't the hero Madison had looked up to, and that made her sad.

She'd set out a platter with a bit of charcuterie, roasted peppers, some black olives. The judge took a seat at a bar stool.

"Come, sit. I can't eat this lavish spread all by myself. It's absolutely gorgeous. You even got my favorite olives. How did you know?"

"I think we have the same taste."

"Well, it's good taste," the judge said, popping an olive in her mouth.

"Hold on, I'm just draining the pasta. Oh, I got sardines for Lucy. I hope that's okay. I mixed a couple in with her food."

"No wonder she likes you. She's very picky. When Nancy comes over, Lucy hisses and goes off and pees in the corner."

Madison giggled. "No!"

"Oh, yes. She hates that woman with a passion."

The judge's tone suggested that she shared the sentiment. Interesting. As Madison dressed the salad and put the finishing touches on the pasta, she made a mental note to look into the case manager.

Madison carried their plates to the table. The dish was basically elevated comfort food, easier to pull off than it would appear to someone who didn't cook. The judge looked transported as she took the first bite.

"*Luscious.* Where did you learn to cook like this?"

"My mom worked long hours when I was growing up, so I—"

She stopped herself. She'd been on the verge of saying that she cooked for herself and Danny.

"—if I wanted to eat, I had to cook. And I waitressed through high school and college. Not easy work, but I love restaurants."

"This is restaurant quality. So good."

"I'm glad you like it. Did you eat anywhere fun in DC? I hear the food scene there is fantastic."

The judge set down her glass with a clatter, her face going gray.

"How did you know I was in Washington?"

"You mentioned that last night when your friend came to the door."

She took a deep breath, seeming relieved. "*Oh,* I forgot. But I told you, he's *not* my friend."

She sounded like she meant it, and looked genuinely upset.

Madison wondered again if this was some sort of abusive relationship. Maybe the judge needed help.

"What is he to you, then? Is he hurting you?"

"No. And I don't want to talk about it."

"Judge, you can trust me. My aunt was in an abusive relationship. I lived with them for a while, but didn't know until he—"

Her stomach lurched. She'd been about to mention Hector beating Danny. God, she had to stop thinking about her brother, or she'd blow her cover with the judge. From the intent way Judge Conroy was watching her, she worried that she already knew.

"He what?"

"He was violent. Eventually, my aunt kicked him out, but it wasn't easy."

"I appreciate your concern, but you've got it wrong."

"I just want you to know that I'm here to help."

"This pasta helps. Conversation helps. Distract me."

"Okay. What do you want to talk about?"

"Tell me about Chloe Kessler and Ty Evans."

Madison barked a laugh. "Seriously? Why does everybody always ask about Ty?"

"Because he's interesting."

"I'll dish on one condition. I get to ask you something in return."

"Hmm."

"That's the deal."

"Fine. You first."

"Let's see. Well. I noticed Ty the first day of orientation. He was the best-looking guy in our year, and I thought, *I've got no chance.*"

"Oh, stop. No false modesty. You're gorgeous and you know it, too."

"Okay. What I really thought was, *I want that guy, and I'm gonna get him.* So I did a little maneuvering to make sure we wound up in a study group together. Anyway, by the third week of school we were a couple, but we were both so competitive. I just never felt like I could trust him, and that bothered me."

"Trust him how? Was he a player?"

She paused, seeing an opening.

"Not with other women, no. It was more like I'd mention something I wanted, and he'd go after it, too. As a matter of fact, that happened with you, Judge."

"With *me*? How do you mean?"

"With the internship."

"But Ty didn't apply."

"I thought he was going to, because he tried to talk me out of applying. He warned me away from you."

The judge's eyes focused sharply. "Warned you how? Tell me exactly what he said."

Huh. A chill crept down Madison's neck. Judge Conroy wasn't actually interested in her relationship with Ty, was she? She wanted to know what people at the law school said about her. Particularly Ty—and Chloe, Douglas Kessler's daughter. Madison wasn't the only one at this table fishing for information.

"Um—it was nothing. He just said you had a reputation for working interns really hard. At the time, I thought he wanted to clear the field to apply for the position himself. But then I heard the last intern was fired."

The judge frowned. "You heard about that."

"It's getting around. Why was she let go?"

"Come on, Madison, you know I can't discuss personnel matters. Let's just say not every relationship works out. Speaking of which, what happened with you and Ty?"

"I broke it off at the end of the school year as kind of a bluff, to be honest. I figured he'd miss me over the summer and come crawling back all humble, the perfect boyfriend. Instead, I drunk-dialed him one night, and guess what? Chloe picked up his phone and said he was in the shower."

"*No.*"

"Yep. They were both interning in New York. Turns out they got together like two weeks after we broke up. Served me right, I guess."

"She's a sly one. You're not friends with her, are you?"

"I don't have anything against her. I'm cool with Ty moving on. I have my career to think about. Relationships hold you back."

"I used to work with her dad. Does she ever talk about me?"

Madison paused. Her instincts were right. The judge was pumping her for information.

"Chloe? Not that I recall. Why?"

"I just wondered. That's all," she said, taking a bite of pasta.

They fell silent. Madison considered her strategy. So far, her plan to loosen the judge's tongue with wine was not working. They were like two prizefighters circling one another but neither landing a blow. Because they both had their guard up.

"I told you about Ty. Now it's my turn to ask a question."

"Go ahead," the judge said, but she did not look happy.

The judge had shut down any discussion of Wallace. Her best bet was to focus on Raymond Logue. How could she bring him up without revealing that she knew of him through Danny? She had to take a roundabout approach. Logue was someone from the judge's past. He'd danced at her wedding, attended her high school assembly. *High school.* That was it. She'd ask a question about Catholic Prep. Their shared history. How school was a ref-uge when their mothers fell ill. How—

How a family member helped with their education.

For her it was her aunt. For the judge, an uncle.

A light bulb flashed in her head. Could that be Raymond Logue?

"If you have a question, ask. The food's getting cold."

"Okay. So, we talked about how similar our paths have been, right? How our childhoods were difficult, but Catholic Prep was a refuge for us both. I'm interested in, well I'm wondering in particular, what made you want to be a lawyer? You mentioned the uncle who helped you get an education, just like my aunt helped me. Was he a lawyer, too?"

Madison made her eyes wide and innocent. But Judge Conroy wasn't fooled. She knew where this was going. An angry flush spread up from her neck, and her jaw tightened with fury.

"Why are you here, Madison? What do you want from me?"

Pay dirt. But also danger. Just then the doorbell rang.

"Is it Wallace?" Madison blurted in alarm.

The judge's mouth fell open. "You know his name?"

The bell rang again, insistently. The judge got to her feet, her gaze roaming the kitchen. The dark-gray Prada tote that she carried everywhere was sitting on the island. She grabbed it, pulling out a gun. Madison's eyes went wide. She jumped up, ready to run.

"Sit down and be quiet. If it is him, trust me, you don't want him knowing you're still here."

Still? Shit. The implications were clear. Wallace knew she'd been there before. And he was capable of hurting her.

As the judge went to answer, Madison retreated behind the island and took a knife from the block. Not that it would be much help when Wallace and the judge both had guns. Judge Conroy opened the front door, letting in a waft of night air. She was talking to someone. Madison couldn't make out the words, but the visitor was a woman. Thank God. She breathed out. The conversation went on. Their voices were agitated, angry. Eventually, the judge slammed the door, muttering under her breath as she came back to the kitchen.

Seeing Madison holding the butcher knife, she stopped short, eyes wide.

"What are you doing? Put that away."

"You pulled a gun, so—"

"Yes, and I still have it," she said, waving it menacingly.

"No, I meant— It wasn't to hurt you, Judge. I thought you might need help."

"Oh, like you were going to back me up?"

"It's the truth," Madison said, putting down the knife.

Sighing, Judge Conroy returned to the table, laying the gun beside her knife and spoon. She topped off both their wineglasses.

"Sit down, all right? We need to talk."

Madison joined her, taking a gulp of the wine. "Who was that?" she asked. And then realized the likely answer. "Was it Nancy?"

The judge didn't reply.

"Why would she show up unannounced?"

"You ask a lot of questions, Madison. My phone's been off, all right? She got worried."

That made no sense. She was lying again.

"Your case manager comes to your house on a Saturday night because your phone is off? When the doorbell rings, you grab a gun? An armed man tries to break into your house, and I'm supposed to trick him into thinking you're home when you're not? What is going *on*?"

"You tell *me*. You're the one being dishonest. You said in the interview that you're an only child. But that's a lie."

The judge plucked papers from her bag and threw them on the table. The employment form was on top, but there were other documents, too. She picked them up and displayed them one by one, her voice tight with anger.

"This is your background form, in which you strategically left off your brother's name. And these? Your birth certificate and his. Proving that he's your brother. This? His booking form, showing that he's a defendant in a drug case before me. You purposely concealed a connection to a known criminal. That's a crime. I'm very disappointed."

Madison was shaking, more with anger than surprise. *The judge knew about Danny.* How long had she known? What more was she hiding? She wanted to get in the judge's face right now and demand to know where her brother was. Then her eyes fell on the gun, gleaming on the table by the judge's right hand. Was it wise to start making accusations? Judge Conroy wouldn't hurt her, she was certain. Then again, the woman kept a bag of cash hidden in her toilet tank and had a close personal relationship with a corrupt cop. Obviously, Madison didn't know her as well as she thought. It wouldn't help Danny if she got shot. She should defuse the situation first and ask questions later.

She kept her voice calm and her gaze steady.

"You're right, Danny *is* my brother. I apologize sincerely for withholding that information. I should have told you. That was wrong. I hope you can forgive me."

"Why should I? I trusted you, and you lied."

We trusted *each other*. And *you* lied. But she couldn't say that.

"I'm truly sorry for disappointing you. I let my ambition get the better of me. I wanted the internship so bad. I know it's no excuse, but I was afraid you wouldn't hire me if you knew."

"*No.* If this was just about getting the job, you wouldn't be grilling me about my past. You're after something, Madison. What is it? And who put you up to it?"

"Nobody. My only motive is to help you, Judge. Last night,

when Wallace came to the door, I felt in my gut that he was there to hurt you. I feared for your safety, more than my own. I knew his name from Danny's case, so I looked him up online. You know what I found? That he was the lead investigator on your husband's murder, which was never solved. That made me wonder. Does he have some sort of hold on you? Are you afraid of him? Please, tell me what's going on."

The judge's chin trembled. For a moment, Madison thought she was going to cry, but she shook it off, throwing back her shoulders with an angry glint in her eye.

"I won't talk about this," she said. "I can't."

"Did he threaten you? You can tell me."

"Don't push me, Madison. You're on thin ice. I'd be within my rights to inform the dean of your dishonesty. Or the bar association, so you'd never practice law. I could even have you prosecuted."

She'd been so focused on Danny that she'd lost sight of the threat to her own future. Her career hung in the balance, and she still cared about that, very much. She had to head this off.

"I hope you won't do any of those things. I know it's a lot to ask you to trust me again. But I promise you, I meant no harm. I only wanted to help you. Please, give me a second chance."

The judge took a sip of wine, studying Madison thoughtfully.

"The truth is, I could use an ally. In a strange way, the fact that you lied almost makes it easier to trust you again. I have something over you now. You're in a precarious position. The best-case scenario is that you infiltrated my chambers to influence my decision on your brother's case. But there's another interpretation that could lead to very serious criminal liability. If you had a vendetta or were plotting to harm me, that could mean years in prison."

She gasped. "You know I would *never*—"

"I don't really think you would. But it might look that way to an outsider. The point is, with what I know about you, I could destroy you, Madison. But I don't want to. I'd rather make use of you instead."

"Are you . . . *blackmailing* me?"

"Let's not get dramatic. This is a difficult moment for us both. I'm simply suggesting that we'd be wise to throw in together."

"Okay. How?"

"Well, for now, I just need you to stay close by. In fact, I'm going to insist that you stay here so I can keep an eye on you and make sure you don't try to compromise me when my back is turned."

"Stay at your house? For how long? Exams are coming up. I have obligations."

"I'm not asking you to skip school. You need to go to class, law review, the internship. Keep up your normal routine. Don't attract attention. At night, come here and be available in case I need help."

Gooseflesh rose on her arms. "If you're expecting Wallace to come back, I'm not the right person to—"

"No, it's not that. I can't go into specifics right now. This is more like . . . running errands."

"Judge, I *won't* break the law."

The judge smiled mirthlessly. "Funny, I thought you already had. Look, I don't know what you think of me, Madison. What you've taken into your head that I'm involved in, and I'm not sure I want to know. But I'm not asking you to do anything illegal. When the time comes, you can always say no. Plus, I'll pay you. Let's say two thousand for one week, cash up front, plus Ubers back and forth to campus to make it easier to get around without being seen. If the arrangement goes longer than a week, I'll pay more."

"Two thousand dollars is a lot of money. There's something you're not telling me."

The judge sighed. "Of course there is, and there's plenty you're not telling me. We're both hiding things. But sometimes, mutual suspicion can make for a solid partnership. If my offer seems overly generous, it's because I'm compensating you for the risk of being around me. There are people who want to hurt me."

"You mean Wallace."

"It's bigger than one person. And I'm not the only one at risk. They know who you are. They're watching you, too."

The hairs on the back of her neck stood up. "Wallace knows my name?"

"Oh, yes. He's the one who told me you lied on that form."

"Are you suggesting that he'd hurt me?"

"I didn't say that."

Her voice rose. "But it's what you meant."

"I hope it never comes to that. I think your best option is to accept my offer and come stay in this house. At least then I can protect you."

She bought herself a minute by gulping down some water. Obviously, Judge Conroy had a hidden agenda. Hell, it wasn't even hidden. Wallace was implicated somehow. She could almost smell him lurking nearby. The thought of crossing paths with him again filled her with terror. This whole situation felt like a trap, but it was too late to escape. She was ensnared. Her choices were: Destroy her future and leave Danny twisting in the wind. Or willingly go deeper into the judge's world, knowing it was filled with danger, but possibly get answers in the process.

Judge Conroy reached across the table and grasped Madison's hand.

"I need a friend, Madison. I don't have many of those. I understand you're frightened, but I'll do my best to make sure you don't get hurt. And if there's a way that I can help your brother, I will. Say you'll do it, that you'll help me."

Madison felt the ground shift under her feet yet again. She couldn't figure this woman out. Was she a victim, a criminal, a mentor, a savior? Did it matter? Against her better judgment, Madison was going to give the answer that the judge wanted to hear. For Danny, for her mother, for herself. But also for Judge Conroy, because somewhere deep down, she still believed in her. Despite every indication to the contrary.

20

....

On Sunday, Madison went to a regularly scheduled law review meeting, a Securities Reg prep session, and then took up a prominent position in the reading room at Langdell Library, where she studied for several hours. She kept to her normal routine and let herself be seen doing so, as the judge had instructed. The question was—seen by whom?

Late that afternoon, she left the library and hurried toward her dorm, glancing over her shoulder. The sun hung low in the sky. Shadows gathered, and dead leaves crunched underfoot, obscuring other sounds. She heard no one behind her, saw no sign of Wallace. Then again, he was a detective, skilled in the art of surveillance. He could be there, and she wouldn't know.

In her room, she drew the blinds before packing a duffel bag with clothes for the week. Her stomach hollow with nerves, she wondered what Judge Conroy had in store for her. What kind of *errands*? Were they dangerous? Illegal? Both? The judge had threatened her with arrest. And that was terrifying. But the real reason she was doing this was to find her brother. She should have demanded answers last night. She would have, if the gun hadn't spooked her. Danny had been missing from the prison database since yesterday morning. Tonight, she wouldn't hold back. She'd confront the judge, even if it meant putting her own safety at risk.

She should tell someone where she was going.

She called an Uber, texting her mother from the back seat.

> Sorry I haven't been in touch. I got a job working for the judge, kind of like a pet sitter. Going to her house now and will ask about Danny. Will let you know what I find out. Don't tell anyone, don't worry, and most of all be careful. Love you.

She had the Uber drop her several blocks from Judge Conroy's house. Creeping through the streets and alleyways, she watched her back. But she was alone on this frigid Sunday night. The temperature had plummeted. Scattered flurries wafted from the sky. Shivering, she slipped through the back gate and let herself in with the key the judge had provided. After disarming the security system, she turned to find herself staring down the barrel of Judge Conroy's gun.

"*Jesus.*" Madison's hand flew to her throat, her pulse rocketing with fear.

"Oh, it's you. Thank God," the judge said, lowering the gun. "I'm sorry. I didn't mean to scare you."

"That's not okay," Madison said.

"I said I'm sorry. I didn't know it was you. Please, come in. Have some wine. I ordered DoorDash."

The judge walked into the kitchen. Madison followed, watching as she stashed the gun in her bag on the island. All was warm and cheery in here. Candles lit on the table, flames dancing in the fireplace. Lucy rubbed up against Madison's legs, purring. But her heart still hammered in her chest. A terrible thought had occurred to her.

"You thought I was *him*," she said, facing Judge Conroy across the island. The gun was within the judge's reach, but Madison no longer believed that it was meant for her. "Wallace has a key, doesn't he?"

The judge sighed. "It's possible."

"You're not sure? Did you give him one or not?"

"*I* didn't. No."

"Someone else gave him a key to your house?"

"Please, I really don't want to talk about this tonight. It's too stressful. Sit down, have something to eat. I got ramen. It'll warm you up. It's so cold tonight. They're saying snow by Friday."

Taking plastic containers from the warming drawer, she dumped the soup out into bowls, which they carried, steaming, to the table. There was an open bottle of pinot noir. The judge filled their glasses, then dipped her spoon. Madison was too keyed up to eat. She crossed her arms, stone-faced.

"Look, if you're going to point a gun at me—"

"I'm sorry. That was a mistake. It won't happen again."

"I don't believe you. I don't feel safe. Not just because of you. I'm risking Wallace showing up at any minute. If you expect me to stay, I'm going to need something in return."

"Yes, of course. I said I'd pay."

"Not money. I'm concerned about my brother."

The judge's face fell. "Oh, now, wait a minute. This arrangement was not an invitation to sway me on his case."

Her chest swelled with anger. "Stop acting like this is a normal case where normal rules apply. It's not, and you're not a normal judge. Danny was framed. And now he's *missing*. I think you know something about that."

The judge's spoon clattered to the table. "Missing? That's not possible. He's in custody."

Her look of shock seemed genuine. Was she simply a talented actress?

"Well, they moved him, and they won't say where. He's not in the database. He hasn't called home. At this point, we're worried something terrible happened. If you want my help, then I need you to look into this. Find him. Tell me where he is. The Bureau of Prisons is giving us the runaround, but they'd have to answer you."

"That doesn't make sense. They don't relocate prisoners until after sentencing. Your brother hasn't been sentenced yet."

"That's correct."

"Are you sure he was moved?"

"Positive. My mother talked to the guards on duty, and then to an administrator at the prison. I confirmed it online. He's not there."

"And they wouldn't say where they took him?"

"She couldn't get a straight answer. The guards say he was transferred, but they didn't have details. The administrator claims he can't give us the information because Danny's status is confidential."

The judge looked shaken. "*Confidential*?"

"Yes. What does that even mean? I searched the BOP database. He's no longer listed. How can they not tell his family where he is? Is this normal, because it doesn't seem like it."

"No, it's not. Thank you for telling me. I didn't know this was happening."

"Can you do anything? My mother is going crazy."

"Let me make some calls tomorrow. I'll see what I can find out."

Madison thanked her, sitting back in her chair and picking up her spoon. She tried to relax, but it wasn't easy—for either of them. They were both on edge, listening for any threat. When the cat suddenly attacked a squeaky toy shaped like a mouse, they both jumped, and then laughed in unison. But the laughter rang hollow. The second she got news of Danny, Madison vowed she'd be out of here, no matter what Judge Conroy said.

———

The following afternoon, she reported to the courthouse for her internship, eager to hear what the judge had learned. But her office door was shut, raised voices emanating from behind it. Kelsey the receptionist gave her a suspicious look.

"What are you doing here?"

"Monday is one of my days," she said, blowing past her, heading for a desk in the law clerks' office.

Sean was at his computer. He looked up, startled.

"I wasn't expecting you," he said.

Nancy had apparently not conveyed her schedule to others in the office. Still, why the surprise? She sat down at her desk, logging on to the server as she replied.

"Oh, yeah. I'll be working Mondays, Thursdays, and Fridays. Imani's not in today?"

"She went to the Clerk's Office. Hey, did you have some sort of run-in with Nancy?"

She looked up in confusion. Her login ID didn't seem to be working.

"Not that I'm aware of. Why, did she say something?"

"Yeah. I mean, not to freak you out, but I was under the impression you'd been fired."

"*What?* I have no idea what you're talking about. Nothing was said to me at all."

Footsteps were coming down the hallway. As Nancy appeared in the doorway, Sean's eyes flew to his computer, almost as if he was afraid of being caught speaking to Madison. Nancy was slightly built, middle-aged, and mousy. Nothing about her would normally inspire fear. Yet people were afraid. When she'd shown up uninvited at Judge Conroy's door, the judge grabbed a gun. Granted, maybe she didn't know it was Nancy. She might've expected Wallace or someone else. Still, Judge Conroy seemed to despise her case manager. They'd argued that night. And just now, that must have been her quarreling with Judge Conroy behind her office door. What were they fighting about? Why didn't the judge just fire the woman instead of taking so much abuse?

"I'm surprised you'd show your face here," Nancy said in a nasty tone.

Okay. This was about Danny. It must be. The judge told Nancy that Madison had lied. Sean was listening from his desk. She knew from Ty that he was a gossip. If Sean found out she'd lied to a federal judge, it would get back to people at the law school. She couldn't let that happen.

Madison's palms went sweaty as she met Nancy's gaze. Could she brazen her way out of this one?

"Uh—maybe you forgot? We agreed that Monday would be one of my days. Also, I don't know if you're the right person to ask about this, but I'm having trouble logging in."

"Oh, I'm the right person all right. You left important information off your employment form."

"Oh. *Yes.* Right. I'm very sorry. I'm still following up. I'll get you that as soon as possible. I apologize for any inconvenience."

"It's more than inconvenient. It's a problem."

"Again, I apologize. I did speak to Judge Conroy about the form, and she said it was okay to take more time."

The judge would back her up. She'd have to.

"You spoke to her directly, without asking me?"

"I was here late on Friday, finishing up a memo. I just— I bumped into her on my way out, so—" Madison faltered. "She didn't seem to mind."

Nancy scoffed. "Well, she wouldn't, would she?"

The silence lengthened until it felt like a stand-off. Madison cleared her throat nervously.

Nancy shot a glance at Sean. She seemed as hesitant to speak in front of him as Madison was.

"Get up," Nancy said finally, sliding into Madison's chair and typing into the computer for several minutes. "Given the omission on your background form, if it were up to me, I'd let you go. But you have friends in high places, apparently. You're staying—*for now*. I fixed it so you'll be able to do legal research but not get into any case files. But just remember, I'm watching you."

Nancy stalked away. Sean had heard everything. What would he think? Who would he tell? She met his eyes, feeling gut-punched.

"I am *soo* sorry," he said. "When Imani and I advised you to leave blanks on that form, we had no idea she'd go batshit like that."

He thought it was his fault. She wanted to scream with relief, but that wouldn't be wise.

"It's not your fault, Sean. But wow, Nancy is just—"

"She's a lunatic since Olivia. We know. She's so overprotective of the judge that she's making it very difficult to work here. I cannot apologize enough. We'll do our best to keep her off your back. Just, please don't tell anyone at the law school, or we'll never get another internship application."

"Of course. No worries at all."

Imani returned. As Sean filled her in, she apologized to Madison and made a few choice comments about Nancy under her breath. For the rest of that afternoon, the three of them worked in silence. There were no cases on in court that day. Everybody kept a low profile in the wake of the confrontation. The judge remained behind closed doors, not showing her face. Madison had hoped to find a moment to speak to her alone and hear what she'd learned about Danny, but it proved impossible.

When she let herself into the town house that evening, she found the judge sitting on the sofa with Lucy on her lap, staring into the fire.

"Nancy wanted me to fire you for lying about your brother. But I refused. We had an argument."

"Why did you tell her?" she asked.

"I didn't. She found out . . . on her own."

The judge's tone was hollow. She seemed listless and depressed. The incident had obviously upset her. Well, that made two of them. Was Madison supposed to feel grateful? At this point, if not for Danny, she would quit the internship and have nothing more to do with Judge Conroy. Though Danny wasn't the only consideration. There was also the not insignificant question of whether they would turn her in for lying.

"Is she going to report me?" Madison asked.

"That's what you're worried about?"

"Not the only thing. I'm worried about Danny, too. Did you find out where he is?"

The judge heaved a sigh.

"*You're* going to be fine."

"What does that mean?"

"Just keep your head down. Stay away from Nancy and I can keep her from reporting you."

"And Danny?"

"I believe he's safe."

"Where is he?"

"I told you what I know," she said, but she wouldn't meet Madison's eyes, and her expression was guarded.

"You don't know where he is?"

"They moved him. The database doesn't say where to, and I was not able to get that information."

"Are you serious? *I* could've told you that much."

"I'm sorry my efforts don't meet with your approval," Judge Conroy said acidly.

"You think he's safe, but you're not sure?"

"He's safe for now."

"For now? What does that mean? Is someone trying to hurt him? And how can they refuse to tell you his location? You're the judge in his case. There's something you're not saying."

Her eyes flashed. "I go to bat for you with Nancy, and this is the thanks I get? You're right, there are things I'm not telling you. I can't. I won't. This topic is closed. Don't ask me about him again. Now I'm going to bed. *Good night.*"

It was just seven o'clock, but the judge picked up Lucy and hurried up the stairs. Madison heard her bedroom door slam. The dramatic exit left her shaken. The topic of Danny was now off-limits with the judge, and she hadn't learned anything new.

She went up to the attic bedroom and called her mother. Mom had been suffering terribly over Danny's absence, unable to eat or sleep. Madison wished she had more news. She did her best to put an upbeat spin on it, leading with the fact that Danny was safe, just leaving out the part about "for now."

Her mother gave a half sob, half sigh. "*Gracias a Dios.* Where is he? Is it close enough to visit?"

"She doesn't exactly know where he is. They moved him, possibly due to overcrowding or something. That wasn't clear."

"She's the judge in his case. How can she not know where he is?"

"I hear you, Mom. When I tried to press her on that, she got mad. Like I said, judges are sensitive about people trying to influence them."

"What are we supposed to do? This isn't okay. I need to talk to him. Can we get a phone call, at least? Did she say when that might happen?"

"I'm afraid not."

"Can you ask again?"

"No. Not for a while anyway. It would be counterproductive."

"Madison, please. I can't go on not talking to my baby. Not knowing how to reach him. It's killing me. Isn't there more you can do?"

There really wasn't. There was nobody to ask beyond Judge Conroy, who now said the topic was closed. And if she'd had any hope of looking into Danny's case herself by searching court records, Nancy had squelched that by cutting off her computer access.

"I'll think of something, Mom. Get some rest," she said, and got off the phone.

———

The next day, Madison was grabbing a salad from the cold case at the law school café when her phone buzzed. As her mother's number flashed across the screen, the guilt hit. She had nothing new to report. Sighing, she swiped to answer.

"Hello?"

"Is this Madison?" a woman's voice asked.

It wasn't her mother.

"Yes. Who's this?"

"My name is Regina. I work with your mom at the nursing home."

She put the salad down. "Is something wrong?"

"Yolanda's in the ER. She was having chest pains. I came with her. They're examining her now."

"Oh my God. Where? Which hospital?"

"Mass General."

"I'll be right there."

She was running, trying to order an Uber on her phone, when she nearly crashed into Ty coming into the café.

"Whoa, slow down there," he said, steadying her. "Where you running off to? The law review meeting's not for half an hour."

"I forgot about that. I can't make it today. Will you let them know?"

"Not a good idea to miss meetings unless you want to give me a clear shot at president."

Great, just what she needed—a reminder that she was falling behind. Exams started next week also, and she was having a hard time concentrating on studying.

"I have to go," she said, trying to push past him.

"Wait, I have a question," he said, blocking her way. "I heard you haven't slept at the dorm the past few nights."

Anger flared. "Oh, are you keeping tabs on me now?"

"You can tell me if you're seeing someone. I've been open about my relationship with Chloe."

"Yes. You have. Now, get out my way. I have to be somewhere."

She got an Uber, hit bad traffic on the bridge into Boston, got out and ran for blocks and blocks. Breathless and sweaty, nearly in tears, she plunged through the sliding glass doors of the ER and hurried to the reception window, where she gave her mother's name.

"Your relationship to the patient?"

"I'm her daughter."

"She's being examined. Take a seat."

"Can I see her?"

"I said to take a seat, please. We'll call you," the woman snapped. "Madison?"

A woman in a puffer coat beckoned to her from a row of plastic chairs. Madison ran over to her.

"Are you Regina?"

"Yes."

"Thank you for bringing her here. What happened? Did she collapse?"

"Nothing like that. She just felt funny, said her chest felt tight. Our staff nurse said better safe than sorry, so we came here. They're doing tests to confirm if it was a heart attack, but the—"

"Heart attack. Oh my God."

"I don't want to alarm you. It could be the stress. I'm sure you know, she's beside herself over your brother."

"She said that?"

"Oh, honey. He's all she talks about. Now if you don't mind, I'll get back to work. We're short-staffed."

"Of course."

"Here's her phone and her pocketbook. She gave it to me for safekeeping."

"Thank you. For everything."

She hugged Regina then sat down to wait. Flicking on her mother's phone, she saw that the screensaver was a picture of Danny as a little boy. Those ears, that goofy grin, the big, dark eyes. He was adorable.

She put it back in the bag.

An hour passed. She went up to the window several times, but got nowhere. Eventually, a different clerk came on duty. The next time she asked for information, he simply gave her Mom's room number and buzzed her through. She located her mother lying on an examination table with her eyes closed, in a room cordoned off by thick curtains.

"Mom?"

Yolanda's eyes shot open. There were dark circles under them. Her cheeks were hollow. She looked old and frail.

"I didn't know if you would come," she said, her voice weak.

"Of course I came. I've been here for hours. They just let me back now. How are you feeling?"

Madison pulled over a rolling chair and sat down, taking her mother's hand. It was small and cold to the touch, the hospital wristband flopping around on it. Her heart turned over. What if Danny never came home? What if her mother died? She'd be all alone in the world. She had to do more to find him and fix this situation.

"From the ECG, it's not a heart attack. They're just waiting to confirm that with the results of the blood tests."

"When do they get those?"

"Not for a few hours. The doctor was ninety-nine percent sure it's just stress. She's giving me some meds and discharging me. I'm just waiting for the papers."

"Okay. I'll take you home and stay with you tonight."

"That's not necessary. I know you're busy."

"Not too busy to take care of you, Mom."

Her mother fixed Madison with a grim look.

"You want to take care of me, don't sit by my bedside. *Do* something. Find your brother. That's how you can help. The stress is eating me alive. Next time, I might not be so lucky."

21

Madison stayed at the hospital until her mother was discharged, then hurried back to campus for a Corporations review session that she couldn't afford to miss. The turmoil in her life was beginning to affect her academic performance. She forced herself to go to the library afterward, which meant she didn't get to the Back Bay until nearly eleven. The judge's car was parked in the alleyway, but the town house was dark. She dealt with the litter box, then went upstairs, pausing on the second-floor landing. The door to Judge Conroy's bedroom was closed, and no light showed in the gap beneath it. If the judge had been awake, Madison would've told her about the afternoon in the ER with Mom. They'd bonded before over their mothers' difficulties. Maybe if the judge understood that Danny's troubles were destroying her mother's health, she'd try harder to help. Or not. She'd seemed so caring when they connected over dinner, but that could've been an act.

The next morning, Madison was sitting on the bench in the back hall, pulling on her boots before heading to campus, when Judge Conroy came running in, still in her bathrobe, looking flustered.

"There you are. I'm glad I caught you."

"What's the matter? Did something happen?"

"It's just, I have an extra ticket for the Pro Bono League reception at the MFA tonight, and I'd like you to attend."

The most glittering event of the year in the Boston legal community, the Pro Bono League reception showcased the charitable work done by major law firms. It was always held in a fabulous venue, with an open bar and food catered by the most notable chefs in the city. Madison dreamed of attending once she was an established attorney. To go as a law student was rare. The only person she knew who'd ever managed to snag an invite was Chloe, because her father was a name partner in one of the sponsoring firms. Normally, she would have jumped at such a rare opportunity. But she suspected that this one came with a catch. Judge Conroy insisted that their deal remain secret. She wanted Madison to tell nobody, sneak into the town house through the back alley, keep up her normal routine. It didn't make sense that she'd invite her to the social event of the year where people would see them together—unless she had an ulterior motive.

"I'd kill to go to that, but I thought nobody could know about our deal or—" She waved her hand as if to say, *Whatever this is.*

"That's right. The fact that you got your ticket from me will remain our secret. We'll arrive and leave separately."

She wasn't surprised. Like all of the judge's invitations, if it seemed too good to be true, it was.

"I assume you're not inviting me simply for my own enjoyment. Is this one of those *errands* you mentioned?"

"Let's call it an assignment. Meet me back here by five, and I'll give you the details. Oh, and you'll need to get dressed up for this. The invitation says 'cocktail attire.'"

"I'll do my best."

Madison was distracted at school all day, worrying about what this "assignment" might entail. At five on the dot, she let herself in through the back, decommissioning the alarm. The house was dark. They kept the shades drawn still, but the threat of Wallace seeped in anyway, like the smell of a dead animal through the cracks in the walls. She went around turning on the lights. She was refreshing Lucy's food bowl when she heard a key in the front door. Judge Conroy swept into the vestibule on a wave of metallic air, cheeks bright from the cold and arms full of shopping bags. Saks, Neiman Marcus. It was a spree.

"Oh, good, there you are," she said, catching sight of Madison. "I've been thinking about what you should wear."

"I was thinking about that, too. My interview suit is probably best."

"That thing? It's all pilled. It sags at the knees. It won't do. I have some other options. Hurry up, we're running late."

Did the judge mean there was something in the shopping bag for Madison? She rinsed the cat-food tin under the faucet and threw it in the recycling bin, following Judge Conroy up the stairs with growing anxiety. In the dressing room, the judge was pulling pieces from the bags, draping them over chairs, hanging them on racks and smoothing out wrinkles. There were dresses, jumpsuits, pants, blazers, blouses, all in gorgeous fabrics and cuts, but subtle, and sexy only in the classiest way, like what the most beautiful lawyer in the world would wear to an important professional social event. Stroking the satin lapel of a white, tuxedo-style blazer, she snuck a peek at its price tag and blanched. $2,290. These were from the couture floors of the department stores that Madison never set foot in.

The judge looked Madison up and down, then walked around, thoughtfully perusing various items.

"This one," she said, snatching a jumpsuit from a hook and holding it up against her. "It's something you could plausibly buy for yourself."

Madison fingered the price tag, fighting a laugh. $895! Was she kidding? Though the question remained how the judge afforded these clothes herself. There had to be ten or fifteen thousand dollars in purchases here, in one afternoon, by a public servant who made two hundred grand before taxes and owned piles of designer clothes already. The likely answer was, Judge Conroy was a criminal, bought and paid for with dirty money, just like these clothes. Why did Madison continue to resist that obvious conclusion?

"Try it on," the judge commanded.

She undressed quickly and stepped into the jumpsuit. As the judge zipped her up, they fell silent, staring in awe at her reflection in the mirror. The jumpsuit was black with filmy, diaphanous sleeves and beading at the neckline, cuffs, and belt. With its restrained, elegant sparkle, it was the most exquisite thing she'd ever worn. It wasn't the outfit that struck them, though, but how she seemed like a different person in it. More beautiful, more mature. *Rich*. Like she belonged. She loved it. And yet it was a fraud, a costume, to be worn for some nefarious purpose that had yet to be disclosed.

"That looks amazing on you," the judge said.

Judge Conroy was sending her to this event for a reason. Until she understood what it was, she couldn't agree to attend at all, let alone accept a gift this extravagant.

"It's generous of you, Judge. *Too* generous. Why are you doing this?"

"This is the most important networking event of the year in the legal community. I want you to look nice."

There was more to it than that, obviously.

"You're avoiding my question," Madison said, holding her gaze, demanding an answer. "If there's something you expect me to do while I'm there, you need to tell me what it is."

Breaking eye contact, Judge Conroy busied herself cutting tags off the garments.

"There are a couple of people I'd like you to speak to on my behalf. That's all."

"I see. Is there some reason you can't talk to them yourself?"

"It would be—inadvisable."

"I don't understand. Inadvisable how?"

"These are people I can't be seen with. Or who can't be seen with me."

That didn't sound good.

"I want to help. I really do. But if it's inadvisable for you, wouldn't it be for me as well? I'm worried I'd be walking into a trap or exposing myself to prosecution. Can you promise me that won't happen?"

The judge's eyes flashed. "I need a favor, Madison. We had a deal. I've remained silent about your indiscretion. Your *crime* of lying on that form—"

"I didn't lie. I left it blank."

"That's a technicality. You lied in the interview. I could get you expelled, or worse, but you begged for a second chance. And I gave it to you. Now I'm asking you to do something for me."

Madison felt the rope tighten around her. She should have foreseen this. The judge was presenting her with an awful choice—get turned in for lying or be forced to do something of even greater risk that could destroy her legal career and possibly send her to prison. Her only option was to call the judge's bluff. She couldn't see any other path out of this nightmare.

"Something that's probably illegal. You said if I was uncomfortable with what you asked me to do, I could say no. I'm saying no now."

She reached back to unzip the jumpsuit. The judge stopped her hand.

"Listen to me. This is not *illegal* per se. I'm not asking you to carry drugs or anything. Is it risky? Yes. Could you go to jail? Let me remind you, that possibility also exists if I decide to turn you in. Think carefully before you walk out on me. I'm desperate, and as much as I would hate to destroy your very promising career, I will."

"You should think carefully, too. If you turn me in, not only will you lose an ally. You'll gain an opponent. You know things about me, but I know about you, too. If you force me, I'll have no choice but to defend myself."

"You'd cooperate against me?"

"Not by choice. But if you report me, what else can I do?"

The judge crumpled at the knees, sitting down hard on the vanity chair.

"Please, Madison. I'm in a very tough spot. I'm appealing to our friendship. Can't you help me out?"

"Can I ask you something? If our friendship is important to you, then why, when I told you that my brother was missing, did you refuse to help me? And don't say it's because of ethical rules. I won't believe that."

"I did try. I tried to locate your brother."

"You're a federal judge. He's a defendant in a case before you. How is it possible that you can't find him?"

"Because they have him squirreled away somewhere."

"*Who*, they?"

"The people investigating me for corruption."

Madison took a step back, hand going to her heart. She wasn't surprised at the bare fact, just shocked that the judge would admit to it, after all the cover-ups and lies.

"You're being investigated? For what, fixing cases?"

"Something like that. Anyway, it's not true. I'm innocent, just like your brother."

"If you're innocent, why are they hiding Danny from you?"

At a loss, the judge shook her head, her mouth open but no words coming out.

"They're trying to protect him, aren't they?" Madison said with dawning horror. "They think you'd silence him if you could get to him."

The judge's eyes burned into Madison's.

"I wouldn't hurt anyone, and certainly not your brother. You have to believe that. I want justice for him as much as you do."

Despite everything, she did believe her. And yet—

"If that's true, why are you mixed up with the people who framed him?"

"I hate them. They put me in this position. They forced me."

"Then why not turn them in?"

"It wouldn't work. They'd kill me first."

Judge Conroy's eyes glittered with unshed tears. As her words hit home, Madison fully grasped an idea that had been forming in her mind these past days. Wallace, Logue, whoever else they worked with—they were probably the ones behind the murder of the judge's husband. If that was true, it put everything in a different light. Then Kathryn Conroy was indeed a victim, and yet the stakes were higher than she'd imagined, because the enemy was that much more dangerous.

"I want to help you. I really do," Madison said. "The risk just feels too great."

"Too great for the reward I'm offering. I understand. You're not willing to do it to save your career. But would you do it to save your brother?"

"You said you don't know where he is."

"I don't. But I can sign an order vacating his guilty plea and dismissing the charges against him. Then it won't matter where they're hiding him. With no pending charges, they'd have to let him go."

"Won't the authorities stop you from doing that?"

"I don't see how they could. I may be under investigation, but I'm still a judge in good standing with full powers. I'll make you a promise. I'll sign that order first thing tomorrow morning, as soon as I get to chambers. Family is everything, Madison. I think you and I agree about that. You'd be taking a risk, but your brother would be safe. Now, is it worth it to you? What do you say?"

As she considered Judge Conroy's offer, the face that flashed before her eyes was not Danny's, but Mom's, hollow-eyed and wan in the ER yesterday. After her father's death, her mother had had a breakdown. With the stress of Danny's disappearance, the symptoms were recurring. The consequences of turning down Judge Conroy's offer went beyond Danny. She feared that her mother would not survive her brother's death.

The calculus was clear. Jail for herself was nothing compared with the lives of her family.

"You've got a deal," she said.

22

The Museum of Fine Arts was free with a student ID, and Madison had spent many a rainy afternoon in high school and college wandering its galleries or studying in the café while nursing an overpriced coffee. Given her workload in law school, it had been a minute since she visited. Under other circumstances, she would be thrilled to be back.

Not tonight.

She walked into the atrium with a belly full of dread. If not for the spiky, forty-foot-high tree sculpted from lime-green glass, she wouldn't have recognized the place. Dramatic swooshes of colored silk draped from the soaring ceiling, making it look like the inside of a circus tent. Potted palms, lavishly decorated tables with tall floral centerpieces, a bandstand, and a thousand twinkling lights completed the décor. More important, it was jammed with hundreds of strangers who—no surprise for a bunch of successful lawyers—looked a lot alike. More men than women. All decades older than her. Clad in tuxedoes or, like Madison, slinky pantsuits and dresses. Finding her two targets in this crowd would require seeking them out aggressively, which could draw attention to herself. People might remember later, if asked by investigators.

Uniformed staff were passing hors d'oeuvres and champagne. Grabbing a glass, she drank it down, hoping the fizz would steady her nerves. It didn't. There was no point in stalling. This wouldn't get easier. If she wanted to save her brother, she needed to jump in the deep end and pray she floated.

A waiter carrying a tray of lobster in puff pastry approached and handed her a cocktail napkin. Taking a canapé, she made a snap decision about which target to start with.

"Thank you. Can you point me to the Bixby, Kessler, and Moore table?"

"Tables seventeen and eighteen, right under the Chihuly."

She pressed onward toward the glass tree, savoring the rich lobster and flaky pastry, admiring the beautiful clothes, noting the famous faces. A TV news anchor, a U.S. senator, the mayor of Boston. This could be her world, so long as what she did here tonight didn't destroy her.

She recognized Douglas Kessler from twenty yards away, despite having seen him only once before at a law school event where he received an award. The managing partner of the law firm she'd be clerking at next summer, and Chloe's father to boot, he had that master-of-the-universe look. Silver-haired, unnaturally tan for the season, wearing a perfectly tailored tuxedo, with the sharp profile and hawk-like gaze of a powerhouse of the bar. He was holding court, surrounded by a gaggle of fans. She moved closer. It would be difficult to get a word with him at all, let alone privately. A managing partner didn't normally speak to lowly summer associates, even if they happened to be classmates of his daughter. But in a stroke of luck, it turned out he was discussing a case he'd argued before the Supreme Court years before that she knew by heart because it was taught in her Securities Regulation class. She waited for an opening and then asked a pertinent question, making a show of listening raptly to the answer. Kessler looked her up and down as he spoke. When he finished pontificating, he asked her name.

"Madison Rivera. Pleased to meet you, sir. I'll be a summer associate at Bixby starting in June."

She held out her hand. He took it, drawing her aside and looking into her eyes in a way that made her wonder if he followed the firm's anti-fraternization policy. She should've known he'd be a hound.

"*Very* pleased to meet you. I see our recruiting team hasn't lost its touch. That was a very astute question you just posed. You're interested in securities litigation, I take it?"

"Very much so. I'm taking Securities Reg right now at HLS. Your daughter Chloe is in my class."

He dropped her hand like it was radioactive.

"A Harvard woman. Glad to hear it. At Bixby, we like our lawyers bright and ambitious. Good luck this summer."

She'd lost his attention with that comment. He was looking over her shoulder for someone else to talk to.

"Sir—"

"Pleasure to meet you, Madeline," he said, moving away.

"Judge Conroy sends her regards."

His eyes flicked back to her warily. "Oh? How do you know her?"

"I'm taking her class and also interning in her chambers this semester."

"Very nice. Now if you'll excuse me—"

"She asked me to give you a message."

He frowned. "A message? Isn't she here tonight?"

"I believe so."

"Then why not tell me herself?"

"I don't know. I'm just the intern. She said it was important."

"All right, let's hear it, then."

She took a breath, knowing that she was about to cross a line. But she had to do it, for her family.

"The judge asked me to convey that people in high places are interested in your work on the Fiamma case. And that's making some other people very nervous."

He went white, his mouth falling open.

God, this was worse than she imagined. Without knowing the specifics, Madison had recognized the message as a warning of some kind. Seeing Kessler this terrified, she realized—he was a co-conspirator. And she'd just tipped him off that he was under investigation.

That was obstruction of justice.

Madison had just committed a crime. And there was no turning back.

"*Who's* concerned?" Kessler said.

"I don't know. I was tasked with delivering that message in those exact words and wasn't told anything beyond that."

"A word to the wise, Madeline. Forget this conversation ever happened. Never mention it to anyone, or you could be in real trouble. Understand?"

Shit. He'd just proved her theory right.

"Yes, sir."

"If I hear you talked about this, you'll regret it. And that's a promise."

Kessler walked away, leaving her standing conspicuously alone. Hearing his angry tone, a couple of people in the immediate vicinity had turned to look. Bixby lawyers, presumably. God, let them forget her face by next summer, when she'd have to work with them. If she wasn't locked up by then.

Cheeks blazing, she was slinking away when she heard her name. Chloe swanned toward her, trailing Ty in her wake. In evening clothes, champagne in hand, they were a glamorous pair. But the sight of them after what just happened made her want to run.

"What was that about?" Chloe said, looking shocked. "My dad seemed angry."

"I don't know. It was odd, actually. I mentioned I was interning for Judge Conroy, and—"

"Oh, that explains it. There's bad blood between those two."

"Why? Did something happen between them?"

Chloe looked over at the Bixby tables, realized that she was surrounded by lawyers from her dad's firm, then turned back to Madison with a guarded look in her eye.

"I'm surprised to see you here," she said.

Maybe that was her way of avoiding an awkward question, but it came off as condescending. Madison wasn't having it, not after Chloe's father, who turned out to be a criminal himself, had just threatened her.

"You're here. Why not me? Am I not worthy?"

Chloe flushed. "I didn't mean it like that. I just wondered where you got your ticket."

"Where did you get yours? Oh, wait, your dad sponsored tables."

As Ty took Chloe's arm, his eyes lingered on Madison in the black jumpsuit.

"We should find our seats. Enjoy the party."

She could hear them bickering as they walked away.

The encounter with Kessler spooked her enough that she wanted to go hide in the bathroom. But she wasn't done with her espionage. She had to find the second target before cocktail hour ended and the guests repaired to their assigned tables. The judge had been clear that she would only sign the order releasing Danny if Madison succeeded at both tasks.

Pulling out her phone, she glanced surreptitiously at the photograph the judge had provided of Andrew Martin. The young prosecutor was in his thirties, clean-cut, with dark hair and a square jaw. Trouble was, at a party full of lawyers, dozens of men fit that description. She grabbed a glass of champagne from a passing waiter and began a circuit of the room, trekking from one end to the other of the vast space. She spotted several lookalikes, but none of them was him.

The band took a break. A woman stepped up and tapped the microphone, eliciting ear-splitting feedback.

"Please take your assigned seats. Dinner service is about to begin."

Time was running out. Because her assigned seat would normally have been next to the judge at a table full of people from the courthouse, she was supposed to leave the event before dinner was served. Otherwise, people would find out the judge gave her a ticket, which would look strange, since she was only an intern. That meant she had to find Martin in the next few minutes, or she would fail at her task, giving the judge an excuse not to fulfill her end of the bargain. She'd be exposed to criminal prosecution for warning Keooler and get nothing in return.

Suddenly, the throng parted, and she saw the judge coming toward her, looking like a movie star in that white tuxedo. Their eyes met.

"Martin," Madison mouthed, shrugging.

The judge continued walking, looking straight ahead like they'd never met.

Okay.

She was heading for the exit when she spotted her quarry at the bar. Mobbed earlier in the evening, it was now empty except for the bartender and one patron—Andrew Martin. She abandoned her champagne glass in a potted palm and approached him. Busy checking his phone as the bartender mixed him a drink, he didn't notice her. She was supposed to identify herself as Judge Conroy's intern and ask for a private meeting later that night in an alley not far from the judge's house. She worried that would not go over well. No matter how impressive she looked in her finery, she was a stranger to him. And he had the sort of job that made him a target. He could perceive it as a threat. Worse, it might actually *be* a threat. She wanted to believe that Conroy was a victim. But she had new doubts after witnessing Kessler's reaction. She couldn't be sure whether the judge herself planned to show up to that alley. Or, whether it would be Wallace and his gun.

What if they were putting her in the middle of an assassination plot?

The lights flashed, like in a theater, herding the attendees to their tables. Still, Martin hadn't turned around. She'd just made up her mind to leave without speaking to him when he suddenly turned, drink in hand, and nearly crashed into her.

"Excuse me," he said.

Then he looked at her, and his expression transitioned from recognition to shock in the space of a second. Andrew Martin knew who she was. And that was not a good thing.

"Miss Rivera. I'm surprised to see you here. You have something to say to me?"

She was struck speechless, her mind filling up with an image of a room in the U.S. Attorney's Office, windowless, full of evidence boxes, with an enormous bulletin board featuring photos of the suspects. Judge Conroy's picture was in the center, with pieces of string stretching between her and the co-conspirators: Wallace, Logue. And Madison.

His eyes scanned the room, alert for threats.

"You're afraid. And for good reason. We shouldn't talk here. Call my office," he said, and walked away.

Madison fled the MFA like she'd seen a ghost, with Martin's words echoing in her ears. *You're afraid. And for good reason.* Did that mean she should fear arrest? Or something worse?

The Huntington Avenue T station was above ground, right across from the museum. A train pulled up and opened its doors, beckoning her to escape. She ran for it, barreling into the empty car and collapsing into a seat. With shaking fingers, she pulled out her phone and deleted Andrew Martin's photo. Having it in her possession felt dirty and incriminating, like—yes—a bag of drugs. She wanted it gone. She looked over her shoulder to make sure that Martin hadn't followed her. There was no sign of him.

But just then a pale man with red hair stepped into the halo cast by a streetlamp. Lighting a cigarette, he looked up, deliberately making eye contact with her.

Wallace.

Her stomach plummeted. As the tone sounded indicating the doors were closing, he took a deep drag, tossed down the cigarette, and boarded a car somewhere behind her. She got up to run. But it was too late. The doors had shut.

Maybe that's what Martin meant. She was right to be afraid, because Wallace was coming for her. *Fuck.* Where could she go to get away from him? Not back to Judge Conroy's town house while the judge was still at the party. The place would be dark and empty, nobody there but the cat. She couldn't go home to Mom, obviously. That would put her at risk. The only option was her dorm. There were lots of people around. If she could make it there, she'd be safe.

The doors opened at Park Street. She took off for the Red Line like she was running for her life. The *thunk-thunk* of footsteps behind her must be him. The stilettos she'd borrowed from the judge were slowing her down, and he gained on her through the maze of tunnels—narrow, low-ceilinged, lined with blood-red tile like something from a house of horrors. Thank God she wasn't alone. A train had just let out, and a number of people passed by. It sat on the platform, exhaling stale air, growling. She plunged through the doors and collapsed into an empty seat. As the train pulled out of the station, her eyes darted nervously. He hadn't made it into this car, but he could be in the next one.

At the Mass General stop, most of the passengers exited. The train picked up speed and passed under the Charles. It was dark outside the windows, and she felt trapped. There were only two other people in her car, and they were glued to their phones, unlikely to help if he came for her. There weren't even doors between the cars to give her a false sense of security. Three more stops to Harvard Square. She got up and stood by the doors, her hand sweaty on the strap as the car bucked and swayed. When the doors opened at Harvard Square, she ran. Up a ramp, through the turnstiles, up one escalator, then another, not looking back until she hit the misty, diesel-smelling night.

He wasn't behind her. Had he given up? The Starbucks was just a few steps from the exit. She could duck in there. But the

interior was lit up like a Broadway stage, the people inside spot-
lighted for all to see. Better to slip away into darkness while she
had the chance. Though, if he caught her alone at night in the
emptiness of Harvard Yard, she'd be in trouble.

The door to the Starbucks flew open with a blast of coffee-
scented air. Two people emerged, law students, one of whom had
been in her Civ Pro class last year. What the hell was her name?
Think.

"Hannah!"

The girl turned, looking confused. They were nodding ac-
quaintances at best.

"Madison?"

"How's it going? Long time, no see."

"Uh, I'm in your Securities Reg class. I sit behind you."

She fell into step beside them. "Right. Are you feeling ready
for the final?"

"No, I've still got a ton of studying to do. What about you?"

She kept up the chatter as they cut through Harvard Yard,
sticking to her companions like a barnacle on a ship, alert for
footsteps behind her. But the damp night and wet trees muffled
the sound. At Langdell, Hannah and her friend peeled off with a
firm goodbye, heading for the library. Madison got out her card
key and ran the rest of the way to her dorm, swiping the key with
a pounding heart. She was in. As the door locked behind her,
she took a deep breath. If Wallace had followed her here, he'd be
looking for a way in. Sneaking in behind a student swiping their
card. Or flashing his badge and demanding admittance. Wallace
had *cop* written all over him, though, and her gut told her that a
bunch of law students would at least ask for a warrant. She *hoped*.
It would slow him down.

Climbing the stairs, walking down the dingy hallway, she realized that she'd been missing this old dump. It was home, not the

glitzy town house. As she unlocked her room, the familiar smell of carpet cleaner and books made her want to turn back time. To before Danny's arrest, before she'd ever met Judge Conroy, to when things were simpler. She wanted her life back. The blinds were open. He could still be out there. She couldn't turn on the light for fear that he'd see which room was hers. Creeping to the window, reaching for the cord, she looked out.

He was there, staring back at her.

The sun shone in her eyes, and she sat up, momentarily stunned to find herself in the lumpy dorm-room bed, still clad in her finery from last night. The blinds were wide open. Memory hit. She jumped up to look out the window.

Wallace was gone. *For now.*

She checked her phone, surprised there was no text from Judge Conroy. Madison hadn't returned to the town house last night, despite an agreement to meet up after the reception. She was supposed to report on delivering the messages, which would cue the judge to sign the order releasing Danny. Of course, Madison had failed to complete the second task. She hadn't told Andrew Martin about the meeting in the alley. If Judge Conroy showed up, she would have waited there alone to no avail. Why hadn't she texted to find out what went wrong? Maybe she assumed it was a disaster. That Madison got arrested. Or flipped. Or else, maybe she was really in league with Wallace, and he had already told her everything.

In the shower, she stood under the pounding water, quietly freaking out. A corrupt cop had followed her home last night. Whether or not he planned to attack her physically, he meant her harm. Andrew Martin confirmed that she was right to be afraid.

Could she turn to the feds for help, ask to be placed in witness protection or something? But they wouldn't help her unless she had valuable evidence to offer, and how much did she know, really? That Judge Conroy and Detective Wallace were on a first-name basis? Big deal. That the judge tipped off Douglas Kessler to the investigation last night? Better, but she'd have to out herself as the go-between. She'd have criminal exposure of her own. They'd be just as likely to arrest her as protect her.

It was the final Securities Reg class of the term, and she should've been paying close attention. Instead, she was distracted to the point of near-hysteria. Chloe was a no-show, which felt like a bad omen. She replayed in her head over and over that sick moment when Doug Kessler threatened her last night. She wanted to scream at Judge Conroy. *I did what you asked and what did I get? Kessler threatened me. Martin knew who I was. I risked jail for you. Now pay up. Release my brother, or I'll tell the feds everything.* She was a law student, not a thug, but lately she didn't recognize herself. Passing secret messages, getting followed by the police. Why not extortion? It was just one more step in this brave new world.

She'd confront the judge that afternoon, at the internship.

But when she got to chambers, Imani told her the judge had not come in that day.

"Where is she?" Madison said.

"I don't know. Sean and I showed up as usual this morning, and chambers was dark. No judge, no Kelsey. No explanation. Just a note on my desk from Nancy saying court was canceled. Sean went home, but I've been here all day catching up on paperwork."

"That's weird."

"Yeah, it is."

"It's kind of worrisome. Do you think she's okay?"

"That's not a subject I'm comfortable speculating about. Not here," Imani said, turning back to her computer.

Unease settled in Madison's chest as she considered why the judge might be absent. Not illness. More likely, arrest. Or fleeing the jurisdiction. Or, God forbid, kidnapping, or worse. And what did Imani mean, that she wouldn't speculate here? They were alone in chambers. Did she think the place was bugged?

The afternoon crawled by, punctuated by the clacking of keyboards. At five, Imani shut down her computer.

"Well, I think I'll head out."

"Me too," Madison said.

She wished she could get Imani talking. Whatever the law clerk knew, she wasn't comfortable spilling here.

"Would you like to grab a drink? I've been dying to try that new martini bar. My treat."

"Really? I heard that place is pricey."

"It's fine. I picked up a second job."

"No kidding. Doing what?"

"Um, kind of like a personal assistant thing."

"Is that wise with your workload?"

"I got tired of being broke."

"I feel you. I remember those days."

"I just got paid, and it's burning a hole in my pocket. So let's go."

It was already dark, and the night air was frigid. They walked the few blocks to the bar, which was just past the T stop, talking about clothes and the weather. Imani hated winter and was planning to go back to Atlanta after the clerkship to work at a law firm.

"That day can't come fast enough," she said.

"That doesn't sound like it's about the weather. Are you unhappy with the clerkship?"

"Let's have a drink first."

The bar was jam-packed with lawyers and other people from the courthouse. Nobody wore ties anymore except in court, but this was still Boston, and there were a lot of conservative dark suits. They pushed their way up to the bar, where blue light shone out from shelves lined with crystal decanters, making it feel like the inside of an aquarium. A couple of thirtysomething guys gave up their seats to them and tried to buy them drinks. They shut them down and ordered Vespers, along with a cone of frites to share. The prices were hair-raising, but the martinis lived up to the hype, ice-cold with the whoosh of rocket fuel. Madison's tolerance for alcohol was not the greatest, so she sipped carefully. Imani was not so cautious, and her eyes quickly took on a cocktail glaze. Time to start digging.

"You mentioned earlier you didn't want to talk about the judge while we were in chambers. But nobody was around. I almost got the feeling you thought the place was bugged."

"I wouldn't put it past her."

"Past who?"

"Nancy. That woman is a little dictator. Just look at how she treats you, limiting your computer usage like you're gonna access porn or something. She thinks she runs the place, and who can blame her? Judge Conroy is so checked out."

"Do you think it's burnout? Teaching on top of her case load is a lot."

"All I can say is, she's changed drastically just in the past month. Even when she's there, she's not there. Maybe something happened. Maybe she suffers from depression. The reason doesn't matter. There's a power vacuum, and Nancy is taking advantage. She's been telling us how to decide cases. Civil, criminal, you name it. And the judge allows it. That's what I object to. She's leaving her docket in the hands of someone who is not qualified. If Nancy knew what she was doing, that would be one thing. But she does things that don't conform to the law."

"You're saying Nancy is deciding cases, and the outcomes are legally wrong?"

"*Yes.* Are you listening to me?"

"I hear you. It's just hard to believe. Don't the rulings get over-turned on appeal?"

"Not everybody appeals when they lose, because of the time and expense involved. And when a ruling does get reversed, it's bad for Judge Conroy's reputation. A friend of mine clerks on the Court of Appeals, and she asked me just the other day what the hell is going on in our chambers. People have noticed. If Judge Conroy flames out, it reflects on us."

"Have you tried talking to the judge?"

"Sean went to her a couple of weeks ago and said, 'Nancy's butting in, and Imani and I are uncomfortable.' Big mistake. The judge said, work it out amongst yourselves, then turned around and told Nancy we complained. She's been taking it out on us ever since, and the judge does nothing. It's nuts. Sean and I are trained lawyers. Nancy is a glorified secretary. If the judge doesn't want to do her own work, she could let us handle things. But Nancy has some weird hold over her. We don't trust her. We think— Well, Sean thinks—"

Imani's voice dropped as she looked around nervously.

"This might sound crazy, but he thinks she's on the take."

"The judge?"

"*Nancy.* Maybe not cash bribes. Maybe just someone cozies up to her, does her favors, manipulates her. That's the only way to explain some of the wackadoodle outcomes in these cases."

It sounded like Nancy was part of the conspiracy. She needed to ask Imani about Logue and Wallace. If Nancy knew them, too, that would say something.

"So, this might sound like a weird question, but have you ever seen a defense lawyer named Raymond Logue around chambers at all? Or a Detective Wallace?"

Imani set her glass down, a shocked look on her face.

"How do you know those names?"

"I just . . . ran across them on a case."

"Are you serious right now? God, I'm disappointed. You're lying to me, Madison."

"Why do you say that?"

"Because. Olivia asked about them, too. She took me out for drinks one night and dropped their names, just like you're doing now. Pumped me for information. Then disappeared."

Madison's scalp prickled.

"*Disappeared?* You mean, got fired? Or—"

"I'm not comfortable saying another word until I know who you work for."

"What do you mean? I work for Judge Conroy. And for you and Sean."

"I don't believe you."

"Imani, I'm an intern, a two-L at Harvard. I'm legit. You know that. We met last year when I wrote onto law review."

"So what? You could still be a sleeper agent. Maybe they planted you."

"You think I'm an undercover agent?"

"Very possibly. After all, Olivia was."

"How do you know that?"

"I'm not telling you anything until you say who you work for."

Madison took a deep breath. She would have to risk sharing some basic facts if she wanted more information.

"I don't work for anyone. This is personal for me. Someone close to me was screwed over by Wallace and Logue. And the judge allowed it. I'm worried that they have some kind of sway over her.

That they're influencing her inappropriately. Honestly, I'm worried for her."

Imani's eyes narrowed. "That's the truth?"

Madison raised her right hand. "I swear on my mother's life that I am not an undercover agent. I'm just a dumb student in over my head because somebody I care about is mixed up in this nasty business. I can't say more without putting that person in danger, or I'd tell you everything. Now, please, what do you know about Wallace and Logue?"

"Wallace I don't know much about, except he skeeves me out. Logue was in the judge's courtroom enough that it piqued my curiosity. I did some research and found some old articles on him. Like ancient, microfiche-type stuff. He was a fixer back in the day, with ties to city hall, representing high-profile organized crime clients. Today, his practice is mostly narcotics. And he's got corruption written all over him."

"You said he piqued your curiosity. Why?"

"Because he has a boatload of cases before Judge Conroy. Like more than normal, like his cases are not getting randomly assigned. I think he has someone on the inside steering his cases to the judge. The docket is Nancy's purview, so it's probably her. I haven't looked into it further because, quite frankly, I'm scared."

They locked eyes.

"*Scared*," Madison said.

"Mm-hmm."

"And you think chambers might be bugged?"

"Oh, that's just rank speculation. I have no idea."

"Imani, what happened to Olivia?"

"I honestly don't know. What I can tell you is, she vanished into thin air, owing me three memos. I tried to track her down. I called her cell. And when it was out of service, I asked Nancy if she had any other contact information? Nancy went ballistic, like eyes bulging, frothing at the mouth. *Don't you dare go near that goddamn so-and-so, this-and-that, or you can quit right now.* Singed my eyebrows. After that, I confess, I was worried enough about Olivia to keep looking. And I'm a damn good researcher. But no luck. I'm pretty sure she said she went to BU Law. Sean thought BC. I tried both. There's no Olivia Chase enrolled in either one, or any other law school in the greater Boston area, for that matter. She's not on LinkedIn, Insta, TikTok, Facebook, Twitter, Snapchat, you name it."

"Does Chase have the usual spelling?"

"C-H-A-S-E. But I'm warning you. Don't try to find her."

"Why not?"

"You won't succeed. She's a ghost. That's why I think she's an undercover. Which begs the question: Working for who, investigating what? And what would they do to her if they found out? I wouldn't stick my neck out if I was you."

"What did Olivia look like?"

"I'm serious, Madison. Don't be foolish. Drop this, or you'll wind up in trouble."

She stared at Imani pointedly. "Tell me what she looked like."

"Fine, it's your funeral. Average-looking. Brown hair. Medium height. Buff, like she works out. Regular features. Boring dresser. Mature for a law student, meaning older than average in appearance. But I'm telling you, you'll never find her. And if you're not careful, you'll wind up just like her, which could be really bad. Olivia is not currently registered in any Boston-area law school. Now, maybe she got caught snooping, Nancy reported that to her dean, and she was expelled. But maybe she's floating in a river somewhere, and that's only partly a joke."

In the heat of the bar, Madison shivered. Imani got to her feet.

"I've got a headache, and this place is making me claustro-
phobic."

"Go. I'll get the check."

"Thanks. Watch your back, hear me?"

"You too."

They hugged goodbye. Madison signaled the bartender. She
was waiting for the bill when she caught a flash of red from the
corner of her eye.

Wallace.

But when she turned in a panic to scan the room, he wasn't there.

Watch your back. Out on the street, Madison heeded the warning, walking for a good ten minutes in well-lit, high-traffic areas,
ducking into doorways to scan the street behind her. Only once
she was certain Wallace wasn't following did she call an Uber and
go to the town house.

The lights were on in the town house as she passed by on the
other side of the street. Her shoulders relaxed when she saw it.
Nightmare scenarios had been running through her mind all day.
Judge Conroy behind bars, talking to the feds, giving up anyone
and everyone, including Madison herself. Judge Conroy kidnapped by Wallace, in the trunk of a car, chained in a basement.
Ridiculous. The judge was at home, keeping a low profile because
of the chaos all around her. Well, Madison would give her an earful. She'd demand that dismissal order for Danny, then quit on the
spot, making a break with the judge before things got worse.

She took a roundabout route to the alley behind the town
house until she was certain that she was not being followed. The
judge's white SUV was in its parking spot. She crossed the empty
courtyard, feeling exposed in the blaze of light that spilled from

the house. In the back hallway, she went to disable the alarm. But it hadn't been armed in the first place. Odd. The kitchen smelled stale, a faint tang of garbage in the air.

"Hello? Judge, it's me, Madison."

No reply. She stopped and listened. The silence was thick and heavy. It was a bit after nine. Every light was on, so the judge was not asleep. Was she sick?

In the back hall, Lucy's food bowl was not just empty, but licked clean. Madison had never known Judge Conroy to let the cat go hungry. The water bowl was dry. Behind her, feet pattered. Lucy rubbed up against her legs, meowing. She seemed eager for Madison to pick her up.

"Where's your mom, huh? She didn't feed you?" she said, picking up the cat and kissing her head.

Lucy never normally let Madison cuddle her like that. She opened a can and dumped food in the bowl. Lucy attacked it. Madison filled the water bowl, then tiptoed to the bottom of the grand staircase, looking up. The second-floor lights were on.

"Judge?"

Nothing.

Suddenly afraid of what she might find, she got out her phone and tapped in 911, poising her thumb over the Call icon. A pulse beat in her throat as she climbed the stairs. The door to the master suite was ajar. She stopped on the threshold, gathering her nerve, and shoved the door with her foot. It swung open. The room was brightly lit. The bed had not been slept in. Breathing out, she walked into the dressing room. It was strewn with empty shopping bags and evening wear. A sleek black dress. A red pantsuit. A sequined skirt and several slinky tops that went with it. Clothes they'd considered for the reception and rejected. Judge Conroy had been planning to return them the following day at lunchtime. Meaning today. She hadn't, obviously.

In the bathroom, the lights blazed. Madison had packed up her cosmetics bag and brought it upstairs before they left. But the judge left her things in disarray. Lipsticks and compacts and makeup brushes littered the vanity top. They'd stood there, side by side, applying bronzer and highlighter and blush. There was a Kleenex in the sink. She remembered debating lipstick colors. Madison said to go bold—Ruby Woo, the classic red from MAC. But the judge preferred subtle, a peachy nude from Chanel. She'd applied it and blotted it, tossing the Kleenex into the sink. It was there now, her kiss still visible.

Was it possible that Judge Conroy didn't make it home from the reception? But her car was parked in its spot in the back alley. Though, since they hadn't gone over together, she didn't know for sure what mode of transportation the judge had taken. Maybe she'd Ubered. Or she drove there and back, made it to the house, and then something happened. Someone came in and took her. Yet the alarm was off, and there were no signs of struggle.

Someone she knew, then, whom she'd let in voluntarily?

Wallace?

The hairs on Madison's arms stood up.

24

....

On the T back to Cambridge, she composed multiple texts and deleted them unsent. It was hard to say what you meant when you were worried about incriminating yourself.

Judge, could you get in touch? I have a question about an assignment . . .

Dear Judge Conroy, I noticed you were absent from chambers and am checking in to see how you're doing. I hope you're well . . .

You never came home from the reception. Where are you? Are you okay?

Please call, I'm worried about you . . .

The problem was, texts could be intercepted. Federal investigators could be tapping the judge's phone. Wallace or Logue might be monitoring her communications. Madison couldn't risk having her message fall into the wrong hands. If any of those people learned the extent of her involvement with Judge Conroy, she'd be in trouble, possibly in danger.

She decided to do nothing. It was safer to wait. Tomorrow afternoon, the final class was scheduled for the Fourth Amendment seminar that Judge Conroy taught. Madison would see the judge there. Unless Judge Conroy was a no-show, which would mean something dire had definitely happened.

The next day, she was en route to class when her phone dinged with a notification. It was from Canvas, the course website. "Update re: Fourth Amendment Seminar." She opened the app with a sick feeling, reading the message from the registrar's office.

CLASS CANCELATION. We received word that Prof. Kathryn Conroy is out of town until further notice. Class is canceled. We are following up to get further information.

A chill went through her. Who sent "word"? It didn't sound like the judge herself had contacted the registrar. Someone from chambers? Nancy, maybe? That didn't bode well. Besides, if Judge Conroy had been planning a trip out of town, wouldn't she inform the law clerks? And wouldn't they tell Madison? Wouldn't the judge tell Madison herself, to make sure Lucy got fed? That was the most alarming fact of all. The woman loved her cat more than any human in her life. She would simply never go out of town without arranging for Lucy to be cared for. No, something unexpected—possibly catastrophic—had come up. Arrest, or worse.

The judge disappearing was the fall of the first domino. Madison had to protect herself, or she'd be next. But how? Going to the authorities was complicated when you had criminal exposure of your own. She'd passed the warning to Kessler, and now she was mixed up in the conspiracy. How big a conspiracy? She had no clue. She'd agreed to carry a message without verifying what it meant, or what the implications might be. And yes, she did it for Danny, and for Mom, but she was beginning to realize how stupid she'd been. It wouldn't help either of them for her to go to jail.

She should look into that case the judge made her ask about.

She exited the T, heading straight for Langdell. The silent magnificence of the law school reading room normally calmed her. But this time, the glittering chandeliers, the soaring columns, and the mahogany tables just reminded her of all she stood to lose. If she got arrested, she'd be expelled. And everything she'd been working toward for so long would come crashing down.

Ty was coming toward her down the long aisle between the rows of tables. She felt a small flame-lick of longing. Not just for a shoulder to cry on, but for the past, before things were so terribly screwed up.

She gave him a nod and half smile, preparing to pass. But he stopped her.

"I'm glad I ran into you. Can we go somewhere to talk?" he whispered.

"Sorry, I'm really busy."

"It's important. Please?"

"All right. The carrels?"

He nodded. Heads were turning, seeing them together, but that was not her problem. They set off for the dank study carrels in the depths of the basement, which were usually deserted, and found a quiet corner.

"By the way, I apologize for Chloe, how she treated you the other night. She doesn't know how she comes off sometimes."

"Is that what this is about? If she feels bad, she can apologize herself."

"No, it's actually not about that. We need to talk about Judge Conroy."

"Oh." She hesitated. "I suppose you saw class is canceled? Have you heard anything about where she is?"

"I have no idea. Do you?"

"No. But I think it's concerning. Her chambers don't seem to know, either. I'm worried something happened to her."

"Okay, yeah. That's exactly why I need to talk to you. She's not the only one who vanished into thin air. Chloe's dad went missing, too."

"*What?*"

"After the Pro Bono League reception, he didn't come home. Didn't go to work the next morning. His phone is going straight to voicemail ever since. They're freaking out. Her mother is considering filing a missing person report."

"But she hasn't yet? Why not?"

"Because something weird is going on, and they don't know the extent of it. Which is where you come in. Chloe and I saw you talking to Doug the other night. Whatever you said upset him a lot. We sat with him at dinner, and he was extremely distracted. He was on his phone the whole time, really agitated. Halfway through, he just got up and walked out—of a major event where he sponsored two tables and was scheduled to give remarks. And he hasn't been heard from since. So I have to ask. What the hell did you say to him?"

Her mouth fell open. "I—I. *Nothing.* It wasn't me. I was just networking."

He struck the nearest carrel with his fist. A sound rang out like the report of a gun, making her jump.

"Don't lie to me, Madison. This is too important."

"I just— I passed a message from the judge. She asked me to."

"And now they're both missing? What did it say?"

"I can't. It's confidential."

"You're in way over your head here. I warned you that Conroy is trouble. Don't you understand you could end up facing criminal charges?"

She knew that already. Hearing Ty say it just made her panic.

"You're scaring me," she said, and started to cry.

He sighed, patting her shoulder.

"Hey, hey. It's okay. We'll get to the bottom of this. Listen, I'll tell you something in confidence, okay, but you have to promise not to tell anyone."

She sniffed, nodding.

"Doug is under criminal investigation. The Kesslers are on the verge of divorce over it. Chloe's mom confided in her, and Chloe told me everything. It's all about Conroy. Apparently, years ago when Doug was a prosecutor, he worked with her, and they were close. *Inappropriately* close. She did something wrong, and either he knew about it or was in on it. Covered it up. Something, I don't know. Now they're both missing. Chloe thinks they ran off together."

"The judge and Doug Kessler? *No.* I'd be shocked. I know enough about her to say pretty certainly that he's not in her life. As far as I know, she's obsessed with her late husband. And any other men in her life, well—"

She paused, thinking of Wallace. As with all Judge Conroy's troubles, he was probably behind this.

"What men? Conroy confides in you about her personal life?" Ty said.

"No. Not at all. I just— I heard gossip around chambers. But she and Doug Kessler are not an item. I promise."

"What did you say to Doug at the reception? You have to tell me."

"The judge asked me to speak to him."

"Like, deliver a message?"

"I'm sorry, but I can't break her confidence."

"Why would you cover for that woman? You're telling me she had you speak to Doug. Do you understand the implications? Instead of making a phone call that could be intercepted, or speaking to him in public where she might be seen, she used you to do her dirty work."

"I know. You're right. It's just—"

She was shaking her head. He took a step closer, his hands

on her shoulders, gazing into her eyes. Despite herself, her heart thumped. At some level, she would always have feelings for Ty.

"You didn't know any better, Maddy. But now you do. You're mixed up in some dirty business. Two prominent people are missing. If you won't tell me what the message was, then go to the authorities. Talk to them, before it's too late."

She pulled away, a mist in her eyes.

"Thank you. I appreciate the heads-up. Now, I should go."

"That's it? Thank you and goodbye?"

"No. Of course not. You're a good friend. I'll think very seriously about what you said. And I promise to be careful. See you later."

She stood on tiptoe and kissed him on the cheek, then hurried away, leaving him gazing after her.

Upstairs, at the far end of the reading room, were computers with Wi-Fi that any student could use. They didn't require entering your ID and so would leave no trace. That's what she needed—to act like a criminal, cover her tracks. She remembered the case name. *Fiamma.* Holding her breath, she typed it into the database and watched as the result loaded. A headline from years earlier hit her like a Mack truck.

Bomb Blast Kills Mob Prosecutor

Boston, April 21—A car bomb exploded in the North End late last night, claiming the life of Bradley McCarthy, Chief of the Organized Crime Section in the Boston U.S. Attorney's Office. McCarthy, an experienced and highly regarded prosecutor, had recently indicted alleged mafia boss Salvatore Fiamma on racketeering and murder charges.

Fiamma's attorney, Raymond F. Logue, Esq., denied that his client played a role in the killing.

"Any suggestion that Mr. Fiamma was involved in this tragic incident is a lie. It's impossible. My client has been under constant surveillance for months. He's as disturbed by the violence as anybody and sends condolences to the family," Logue said.

Deputy Chief Douglas Kessler was appointed Acting Chief of the Organized Crime Section upon McCarthy's death. The Fiamma case will now be handled by Assistant U.S. Attorney Kathryn Conroy, formerly second chair on the case.

How the hell had she missed this case? That night she stayed up till dawn, researching Logue and Wallace, her head on fire from the sake, there had been a hundred news articles. This one was so old it would have been at the end of a long queue of results that she was too tired to wade through.

She'd pay a terrible price for that moment of weakness.

A photograph of McCarthy and the rest of the prosecution team accompanied the article. She clicked to enlarge it. Doug Kessler stood at McCarthy's right hand, his silver hair still dark back then. Next to him was an exquisite young woman, the only female in the group of stone-faced men—Kathryn Conroy. And in the very back row, with the Organized Crime Task Force, another familiar face—Detective Charles Wallace.

And Ray Logue was the mobster's defense attorney.

They're all in on it.

And now Kessler and the judge were both MIA.

Madison was shaking. This was worse than she could ever have imagined. An influence-peddling conspiracy stretching back decades, involving the murder of a federal prosecutor with a car bomb. Possibly connected to the murder of the judge's husband. And now, years later, the disappearance of Judge Conroy and Douglas Kessler.

The message she'd delivered was enough to implicate her. Or

put her in danger. If Conroy and Kessler were missing, Madison was probably next. Between Wallace on the one hand, and the feds on the other, she knew which scared her more. Her only hope was to go to the feds. But they could decide to lock her up. *Unless* she had evidence to trade.

Based on what she'd learned in Crim Pro, the bar for immunity from prosecution was high. The evidence she offered had to be valuable enough to outweigh her own culpability for passing that message. She could testify about what she'd seen in the judge's house. The cash in the toilet tank. The photos of Ray Logue with Judge Conroy at her high-school recital, dancing at her wedding. Wallace pounding on the door in the middle of the night. But she feared that wouldn't be enough. It was too vague. They'd want documents. Phone records. Evidence of money changing hands. Files on specific cases that the judge had thrown. She'd searched the town house high and low, and that stuff just wasn't there. Where could it be?

In chambers, probably.

She would wait until later tonight, after the courthouse closed. Then she'd go and search the judge's office. Wherever she was, Judge Conroy would not be riding to the rescue. Madison had to look out for herself.

....

25

The lights were off in chambers, but ambient light from the city lent a bright glow to the reception area. She decided it was wise to leave the lights off. She could search the drawers and filing cabinets using her phone flashlight if necessary.

Out of an excess of caution, she checked the law clerks' office, the break room, and the restroom. All were deserted.

Back in the reception area, no light showed beneath the door to Judge Conroy's private office. She tried the handle. Locked. She went back to the reception desk. In addition to answering phones, Kelsey handled things like travel vouchers and expense accounts. She kept files. Maybe there would be something revealing in them. Madison sat down and methodically searched the desk drawers. The top drawer held pens, pencils, office supplies, and a large stash of gummy candy. The second was where the files were kept. Thumbing through, she found a folder labeled "Employee Background Forms" and got a rush. She could shred hers. On closer inspection, the folder proved to be empty. Of course—Judge Conroy had it somewhere.

Madison went through page after page of copies, finding nothing at all incriminating. At the very back of Kelsey's files, a hanging folder felt heavier than it should. She plucked it out. *Voilà!* A Patriots key ring with a bunch of keys. Of course. Kelsey had keys to the entire office. She tried them in the lock on the judge's door until she found one that fit.

The office was bathed in cool blue light reflected from the skyline, bright enough that she didn't need her flashlight. She sat down at the judge's desk, perspiring with nerves and shrugging out of her heavy coat. The drawers were unlocked. She took a deep breath and opened the top one, the whisper of rose perfume in the air reminding her of that first interview. Judge Conroy sitting with her feet tucked under her, chatty and welcoming. She'd wanted the internship bad enough to ignore the warning voices in her head. If only she'd listened, she wouldn't be here now, a burglar in the night, rifling through the judge's desk. She went through the drawers methodically. A stash of official stationery with a gold seal. The judge's favorite Uniball pens in dark blue. Some Kleenex, a tin of mints, lip balm, a nail file. In the drawer that would normally hold hanging files, there was a stash of Manolo Blahnik heels in different colors. The woman had good taste in shoes, you had to give her that.

The desk was a bust.

Behind her, a credenza gleamed in the moonlight, its dark gray enamel surface as sleek and perfect as the judge herself. The face of it was flat, without handles or pulls, but a vertical line suggested it was divided into two compartments. She pressed a spot at the top right, and a door sprang open. The cabinet was divided into two sections, each outfitted with three levels of pull-out shelves full of file folders. She spent the next half hour going through the judge's files. They were meticulously organized, containing memos and draft opinions, all perfectly legitimate. Nothing of interest there. She stood up and looked around. There were no other filing cabinets in the office. Just rows of bookshelves lined with *Federal Reporter*s, their spines crisp and shiny with gilded stripes. She pulled out a volume at random and rifled the pages, looking for documents tucked inside. All she got was the smell of books and a jolt of melancholy, thinking about how far she'd sunk—from learning the law to breaking it.

She'd struck out in chambers. The evidence better be in Nancy's office, or it was hidden somewhere else entirely, and she'd never find it.

The case manager's office was not part of chambers but was located behind the courtroom on the other side of the floor. Madison walked down the public hallway on tiptoe, trying not to make a sound. One of the keys on Kelsey's ring opened the courtroom doors. Inside was hushed and dim, with a row of small windows placed high up on the towering outer wall, making the space feel almost like a cathedral. She walked down the center aisle with a lump in her throat. If she couldn't figure out a way to save herself, her future as a lawyer was dead.

A door behind the judge's bench led to a small hallway containing the jury room, a restroom, and Nancy's office. The office was locked. She found the key on the key ring and let herself in. It was windowless and pitch-black, but she was afraid to turn on the light. Shining her phone flashlight around, she saw a narrow room sparsely furnished with a desk, a chair, and a bank of metal filing cabinets. The cabinet drawers were all locked. None of the keys fit. This was a dead end if she couldn't get them open. Maybe the key was in Nancy's desk? She tried the top drawer. But it was locked, too.

She couldn't afford to abandon her search without finding the evidence. She had to get into those filing cabinets.

A glass dish full of paper clips on Nancy's desk made her think about picking the lock. That seemed far-fetched, like something from a film that would never work in real life. Then again, this was just a desk drawer, not Fort Knox. She watched a quick how-to video on her phone. It looked simple enough but required two hands, which meant she couldn't hold her phone flashlight. She closed the office door and flipped on the light. A gap at the bottom of the door would let the light shine through, but that shouldn't be a problem. She highly doubted the security guards patrolled the private hallway behind the judge's courtroom after hours.

She unraveled a paper clip, straightened it out, and bent a second one at a ninety-degree angle to make a rough lever. So far, so good. Taking a deep breath, she inserted the flattened paper clip into the keyhole on the top drawer of Nancy's desk. There should be pins in there that she could locate by probing. But she couldn't feel a thing, probably because there wasn't enough tension with just one clip. Inserting the second clip on top of the first was supposed to ratchet the tension. *Okay, yeah, there we go.* She felt it now. She could turn the bent clip like a key. A little more, a little more. *Click.*

Surprise. It worked.

Pulling open the desk drawer, the first thing she saw was a gun. She stared at it for a second. It seemed strange for a bureaucrat to keep a gun in her desk, even one as paranoid about threats as Nancy. It supported the conclusion that Nancy was implicated in the corruption. Better get what she came for and get out of this office before she got caught. Ignoring the gun, she lifted up the plastic pencil tray and found a set of keys to the filing cabinets. Starting with "A," she reviewed file after file of legal documents for the cases assigned to Judge Conroy. Indictments, guilty pleas, sentencing reports, case dispositions. Duplicates of every paper Nancy sent to the Clerk's Office for recording. A place for everything, everything in its place—the woman was a marvel of organization. Under "C," she did find one unexpected item, a file called "COMM AVE HOUSE" containing the deed to Judge Conroy's town house on Commonwealth Avenue. Except, turned out it wasn't the judge's house. Judge Conroy didn't own her home in her own name. The town house was held by something called Gloucester LLC. Madison had learned about limited liability corporations in school. They shielded owners from liability for taxes, debts, criminal acts, you name it. It could be virtually impossible to find the man behind the curtain of an LLC, which made it the perfect form of ownership for people with something to hide. It was suspicious that the judge's house was owned by an LLC, but not proof of a crime in and of itself.

Why did Nancy have the deed in her files?

Just in case it was of interest to the feds, she snapped a photo before moving on. It was all a big nothing burger until "P" for "Peña," the file on Danny's case. At first glance, everything looked neat and tidy like the rest, with the level of organization she expected from Nancy. Documents on each defendant organized alphabetically by last name, and chronologically by date of filing with the court. Except that where Danny's documents began, an oversized manila envelope protruded, marked "Rivera Photos" on the front in thick black marker.

Were there surveillance photos of Danny? The official documents from the case hadn't mentioned any.

She fanned the sheaf of photos on the desk and gasped. These were not photos of Danny. They had nothing whatsoever to do with any drug case. They were of Madison herself, going about her life, in Boston and Cambridge. Getting coffee. Walking to class. With Ty. With her law review mentee. With *Judge Conroy*.

The night they went for sushi, the judge had been on edge, looking over her shoulder the whole time. For good reason, it turned out. They were being followed. One photo showed them running into the sushi place in the rain, another getting into Judge

Conroy's car. There were multiple photos of Madison entering Judge Conroy's town house through the back gate.

Why? And where the hell did Nancy get these?

That question was answered by photos of Madison, all dressed up on the night of the reception, the night Wallace followed her home. There were shots of moments when she knew he'd been there. Her getting on the subway across from the museum. Walking with Hannah and that other girl when she felt him behind her. Accessing her dorm with the card key. She'd looked out the window and seen him there. He wasn't just following her. He was taking photographs. And he'd started earlier than she knew. There were photos of Madison inside the event. Talking to Douglas Kessler. And that prosecutor, Andrew Martin.

Those photos could be used to incriminate her.

She'd come here looking for evidence against the judge. And ended up finding evidence against herself.

The envelope wasn't empty yet. And the horror wasn't over. Another photo was stuck inside. Pulling it out, she held it up, staring at the middle-aged woman with graying dark hair getting into an old Toyota on a rainy night, in her well-worn winter coat.

Mom.

That asshole wasn't just stalking her. Her mother was in his crosshairs, too. She recognized that parking lot. The building in the background was the nursing home where her mother worked. He didn't just catch a picture of Mom by accident while tailing Madison. He'd purposely followed her to work. She turned over the photo. There was writing on the back. "Yolanda Rivera, aged 52 years, works at Sunrise Senior Living, home address . . ."

Rage throbbed in her head, filling her ears with a sound like the inside of a seashell. She didn't hear footsteps until they were right outside the door.

"Don't blame me for your screw-up, kiddo. Hold on," a voice said.

It was Nancy, and she was on the phone. Madison froze, listening to the jingle of keys, the scrape as one was inserted in the lock. The office was on the tenth floor, and windowless. She was trapped, with no way out.

"Hey. Wait a minute. . . . That's weird, the lights are on in my office. . . . I don't hear anyone. You think someone could've broke in? . . . You know I always lock it, Charlie."

Charlie. She was on the phone with Wallace. And from the sound of it, she knew him well.

"You think I should call security? . . . I don't have it on me. I left it in my desk drawer."

She was talking about the gun. Madison thought briefly about grabbing it to protect herself and immediately rejected the idea. She'd wind up with a weapons charge.

"I probably just forgot to turn 'em off. But do me a favor, hold on while I check that nothing's been disturbed, okay? It's making me nervous."

Madison stared in horror as the door handle began to turn.

26

....

The blood pounded in her ears as she advanced on the door, careful not to make a sound. It swung open.

Now.

Madison exploded through the doorway, slamming into Nancy, knocking her backward into the wall. Nancy's phone flew from her hands, and Madison scooped it up as she ran, ending Wallace's call. She hoped whatever he heard didn't bring him running. But it probably would. She had to get out of here. She sprinted through the courtroom out to the public hallway. At the elevator, she jammed the button over and over. But it couldn't come fast enough. She was hearing footsteps. Nancy? A security guard? *Run.* Turning for the stairs, she bolted down, half sliding, breath rasping in her throat. On the floor below, she forced herself to slow down. There were cameras everywhere in this building. Running like a maniac would achieve nothing but alerting the security guards that she ought to be stopped. Every cell of her body cried out to run, but she forced herself to walk all the way to the lobby, where she waved her intern ID at the guard on duty and exited through the employee door.

When she hit the frigid night air, she realized she'd left her coat draped carelessly over Judge Conroy's desk chair, proof of her break-in. *Idiot.* Looking over her shoulder to see if Nancy was behind her, she stepped into the street. Brakes screeched. A driver leaned on his horn. No Nancy, but she'd almost been hit by a car. Heart jackhammering, she ran across the street toward the bus that waited at the curb, reaching the door just in time. It didn't matter where it was going, as long as it was away from here, before Nancy brought Wallace down on her head.

Wallace. And Nancy? Was that really a surprise? She should have expected the two of them to be in league. Walking unsteadily toward the back of the moving bus, Madison clutched the manila envelope in one hand. Madison herself might be fair game, but they were following her *mother.* The photos were an abomination. She'd intentionally confiscated them. Nancy's phone she'd swiped by instinct on the spur of the moment, to cut off the call before Nancy put Wallace on Madison's tail. She pulled it out, wondering what to do with it now. A text had come in about five minutes earlier, its first line visible on the home screen.

What happened? Call me back. I need Kathy's . . .

Kathy's what? It was from Wallace. She swiped at the screen and got a prompt to enter Nancy's passcode. Maybe she could draw him into a conversation. She tried some obvious ones. 1234. 0000. A couple of possible birth years for Nancy. Nothing worked, and she gave up.

There was nobody sitting near her. She pulled out her own phone to call her mother, who answered on the first ring, despite the hour.

"You're up late, Mom. You need your rest."

"You know I can't sleep. Any word on Danny?"

"Not yet." She hunched over the phone even though no one

was near her. "Mom, I need you to listen carefully. I haven't been telling you everything because I didn't want you to worry."

"Oh, God. What happened? Is he—"

"It's not about him. You know how I've been trying to get close to the judge in his case to get information? I found out she's involved with the dirty cop. I don't know if he's her boyfriend, or what. But he's following us."

"The cop?"

"Yes."

"Following—*who*?"

"Mostly me. But you, too. He went to your work. He took a photo of you. I found it, and on the back of it, he wrote your home address."

"My God, that's what Danny said. Remember? The guys who beat him up had my address. You think that's connected?"

"I do. I'm worried for your safety."

"Oh, no, honey. Worry about yourself, your brother. Not me."

"We can relax about Danny. I'm a hundred percent sure he's in protective custody, where nobody can hurt him."

"Why do you say that?"

"The judge told me. The danger now is to you and me, from Wallace. He knows I'm snooping. He wants to stop me. And he might take it out on you. I think you should leave town. Go to Aunt Nilda's for a few days."

Even as she said it, Madison knew her mother would never agree.

"Leave? When your brother's still missing? When this *cabrón* is following you? No way. I'm staying here to help."

"How does it help me if something happens to you?"

She looked up to see that the bus was pulling into South Station. From there, she could catch a bus to Revere, to Mom's apartment.

She would drag her out kicking and screaming if she had to, rather than risk Wallace coming for her.

"Oh. I'm at South Station. I'm coming to you now, you hear me?" Madison said.

"Coming to the apartment?"

"Yeah, I'll be there in an hour at the latest. Mom, you don't open your door for anyone but me. Understand?"

"Okay. Be safe."

She dropped the call and ran toward the Chelsea bus, only to see it pulling away. To add insult to injury, it had started to rain, a frigid downpour that hit the icy ground, making walking treacherous. Tucking the envelope under her sweater to protect it, she scanned the street. Passengers, Uber drivers, people walking by. At least she wasn't alone. A dark, late-model sedan pulled up at an odd angle, wedging nose-first into a parking spot that was too small for it. She backed up, eyes glued to it as the passenger door flew open. It was Wallace.

He hadn't seen her yet. But how the hell did he find her so fast? *Nancy's phone.* He must've tracked it.

She turned and ran into the bus station, dumping the phone in the first trash can she passed. The echoing lobby was mostly deserted, no crowd in which to take cover. She sprinted for the escalator, running up the treads two at a time, and dashed blindly into a newsstand. Peering out from behind a rack of books, she saw a shock of rust-colored hair floating up the escalator. *Him*, coming toward the newsstand, eyes lifted, looking at the back wall of the store. She glanced over her shoulder. The wall was mirrored to catch shoplifters. He had a perfect view of Madison crouching behind the rack. *Shit.* She was an incompetent criminal. Every decision she made tonight was wrong. She had a split second to choose—stay, or run? The only other person in the store was the cashier, an older woman in a hairnet who looked exhausted and beaten down. She'd be no help against a cop.

Madison bolted. He wasn't expecting that. She slipped by him, reaching the escalator before he realized what was happening. But the split-second advantage instantly dissipated. She could hear and feel his feet pounding the metal treads as he raced down behind her. She made it to the concourse. The crowd was sparse, but every one of them turned to look. Her instincts might be terrible. But she knew one thing in her gut. He was capable of killing her to shut her up.

In the time it took to see the flash of red from the corner of her eye, he tackled her. She was on the filthy floor, cheek in the muck, the breath knocked from her, arms twisted above her head, crying out in pain. His clothes smelled like cigarettes. There was only one thing to do. Scream bloody murder.

"*Help! Help me! He's kidnapping me! Help!*"

He tried to get his hand over her mouth. She bit down. He grunted and twisted her arm behind her back.

"*Help! Call the police!*"

"I am the police," he said, holding her down with one hand, flashing his badge with the other.

Most people averted their eyes or backed away. But a few came closer. And one starting filming with his phone.

"He's lying. He's kidnapping me. Call the police, I'm begging you," she said to that man.

"I am the police. This woman is a heroin dealer."

He got to his feet and yanked her up. She looked directly into the camera.

"That's a lie. My name is Madison Rivera. I'm a law student at Harvard. He's a dirty cop. He—"

Wallace slapped the man's phone to the ground and stamped on it, cracking the screen.

"What the hell! Fuck you, cop."

"No, fuck you," he said, pulling his gun on the guy.

The man backed away, raising his hands in the air. Wallace slapped handcuffs on her. The ratcheting sound as they closed echoed in her skull. He dragged her outside to his car, shoving her against it, kicking her feet apart, and patted her down, plucking out her phone, her ID, subway card and debit card, and the manila envelope of surveillance photographs she'd hidden under her clothes.

He paused when he found that.

"This? *This* is what you were looking for? Where's the phone?"

She nodded toward her own phone, which he had in his hand.

"Not yours. Nancy's. What did you do with it?"

She shouldn't admit to having the phone. That was actually a crime, and this was a police interrogation, by a dirty cop. Anything she said, he would not only use against her, he'd twist it, lie about it. He hadn't read her her *Miranda* rights, but he'd lie about that, too. She clamped her mouth shut, determined not to make it easy for him.

"Fine, be that way. I can escalate, too, and you're not gonna like it."

He opened the door and shoved her toward it so she hit her head. Her eyes watered, but she refused to cry out. Fuck him, she wouldn't give him the satisfaction. The car reeked of cigarettes and stale coffee. Getting in the front seat, he glared at her in the rearview mirror.

"That was some stunt you pulled back there. You're lucky I didn't blow your brains all over that filthy floor. Just so you know, give me trouble again and I *will* kill you."

Fear turned to rage. And rage got her talking.

"Then you're *stupid*. Twenty people saw you arrest me. People will notice if I disappear. I'm a Harvard Law student."

He laughed. "You want to know one thing people hate more

than cops? *Harvard.* I'll just claim I had to shoot because you grabbed for my gun. They'll throw me a parade."

Whether he was right or wrong, he believed what he was saying. He thought he could kill her and get away with it, which made him deadly.

He pulled out into traffic.

"I'm gonna ask you some questions. If you answer to my satisfaction, things will go easier. If you don't, they'll go harder. Your choice. Is that clear?"

She stared back at him, hate in her eyes.

"I'll take that as a yes. First question. Where's Kathy?"

The question shocked her. And that shock made her realize that, deep down, she'd been thinking that Wallace had kidnapped or murdered Judge Conroy. She just hadn't verbalized that to herself because it was too scary. If he didn't know where the judge was, then obviously she was wrong. Small mercy.

Madison didn't know where Judge Conroy was, either, but she should pretend to. He'd be less likely to kill her that way.

Slowly, deliberately, she turned her head and stared out the window.

"*Hey.* Look at me. I'm talking to you. Where is she? And what were you doing in her house while she was gone?"

She didn't say a word.

"If you don't start talking, we'll go somewhere private, and I'll beat the answers out of you. I'm not kidding."

She believed him. Screw strategy. Screw *Miranda.* This wasn't an arrest. It was a kidnapping. She needed to stay alive.

"I was feeding the cat."

"The *cat.* You expect me to believe that?"

She shrugged. "It's true."

"Bullshit. Kathy knows you're a liar, that your brother is a criminal. She was told you're a threat. Given all the information. She agreed to fire you, but then she didn't. It makes no sense. *Unless* you have something over her. I want to know what it is. And you're gonna tell me one way or another."

"I'm her student and an intern in her chambers. She asked me to take care of her cat. Run errands. She pays me to do that. Nothing more."

"Who do you work for?"

"Did you hear what I said? I work for Judge Conroy."

He pounded the steering wheel, making her jump.

"Brooke Lee? Olivia? Who told you to break into Nancy's office? What were they looking for? What did they do with Kathy?"

Olivia *was* an undercover, then, like Imani said. Brooke Lee must be from law enforcement, too. If he thought Madison was passing information to them, he'd kill her.

"I don't know who you're talking about. The only Olivia I know of was the intern before me, and I never met her. I don't know *Lee*, or whoever that is. And I didn't *break in* to Nancy's office. I needed some documents for a memo. I used Kelsey's keys that were readily available. I thought it was okay. Sorry if it wasn't. I'm just a student. I didn't know better."

He scoffed. "If you're so innocent, why run? You knocked the old lady over, you were in such a rush."

"It was late. I thought I was alone, and suddenly the door flew open. I got spooked, that's all."

"That's a load of crap. You were looking for something. Was it the surveillance photos, or something else?"

"I told you, I was looking for documents on a case."

"That's not what you took, though, is it? What are these?"

He waved the envelope.

"They're photos of *me*. Of my *mother*. Stop blaming the victim. You're the one in the wrong. Why were you following us?"

"Because you're a goddam snitch, that's why. Andrew Martin. Doug Kessler. What are you doing talking to the likes of them?"

"It was a party. I was networking. They're influential people."

He smashed his fist against the steering wheel. "Bullshit. Tell me now, or you'll end up at the bottom of the river."

He wasn't joking. Dizzy with fear, she struggled to keep her voice steady.

"I only did what Judge Conroy told me to do."

The car swerved hard enough to draw a blaring horn from an oncoming truck. Wallace looked haggard in the rearview mirror.

"Kathy sent you in to talk to them? She's working with them?"

Jesus, she'd get the judge killed if she wasn't careful. On the other hand, the judge wasn't in the car with this lunatic. She had to protect herself.

"There was no mention of *working*, nothing like that. She said the party would be a good networking opportunity, and those were the people I should talk to."

"What were you supposed to say?"

"Just introduce myself and say I work for her. Look, I don't know anything. I'm a lowly intern. The judge doesn't confide in me. I haven't seen her in two days. I don't know where she is. I went to the house to feed Lucy, to make sure she didn't starve. That's all."

"Right." He scoffed.

They pulled up in front of a small, modern office building, the parking spaces in front of it filled with police vans and cruisers. *The police precinct.* She nearly fainted with relief. He wasn't going to kill her. But the next second, she wanted to cry. She was under arrest. If he took her inside and actually booked her on a criminal charge, the thing she'd been so afraid of would come true. It would destroy her legal career, ruin her life. Would he really do that? Arrest her for stealing those surveillance photos from Nancy? The photos implicated *him* in a conspiracy. He'd be crazy to broadcast that. Yet here they were.

He came around to her door and pulled her from the back seat.

"Where are you taking me?"

"Where snitches go."

He led her inside, through a glass door marked "Booking and Processing," to a large open area. A uniformed female officer with short hair and no-nonsense body language came out from behind the desk.

"Charge?" she said.

"Narcotics conspiracy. Federal. Log this as evidence retrieved from her person," Wallace said, throwing a clear plastic evidence envelope down on the desk.

Inside were dozens of little baggies filled with a brownish-white powder, stamped with a red rocket ship. Rocket was the brand of heroin that Ricky Peña's crew sold, according to the write-up in Danny's complaint. Madison staggered, her stomach heaving. Burglary she'd expected. That was a charge she could defend against. But narcotics? *Jesus, no.*

She looked at the female officer in desperation.

"He's lying. Those drugs aren't mine. I've never seen them before in my life."

The woman rolled her eyes.

"If it's federal, why you bringing her here?" she demanded of Wallace.

"The feds didn't answer the phone. I'll do a removal order tomorrow."

"You dump all that paperwork on me when I won't even get a stat? No way, Charlie."

"Quit whining and do your job," he said. "Here, log this, too."

He threw Madison's wallet onto the counter. But not her phone, she noticed. Was he keeping that? He would rifle through her photos, read her texts, track down her mother, her friends. No one would be safe.

"Where's my phone?" she said to the officer. "He can't just walk off with it, can he? That's stealing."

The officer sighed. "You got her phone or what?"

Wallace's eyes narrowed. "Yeah, so? I need it for a warrant."

"You're kidding me. You walk off with evidence, I take the hit for the lost item. They'll dock my pay for an iPhone. You need to log it in and submit a requisition."

"Oh, for fuck's sake. Fine. I'll be back with the form," he said, slapping Madison's phone down on the counter.

About to leave, he turned back.

"And I'm requesting a body cavity search on her, you hear? Probably got drugs up her cooch."

Wallace stalked away. He knew that wasn't true. It was sheer harassment.

The officer waved Madison toward a bench along one wall. "Have a seat and don't move."

Sitting there, reality hit, and she started hyperventilating. Body cavity search. *Jesus.* She'd be stripped naked. They'd take her clothes, make her wear an orange jumpsuit. Fingerprint her, take a mug shot. Tell the law school. She'd get expelled. And then what? Go to jail. Not just for one night, but every night for a long time, for a crime she didn't commit. Her life would be over. Just like Danny's. She used to think they were so different. But they weren't. They were the same. Equally at the mercy of that criminal with a badge. Her mother would have two children in jail.

Oh, shit. Mom.

More than an hour had passed since their phone call. Mom didn't know where she was. She'd be in agony worrying. Just like with Danny. *Argh, Danny.* Madison finally, truly understood how her brother felt, and it was unbearable.

She had to get out of this situation. Not just for herself, but for him. And for Mom.

She put her head between her knees to get her breathing under control. By the time she raised it again, she knew what she had to do.

"Excuse me, Officer. Can I have my phone call now, please?"

"What d'you think this is, a hotel?" the woman said.

"I'm entitled to one phone call. I'm a law student, and I know that's the law. I'd like it now, please."

"Well, too bad. I'm swamped with paperwork because of you. You'll get your call when I'm done. Now be quiet."

"I can make all that paperwork go away. Let me have the call, and I guarantee the feds will come pick me up. They'll take the case over before you lift a finger."

"I got news for you, honey. The feds aren't about to come pick you up at this hour when they could wait for us to bring you to them tomorrow. I'll have to book you anyway."

No. Getting booked would create a criminal record. She had to head it off.

"I promise they will, because they're looking for me, and they're really anxious."

"I just entered you in the database. There's no federal warrant out for you."

"They want me as a witness. That's why there's no warrant. They don't want it getting out, or I won't be valuable. I'm telling the truth, I swear. The U.S. attorney is Andrew Martin. Call him yourself if you don't believe me."

The officer was wavering. Madison went with her gut, hoping this time, it would work.

"Just, whatever you do, ma'am, don't tell Wallace that you called the feds," she said. "That would piss him off so much, because he's in a competition with them to make this case."

"Me calling the feds would piss off Charlie?"

"Yes."

"*Good*. Guy's an ass." The officer picked up the desk phone. "What's that U.S. attorney's name again?"

A couple of hours later, Madison was dozing on the bench when a dark-haired woman in a gray pantsuit walked up to the desk officer and flashed a badge.

"I'm here for the prisoner transfer on Madison Rivera. Special Agent Olivia Chase, Federal Bureau of Investigation."

Olivia.

Madison's head snapped up.

"That's her," the officer said. "I'll need chain-of-custody on both prisoner and evidence."

"Just show me where to sign."

Agent Chase took custody of Madison's wallet, phone, and the bag of drugs. Hauling her to her feet, she marched her out to an SUV in the parking lot.

"Let me see those cuffs."

Taking a key from her pocket, she unlocked the handcuffs. As Madison shook out her hands, tears glazed her eyes. She was free.

Or was she?

"I'm no longer under arrest?" she asked.

"I'm tasked with bringing you to DC for an interview, and I want you to be comfortable. Doesn't mean your status has changed, so don't try anything."

"Oh," Madison said, not bothering to hide her disappointment.

Olivia's face softened. "So you understand, no charges have been filed yet. Who knows, maybe they won't be. That's above my pay grade. The prosecutors will decide."

She opened the passenger door. "Hop in, we're booked on the first flight. There's folks at Main Justice who are dying to talk to you."

27

....

The plane came in for a landing as the sun was rising over the Washington Monument. The view would've been thrilling under better circumstances, but she just felt sad. Outside, the air was soft and balmy, like a different country in a different season. A car waited to whisk them to the Justice Department. She recognized the building from photos she'd seen, the trapezoidal hulk of it looming over the block, its white marble glowing pink in the morning light. She'd imagined arriving there in glory as an attorney on a high-profile case. Instead, she was being escorted in custody, to give evidence against a woman she'd once revered.

How the mighty have fallen.

They passed through heavy metal doors that belonged on a bank vault, into a dark, imposing hallway where they presented identification, through a metal detector, up in a secure elevator to an entry floor with a plexiglass window, where they were given visitor passes and told to wait for their escort.

"I understand why *I* have to go through this," Madison said to

Olivia as they took seats in uncomfortable chairs lined up against a sterile, white wall. "Why do you? You're FBI."

"They're careful. Have to be, when the targets have been known to assassinate prosecutors," Olivia said, quirking an eyebrow.

That reference—to the car bombing of that prosecutor years ago—caused the bottom to fall out of her stomach. She wasn't in the clear yet. Even if the feds believed that Wallace had lied about finding drugs on her, there was still the matter of conspiring with Judge Conroy. Did they know she'd delivered that warning to Doug Kessler at the reception? With Kessler and the judge missing, would they care that she did it out of fear for her brother's life?

Andrew Martin came out to get them.

"Madison, nice to see you again. Come on in."

He smiled like an unusually handsome dentist, reassuring her before he drilled her teeth. The conference room he took them to was out of central casting. The long table, the whine of the HVAC, a smell of burnt coffee, and—as she'd feared—an enormous bulletin board marked "McCarthy Assassination." So, the focus of their investigation really was this crime Madison hadn't known about until yesterday. Not something bloodless like bribery or corruption, but the murder of a prosecutor, with graphic photos of a burned-out car and bloody bits of flesh that made her stomach heave. And that wasn't the worst part. She took a step closer, her mouth falling open. Among dozens of photos of suspects, most of whom she didn't recognize, she saw Judge Conroy, Detective Wallace, Ray Logue, and Nancy. But Danny's mug shot was also there. And next to it, Madison herself, her Harvard Law School ID photo with "The Intern" written under it.

She was on a bulletin board for assassinating a prosecutor.

"Madison, so glad you could join us."

She turned, noticing for the first time the petite, pretty female prosecutor at the head of the table. With a sleek, black bob and immaculate clothing, she looked ready to address a jury. Meanwhile Madison hadn't slept, showered, or combed her hair since yesterday.

"Morning, boss. Special delivery," Olivia said, dropping the plastic evidence envelope full of drugs on the table in front of the woman.

"How'd you get *that* on the plane?"

"I have my ways."

"Thanks, it'll make a nice conversation starter. Miss Rivera, Brooke Lee. Department of Justice."

Brooke Lee. Wallace had mentioned her.

"I work with AUSA Martin on this investigation. I'm sorry we're meeting under such unfortunate circumstances. Not long ago, you would've been someone I'd love to hire. But now."

Picking up the evidence, she clucked her tongue. Madison's legs went weak, and she fell into the closest chair.

"You can't possibly believe those are my drugs," she said.

"I admit, Detective Wallace has been known to lie. On the other hand, your brother *was* arrested for selling Rocket heroin, so it would make sense that you're involved in his operation. Despite the Harvard Law pedigree."

"Danny is innocent. The drugs were never his."

"Look, I get it. He's your little brother. You probably have fond memories of reading him bedtime stories. That doesn't make him innocent. There's not a narcotics case in history where the defendant doesn't claim they're not his drugs."

"This time, it's true. He was in the wrong place at the wrong time. It was just bad luck."

"I'll say. He's facing ten years. But if you're willing to talk, and you give us hard evidence against Judge Conroy, you might be able to help Danny out. Help *yourself* too. Because the penalty for possession of these drugs here," she said, holding up the plastic envelope, "is a minimum of five years in federal prison."

Madison realized that her teeth were chattering. She'd been freezing since forgetting her coat in the judge's office last night. The cold blast of air from the vents didn't help. It was almost like an enhanced interrogation technique, the equivalent of bright lights or sleep deprivation. Brooke Lee was staring her down. The feds were sharks, as dangerous as Wallace in their own way. Desperate and exhausted, not knowing what to do, she did the thing they always said not to. She started talking.

"Wallace kidnapped me last night. He planted the drugs on me. Please, you have to believe me."

"What I don't understand is, if you're just a humble law student, and so innocent, why would Wallace waste his time framing you?"

"To stop me from cooperating. He thought I was working for you and wanted to destroy my credibility. And you're scaring me, because I'm afraid he succeeded."

"Your credibility is yet to be determined. It really depends on you. On your willingness to answer questions truthfully."

"Ask me anything. I'll answer. The whole truth, I promise."

"Okay. What exactly is the nature of your relationship with Kathryn Conroy?"

"I'm her student and an intern in her chambers."

"Why are you living in her house?"

"I'm not living there. I just stayed over a couple of nights."

"Why?"

"She hired me as a pet sitter."

"Hmmm." Brooke looked skeptical, shaking her head.

"I swear, that's the truth. She's my professor. I got an internship in her office. Then she asked me to watch her cat."

"What were you doing at the Pro Bono League dinner?"

"The judge gave me a ticket. I was networking."

"You were seen speaking with Douglas Kessler. Why were you talking to him?"

"Again, networking. I'll be working at his law firm next summer."

"What exactly did you talk about with him?"

Her mouth fell open. What the hell was she doing? She should ask for a lawyer before she incriminated herself.

"Brooke, may I?" Martin interrupted. "I think rather than focusing on Kessler, we need to get Conroy's whereabouts. She's been MIA for two days now, and we urgently need to speak with her. Madison, tell us where she is, and you'll go a long way toward restoring your credibility. Hold back, and we'll have reason to think you're involved."

"Involved in *what*?"

"Murder," Lee said, and the word seemed to hang in the air.

Madison looked at the bulletin board in disbelief.

"How? That happened when I was a child."

"No. It happened the night of the Pro Bono League reception."

"What are you talking about? I'm really confused. That murder on your poster—McCarthy—wasn't that years ago?"

"We're talking about Douglas Kessler. He was murdered the night of the Pro Bono League reception, shortly after getting into a very public argument. With *you*."

Madison reeled back in her chair, the breath forced from her body. The world went dark.

A moment later, Martin was pouring her a glass of water.

"Are you okay? Here, drink this."

She picked up the glass with a shaking hand.

"I take it you were unaware of his death," he said.

But Brooke leaned forward with a "gotcha" gleam in her eye.

"Stop it, Andrew. She's just a good little actress. She was seen talking to him right before it happened. We need to know about that conversation, Madison. Kessler's daughter claims that whatever you said to her father got him so upset that he ran from the event without giving his speech. By then, you'd already left, hadn't you? And Kessler was found murdered not long after."

Her teeth chattered so hard that she had to fight to get the words out.

"I-I—want a lawyer."

Martin threw up his hands. "Great move, Brooke. You got her to invoke. Now we waste days with her consulting a lawyer, while Kathryn Conroy flees the country."

For a moment, Madison thought they were playing good cop/bad cop. But then she realized—Andrew Martin was genuinely not on board with Brooke Lee's approach. Because he believed Madison was innocent.

"I didn't have anything to do with Mr. Kessler's murder," she said, looking into his eyes desperately. "I would never hurt anyone. Please believe me."

"It's okay, Madison. I do believe you."

Lee sighed irritably.

"Well, *I'm* not so sure. I'd be willing to listen to your side of the story, if not for the fact that you invoked your right to counsel. Now we can't talk to you unless you sign a waiver. You have to decide that of your own accord. I'm not going to pressure you and get accused of violating your rights."

"What do you say, Madison? Will you sign a waiver?" Martin asked.

"I don't know. I'm upset. I'm tired and hungry and cold. I can't think straight."

"Food can be arranged. Coffee. A warm sweater," Andrew said.

"And if she wants to talk to someone," Olivia said, "it doesn't have to be a lawyer. Her brother's down the hall. She could consult him. I bet he'd get her talking."

"*Danny?* He's here?"

The prosecutors glared at Olivia like she'd divulged a state secret. But it was the only good thing Madison had heard in days.

"Yes, let me talk to him. I need to. Now. *Please*," she said, tears in her eyes.

"Can we consult?" Lee said, gesturing at the door.

The prosecutors and Olivia stepped out. Madison heard their voices in the hall, low and urgent. She couldn't make out the words, but the sound was like white noise, lulling her. Her eyelids were heavy. She rested her head on the table. When the door opened a while later, she jerked up. Despite the tension, she was so exhausted that she'd dozed off.

"We're all set. Come with me," Olivia said.

"Where?"

"You'll see. You'll be happy, promise."

She followed Olivia down a hallway that seemed to go on forever. High ceilings, marble floors, identical-looking doors, numbered but otherwise indistinguishable. It was like a bureaucracy conjured to life. As they walked, Olivia handed Madison a black puffer jacket.

"I got this from the lost and found. A bit large, but it'll keep you warm."

"Thanks."

They stopped in front of a closed door. After the trauma of Brooke Lee's interrogation, she braced herself for a letdown.

"It's true? I'm really going to see my brother?" she asked, eyes welling.

"Yes, ma'am. See for yourself."

Olivia pushed open the door.

"*Danny.*"

He was up and out of his chair, his well-loved face bright with a fierce joy, grabbing her, lifting her in the air. She threw her arms around his neck. They were smiling, sobbing, talking over each other.

"We'll wait outside, give you guys some family time," Olivia said, motioning to the U.S. Marshal who'd been guarding Danny.

They were alone in the room. Tears streamed down Madison's face.

"They wouldn't tell us where you were. We thought you might be dead."

"I never thought I'd see you or Ma again."

She stepped back to get a better look at him. His eyes were sunken, his skin dull, his thin frame verging on emaciated.

"What did they *do* to you?"

"Hey, you don't look so great either."

"Yeah, I've been through the wringer."

"But here we are, still standing, and *together*. That's what matters. Seeing you now, Maddy, I just—"

He started to cry, digging his fists into his eyes.

"C'mere."

She hugged him again, tighter this time.

"Dude, I can feel your bones sticking out. I want to feed you."

"You already did. Look at this spread. You got mad connections."

A large platter of breakfast pastries sat on the conference table, along with a carafe of coffee and paper cups.

"Danishes, donuts, muffins, mini banana breads. I feel like I won Powerball. I tried three different kinds already," Danny said.

They sat down at the table, clasping one another's hands. Only the desire to take care of him made her let go. She blotted her eyes with a napkin, then poured his coffee, dumping in three creamers and two sugars.

"That's how you take it, right?"

"Perfect," he said. "And I'm guessing you want a blueberry muffin."

She laughed through tears. "You know it. My childhood fave."

"I know what you like. It's up here," he said, tapping his temple as he carefully selected a muffin for her.

His sunken cheeks and shadowed eyes revealed a man who'd been through hell, physically and mentally. How close had he come to dying? What scars would he carry for the rest of his life? If she'd done more, sooner, this wouldn't've happened to him.

"I feel sick thinking about what you've been through," she said, a rush of words spilling out. "You told the truth about everything. I should never have doubted you. I should have done more, tried harder to get you out. I should have—"

He squeezed her hands. "Stop it. What could you've done? It happened so fast. A week after I was arrested, Logue pled my case out. And that judge let him. None of it was normal. You said yourself, it's not how the system is supposed to work. You couldn't've predicted."

"But I should've known better. So much happened just in the past few days that made me out to be a fool. And *naïve*. I couldn't believe you until I went through the same thing myself. I'm so sorry."

Her tears started up again.

"Hey, hey, come on. Eat something, okay? You'll feel better. I forgive you for whatever you think you did. For every imaginary sin. Hear me? Let's not waste our time with regrets. One thing I learned from this experience, life is too short. Family is what matters."

There was a noise outside the door. They snapped around, staring at it, faces going grim.

"We should talk before they come back in," he said.

"Yes. Tell me what happened. I'm so behind. When did they move you? Where have you been, and what's going on with your case? Catch me up, so we can figure out what to do."

"Right. So, you remember when you and Mom came to visit, and I was beat up?"

"Are you kidding? I'll never forget. That took a decade off my life, not to mention Mom's."

He shook his head, his eyes misting over. "*Damn.* Mom. I can't even—"

She put her hand on his.

"Danny, she's okay. I talked to her right before I got on the plane to come here and persuaded her to go to Aunt Nilda's as a precaution. She's leaving today."

"Thank God. Because those people know where she lives, and they don't play."

"I know."

"Okay, so what happened is, after I got beat up that time, one of the COs starts looking out for me. He's Puerto Rican, from our neighborhood, and I knew his nephew in school. So it made sense why. But still, I didn't trust him at first. I didn't trust *anyone*. One night, he comes to me and says, 'Son, I heard there's a target on your back. They put out a hit on you, so we got to move you right away.' He had me transferred to Ad Seg that night. The whole time, honest to God, I was shitting my pants. I didn't know if he was for real, if he was in on it, or what. Because Ad Seg, it's solitary, right? You're all alone. If that CO was dirty, that's the worst place I could be. I didn't close my eyes that night. At first bell, the cell door opens, and it's him. He goes, 'You're going to court.' And I'm convinced this is the end. Because I know my sentencing's not for months, so it has to be a lie, right? The next few hours while they transported me, I died a thousand times. Every new person.

Every sudden move. I thought I was done. But then they took me to court for real. Not to *your* judge. Some guy I never saw before. And he says this is a—what do you call it, ex something?"

"Ex parte?"

"Yeah, an emergency hearing, just me and the judge. And he says, *I heard you're being threatened. Is that true?* Long story short, he gave me a new lawyer, who hooked me up with Ms. Lee and Mr. Martin. I went in for an interview. They asked what I knew about Wallace, and Logue, and your judge. I told them everything, but it wasn't enough. Truth is, I don't know shit about the big shots. I could tell them if Adrian smokes weed, or if he sells bundles for Ricky Peña. That's small-time stuff. The feds want the big fish. The judge, the lawyers. That's when I told 'em, my sister goes to Harvard Law. Judge Conroy is her teacher. I said, you *know* her. Mom had told me that, so I told them."

Remembering the shock and recognition on Andrew Martin's face when she approached him at the reception, she realized Danny must have told him about her.

"So, that's how the feds knew about me. From *you*."

"I was never trying to hurt you or drag you into my problems or anything. I just didn't know what else to say."

"No, it's okay. Your problems *are* my problems. That's what family means."

"Still. I'm sorry, Maddy."

"Don't apologize. The feds got me out of a tight spot last night, which they might not've done if they didn't think I could help their investigation. So really, you did me a solid in that regard. On the other hand, now they're accusing me of things I didn't do."

"Like what?"

"Well, for one thing, Wallace planted drugs on me."

The sadness in his eyes turned to horror. "What the hell? On you? *Why?*"

"Oh, it's a long story. But then this lawyer got murdered, and—ugh, I can't even."

"You didn't have anything to do with any of it. Right?"

"Of course not."

"Yeah, that's just like me, when they threw that bag of drugs at me. Now I'm worried they're trying to play you, and it's my fault."

"Who's playing me?"

"The prosecution."

"You mean like a negotiating tactic?"

"Exactly. I convinced them you were valuable. Now they want to force you into a cooperation agreement because they think you can really help their case. They say you work in the judge's office and spend time at her house. Is that true?"

"Yes, I'm her intern. And I take care of her cat."

He laughed. "A cat? Seriously?"

"I only did it to try to help you. To get close to her and see what I could find out. The cat's cool, though."

"I don't think the feds care about the cat, sis."

"Probably not."

"They want to know about her crimes. When they first brought me in for an interview, they asked about Judge Conroy and Ricky Peña. Like, did he bribe her to put the weight on me, and let him go? I can't answer that. I'm no insider, no mastermind. I only met Ricky once for five minutes. I don't know the judge at all. They don't tell me secrets. All's I could say was that my lawyer railroaded me, and she went along with it. Turns out, that information's not worth enough to get me a deal. Now, they're saying I have to get *you* to cooperate. That's why they brought me here."

"Wait a minute, what?"

"I'm here to talk you into signing up with them."

"They planned this? Like, brought you here ahead of time?"

"Yeah, I'm housed in Pennsylvania now, in a secure facility.

They brought me down to DC this morning at the crack of dawn. What I'm saying is, these people are not looking out for your interests. They want to put pressure on you. You got to be careful. From what I've seen of them, they'd tell you they got evidence on you just to get you to wear a wire."

"A wire?"

"Yeah, they want you to record this judge, get her to confess. They told me so. And said I should tell you to do it, for my sake. But I won't. You got to make up your own mind. I've been inside. I've seen what can happen. Snitches get retaliated against. It's dangerous, and I don't want anything to happen to you. So I'm here to tell you, don't do this for me. Really. Maybe don't do it at all. I'll survive somehow."

"To help *you*? I'm sorry if I'm slow, but how would me wearing a wire help you?"

"They didn't tell you?"

"They haven't explained the deal to me yet. We were at kind of an impasse when they brought me over to talk to you."

"From what I understand, they're willing to count your cooperation for my benefit."

"Count it how?"

"Big time. If you get this judge on tape, they'll dismiss my case. I could walk out of here a free man. They'd expunge my record. I could start my life over, instead of rotting in jail for something I didn't do. It would be like this nightmare never happened."

"Wow. That's huge, Danny."

"Not huge enough to risk my sister's life."

"That's my decision, isn't it?"

"It affects us both. In Ad Seg, you're all alone. I had a lot of time to think, and I realized I need to be better for my family. Going to the bar that night wasn't just foolish. It was selfish. It put you in a position where you had to take risks to help me. Saving my ass should not be your problem, Maddy. I'm the one who screwed up my life."

"Well, I screwed up mine, too. I should have done things by the book. Tried to get you a new lawyer or something official like that. Instead, I inserted myself into Judge Conroy's operation like I was some spy or something. I thought I could help you, but I was just a fool."

He put his hand on his heart. "I'm touched you would do that for me. But also, it makes me feel guilty."

"Don't. To be totally honest—I did it for myself, too. I wanted the internship for my résumé. And I wanted to get close to the judge. She's a fascinating woman with an important job, and I admired her. My head was turned. I never believed you when you said she was corrupt. I had to learn the hard way."

"I think we both learned our lesson, huh? Stick to what we know. Be humble, be grateful. Take care of each other, and of Mom."

"That's exactly what I'm going to do. Take care of you. And Mom. Because she'll never be okay until you're out of jail."

"Madison. No."

"Hey, if it was me in trouble, and you in a position to help, you'd do it. Besides, like I said, I've got legal problems of my own. Brooke Lee seems to actually believe I'm a murderer."

"Nah, she's playing you."

"I'm not so sure. Anyway, I'm going to tell them yes. That I'll wear a wire. There's just one problem. Judge Conroy is missing. The feds seem to think I know where she is, but I have no clue. If I can't find her, then I can't get her on tape, and the whole deal falls apart."

There was a knock on the door, and Olivia marched in.

"Time's up. We just got word that Kathryn Conroy resurfaced in Boston."

Danny nodded. "Problem solved, sis. But are you sure?"

She met her brother's eyes. "I'm sure."

She turned to Olivia. "I've decided to waive my right to an attorney and fully cooperate."

"That's great news. Say your goodbyes for now, Madison. They're waiting in the conference room. We have work to do."

28

....

The sun had set, and the temperature was plummeting. Madison crossed the courtyard and fit her key into the back door, huddling into the borrowed puffer jacket. The lights were off inside the town house. She stepped into the darkened back hall.

"Hello?"

Nothing. The feds had assured her that Judge Conroy would be at home when she arrived. They were wrong, apparently.

As the *beep-beep-beep* of the alarm started up, she entered the code into the keypad near the back door. It should've turned off immediately. But the beeping didn't stop. An error message flashed on the panel. She input again, more carefully this time, but it still didn't work. There was a second keypad by the front door. She ran to it and tried the code there. Nope. As the beep turned to a shriek, her heart rate skyrocketed. The code had been changed.

A light switched on behind her. She whirled to see Judge Conroy, Lucy in her arms. She'd been sitting in the dark. Waiting. *Hiding.*

"Judge. You're back. I was worried. Where have you been?"

She stared accusingly with those ice-blue eyes. "The more interesting question is where *you've* been."

She knows.

"Did you change the code?" Madison asked, and her voice was high and shaky.

"Why, yes, I did. I can't have just anyone coming into my home. People are dangerous, the ones you trust most dangerous of all."

Any second now, the alarm system would send an alert to the security company, which would in turn call the police. That could bring Wallace down on their heads.

"It's about to call the cops," Madison said.

The judge didn't want that either, apparently, because she walked decisively to the panel and tapped in the new code.

The beeping stopped.

"Come in. And take off that extremely large coat."

Madison advanced hesitantly into the darkened living room. It looked like Judge Conroy had been about to flee. She was wearing a dark raincoat that Madison had never seen before. A pet carrier sat on the sofa, unzipped, yawning open. The judge tried to force Lucy into it, but the cat struggled, jumping down with a yowl and taking off.

"I'll get her later," she said. "After I deal with you."

In the harsh light of the single lamp, she looked like she'd aged a decade since the night of the reception. There were purple shadows under her eyes and lines around her mouth. In spite of everything, Madison was worried for her.

"Are you all right, Judge? You look—"

"Oh, spare me the phony concern and take off that ridiculous coat."

The borrowed black puffer was bulky enough to conceal a wire. That was why Judge Conroy had fixated on it. Madison shucked the coat. The judge looked her up and down skeptically.

"Now the rest of it."

"What?"

"Take off your clothes."

"Are you kidding?"

"This is no joke. I know where you've been, and I'm not taking any chances."

"Where I've been?"

"Don't lie. You'll just make me angry and destroy what's left of our friendship. I know you went to DC. You met with the feds. You turned on me. And I know how that goes. You're wearing a wire."

"It's not true."

"Prove it, then. Take off your clothes."

"That's absurd. I refuse."

Judge Conroy sighed and leaned sideways, reaching for something hidden in the murk, outside the circle of lamplight. She stood up with the gun in her hand, leveling the barrel at Madison's chest.

"You wouldn't shoot me. You couldn't," Madison said, but she was shaking.

"You have no idea what I am capable of when pushed. Do it."

When Madison returned to the conference room after meeting with Danny, Brooke Lee told her that Judge Conroy had murdered Douglas Kessler. The prosecutors showed her evidence, but it was all circumstantial. A text from Kessler to the judge arranging to meet. Photos of Kessler's car in a parking garage with the windows shot out. A woman they claimed was the judge in a dark wig, at what they said was the same garage. Madison hadn't believed them then because the Kathryn Conroy she knew was no killer. Maybe it was time to reevaluate that.

Kicking off her sneakers, she stepped out of her jeans, and pulled the sweater over her head. She stood in her underwear, numb with disbelief that it had come to this.

"Turn around," the judge said, gesturing with the gun.

She pirouetted. There was no visible wire taped to her chest or back.

"I suppose they think they're clever," the judge said, picking up the puffer coat and checking the pockets, patting down the fabric for anything concealed in the lining.

She clicked her teeth impatiently.

"You're making this harder than it needs to be. Tell me where it is."

"If you mean a wire, I'm not wearing one."

"You're not *wearing* it. Okay. Hand me your backpack."

Madison retrieved the backpack, which she'd dumped in the hall, and advanced on the judge.

"Stop there," she said, brandishing the gun. "Slide it over and back up."

Madison propelled the backpack across the smooth parquet floor. The judge turned it upside down and shook everything out onto the coffee table. Her phone, papers, notebooks, pens, a hat, an empty water bottle.

The judge picked up the phone, which Olivia had returned to her before she left DC.

"Is this it? It's set to record?"

"No."

"What's your passcode?"

She said it. The judge unlocked the screen, checking to see if the voice note function was enabled. It wasn't.

"What is it, some special software you downloaded?"

"There's nothing."

She was telling the truth. Not believing her, the judge took the phone and smashed it against the corner of the coffee table. The screen cracked. Madison winced, but Judge Conroy wasn't satisfied. Slipping past Madison, she opened the door to the powder room and tossed the phone into the toilet.

"My phone. *No*."

It was her most prized possession. Her life was on that thing.

"The FBI can buy you a new one," the judge said.

"You destroyed it for nothing. It wasn't recording."

"Well, then, I'd better keep looking."

The judge was relentless. She went through pockets and compartments, throwing anything else she found on the pile and then examining everything meticulously, including looking inside the Kleenex pack and the earbuds case, the ChapStick and tin of breath mints.

Nothing.

"Hand me your clothes."

Madison tossed her jeans and sweater onto the sofa. The judge went over them with equal zeal, coming up empty.

"Your underwear."

"Judge. No."

"I'm not giving up till I find the damn thing. If you don't want to strip down, just tell me where it is."

"You can see there's nothing. There's nowhere to hide it. Look."

She drew within a couple of feet of the judge, tugging her underwear away from her skin and shimmying, doing the same with her bra, which was lacy and sheer anyway.

Judge Conroy slammed her hand on the table. "I'm tired of this stupid game. Where is it?"

"I don't know what else to say to convince you."

"You could tell the truth about where you've been."

"Fine. Yes, I went to DC. I met with them. I'll tell you exactly what happened if you'll just let me get dressed. Please? It's cold in here."

Sighing, the judge sat back. "All right, go ahead."

Now that the argument was over, Lucy strolled in and rubbed up against Madison's legs, getting in the way as she tried to put on her jeans.

"Lucy, here. Stay away from her."

The cat looked skeptical. Judge Conroy had to put the pet carrier aside before Lucy would agree to get on the sofa. Their negotiation gave Madison a moment to catch her breath. To be forced to disrobe at gunpoint had shaken her, but it shouldn't have. Olivia had warned her that might happen. *Wallace knows we took you from the police station. He'll assume we met, and that you're cooperating. If he knows, she knows. She'll probably pat you down, so we won't send you in wired yet. Your job is to allay her suspicions. Talk her around, win her trust back. Once she trusts you, that's when we wire you up.*

Madison sat down, a nervous flutter in her chest. She'd rehearsed what to say and how to say it. Tell enough of the truth to be credible. Don't apologize. Let your anger show. The advice helped with the fear but not the guilt. She didn't want to be responsible for bringing Judge Conroy down. That was foolish, even self-destructive. She needed to overcome her schoolgirl hero worship of the judge and do the right thing for herself. Or else Kathryn Conroy would walk away unscathed and leave Madison and her family to pay the price.

"Go ahead, I'm listening," Judge Conroy said.

"You want to know why I met with them?" Madison said, the anger rising in her voice. "Because your psychotic boyfriend kidnapped me and threatened to kill me. Was I supposed to just sit back and accept that?"

"If you mean Charlie, he's *not* my boyfriend."

"I don't care what he is to you. He's a complete psycho. He planted drugs on me. *Me*, who's never been in trouble a day in my life. Then he threatened to murder me for snitching to the feds, which I was totally innocent of. And he might've succeeded, if they didn't pick me up on a transfer. *That's* why I agreed to meet with them. He gave me no choice."

Judge Conroy dropped her head into her hands, rubbing her eyes.

"I understand. I believe you, and I'm sorry that happened to you. But I still need to know whose side you're on. Keep talking. You met with them. They asked about me, obviously. What did you say?"

"You know, not everything is about you. I was more interested in convincing them not to arrest *me*. Come to find out, you're implicated in the assassination of a federal prosecutor, and because of my association with you, I am too. I had nothing to trade. No proof to give. No testimony. Because you don't confide in me. You know that better than anyone. I'm a target, and useless to them as a witness. Because of *you*. They let me go. But they said they're not done with me, and I'm sick over it."

The judge looked genuinely upset.

"Madison, I'm sorry. I never meant for any of that to happen to you. I want you to know I had nothing to do with that murder. Brad McCarthy was my friend."

"Yes, well. Being your friend gets people killed, apparently."

Judge Conroy exhaled, hard and sharp, like she'd been slapped. Her eyes filled with tears. She made a valiant effort to hold them back, but a few spilled over and rolled slowly down her cheeks, sparkling in the lamplight.

"I can't argue with you. Brad. Doug. *Matthew*. They died because of me. I don't want that to happen to you. I can't deny you're in a horrible position. That's why I'm concerned about a wire. I wouldn't blame you if you flipped on me."

"You say they died because of you. What does that mean? The feds say you killed Douglas Kessler. Is that true? You know I'm not wired. I'm asking because it matters to me. And if you're worried that if you confess, I'd testify—"

"I can't confess, because I didn't kill him," the judge said. "Completely the opposite. I tried to warn him. Charlie wanted proof that Doug was working for the feds. I was supposed to get that for him, and then they were going to kill him. I just couldn't handle another death on my conscience. So I sent you in to warn him instead. That was the message you delivered at the reception. A warning that the feds were investigating. And that Charlie and his people thought he was snitching and wanted him dead."

"But it didn't work?"

"He panicked. He ran out of the party, which spooked Charlie, I guess, and then they—well."

Madison felt like she'd been punched in the stomach. Even if the message was intended as a warning, by delivering it, she'd played a part in a man's death. She looked at the judge with horror in her eyes.

"Brooke said you killed him. Maybe you didn't pull the trigger—"

"Madison, I tried to save him."

"—but you put me in the middle of a murder."

"It was going to happen anyway. The slightest hint that some-one might rat, and the order goes out. Eliminate the risk. They got to Doug. They're coming for me next. I've been under their thumb since I was a kid. You can't fight them. The feds won't help you. They'll turn on you if it suits them, like they turned on me. Brooke flipped you without explaining the risks. And now she's dangling you like bait. Is there even a unit outside protecting you?"

The answer was no. Olivia said it was premature to station a unit at the town house until they'd allayed Judge Conroy's sus-picions. Monitoring too closely could blow the investigation. So they'd sent her in alone. Unprotected. The judge was right. She couldn't trust the feds. So, where did that leave her?

"That's what I thought," the judge said. "They don't care what happens to you. But *I* do. I don't want you to pay for my sins, Madison. I came back here to get Lucy, knowing it was a risk. But it's *my* risk. I don't want you here when he comes for me."

The hairs rose on the back of Madison's neck. "Wallace is coming here?"

As if on cue, a red flash lit up the dimness of the room. Their eyes flew upward. A motion sensor mounted near the ceiling had switched on suddenly, seemingly of its own accord. Its red eye glowed. Madison's hackles rose.

"Why did it do that?"

"*Shhhh.*"

The judge went to the alarm panel in the back hall and studied it, tapping in a complicated sequence of codes. As mysteriously as it turned on, the red light blinked off. They both visibly relaxed.

"I've always wondered—" Madison began, but the judge put her finger to her lips and shook her head.

She'd meant to ask, *Do those things have cameras in them? Is somebody watching?* The judge's behavior suggested that the answer to both questions was yes. The red light was off now. A phone sitting in a charger on the kitchen island began to ring. It wasn't the judge's normal phone, or her normal ringtone. She could see the screen from where she sat. NANCY, it read. They exchanged glances. Judge Conroy looked gutted, terrified. She silenced the phone, but it rang again a moment later. CHARLIE, it said this time, and she switched it off. There was a pad of paper on the island next to the phone charger. She grabbed a pen and scrawled a note, putting it under Madison's nose, at an angle the camera couldn't see.

They know we're here. We need to leave NOW.

Judge Conroy chased Lucy down, dragging her out from under the sofa and getting clawed in the process.

"Do you need help? Will she come to me?"

The cat settled into Madison's arms.

"She hates the carrier. She thinks she's going to the vet," Judge Conroy said. "Come on, let's go."

They ran out the back door and through the courtyard. In the alley, Madison stopped.

"I'm not going with you."

"We can get away, I promise. I've got a plan."

"I'd feel safer on my own."

"You think you can hide? Where—in your dorm? Your mother's house? He'll find you. The feds won't save you. They're doing nothing to protect you. You must see that."

Madison hesitated. The judge reached into the pocket of her raincoat and pulled out the gun.

"I'm sorry to do this, but you're coming with me, whether you like it or not. If I leave you behind, they'll use you to find me. And when they're done with you, they'll kill you, which I could not abide. Now, *move.*"

The judge waved the gun. Madison headed for the white SUV.

"No. They know that car. Follow me," Judge Conroy whispered, yanking the hood of her raincoat over her bright hair.

It was a cold night with the taste of snow in the wind. Their breath came out in clouds as they hurried down the alley, around the corner, and down a few blocks. Madison thought about making a run for it. Despite the threats, she didn't believe that Judge Conroy would shoot. But the judge's warning had gotten through to her. It was true—the feds weren't protecting her. She could try to run on her own. But Wallace had found her before. He could do it again. And she couldn't count on outsmarting him twice.

They ended up in a grimy parking lot behind a restaurant.

An old Volvo with New Hampshire plates was parked beside a dumpster. The judge unlocked the car with a fob, opening the passenger door.

"That's your car?"

"It belongs to a friend of mine. You're driving. Get in."

"Can you take her?"

Madison held out the cat, who took one look at the open car door and dug her claws into Madison's hands. Leaping, Lucy hit the ground running and disappeared behind the dumpster. The judge went after her.

"Goddamn it, Lucy. Get out here *now*."

The cat shot out suddenly, avoiding both their attempts to grab her. In the blink of an eye, she was gone.

"Did you see where she went?"

"Down the street, I think."

Judge Conroy ran after Lucy, returning a few minutes later, looking frantic.

"I don't see her anywhere."

"What should we do?"

"We have to get out of here before Charlie finds us. We'll drive around and look for her."

They got in the car, with Madison driving, and squared the block several times without a single sighting of Lucy. They stopped at a red light. The judge was distraught.

"I don't know what to do. We can't stay. It's too dangerous. But it's below freezing tonight. And I won't be there to let her in if she comes home."

"Let me get out. I'll keep looking, I promise. I won't give up."

They were several cars back from the intersection when the light changed. A dark-colored sedan passed them, going in the opposite direction, toward the town house. They turned in unison to watch it go.

"Was that him?" Judge Conroy said, her voice cold with fear.

"I think so."

"Did he see us?"

Madison's eyes were on the rearview mirror. "I'm not sure. He hasn't turned around yet."

The light changed. The car behind them honked.

"*Go*. Take 93, heading north," Judge Conroy said.

As Madison stepped on the gas, she tried not to think about the fact that she was driving off with a woman who was at the center of a vast conspiracy, whose closest associates were criminals and dead men. In the moment, there didn't seem to be any alternative. Merging onto the interstate, she kept glancing in the rearview mirror. There was no sign of Wallace yet. That didn't mean she was safe, any more than getting on the interstate meant she'd decided to flee. They were heading north. To where, *Canada*? She had no intention of leaving the country, no matter who was chasing her.

"Where are we going? You can't just take me hostage. I have my family. School. Exams start next week."

The judge's mouth fell open. "Finals. Right. I guess that slipped my mind," she said.

They looked at each other, dismayed at how crazy things had gotten.

"You say you can't run because of your family," Judge Conroy said. "That's exactly why I have to. We're going to New Hampshire. There are people there I love, who I need to protect."

As far as Madison knew, Judge Conroy had no family left. Her mother and her husband were dead, and she'd never mentioned any other relatives. She seemed to be alone in the world.

"Who are you talking about?"

The judge shook her head. "I've said too much already."

"If you don't trust me, then why am I even here?"

It was starting to snow, fat flakes drifting down and melting on the windshield. As Madison turned the wipers on, the silence lengthened.

"You asked why you're here," the judge said finally. "I didn't want to leave you behind to face Charlie. But the bigger reason is, I need your help. You and I are in very tight spots. There's a chance we could save each other, but it would require total honesty. If I tell you about—about *them*—well, I'd be putting their lives in your hands. That's hard to do when I'm not sure you've been honest about what happened in DC."

"If I told you everything, and you didn't like it, where would that leave us?"

"Maybe in a better place to make a deal? I'm not going to harm you, if that's what you're worried about. And the people who would are my sworn enemies."

Madison nodded. "I know."

"Tell me about DC. And I'll tell you about my family."

So she did have family. Madison glanced over in surprise to find the judge watching her, looking as nervous as Madison felt, and knew deep down that she could trust her.

"For me, this is about my brother. He would have been killed in prison, but the feds moved him into protective custody. In DC, they let me meet with him. I was told if I agreed to cooperate against you, they'd dismiss his case. They wanted me to wear a wire, just not yet. I sort of said yes. Now, I'm wavering. And that's the truth. Do you hate me?"

"I completely understand. I've said before, family is everything. So, in order to help your brother, you need to hand me over to them, wrapped up in a neat little bow?"

"Something like that."

"That's good news. It means you need me as much as I need you. We can work together. Okay, my turn. You know by now that I'm not a saint, Madison. I've committed crimes. I've done so knowingly, but not willingly. I was manipulated at first. Later, I was forced. And there was no way out except cooperating with the government, but I knew that if I did that, they'd kill me. So, five years ago, I tried to run. They found out. They didn't kill me, because I still had value for them. They did something much worse. They murdered Matthew. I would have turned them in then, even if it resulted in my death. Honestly, I would have been happy to die at that moment if it meant getting revenge. But I wasn't free to think only of myself. There were two people, very dear to me, who needed my protection."

The judge took a deep breath, her eyes far away.

"My mother. And my daughter."

Part Four

Kathryn

29

....

Six years earlier

Once she became a judge, and in charge of her own schedule, Kathryn took up running. At lunchtime, if the weather was good, she would jog along the Esplanade. The wind coming off the water smelled clean and pure. The rhythm of her feet against the pavement emptied her mind. For an hour, she felt free.

It was a sunny day in May, and the wind was at her back the first time she saw Matthew. The first thing she noticed was his stride—long, fast, focused, like a serious runner. *I could learn something from the way that guy moves*, she thought. Her eyes traveled up his body, which was strong and lean, to his face. Their eyes met. She blushed at being caught checking him out. He smiled at her, and he was so handsome that she smiled back.

She started looking forward to seeing him. And then thinking about him when she wasn't running. One day in midsummer, he finally stopped to say hello.

"Hey, hold up," he said, like he wanted to have a whole conversation.

She hadn't anticipated that. She should never have made eye contact, never have smiled. She shook her head like an idiot, pointed at her watch and kept running.

Kathryn didn't allow herself normal relationships. After Brad McCarthy was murdered, she broke things off with the law school classmate she was seeing. For years ever since, her only entanglement was an affair with Doug Kessler, whom she'd chosen for the simple reason that he was already compromised. Ray told her that Doug was taking money to steer the results of cases, including the Fiamma case. He was damaged goods like Kathryn, which meant she wasn't putting him at any risk he hadn't undertaken voluntarily. He was married, and she felt bad about that, but she was too lonely to care. All she knew was, if something happened to Doug, it wouldn't be her fault. The runner was different. She had to keep her distance.

The next day it rained. The day after, she ran but didn't see him, and she felt more disappointed than relieved. What if he stopped coming to the Esplanade? What if she never saw him again? It made her realize how much she wanted to.

The third day, she saw him at the same spot. She couldn't run away a second time. It would seem too weird. When they reached each other, they smiled. And both stepped off the path. People ran by them on all sides, but it was like they were alone.

"Finally, we meet. Matthew Latham."

He held out his hand, and they shook. There was a flutter in her stomach as she looked into his eyes, which were unusual and arresting. Sea-green with dark lashes, full of humor and understanding.

"Kathryn Conroy."

"It's about time we said hello. You wouldn't happen to be training for a race?"

"No, I wish. I have a demanding job, and I can only get away at lunch."

"What do you do?"

"I'm a federal judge."

He took a step back and broke into a wide smile that was like sunshine on water. His eyes crinkled. A dimple appeared in one cheek. And she felt at ease, like she'd come home after being out in the cold for a long time.

"*Wow.* You know, I had my theories about you. But federal judge was not on the list. Very impressive," he said.

She laughed. "Do I look like a lightweight or something?"

"Not at all. I just think of federal judges as old, white-haired guys who look like toads. You're much too beautiful to fit my stereotype. Very impressive."

"What do you do?"

"I just embarrassed myself. Your turn. All these weeks we've been passing each other on the Esplanade, you must've formed an opinion about me. What do you think I do?"

"Hmm, not a lawyer. I can spot those a mile away. I'm thinking finance. Or consulting. Something high-powered and well-paid."

"Sadly, I'm about as far as you can get from well-paid. I'm a teacher. Social studies and history at St. Alfred's."

"That's lovely. Though I guess you won't be springing for dinner, then."

"If I'm taking out a federal judge who's used to high rollers, you bet I will. Even if I have to eat beans for a week. Saturday night at La Voile?"

It was fall, and they'd been seeing each other for several months. They were out to dinner at their favorite restaurant. The waiter had just opened the wine. She raised her glass to clink and found Matthew gazing at her with pain in his eyes.

"What?"

He took her hands in his.

"I need to ask you something."

Her heart raced. This couldn't be a marriage proposal. It was too soon, and he looked too unhappy.

"Okay."

"Kathryn." He paused, like it was difficult to go on.

"Just say it; you're scaring me."

"You'd tell me if you were married, right?"

She took her hands away. "*Married?* Like, to someone else, and this is an affair?"

"Yes."

"You can't possibly think I've been lying this whole time."

"I don't know what to think. I've never spent the night at your place. We always go to mine. I've never met your friends or your family, though I've introduced you to mine. When I ask about them, you avoid my questions. You won't talk about past relationships. It's like there's a wall between us that I can't get through, and it's really bothering me."

"If there is, and I'm not saying I agree . . . but if there is, it's only because I want to protect you."

"Because you're a judge? That makes no sense. Judges have normal relationships. They get married and have children. They lead normal lives. Am I wrong?"

"No."

"Then I don't understand. And I don't want to be protected. I want to get closer. Know you better. Have more than just dinner and sex, though those are great. I could imagine a life together, but not like this. I don't mean to be dramatic, but it feels like you're hiding something. Being married was just the most obvious conclusion."

"I'm not married. I promise you."

"Then, what is it? Why do you push me away?"

She wanted so badly to tell him the truth. The *whole* truth. Not just that she was born to the wrong family, or that she grew up under the influence of dangerous people. But that she'd made bad choices. Accepted Uncle Ray's money to pay for her education. Broken the oath she took as a prosecutor. Watched a good man die before her eyes, in part due to her own sins. A braver woman would tell. A truly brave woman would have turned herself in by now. But she was afraid they'd do to her what they'd done to Brad. And not only to her, but to her mother. So she kept silent. After Brad, a few years had passed in which they didn't ask for much, and she almost believed she was free. But it turned out they'd been waiting and watching, as her influence grew. She never should have accepted the judgeship. Once that happened, they pounced, and she was caught like a fish on a line. After Brad, she was complicit. After Brad, they owned her, which meant that, yes, she couldn't give herself completely to Matthew.

"It's . . . because of things in my past."

"What *things*?"

If only she could tell him, what a weight off her mind it would be. He would still love her if he knew the worst. She believed that. But the information would be dangerous in his hands. He'd feel compelled to play the hero. He was innocent enough to believe you could oppose these people and survive. She knew better. Telling him would put him in danger.

She had to come up with a lie.

The most convincing lies were built on truth.

"I'm . . . *illegitimate*."

He cocked an eyebrow. "You mean, born out of wedlock?"

"Yes."

He laughed in relief. "Is that all? Wait, what year is this?"

"Please, don't make light of it."

He took her hand again, and she let him.

"No, of course, love. I'm sorry. But you must know I don't care about that. I can't believe anyone does, in this day and age."

"Thirty years ago, in my Irish Catholic neighborhood, people cared. Everyone knew that my mother was my father's mistress. I grew up ashamed. Nobody stood up for me. Nobody told me that it wasn't my fault. It made me skittish about relationships. And there's something else."

"Go on."

"When I was a prosecutor, I had an affair with my boss. Who was married. Classic, right? Repeating my mother's mistakes. I'm sure a therapist would have something to say about that. It ended a while ago, but I'm scarred by it. The guilt—it's crushing."

She shook her head, tears in her eyes. The guilt *was* crushing. It was just about different things. And now it included lying to the man she loved.

"Thank you for trusting me enough to share that. We all do bad things sometimes. It doesn't make us bad people."

"I'm not sure I agree."

"You're not bad. You learned from your mistakes. You changed. I think you're perfect in every way. And I don't want you to worry. I won't push, okay? We'll take things as slowly as you like."

As he lifted her hand to his lips, her heart filled with love. He wanted a future together. She wanted that, too. So much that she decided then and there to find a way. He was right. She'd made mistakes, but anyone would have, in her position. She didn't choose the circumstances of her birth. The pressure she was under had been unbearable. But she could change. She could learn, get better. And she would. For him.

The next time they asked her for something, she'd say no.

30

....

It was a sunny day in June, and they were in a charming room in a quaint inn on the Cape. She could hear the crash of waves on the beach below. The string quartet tuning their instruments. And Matthew's laugh as he arrived with his brother, who was to be the best man. Her mother was doing Kathryn's makeup.

"Close your eyes," Sylvia said, and the touch of the brush was like a kiss from childhood.

If she could have, Kathryn would've skipped the wedding and gone straight to the marriage. She didn't need a striped tent or a luncheon buffet with a choice of entrees or a cake trimmed with fresh flowers. All she needed was Matthew. Just the two of them at city hall with a justice of the peace and kind strangers as witnesses. Get it done before anyone could come along and destroy their happiness. But Matthew wanted a big celebration, and she loved him enough to compromise. So here they were. A beachfront wedding with fifty guests. A white lace sheath dress with a beaded bodice hanging on the closet door. A bouquet of peonies and blush roses in a box on the armchair. And Kathryn, sitting at the vanity, holding her breath, waiting for the thing that would derail them.

"Oh, you look so pretty, Kathy."

She opened her eyes. Her mother had an expert touch with makeup. Kathryn looked young and fresh and natural, a better version of herself.

"Thank you, Mom. That's lovely."

"Let me help you into your dress."

"It's just a zipper."

"I know, but I don't want you to muss it," Sylvia said.

Kathryn stepped out of her bathrobe, and Sylvia slipped the dress on over her head and zipped it.

"Beautiful," Sylvia said, her eyes bright.

As they admired her image in the mirror, someone knocked on the door. Kathryn's face changed.

"No visitors. Tell them I'm still getting dressed."

Her mother went to answer. It was Ray. She could hear his voice. Sylvia swung the door wide.

"Mom, I said no."

"It's just Ray. He has a present for you. I'll go get us more champagne," Sylvia said, slipping out the door.

Ray leaned in to kiss her cheek with a whoosh of bourbon and aftershave. He was carrying a battered leather duffel bag in one hand.

"You're a vision, kid. Your dad is looking down from heaven and smiling."

As if Fast Eddie made it to heaven. But she wasn't going to argue. Not today.

"Thanks for coming, Ray."

"Are you kidding? I wouldn't miss it for the world. Hey, you know I'd be happy to give you away, unless Charlie's doing it?"

"Charlie's not invited. Mom is standing up with me. I don't believe in the whole handoff thing anyway. But thank you."

"Suit yourself. Well, I just wanted to drop off a little wedding gift. It's not the sort of thing I can leave on the table next to the cake. Hope you don't mind, it didn't fit in an envelope."

He lifted the duffel bag onto the table and unzipped it. She stared in horror. The tightly packed bundles glowed in the light from the window, giving off the musty scent of ink. From the size of the bag, there had to be several hundred thousand dollars in there.

"A suitcase full of cash? Are you crazy? *No.* Get it out of here right now."

He was taken aback. "No need to get mad. Maybe I shouldn't've brought it to the wedding. I can put this somewhere safe. A secure account that can't be traced to you."

"That's not the point. If you want to give me a gift, I have a registry. I can't take your money."

He looked hurt. "Well, I don't know why not. You been taking it for years, and it's not like I'm slipping you something for no reason. This is a special occasion. Your wedding day. Your future. You could start looking at real estate. It's enough for a down payment on something nice. I always said I consider you like my own, Kathy."

"I feel the same way. You're the closest thing to a father I had."

"Don't say that. Eddie did what he could."

"You did more. It's not that I don't love you, Uncle Ray. I do. But I can't accept this. Since what happened with Brad—"

He put up his hand as if to ward off a blow.

"I get it. That was a terrible mistake, putting you at risk that way. Those guys were careless. You were never supposed to be there when it happened. Just so you know, I never worked with that particular syndicate again."

"Okay, but that's not the point. I appreciate everything you did for me in the past. I did things for you, too. Things I wish I hadn't.

Water under the bridge, okay? Going forward, it needs to be different. I'm a judge now. There's too much scrutiny. I can't accept your money. And I can't do any more favors."

"Aw, honey. I wish it was that easy. This isn't just about me. There's a whole network of people who invested more than dollars in you. They pulled favors, at great inconvenience to themselves, great risk. Your background check. Your promotions. Your nomination to the bench. They put their network at your disposal, their powerful friends. I mean, Charlie you know about, of course. Would he maybe let things slide, out of love for you, his little sister? It's possible, though I can't say for sure. But there are too many others involved. People you've never met, and you don't know their names for good reason. You can't just take the goodies and go home. Not with those guys."

Was Ray telling her that her hard work and talent counted for nothing? Year after year of late nights at the office, early mornings in court. The case files, the legal briefs, the witness interviews, and oral arguments—all meaningless because she had shadowy people in her corner, whom she'd never even met, and never knew about? It couldn't be.

"That can't be true. I worked hard. I had the Harvard degree. I played by the rules. I—"

"Yeah, and so did plenty of other schmucks who never got anywhere. Look, Kathy, I'm not disparaging you or saying you weren't qualified. Just, things go on behind the scenes. What happened for you was no accident. You had help. And that's the truth."

She thought about Brad McCarthy's murder. How that douchebag cop, Morelli, tried to stop her from getting in Brad's car that night. How Doug Kessler waltzed into Brad's job and dismissed the case against Fiamma, just like the mobsters wanted. Ray was telling it to her straight. Behind the scenes, there was play upon play. Her meteoric rise was not her own. It just made her want to quit. Run away and start over, a million miles from here, with Matthew and the clothes on their backs, nothing else.

"If that's true—"

"It *is* true. Cross my heart," he said.

"Then I never asked for it. And it stops now."

"*Now?* You're kidding me. Now you're a judge. You're finally in a position to pay off the debt. Now you're too valuable to let go. Do I need to remind you of the stakes? Kathy, you're implicated in the murder of a federal prosecutor, and they will use that against you."

"So turn me in."

His jaw went slack. "*What?*"

"You heard me. For all I care, you can turn me in, and I'll tell them what I knew in advance, which was nothing. And who was involved. Which was you and Charlie."

"You'd rat on your own family?"

"Matthew is my family now. He's an honorable man. I need to follow his example."

"Ah, well. I'm sorry to be the one to tell you this. But that's a problem. Not for me. For you. And most of all, for Matthew."

"What is that supposed to mean?" she said, going cold.

"You know what it means. You're too valuable to dispose of. But him . . ."

She burst into tears just as Sylvia came back with the champagne in a bucket.

"Kathy, what are you doing? Your mascara's running," she said, rushing over with a Kleenex. She turned on Ray. "Did you make my daughter cry on her wedding day? Get out of here, you bum, before I smack you."

Sylvia pushed him toward the door and slammed it behind him.

"He's gone. Let me fix your mascara, hon."

"No, get Matthew. I have to talk to him."

"He can't see you in your wedding dress. It's bad luck."

"Just do it. I have to call off the wedding."

"You're serious?"

"Yes."

"Jesus, that fucking Ray. He pushes things too far."

Sylvia left the room, muttering. A few minutes later, there was a knock on the door. Matthew came in and sat down on the bed across from her, looking like he'd been punched in the stomach.

"Your mother told me you're having second thoughts. Is that true?"

She looked into his green eyes, so full of love and pain, and almost couldn't continue. If she lost him, her life going forward would be desolate, empty, a field of ash. There was almost nothing she could think of worse than life without Matthew. *Almost* nothing. Except one thing. Knowing that he'd died because of her.

"I can't marry you, Matthew. I'm very sorry."

"Well, I don't accept that. I love you. I know you love me, too."

"I do. More than anyone or anything. More than life."

"Then, what is it? I deserve an explanation."

She took a deep breath and told him the truth. He listened intently, his face pale and serious, his eyes locked on hers, for half an hour. At the end of it, he thanked her for her honesty and told her that the circumstances didn't make a difference to him. He would never choose to live his life without her, no matter what the risk. This was a serious problem, yes. But that's what vows were for. Richer, poorer, sickness, health, till death do you part. They would face this together, and together they would overcome.

He was so pure, so persuasive, that she believed him. He took her hand, and they went downstairs to get married.

....

31

They were living in a rented house in Wellesley and going to open houses on the weekends. They loved the town, which was leafy and quaint, with cute shops and a fabulous school system, all within a reasonable commute to Boston. Between what they'd each saved over the years, and a wedding gift from Matthew's parents, they had enough for a down payment. They were looking for three bedrooms and a real backyard, for kids. They'd started trying on their honeymoon.

You could feel fall coming on, with its sparkly days and chilly nights. The first bits of color were appearing in the trees, and it got dark earlier every night. On the way home from the courthouse, she stopped to pick up a pregnancy test. Her period was late, she had a touch of nausea and a strange fatigue that made her feel heavy and slow. When she walked in the door, the smell of chicken roasting turned her stomach. Matthew had left a note on top of the mail on the island saying he'd gone out for a run. She hurried to the bathroom to do the test before he returned. If it was negative, she wouldn't tell him. They'd had a couple of false alarms. For days after the first one, he treated her like she was made of glass. After the second, he brought home a kitten with eyes as green as his own, who was adorable but proceeded to scratch up all the furniture. She didn't want to find out what happened after another.

She was in the bathroom staring at the plus sign in disbelief when he came back from his run.

"Hey, babe. Come in here," she called. "Look."

She pointed to the wand sitting out on the vanity.

"A plus sign. Does that mean it's—"

She nodded. "*Positive.*"

"Are you sure?"

"As sure as these things get. They're pretty accurate."

"It's *real*?" He put his hands on her stomach, joy blazing in his eyes.

"Are you happy?" she said.

"So happy I'm speechless. C'mere."

He kissed her hair, her eyes, her mouth.

"Let's have a toast," he said.

In the kitchen, he poured Sanpellegrino into champagne glasses. They toasted the future over the roast chicken dinner at the kitchen table. Normally, she found it impossible to appreciate life while she was living it. Her mind was always either ahead or behind. But for the space of that dinner, for once, she knew she was happy.

Afterward, sitting at the island, watching Matthew load the dishwasher, she shuffled through the day's mail. A circular from the local garden center. Something from the ABA. The cable bill. And a plain white envelope addressed in block letters to "JUDGE CONROY," with no return address.

It was heavy. There was something inside other than a letter.

"Did you see this?" she said, her voice rising.

He took it from her and held it up to the light.

"There's something in there."

"No, don't open it," she said, but he was already tearing off the end.

He spilled the contents onto the island. They rolled around, glinting in the light. Two bullets. One for her. One for him.

"What is that?" he whispered.

"It's a message. A threat."

Whoever sent that envelope could be charged with multiple crimes. Threat by mail. Threatening a government official of the United States. Obstruction of justice. They could wind up doing ten years in jail, but only if Kathryn called in the FBI. Matthew begged her to, but she was terrified.

"If I report it, they'll start digging. And they'll find things about *me*. They'll reopen the investigation into Brad McCarthy's death."

"From what you've said, you did nothing wrong."

"I passed information to my half brother, who passed it to the mob. Including where we were going for dinner the night they killed him, and the make of his car. That's enough to charge me with the murder conspiracy."

"But you didn't know."

"I knew *enough*. I knew what they were capable of. Any jury would convict me. Our baby will be born in jail. I can't bear that. Can you?"

"It doesn't have to be that way. You told me so. You said there's a way to get them not to prosecute you."

"Right. I flip. On Ray. On Charlie. Doug Kessler. *The mob*. They'll kill us both."

"Not if we ask for witness protection."

"Do you have any idea what it's like to go into hiding? The feds give us new identities and send us somewhere random. It's like living a stranger's life. You'll never see your family again. I'll never see my mother. Our child will grow up with no family. And besides, it's not foolproof. These people are relentless. They'll never stop hunting us. And they have moles everywhere. Somebody someday will leak our location, I guarantee you. And we'll spend the rest of our lives looking over our shoulders."

"Like we're not doing that already? I watch the rearview mirror when I drive. I hesitate to answer the door, and now I have to worry about opening the mail. I can't live with the constant threat of violence, and I don't want to bring our child into this situation. Do you?"

"There has to be a solution. I'll talk to Ray."

"*No*. You already tried that—on our wedding day, remember? And he told you to play ball. Which you haven't, and now we get this threat. He's no savior, Kathryn. He's the one holding you captive, and no matter what you say, he won't let go."

She rubbed her temples, struggling to think clearly. *Is he right?*

"But he's a sentimental old bastard. What if I told him I was pregnant? Maybe—"

"Jesus, are you crazy?" he said. "Absolutely not. You can't tell *anyone*, not even your mother. Once they know about the baby—"

The terror in his eyes was catching. Her heart clutched.

"Oh my God, you're right."

"I am right. You know I am."

"I can't tell them. He won't be safe."

His face crumpled as he touched her belly. "*He*. You think it's a boy?"

She nodded. "I have a feeling."

"That makes him seem so real."

"I know. A person, growing inside me. *Our* person."

"It's our job to protect him. Don't you see? For his sake, we have to get away from here. Take the down payment money and run. We'll do it ourselves, so there are no leaks, no one who can give us up."

"Yeah, there's a problem with that. Not only will we have the bad guys on our tail, we'll have the FBI."

"I agree it would be tough to pull off. We'd have to plan carefully. Identify a place to go. Find a secure way to get false documents. It could take months, and nobody can know. But we're smart and resourceful and determined. And we have the greatest motivation in the world now. We can do it. I know we can."

He took her in his arms, stroking her hair. She listened to his heartbeat and thought about a life far away. A backyard, a swing set, a little boy with Matthew's eyes. In that moment, she believed it was possible.

———

Kathryn stood in the dim light of the funeral home, her hand on Matthew's casket. It was the first time she'd seen him since identifying the body. He'd been found shot dead in the driveway of their rental house in Wellesley, not by Kathryn, but by a neighbor who'd heard shots fired and called the police. The neighbor didn't see much. Just a car speeding away. There was no description of the killer, no license plate, not even a reliable model on the car. But Kathryn knew exactly what happened. The people who pulled her strings, who sent those bullets in the mail, made good on their threat. They murdered the man she loved to send the message that there was no escape.

That was two days ago, and she hadn't slept or eaten since. The service was tomorrow. This was her last chance to be alone with him. Soon Matthew's parents would arrive. It might even become contentious. They wanted a closed casket, but Kathryn preferred to show the world how they'd murdered her beautiful love. The bullets shattered his skull so badly that no amount of sutures or putty or pancake makeup could hide the wreckage. She had to look past it, to see the familiar lines of his face, so they could talk. She told him about visiting the graveyard where he'd lie, and how she wanted to join him there as soon as possible. *The ground is hard at the moment. It smells like snow is coming. But we can handle seasons, right, babe? In spring, I bet it's pretty there. Daffodils, robins. In summer, the sun will be warm on the grass, like on the Common when we'd walk, do you remember? I want to come with you so bad. I hate that you'll be alone. It's only Ollie holding me back.*

Oliver. *Ollie.* Their son. They'd taken to calling the baby that even though it was too soon to find out the sex, picking Grace for a girl just in case. How to protect Ollie should be at the forefront of her mind right now. But all she could think of was Matthew.

Hearing footsteps, she turned, composing her expression for Matthew's mother. But it wasn't her.

"How dare you show your face," she said, spitting with rage as she advanced on Ray. "Get out of here before I fucking kill you."

She picked up an empty vase from the table where the guestbook was displayed, hefting it in her hand, ready to smash it into a cutting blade. She would slash his throat with it and laugh while he bled out.

He backed away, raising his hands defensively.

"Whoa, whoa, Kathy, this is not on me. You must know, no matter how you disappoint me, I couldn't do that to you. Or order it, or even know about it advance. They kept it from me."

"Who did? I want names."

"What good would that do?"

"It was Charlie, wasn't it? That fucking pervert. He was jealous."

"You don't know what you're saying. They wouldn't ask him, and he would never agree."

"Bullshit. *Them. They.* These shadowy people don't exist. They're ghosts you make up to cover your own ass. This conspiracy has only ever been Eddie, and you, and Charlie, and *her*. Anyone else is hired help."

"That's just not true. If it was, would I have warned you? I told you what would happen. I tried to head it off. But you wouldn't listen. Instead, you did the worst thing possible. You decided to run. You think they weren't gonna find out?"

The vase slid from her hand, bouncing on the rug.

"*No.*"

"Yes. The guy you went to, to get your passports done? He narced on you."

She sat down on the nearest chair and started to cry, struggling to get words out.

"How . . . do you know that . . . if you're not involved?"

"They told me afterwards. When I heard what happened to Matthew, well, to put it mildly, I was not happy. So they explained to me why they felt that step was necessary. That doesn't mean I was on board with it, even if I could see where they were coming from. I wasn't, and I definitely didn't know in advance. Swear to God."

"I don't believe you, Ray."

He shook his head sadly. "That hurts my feelings, Kathy."

"Please, just go. Leave me alone."

"I can't do that. Look, I know you're angry. It's natural. But we're at a dangerous moment, and there are things you should know for your own safety. The feds are circling the case to see if someone killed Matthew to retaliate against you. An attack on a judge is a federal case, and if they grab jurisdiction, we're screwed. Not just me. You too. And Charlie. Doug Kessler. A few other people who look to me for protection. We have to head it off. If the feds interview you, I need to know I can count on you."

"Count on me how?"

"Steer them to thinking this was a personal dispute. Someone with a grudge against Matthew, that type of thing. If we can get jurisdiction locally, then Charlie takes the lead on the investigation, and it all goes away."

She stared at him in shock. That anybody would be so callously pragmatic about her husband's murder was terrible to her. But the man whom she'd thought of as a father? She put her hand to her mouth and swallowed to beat back the bile that was rising. If Ray saw her throw up, he might start to wonder.

"This isn't just business, you know. I'm thinking of how to keep you safe. Are we on the same page?" Ray said.

Collecting herself, she took her phone from her jacket pocket.

"Leave now, or I'm calling the feds," she said, her voice shaking.

"Kathy, listen to me. There's no way out. If you disappear, they'll never stop looking. And when they find you, they won't play nice."

"By *they*, you mean you."

He sighed. "I don't know how to get through to you. If this was just me, we'd be having a very different conversation. If you won't listen, the next funeral will be yours. I couldn't stand that. And neither could your poor mother."

"Get out. And never contact me again."

....

32

The day had been raw and ugly, with a mix of rain and snow. As the cab pulled up to the apartment building that night, it started to sleet, ice crystals pinging on the windshield. Kathryn reached into her wallet for some bills. Her gaze wandered as the driver counted the money.

Someone was standing in the shadows near the front door to the building.

"What's that person doing, standing there in this weather?" she said, her throat going dry.

The driver ignored her.

"Excuse me, driver? Go around the block."

"Fine, but I have to drop the meter again."

The sleet was blowing sideways in the wind. The shadow moved into the halo of the streetlamp.

It was Sylvia.

"Never mind," she said.

The wind hit her full force as she got out and hurried up the path to the front door. She took out her key, ignoring her mother hovering beside her.

"Kathy, please," Sylvia said, her voice quavering. "I've been out in the freezing cold for half an hour waiting for you to come home."

"You know I won't talk to you. Go away and leave me alone."

"Five minutes. That's all I ask, so I can understand why you cut me from your life."

A savage gust of wind hit, and her mother shriveled into her coat, her eyes watering from the cold.

"I shouldn't've let that cab go. You can wait inside while you call another," Kathryn said.

Her mother followed her into the vestibule, carrying a shopping bag. Out of the wind, it was quiet and overheated, smelling of dust. Once upon a time, the building had been fashionable, but it had fallen on hard times. There was a row of dented metal mailboxes. Kathryn didn't receive mail there, though that precaution was mostly for show. She figured they could find her easily enough simply by following her from the courthouse. The idea was to lull them into a false sense of security. As long as she didn't run, they would have no reason to hurt her. Which meant they wouldn't hurt the baby. They knew where she lived. At regular intervals, she felt that prickling on the back of her neck that meant someone was watching.

Which made her wonder—

"How did you find me?" she asked, eyes narrowing.

"Oh, no. I haven't spoken to Ray since Matthew died, if that's what you're suggesting. I quit the day after the funeral, didn't even give notice. I'm temping, living on a pittance so I can respect your wishes and have no contact with that man. I know you're hurting, Kathy. But I can't understand you taking this out on me."

Tears rolled down Sylvia's papery cheeks.

"Answer my question. How did you find me? And I want the truth."

"It was that girl in your chambers. The case manager, Allison. She took pity on an old lady because it's Christmas. I'm begging you, don't fire her over it. Can I come in? Please? I brought you something. A gift. Some food."

She lifted the shopping bag. A wrapped present was visible inside. Kathryn was about to say no when a wave of dizziness hit, so powerful that she had to grab the wall for support. The room was spinning. She broke into a sweat.

"Are you okay? Here, let me help," Sylvia said, sliding her arm around Kathryn's waist.

Her mother's voice, the scent of her perfume, and the peppermint Life Savers she chewed were all so familiar. Suddenly, she was glad for her presence. She handed her the keys, and together they lurched up the stairs to the second floor.

Kathryn was living temporarily in a one-bedroom apartment at the end of a long hallway. After Matthew's death, she couldn't bring herself to go back inside that house in Wellesley where they'd been so happy. Besides, it looked better to move somewhere anonymous. It played into their expectations for how a hysterical woman should behave. Hide, but poorly, in plain sight. Make them think she'd broken off contact but wasn't planning to run. There was just one flaw in her plan. She was starting to show. She had to get away before they found out about Ollie. But she hadn't figured out how to do that, not with them watching her.

Sylvia let them into the apartment. Inside, harsh lighting bounced off bare white walls, hurting her eyes. She collapsed onto the hard sofa.

"Let me help you off with your coat," Sylvia said.

Kathryn was sweating, but she drew back. She barely showed, but Sylvia would notice the difference right away. *That* was why she'd cut her mother from her life. She didn't trust her not to let her secret slip to Ray.

Lucy came sauntering out from the bedroom. She stopped, contemplating Sylvia.

"Oh, is that the kitty Matthew got you? She's so big now."

She took a step toward Lucy, who bounded back to the bedroom.

"I remember she was skittish with strangers. Or else she just doesn't like me," Sylvia said, laughing nervously.

There was an awkward silence.

"You want something to eat? I brought your favorite. Look."

Sylvia took a Tupperware container from the shopping bag and peeled off the lid. She'd never been much of a cook. The corned beef and cabbage glistened with congealed fat and gave off a meaty smell. Kathryn clapped her hand over her mouth and ran to the bathroom, where she spent the next five minutes heaving into the toilet. When she came out, the corned beef had been whisked away. Sylvia had her coat off and a kettle on the stove.

"Lie down, babe. I'll bring you some tea and saltines."

"I'm better now, thank you. You can go."

Kathryn stood her ground, watching the expressions play across her mother's face. Regret, longing, pleading. Sylvia's eyes welled with tears.

"I know you don't trust me. You think I'm a bad mother for bringing Ray into your life. But I had to keep us afloat somehow. That man pursued me for years. I couldn't bring myself to marry him, so I took a job in his office. To put a roof over our heads and food on the table. I did it for you."

"You put me in his debt forever."

"You mean the money for your schooling? What else could we have done? I wanted you to have an education, something I never had and could never give you. Look, I made mistakes, but they were done out of love."

Kathryn's face had turned to stone. "You're rewriting history. What about the Wallaces?"

"You mean that little shit Charlie and his bitch of a mother? What about them? If they were dying in the street, I'd spit on the ground and walk past."

Kathryn looked away. "You left me with them for months."

"You mean when I was *dying*? My God, I had no choice. And I didn't leave you with them. I left you with Ray. Turns out he was a selfish prick who couldn't be bothered with a kid. I was so out of it, I didn't even know he gave you to Eddie until weeks later. And if it's Eddie you're upset about, well, I admit I fucked up royally there. In my defense, I was too young to know better."

"Oh, come on. You stayed with him for years. You'd still be with him today if they hadn't shot him in the head. Just like they did to Matthew."

"I understand you feel I raised you in a bad environment, and that makes it my fault, what happened to Matthew. Maybe I should've sat you down when you were younger and explained a few things, but the truth was so ugly. I'll tell it to you now, though. If you'll listen."

Kathryn said nothing, but she kept her eyes on her mother. She had to admit, she was curious. After a moment, Sylvia plunged ahead.

"You see, Eddie was my mother's cousin. He started messing with me when I was sixteen and he was thirty-five. I admit, he didn't force me. He gave me alcohol, he gave me money and gifts. And he was a handsome man. But I was underage, with no guidance. Nowadays, he'd get arrested. Back then, everybody looked the other way. And when I got pregnant with you, they blamed me, not him. My own parents blamed me. So, if you're blaming me, too, Kathy, I don't know what to say. I wish I could've given you a squeaky-clean life full of honest people. But that's never who was around me."

The kettle started to whistle, and Sylvia got up to make the tea. While she puttered in the kitchen, Kathryn thought over what she'd said. About to become a mother herself, she saw things in a new light. Ollie would be born into cataclysm. His father murdered, his mother implicated in crimes, his own safety at risk. It was a million miles from what she wanted for her child. But it was beyond her control. Couldn't the same be said for Sylvia, and Kathryn's upbringing?

She'd been unfair to her mother. Though, that didn't answer the question of whether to trust her now. Deep down, she knew Sylvia was telling the truth. If it were only her own life at stake, she'd bet on her loyalty. But with the baby to think of, the stakes were higher. She couldn't afford to be wrong.

The wind rattled the windows. Sylvia carried a tray with two cups of tea and a sleeve of saltines over to the sofa.

"Take off your coat, honey. You're sweating."

Without help, she had no chance of saving her child. Or herself. It was a leap of faith, but one she ought to take.

Kathryn shrugged out of her coat and handed it to her mother. Underneath, she wore a shapeless black dress, with a silk scarf at her neck to draw the eye. Since Matthew died, she couldn't eat. In her fourth month of pregnancy, she'd gained only three pounds. But her waist had thickened in a noticeable way that Sylvia didn't miss. Her eyes went wide.

"*Kathy.* You're pregnant. Oh my God, no wonder you threw up like that. I'm so happy. How far along are you?"

"Four months."

Her eyes glittered with tears of joy. "Thank you for sharing this with me. It's wonderful news. What a special Christmas present."

"It's not wonderful. You can't tell *anyone*. Do you understand? If they find out this baby exists, he won't be safe."

Sylvia wiped away tears, her expression sobering.

"Cross my heart, I won't tell a soul. Does anyone else know?"

"Nobody. I'm hardly showing. I don't go anywhere except work, and there, I wear my judge's robes and sit behind the bench. It's winter, so I hide under bulky sweaters. And my OB is in the same medical building as my shrink, so I say I'm going there when I leave for the appointments. Everyone believes that I'm depressed enough to go to the shrink constantly, so that works."

"Okay, but how much longer? You won't be able to hide it forever."

"I don't need to hide it *forever*. Just long enough to get away from here."

Sylvia looked scared now. "Honey, how you gonna run with a baby? I say this as someone who was all alone and had nothing when her child was born. It's a nightmare even if nobody's after you. And these people will not let you go without a fight."

"I understand that. Ray made it clear there's no way out. That if I run, they'll never stop looking for me. I have to figure some way around it."

"Like what?"

"I don't know. Every day, I wake up terrified about what happens next and no closer to a solution."

Sylvia sighed, and tucked Kathryn's hair behind her ears. They sat for a moment, listening to the hiss of the radiator and the scratching of sleet against the windows. Kathryn picked up her teacup.

"Blow on it first, it's hot," Sylvia said.

Despite the horror of her situation, her mother's presence made her feel better. A small kernel of hope began to glow in her heart.

"What if—" Sylvia said, and stopped.

"What if what?"

"What if it's not you who runs? But me?"

"I don't understand."

"*You're* their investment, Kathy. They care about keeping *you* on the hook to do them favors. They don't care about me. What if I take the baby somewhere? You stay behind like nothing happened. Do their bidding, bide your time. And visit in secret while we figure out a better plan."

"Well, first off, they'd find out about the baby anyway, because there's the rest of the pregnancy and then the birth, which I won't be able to hide. Second, they'd notice that you're gone. Charlie? Ray? They'd put two and two together and figure out you ran with the baby. They'd come looking for you. The baby would still be in danger, but now so would you."

"Not if they never know about the baby, and they think I'm dead."

"I don't understand. How?"

"Women hide pregnancies, and people fake cancer. They do it all the time, as a grift. In my case, it would be easy, because I was sick before. They'd believe it for sure. Say I lose a few pounds. Put on a turban like I lost my hair. We take a picture for the Facebook with an IV in my arm, tubes in my nose, a little contour on my cheeks so I'm gaunt. You take a leave of absence from work to care for me. Say you're bringing me somewhere for treatment. Then disappear till after the baby comes. Nobody will suspect. Your husband just got killed, and now your mother's dying? Who's gonna begrudge you, or think to check your story?"

"Wow. That could actually work."

"It will work. I'm a good actress when I want to be."

"You'd do that for me?"

"For you. And for my grandchild."

"His name is Ollie."

"No," Sylvia said, eyeing Kathryn's waistline. "You're carrying thick in the middle like I did with you. That's a girl in there, for sure."

33

....

Kathryn had thought it would take an effort to cry at Sylvia's memorial service, since her mother wasn't actually dead. But she broke down repeatedly. She'd given birth just two weeks earlier. The bleeding had stopped, but her breasts were still engorged, and her hormones haywire. She longed for that red-faced, scrunchy little baby with a physical craving. *Grace.* Her downy head, her perfect fingers and toes and ears. She understood that they couldn't be together. But the separation hurt worse than anything she'd ever felt. When Matthew died, he was gone forever. It was final. There was nothing to do but accept, and plot revenge. Grace was still here on this earth. She could be touched and held and kissed and cuddled. Just not by Kathryn. Ten minutes after being discharged from the anonymous Midwestern hospital where she'd given birth, she'd waved goodbye under cover of darkness. Her stitches hurt. There was a heavy pad between her legs. But it was her heart that felt like it would explode. If there had been any other way . . . but there wasn't. Sylvia's death certificate was ready. It was time to call Ray, notify him of her passing, and announce Kathryn's imminent return, along with the date of the memorial service.

And that's what she did, because she'd learned the hard way that delay could be deadly.

That night, she watched the people she loved most in the world drive off in a used Volvo, registered in Sylvia's new name of Marie Allen. The Volvo had an infant seat in the back and a portable crib and stroller in the trunk. Also, two cases of formula, three boxes of newborn Huggies, and piles of tiny clothes. Onesies, footie pajamas, little hats and booties and blankies and a shopping bag full of stuffed animals. Things that Kathryn had lovingly collected during the months of Sylvia's fake illness to gift to her daughter. Things that would touch her velvet skin when Kathryn couldn't, comfort her in the night when her mother wasn't there. Though, if she was honest with herself, Grace wouldn't miss her. How could you miss someone you didn't know?

The Volvo's navigation system was programmed with the address of a small house on a lake in remote northern New Hampshire, purchased with the down payment money intended for her family home with Matthew. She'd drained the account to pay for the house in cash, because monthly mortgage payments could be traced. Sylvia complained about the destination. Why pick a place with such brutal winters? Why not Arizona, or better yet, Miami Beach? There was a reason. The house backed onto woods full of hiking trails, less than a mile from the Canadian border. You could step out the back door, walk for fifteen minutes, and cross into Canada without being seen. Besides, it was close enough for Kathryn to visit, if she ever decided that was safe to do. And it was only for a while. They'd live there until she could join them permanently, which hopefully wouldn't be long.

But first, she had to put the logistics in place for the three of them to disappear without a trace. She'd taken some important steps already. She'd bought a gun, unregistered and untraceable, which she'd keep hidden until it was needed. There was a death certificate in Sylvia's name, obtained by bribing a county employee. Once it was filed, Sylvia would cease to exist, legally speaking. They'd paid top dollar for new identification, not just for Sylvia, but for Kathryn too, in the names of Marie and Jenna Allen, a mother and daughter who'd died in a car crash in Tennessee years before. Rather than going through crooks in Boston who might rat her out, she bought the Allens' identities on the Dark Web, using an alias. It cost many times more, but the peace of mind was worth it. Using the name Jenna Allen at the hospital, Kathryn obtained a birth certificate for Grace in the name of Allen, too. But as anyone living in the shadows knows, even the most professional-looking false documents will only get you so far. It's hard to build a life around them if you want to work, go to school, get a line of credit or a mortgage. The risk of being caught was too great, at least in the States. She would be better off retiring to a foreign country. But for that, she'd need money. Lots of money, enough for the three of them to survive on indefinitely. And since she'd just drained her bank account, that would take time to accumulate, more time than she wanted to spend. So she decided to steal it. The people who'd been profiting off her for decades were loaded. She would take their money and leave them broken and destroyed. She didn't know how yet, but that was her vow as she returned to Boston on a warm spring day, with a marble urn in her roller bag that supposedly contained her mother's ashes.

———

Step one in her plan for revenge: lull them into a false sense of security.

There was no coffin at Sylvia's memorial service. Just the urn displayed on a stand next to a photograph draped with black ribbon. The photo showed Sylvia on the Cape thirty years before, looking glamorous in sunglasses and a white dress. The lavish arrangement of white lilies in front of the photo complemented her outfit. Kathryn snapped a picture on her phone. Her mother was going to love this.

"Damn, she was a looker," Ray said from behind her.

Her skin crawled at the sight of him, which reminded her not to overplay her hand. The last time they met was at Matthew's funeral. That ugly confrontation was burned into her brain. It would be burned into his, too. He was the first to arrive. They were alone for the moment. But welcoming him with open arms wouldn't seem natural.

"You weren't invited," she said coldly.

"Kathy. Please, let me say goodbye. Your mother was the love of my life."

"You should have thought of that before you murdered her son-in-law."

He put his hand over his heart like he'd been struck.

"If it was up to me, that would never have happened. I tried to protect you. It was just impossible. I know you'll never forgive me, but please, for Sylvia's sake, let me mourn her. I would have been with her at the end if you had let me. Held her hand while she left this earth. Sung to her. You know she loved my singing voice?"

That voice was shaky now, his eyes red and wet. She had a hard time believing anything Ray said or did, but she had to admit, his tears seemed real. He was an old man, and not in the best of health. She had an image of him dropping dead on the floor in front of her. How satisfying that would be. But it wouldn't serve her purpose.

"You can stay," she said grudgingly. "I agree Mom would have wanted that, and today is her day."

He grabbed her hands and kissed them.

"Thank you. I'm very grateful. I pray that someday our differences will be like water under the bridge. You know I think of you like—"

A daughter? It made her want to vomit.

"Enough," she said, and took her hands away.

She let him stand beside her as the room began to fill. The crowd was bigger than she'd expected. Ray made introductions because Kathryn didn't know most of them. People from the office, the old neighborhood. She was taking mental notes for Sylvia, who'd want an accounting of who showed up for her funeral. Some of them objected to the choice of cremation. She wanted to say, *Mind your business.* Better to placate them than get them focused on what was in the urn—which was nothing.

"It's what she wanted. She was vain of her appearance. And she wasted away at the end, lost her hair and everything. She preferred cremation."

"It denies the resurrection of the soul. She was a sinner to begin with," one woman said.

Kathy was ready to punch her. Ray smoothed things over, and she let him so he'd think that he was back in her good graces.

A Unitarian minister conducted the service, reading from the eulogy that Kathryn had prepared, extolling Sylvia's independence and sense of humor—qualities that this audience probably disliked in her mother. Ray sang "Danny Boy," which he claimed was one of Sylvia's favorite songs. That was news to Kathryn, but she had to admit, he did have a beautiful voice. There wasn't a dry eye in the house, including hers. When the minister thanked them for attending and asked them to sign the guestbook on the way out, they realized there would be no wake. No food. No booze. The grumbling was audible. What a group. She'd be glad to see the backs of them.

Ray remained as the crowd filed out.

"I was thinking we should go to lunch," he said, taking her arm. "The Oyster House? Sylvia loved that place."

"I'm sorry, I'm really not up for it."

"I understand, but we've got business to discuss."

She stepped back like she'd been burned. "What business?"

Lowering his voice, he drew her aside.

"Kathy, while Sylvia was ill, we gave you your space. But now it's time to get back to work. I wish we could trust that you'd let bygones be bygones. Unfortunately, I don't think that's realistic. So, we need to put a few measures in place to keep you on track. Now, it won't be all bad. There's perks that come along with it for sure. For one thing, you won't have to keep living in that dump near the courthouse. We have a new place for you. A beautiful town house in the Back Bay."

"No, thank you, I'm fine where I am."

He thrust out his chin. "This is not a request you can refuse. A lot of thought and work and money has gone into this, to keep you safe."

"Safe? *Please*. You want to keep me where you can watch me. Let me guess, this place has a state-of-the-art security system, with cameras, microphones, everything you need to monitor my every move. Am I right?"

"Be reasonable. The trust has been shaken. I believe it can be rebuilt, but it's only natural that you'd be under enhanced scrutiny for a while."

"So you built me a prison."

"It's no prison. This house is beautiful and befitting of your station. It'll be a wonderful place to entertain when the time comes."

"*Entertain?* You can't be serious." She laughed bitterly.

"I'm talking about eventually, after you mourn your mother's loss. Once trust is reestablished, and you're back in the swing of things, it'll be time to think about pursuing higher office.

Governor, senator, Supreme Court justice. With your qualifi-cations, your looks, the sky's the limit. What I'm saying is, this darkness will pass, Kathy. There are things to look forward to. You can still have the future that I always envisioned for you."

That *he* envisioned. She knew what Ray's vision of her future looked like. Money and position in exchange for a life of captiv-ity, of complicity, of people around her dying because she allowed herself to be compromised. Never. She'd tried to keep her mouth shut and play along, but the provocation was too great. The words came tumbling out before she could stop them.

"That will never happen. I will *never* work for you again."

He sighed. "That negative attitude just won't fly anymore. There's no option of refusing to cooperate. You'll live in the house. You'll go back to work. And you'll do what you're asked. Measures will be put in place to make sure of that."

She'd been vaguely aware of two people lingering in the back row after the other guests departed. Now, from the corner of her eye, she saw them rise and come toward her.

Charlie. And his mother.

She looked at Ray in dawning horror.

"No. Please, Ray."

"Kathy, I'm getting old. It's time that I step back. Besides, it hasn't really worked out, has it, you and me? The view is, you need a firmer hand. That I was too indulgent."

"But Mrs. Wallace? You can't mean that. I hate her. She hates me. It just won't work, and that's bad for *you*. Besides, she's a com-plete outsider. She won't know what to do. She'll mess up. She—"

"She's no outsider. She's always been behind the scenes, keeping the books, mapping strategy. We kept that from you because we knew you'd object. Well, courtesies like that are no longer being extended. There's a new game plan. You're going to let your cur-rent case manager go and hire her as a replacement."

She grasped for any excuse to refuse.

"But people will know she's Charlie's mother, Eddie's wife. They have the same last name. It's too dangerous."

"We thought of that. She'll use her maiden name. *Nancy Duffy*. Now, stop complaining. It's time to bury the hatchet. I want you to shake hands."

They were upon her. She'd seen Charlie not long before Matthew died. But with Mrs. Wallace it had been decades. She was surprised to see that the years hadn't changed her much. She was still small and neat, with boring clothes and a put-upon expression. The only difference was that her dishwater hair had gone gray, which suited her. She was born old.

"I'm sorry for your loss, Kathy," Charlie said, holding out his hand.

She stared at it in disgust for a long moment. Then, under Ray's watchful eye, she shook it.

Mrs. Wallace didn't bother offering condolences, which was just as well. If she pretended to be sorry for Sylvia's loss, Kathryn would have to pretend to believe her. And she couldn't've managed that.

"I look forward to working with you," Nancy said instead, with a glint of triumph in her mean, colorless eyes.

34

....

The day before the Pro Bono League reception

The call Kathryn had been dreading came at the worst possible moment—during the weekly docket review meeting with
Nancy and the law clerks. Kathryn was behind her desk when
the intercom buzzed. Nancy got up from the guest chair and
came around to answer it so fast that Kathryn had to bat her
hand away.

"I've got it, thanks. Take a seat," she said, putting the receiver
to her ear.

"Judge, a call from a Mrs. Katz at the doctor's office," Kelsey
said.

"Put her through. Thanks."

She covered the receiver with her hand. "If you'll excuse me, I
have to take this."

"Who is it?" Nancy asked, frowning.

"It's a private medical matter. Please step out. I'll let you know
when I'm done."

Nancy couldn't very well protest in front of the law clerks. But she shot a livid glance over her shoulder as they left, letting Kathryn know that she would pay for this later.

"Hello?"

"Yes, um—this is Dr. Katz's office calling."

Her heart plummeted. She'd been expecting her mother's voice. "Katz"—because of Lucy the cat—was the code name they used for communications that might be intercepted, rather than risking blowing the cover on their new names, Marie and Jenna Allen. But it wasn't Sylvia on the other end of the line, which meant something terrible had happened.

Kelsey was probably listening in.

"Is there a number where I can call you back?"

"I was told you should call the ER?" the woman said, doubt in her voice.

"The ER" meant the burner phone that Sylvia kept for extreme emergencies.

"Thank you. I'll call back at the ER within five minutes."

There were precautions she needed to take in order to speak safely. She locked the front and rear doors of her private office, wedging chairs beneath the doorknobs for extra security since, after all, Nancy had the keys. Reaching into her credenza, she pressed on a panel and released a false bottom, pulling out a burner phone of her own. In her private bathroom, she turned on the tap full force to defeat any bugs they might've planted. Then she dialed the burner.

"Hello?"

"Dr. Katz?"

"Uh, yeah, I guess."

"We can speak freely now. Who am I talking to?"

"I'm Denise Lamb, Marie Allen's neighbor. Is this her daughter Jenna?"

"Yes. I'm sorry for all the hoops you had to jump through."

"It's okay. She explained about your abusive ex, and I know how that goes. I get being careful."

"Thank you for understanding."

"Listen, I'm calling with bad news. Marie went into the hospital, and it's serious. She left Grace with me. I mean, what a sweet little girl, but I really can't keep her for more than a night or two."

"Yes, of course. I'll come get her. Did they say—?" She drew a ragged breath. "Did they say anything about my mother's condition? How long?"

"They wouldn't talk to me because I'm not family. But I don't think she has long."

Kathryn pressed her hands to her eyes, fighting the tears.

"I have to take care of a couple of things. I'll try to get there by tonight. Tomorrow at the latest. I'll keep you posted."

"Okay."

"And Denise. *Thank you.*"

"I'm happy to help. She's a pistol, your mom."

"That she is," Kathryn said, her chin trembling.

She hung up, trying to hold herself together. There was no choice. She'd leave tonight, for good, which meant she had to put her hands on the money. *Now.*

Since the day of Sylvia's memorial service, Kathryn had been working on funding her escape. Every week, she siphoned money from her official salary and from the household account they allowed her. But she had to keep the diversion of funds small enough that they wouldn't notice. And only some of it had gone to the secure offshore account in the name of Jenna Allen that could be accessed from anywhere. The rest went to Marie Allen and her granddaughter Grace in their New Hampshire hideout. The balance in the Jenna account was only about eighty thousand.

Once they got where they were going, she'd never be able to work again.

It wouldn't be enough.

The real haul was stashed in the bank account of Gloucester LLC, the entity that Ray had set up to launder their profits. The Gloucester account books were kept in a file cabinet in Nancy's office, mixed in with court documents. After discovering them three years ago, she made contact with an insider at the bank and started paying for information, keeping tabs on the profit they were making off the ruins of Kathryn's life. Seventeen million at last count. Eye-watering. Hers by right, and she planned to take it. But information was one thing, embezzlement another. The insider was a woman with a family, nervous, risk averse. Kathryn had in mind offering her half the proceeds to transfer the funds to her own offshore account. Would she do it? Maybe, maybe not, and even asking would be a huge risk.

A risk she would now be forced to take.

She texted the woman at the number they used, entering a code that included the number of the burner phone for a return call. Then she waited.

Over the sound of running water, she heard pounding on her office door.

"Judge, are you okay in there? We're worried. Answer me, or I'll call security!" Nancy shouted in that fake sweet voice that made Kathryn's skin crawl. Fuck that woman to hell and back.

The burner phone rang.

"Jenna?"

"Hi, Andrea. Thanks for getting back to me so fast."

"Yeah, I figured you'd be calling."

Her stomach clenched. "Why?"

"Well, since they moved the money."

"*What?*"

"You didn't know?" Andrea said.

No, that's why I pay you, idiot. But who was the idiot? Kathryn should have anticipated that they'd do this. Not because of Sylvia, who they assumed was dead and buried. Because the feds were breathing down their necks.

"Where did they move it to?" she said.

"An account in the Caymans. Whether it's still there, or got moved again, which would be a standard protocol, I have no visibility into."

"Give me the information on that Caymans account, please."

Kathryn jotted it on a Kleenex and hung up. She knew what kind of bank that was. She used one herself. It would be hardened against law enforcement, resistant to subpoenas, suspicious of anyone who called asking questions. She wouldn't get anywhere with them. And if magically she could, it would take months or years. Not overnight. The eighty grand she had, plus whatever she could sell that wasn't nailed down—jewelry, a few paintings, the SUV—wouldn't get her far. It was plane fare, then rent and food for a year, two at best, even in a cheap country. The Gloucester money was gone, and with it, her escape plan.

She couldn't afford to disappear to a foreign country, it was that simple. But she couldn't stay here either.

That left WITSEC—the federal witness protection program. She didn't trust them, and that was the least of the problems. The feds didn't just set you up with a false identity because you asked nicely. Qualifying for WITSEC was a long, complicated process. She'd have to turn herself in to Brooke Lee, face charges, plead guilty. They'd want her to testify. If something went wrong with the testimony, that guilty plea would be hanging over her head, meaning they could lock her up, and she'd have no recourse.

Grace would be sent to foster care. Or worse, somehow Nancy would get her claws on her.

There had to be another way. But if there was, she couldn't think of it.

Someone was knocking on the bathroom door. Kathryn crumpled the Kleenex and flushed it down the toilet.

"Uh, Judge Conroy, ma'am? Curtis from the marshals. Everything okay in there?"

He sounded embarrassed, as he should.

"I'm having stomach troubles, deputy. I don't know what's wrong with Nancy, the way she overreacts."

"Yes, ma'am. The, uh—the chair blocking the door—there isn't any threat I should be aware of?"

"The threat is Nancy. She won't leave me in peace to use the bathroom."

He chuckled. "Got it. Sorry to disturb you."

"Close the office door on your way out. And tell her to stay away until I call her."

"Will do, ma'am. Feel better."

Five minutes later, they resumed the docket meeting. The atmosphere was thick with subtext. Nancy eyed her suspiciously. The law clerks seemed nervous. Kathryn was distracted, plotting her escape route in her mind. If she wanted to leave tonight, there were arrangements to make. She needed the gun, her documents, a way to obscure her identity. She should leave as soon as possible, not wait until she got home hours from now. But if she walked out of chambers midafternoon, they'd notice. They'd start looking for her, and the first place they'd go was the town house. It wouldn't work. She needed to put events in motion now. Madison could get the items she needed. Put everything in the car. But that wouldn't work, either. Charlie knew about Madison. And he'd be looking for Kathryn's car. She'd have to figure out an alternate stand-in, other transportation. She needed to slip out the judge's exit and be gone before Nancy realized.

But when the meeting broke up, they were waiting for her. Nancy ushered the law clerks out, turning to Kathryn with a smug look in her eye.

"There's been an addition to your schedule, Judge. The detective and defense attorney on the Peña case would like a word."

"I'm afraid that's not convenient."

"Oh, but they're already here. It won't take much time," she said, waving them in, closing the door behind them.

Ray and Charlie took seats in the guest chairs just vacated by her law clerks.

"Before we get down to business, I need to know—who's this Mrs. Katz who called you from a blocked number?" Charlie said.

A blocked number. Thank God.

"It's a private medical matter."

"I'm not aware of any medical issues you have, Kathy."

"You're not. And I plan to keep it that way."

"We wouldn't be concerned," Ray said in a conciliatory tone, "if not for the federal investigation. Be reasonable, honey. Give us some details to put our minds at rest."

She crossed her arms and clenched her jaw.

"If you insist. Mrs. Katz is the receptionist in my gynecologist's office. I'm having unusually heavy periods. It might be fibroids. It might be uterine cancer. It might just be menopause. They need to do an ultrasound. She was calling to schedule that. Satisfied?"

"Uterine cancer," Ray said, looking genuinely upset. "You don't think—"

"I don't know."

He put up his hands. "That's good enough for me. You do what you need to do to take care of yourself."

"I want to know why she called from a blocked number," Charlie said.

"You'd have to ask her that."

"Fine. Give me her digits."

"You're seriously asking for the phone number of my gynecologist's office? Don't you know already? You follow me everywhere."

"C'mon, we're family here, Charlie. The kid came clean with us about the feds. Stop busting her chops."

"She came clean because I caught her in a lie, Ray."

"So you asked about the call, and she gave a reasonable explanation having to do with—uh, lady's business. I know Kathy. She wouldn't make that up if it wasn't true. Now, let's move on to the matter at hand, okay? *Douglas Kessler.*"

"What about Doug?" Kathryn said.

"He's a fucking snitch, that's what," Charlie said.

"You know that for a fact?"

"We *think* he's working for them, but we need proof," Ray said, "which is where you come in. Tomorrow night is the Pro Bono League reception. The likes of me don't get invited to a thing like that. But you do. And so does Kessler. We want you to approach him there and set a trap."

"How?"

"Get him alone in a corner and bring up Greco. Explain that Lee and Martin hauled you down to DC for an interview, you're very worried, yada yada, does he know anything. In other words, smoke him out. Charlie's got a guy inside the phone company who'll be monitoring Kessler's phone in real time. If we're right, he'll turn around and rat you out to Brooke Lee, and we'll see it happen. Then we'll know for sure what we're dealing with."

"Are you crazy? They're already investigating me, and you want me to approach Doug, who you believe is cooperating with them, and act like a mobster threatening a witness? You'll get me arrested."

"No. See, Charlie's guy can stop the call from going through. She'll never hear from him, so she won't find out what you said."

"Okay, say Charlie's guy *does* manage to stop the call. Wouldn't Doug just call her later from another phone?"

Ray shrugged. Charlie raised an eyebrow. And she knew.

They were planning to kill him.

"Oh, no. *No.* I won't be part of that."

"It's not a request," Charlie said. "We need you to do this for us. You're going to do it. And I'm going to make sure of that. We'll get out of your hair now so you can do your work. But know this, Kathy. When you look over your shoulder in the dark tonight, I'll be there, looking right back at you. Whether you see me or not."

35

As Kathryn pulled out of the courthouse garage that night, she saw Charlie's headlights in the rearview mirror. When she parked in the alley behind the town house, he took up position nearby. Inside, she went to the front window and peeked out from behind the drawn blinds. There was a red glow in the darkened window of a car parked across the street. Someone was in there, dragging on a cigarette. Charlie had her surrounded. He wasn't hiding. He wanted her to know they were there, to scare her. It was working. There was no route out where they wouldn't see her leave. As frantic as she was to get north to Sylvia and Grace, she'd be leading him right to them.

For a while now, she'd had in mind a Hail Mary pass, involving the intern, the plaid trench coat, and a decently convincing red wig that she'd acquired during a stop at a wig store in DC. Madison wasn't here now. With exams coming up, she was probably on campus. When she returned to the town house, Kathryn could try to persuade her to switch clothing and drive off in the SUV to divert their attention. But the more she thought about it, the more she realized it wouldn't work. Madison would never agree.

And even if she did, they'd stop the car before it left the block and discover the hoax.

She drew a bath and cried in it, the hopelessness crushing so hard that she thought about opening a vein. But then Lucy came in and settled on the bathmat, licking her paws and staring with those green eyes that reminded her so much of Matthew's. She owed it to him not to give up. Their child's life depended on it. She texted Denise—Sylvia's neighbor—that she couldn't make it that night but would come by tomorrow night at the latest to collect Grace. How she would accomplish that, she had no idea. She'd think of something in the morning.

She woke up the next morning with the answer fully formed in her mind. They insisted she attend the Pro Bono League reception to do their dirty work? She'd go and turn the tables. Everything she needed to do could be accomplished at the event tonight. Warning Doug that they planned to whack him. Making contact with the feds to get resources for her new life. And slipping away into the night to hold her dying mother's hand and reclaim her lost daughter. Charlie might have spies circulating, but he didn't rate an invitation for himself. Few members of law enforcement were invited, certainly not one with his unsavory reputation. The crowd would be thick. She would invite the intern, use her to create a diversion, and disappear before they realized she was gone.

The scent of coffee told her that Madison was downstairs and would be leaving for campus soon. Kathryn threw back the covers and went to issue the invitation.

———

In white, she shone like a star. Standing beneath the towering glass tree, chatting and air-kissing, Kathryn didn't know where the spies were, but she made sure they were watching *her*, not the intern.

Charlie texted, confirming her theory.

I hear you're standing around holding court like the Queen of Sheba. Stop stalling. Go talk to Kessler.

You're having me watched?

You know I am.

I'll do it when the moment's right. Too many eyes.

Do it now.

Fuck off or I won't do it at all.

She'd make excuses, put him off until it was too late, and then disappear. Doug would get a warning, but a different one than Charlie expected, delivered by Madison, telling him to watch his back. Charlie would be left thinking that Kathryn failed to pass along the message. Hopefully they'd back off long enough for Doug to do what was necessary to protect himself.

From the corner of her eye, she saw Madison approach Doug. Laughing loudly, making a show of walking toward the bar, Kathryn drew the attention of the spies away from them. Everything was going according to plan. Then she turned her back. A few minutes later, drink in hand, she heard Doug's voice raised in anger and cast a glance over her shoulder. He was red in the face, and people were gawking. The spies didn't miss it. Her phone buzzed with a text.

What's that intern doing with Kessler??? Charlie texted.

Who?

Your intern is with Kessler causing a scene.

Madison? There must be some mistake. She couldn't get into an event like this to save her life.

Don't BS me, my guy is looking right at her.

I'll see what I can find out, stand by.

Andrew Martin was coming toward her. Their eyes met, and they veered away from one another. That wasn't by any arrangement. Given the way she walked out on the DOJ interview, he probably thought that she wanted to avoid to him. She needed to change that impression, but not here, not now, not with so many eyes on her. Madison had been tasked with setting up a meeting with Martin on her behalf, but now Charlie's spies would see her do that. The situation was deteriorating fast.

Shrill feedback on the PA system accompanied an announcement that dinner was about to begin.

Sorry, I don't see Madison and they just said take our seats.

You're doing this on purpose.

I'm trying to be helpful. Just give me time.

Heading for her assigned table, she crossed paths with Madison. She wanted to warn her off and tell her to go home without speaking to Martin. But the risk of being seen was too great. She looked right through her and kept walking.

Was that her? Charlie texted.

Who???

You just walked right by the intern.

Where? I don't see her.

You're lying to me, you're fucked.

Kathryn tried not to appear alarmed as she took a seat at the courthouse table, shaking hands, greeting colleagues. The executive director of the Pro Bono League went to the mic to make welcoming remarks. Waiters brought baskets of rolls, poured wine, served the salad course. Her heart was pounding. Her phone buzzed again. *Screw Charlie*, she thought, but this time, it was Doug.

I'm not going down for them. Neither should you. Want to run away with me? Meet me at the Belvedere garage near Logan in half an hour but don't let them follow you. I'll have a plane waiting.

Shit shit shit. Charlie's guy was monitoring Doug's phone, reading his texts in real time. This was not the conversation they'd ordered her to have with him. There was no way to respond to his text without tipping them off. She wrote nothing. But Doug kept texting.

Remember Bermuda? You look so beautiful tonight. Say you'll come with me.

She glanced over at the Bixby table and saw him staring at her. She did remember Bermuda—that legal conference years earlier, where they drank too much and fell into bed together. But Kathryn hadn't loved him. Not that night, not ever. After a while, the guilt got to her, and she ended the affair. Doug was crushed. She had to crush him again now—to shut him up, to save his life. Glaring at him, she shook her head no. He threw his phone down and pushed his chair back, knocking over a water glass in the process. Chloe, sitting beside him, clutched his arm, looking concerned. He shrugged her off and made a break for the exit.

A guy in a uniform that read EVENT SECURITY followed Doug out the door. One of Charlie's spies?

Her phone buzzed.

Recognize anyone? Charlie texted.

He attached a grainy photo of a woman boarding the T outside the museum, taken from some distance away. It was Madison. She could tell from the jumpsuit.

If you mean my intern, hard to say if that's her. Too blurry.

I'll get a better picture. Talk to Kessler yet?

Nope, he left. Guess your guy didn't tell you.

She didn't hear from Charlie after that.

Waiters served the main course. Kathryn had ordered the cod, but she was too nervous to eat. The executive director of the Pro Bono League must not have seen Doug leave. She launched into an introduction full of praise for his distinguished career. When she called him to the stage, there was an awkward pause. Heads swiveled in the direction of the Bixby tables. After a long minute, Chloe rose from her seat and glided to the mic.

"Good evening, and thank you for that lovely introduction. I'm Chloe Kessler, a second year at Harvard Law and Doug's daughter. My father sends his apologies. He was taken ill and had to leave. But he asked me to speak in his place about the privilege and responsibility of pro bono work."

This was the moment Kathryn had been waiting for. Chloe—young, blond, pretty, subbing in for her sick father—held the audience spellbound. With Charlie off chasing Madison, and his spy following Doug, it was her chance to disappear. She tucked her phone under a napkin. If they tracked her location, they'd think she was still at her table.

Walking casually into the ladies' room, she peeked under the doors of the stalls to make sure she was alone. Before the event started, she'd stashed a go-bag with clothes and a wig inside the closed infant changing table, on the assumption that nobody would bring a baby to this event. She was right, or in any event, it was still there. In a stall, she stripped down. The items she couldn't afford to lose were taped to her body, under the white tuxedo that she rolled up and hid at the bottom of the trash. Wincing, she ripped off the tape, stowing the valuables in a small backpack. Cash, passports, her gun, and two phones—one registered to Jenna Allen, the other a clone of Kathryn's phone with geolocation features disabled. If it worked like she'd been promised by the guy who sold it to her, it would enable her to send and receive texts and phone calls without being tracked—by anyone, criminal or law enforcement.

Moments later, dressed in black, a dark wig covering her conspicuous hair, she slipped out a side exit. Jenna Allen called an Uber heading for Logan Airport, where she'd catch a bus north, never to return.

That was the plan. Then her emotions got the better of her.

As the Uber neared the airport, she saw that they were in that same no-man's-land of parking lots and warehouses where Charlie had grabbed her and threatened her just the week before. Hatred swept over her. For Charlie. Ray. Eddie. *Mrs. Wallace.* All of them. Since she was a little girl, they'd manipulated her, beaten her, held her back, starved her, destroyed her mother, murdered her husband, separated her from her child. She wanted to ruin them, like they'd ruined her. Just at that moment, the Uber passed the Belvedere garage, where Doug said to meet him. He could be in there right now, not realizing that he was about to take his last breath, that some goon hiding in the shadows was waiting to ambush him. She couldn't stand for that to happen. Not because she loved Doug, but because she hated Charlie and his bitch mother and refused to let them win.

The bus to New Hampshire didn't depart for another hour.

She leaned forward.

"Excuse me, I changed my mind. Let me out over there at the Belvedere garage?"

"You'll be charged for the full trip," the driver said.

"Fine. Around the back, okay?"

It was a cold, moonless night. The Uber let her out behind the garage where there were no streetlamps. A dark figure in the murk, she slipped in through an unlocked door and walked the first level, searching for Doug's car. He drove a silver Porsche with vanity plates that read RAINMKR. If it was here, she'd find it.

She was heading down the ramp to the basement level when the shots rang out. Three loud pops in quick succession, accompanied by a shattering of glass. It came from below. She ran down the ramp and ducked behind a pickup truck, listening for more shots. Those three sounded like they came from a single gun, with nobody firing back. An ambush, followed by silence. Someone was dead. Presumably Doug. Would she be next? Her heart pounding, her breath rattling in her chest, she strained to hear. Finally, a car door slammed. Tires squealed on concrete. She stood up just in time to see the car speed past. The Jenna phone was in her hand. By instinct, she snapped a photo. The car wasn't Charlie's, but she knew it. And she was shocked, though in a way not surprised.

The taillights disappeared out the exit, and the car was gone. She listened for another minute and heard nothing. Emerging cautiously from behind the truck, she walked toward where the shots had come from, sticking close to the row of parked cars. But then the row ended, and she was in the open. Doug had parked in the farthest reaches of the bottom level of this obscure garage, because he planned to run and wanted to maximize his head start. He probably wasn't thinking about the fact that it would take longer for the cops to find his body.

She approached the Porsche like a sleepwalker in a nightmare. The windshield was shattered, but no sound emerged through the gaping hole in the glass. No moans, no labored breathing. Only silence. He was splayed in the driver's seat, his face pulverized to a raw mass of flesh. Unrecognizable. She was too late. They got him. They beat Doug in the end. But Kathryn was still standing. And she had people to protect.

She backed away, then turned and ran. Half an hour later, she boarded the bus north, to freedom.

36

....

Kathryn sat by her mother's bedside, holding her hand while she slept. Sylvia's face was hollow, shadowed by approaching death. The room smelled of disinfectant and was filled with blinking, beeping machines that made her nervous. Her mother's heart rate seemed irregular, her oxygen levels too low. The hospital was understaffed. She couldn't find anyone to ask for help. Even if she did find someone, how much could they do? Sylvia was going to die. That was the reality. Kathryn steeled herself to face it, but it still burned. After a lifetime of low expectations, she'd finally come to appreciate her mother at the exact moment when they got separated. It was so unfair. She was emotionally invested in the dream of their reunion. A new life together in a new land. Now that wouldn't happen, either.

They'd been robbed.

It wasn't the only robbery she'd suffered.

Small children have short memories. Kathryn had visited her daughter twice since giving birth to her. The last time was two years earlier, too long a gap for a little girl's heart. She'd gotten to

New Hampshire in the wee hours of the morning—too early to visit Grace—and went directly to her mother's bedside. Sylvia was unconscious, so she sat holding her hand, whispering her troubles into her mother's ear as if she'd get an answer. She spoke to a nurse who wouldn't, or couldn't, tell her much about Sylvia's condition, and tried without success to find a doctor who would. Eventually, she gave up and drove instead to the neighbor's house to retrieve her daughter.

Kathryn rang the doorbell with a heart full of fierce love.

"Look, hon, your mom came to get you," Denise said.

Grace took one look at her and ran away crying. She hid in the bathroom and wouldn't come out, not even on the promise of applesauce cake, which was apparently her favorite.

"Don't take it personally," Denise said. "With Marie sick, she's had a lot of disruption."

"She doesn't know me from Adam. I wouldn't go with me, either."

Eventually, Denise managed to coax Grace from the bathroom. The little girl sat at the kitchen table eating cake, watching Kathryn warily while Denise made coffee. Later, Grace allowed Kathryn to sit beside her on the sofa as she played with her doll, and Kathryn knew with a blast of gratitude that her daughter would accept her, given enough time.

But time was a luxury they didn't have. Charlie was out there somewhere, tracking Kathy right now. So were the feds. Eventually, one or the other would find her, and rip her away from her daughter. And from her mother, whom she'd left all alone in the hospital. Kathy needed to get back there to spend these last precious hours with Sylvia. She begged Denise to keep Grace for just a little longer, so she could take care of her mother, offering to pay for the woman's time. Denise wouldn't accept money.

"I can't take your money. Marie's been a good friend to me for years. Go, be with your mom. Leave Grace with me for now."

Kathryn returned to the hospital in the Volvo registered to Marie Allen. This time, she managed to track down Sylvia's doctor and get a prognosis. It would be a matter of days, he said, not more than that. She sat with that information for a while, gazing at her mother's face, trying to memorize it for when she was gone. Wherever she went next, Sylvia wasn't coming.

The escape they'd dreamed of together would never come to pass. That terrible truth pushed everything else from her mind, and she sat up through that night, holding her mother's hand. Sylvia drifted in and out of consciousness, occasionally muttering unintelligibly. Kathryn was afraid to sleep, or even go to the bathroom, for fear that she'd miss something important. She couldn't bear for Sylvia to pass away alone. But she could only fight off sleep for so long. Eventually, she dozed, waking with a start hours later, running to get coffee, sitting with Sylvia from when the sun came up to when it went back down. She lost track of time, though she never forgot that in the outside world, things were still happening. Dangerous things. The people who were coming for her hadn't stopped looking.

It was getting light again when her phone buzzed. It was him. Charlie. He'd been texting her at intervals since Doug's murder, demanding to know where she was, making threats, warning her against snitching to the feds or else the same thing would happen to her.

He'd even sent a photo of Doug Kessler's car with the windshield shot out and his pulverized head visible inside. What happens to snitches, it had read.

She was terrified to open this latest text, but it was better to face the truth than let him ambush her. With every moment that passed, she felt him drawing closer. By now, he could be standing in the parking lot outside, preparing to drag her away. She had to know.

Heart pounding, she opened the text.

Got sent an interesting picture from a friend who works at Logan Airport. Thought you'd want to know your little friend is snitching.

The attached photo showed Madison sitting at a JetBlue gate at Logan. The display for the departing flight, visible over her shoulder, said WASHINGTON. Seated beside her, mouth open in midsentence, was Olivia Chase, the FBI agent who'd posed as an intern in Kathryn's office until they found out and fired her.

Madison was cooperating.

She was surprised how much that hurt.

Then again, if Kathryn had any hope of surviving, and rescuing her daughter, she had no choice—she had to cooperate, too. Join the feds, beg for protection. Charlie was off the rails. He would kill her if she didn't. It was that simple.

She went to her list of contacts. Despite the early hour, Brooke Lee picked up on the first ring.

"Hello, it's Kathryn Conroy."

"Judge Conroy. What a surprise," she said.

Her tone was so filled with contempt that Kathryn was taken aback. She was hoping to negotiate a favorable deal, but that would be tough if the lead prosecutor loathed her as much as this woman seemed to.

"Ms. Lee. I know we didn't part on the best of terms last time, but I was hoping we could talk."

"You caught me at a bad moment. Can I call you back?"

Kathryn knew that trick. Brooke needed to get off the line to make arrangements to record and trace the call. Even with the geolocation on the clone phone supposedly disabled, she felt uncomfortable taking that risk.

"I'd prefer to speak right now."

"Go ahead. Say whatever you like."

"Well, uh—when we met in DC last week, you solicited my

cooperation, and I said I wasn't interested. I *might* be reevaluating. I'm now willing to hear you out, at least as far as listening to what terms you're offering in exchange for testimony."

"Circumstances have changed. That deal is off the table. *Permanently*."

If Kathryn had been hooked up to the heart monitor, it would have showed a terrible jolt. Though she shouldn't be surprised that Brooke Lee no longer needed her testimony. Madison was cooperating.

"I see. So, can I assume that another witness came forward?"

"If I had a witness, you think I would tell *you*? Not if I want to keep them alive."

She knew what that meant. The room tilted around her. They'd found Doug's body. And they blamed her somehow.

"I'm texting you a photo taken by the security camera at the rear entrance to the Belvedere garage last night at nine thirty P.M. The same location where Douglas Kessler was found shot to death just an hour ago. Take a look. Tell me if you recognize the woman in the photo."

The clone phone buzzed with a text. Kathryn opened it with a pit of dread in her stomach, already knowing what she would see. Herself, dressed in black, wearing a dark wig. It was almost laughable. She couldn't have looked more like a criminal if she tried.

"I didn't kill him."

"I don't believe you."

"I know who did, and I can prove it."

"I'm sure you do know. Look, I'd love to take your co-conspirators down. But not at the cost of working with someone as sleazy as you. You're entrusted with the most sacred office in our legal system, and you perverted it for personal gain. You're a killer at least two times over that we know of. Brad McCarthy, and now Douglas

Kessler. You could plead guilty to every charge in the book, *Judge* Conroy, and I would still never work with you. But I will bring you to justice, and that's a promise."

Kathryn dropped the call. Her hands were shaking. She felt cold and sick. All along, she told herself that she didn't trust the feds and didn't want their help. Now she realized that she'd been counting on it. There was no plan B. If Brooke Lee wouldn't give her a new name, a new face, a new life, then she lacked the resources to do that for herself. If the feds didn't take her into protective custody and arrest her enemies, she'd be killed. It was that simple. And not just Kathryn. Her mother and daughter, too. Even her cat. She'd left Lucy behind at the town house because she had no other choice in the moment, but in her mind it was temporary. She'd been counting on the FBI to go pick up her cat and bring her to whatever safe house they stashed Kathryn in. She had no plan to get Lucy back.

"*Kathy.*"

"Mom. You're awake."

"Are those tears for me? I'm still here, you know. Let's not waste time blubbering," Sylvia said, her voice weak but clear.

Kathryn hadn't even realized she was crying. She swabbed her eyes with the back of her hand and forced a smile.

"I'm so happy to hear you sounding like yourself," she said.

"Who else would I sound like? Did you see Grace?"

"Yes. She ran away and hid."

Sylvia started to laugh but ended up wincing in pain. Kathryn bent over her in an agony of worry.

"I'm fine," her mother said, waving her off. "You look worse than I do. Is something wrong?"

"You want a list? My daughter doesn't know me. My mother is"—she stopped herself from saying *dying*—"hospitalized. My psycho half brother wants to murder me. The feds want to lock me up for murders I didn't commit. My cat got left behind when I ran. I need to start a new life in a new country that has no extradition treaty, but I don't have the cash."

"Well, that's quite a tale of woe."

"Yes, it is. Any bright ideas for how to deal with it?"

"You need money? I thought you had the funds squared away. Isn't that what you were supposed to be doing all this time?"

"I skimmed what I could. It wasn't enough. They watch too closely. I was planning to rip off Ray's bank account, to be honest. But with the feds closing in, he moved the money offshore. I don't know where it is now."

"Did you look on his computer?"

"How would I do that?"

"I have the keys to his office and all his passwords. Now, granted, they're five years old. But Ray never updated a thing in his life."

"Well, jeez. Why didn't you say so?"

Ray's office was located on a side street near Government Center in a building that had seen better days. Kathryn peered through the streaky glass door into the dingy lobby, then let herself in using Sylvia's key. It was nine-thirty at night. The lights were on in the lobby, but the place seemed deserted. This wasn't the sort of building where people toiled till midnight. Still, she was nervous as she waited for the ancient elevator. The smell of it when she got in—a combination of sweat, brass polish, and the oil they used to keep it running—took her back to that summer after college, working for Ray as a file clerk. She'd been so shocked at the parade of grifters and thugs and losers who were his clients. It was an education all right, but she hadn't learned her lesson.

On the fifth floor, her feet found their way to his door. Suite 5100 was an overblown title for two little rooms with wall-to-wall carpet looking out onto an air shaft. But "Raymond J. Logue, Esq., Attorney at Law" still had a ring to it, of a man with a wad of cash in his pocket, a bottle in the bottom drawer, and connections at city hall. She shook her head, smiling, as she raised the key to the lock.

It didn't fit.

Why was she surprised? With everything that had happened in the last five years, even someone as disorganized as Ray would think to change the locks. She had nothing on her that could be used to force it, and if she had, she wouldn't know what to do with it. As she considered her options, her eye traveled upward. *Shit.* Something else had changed since she'd been here last. Ray had installed a security camera, and it was pointed right at her. Did he check the feed regularly? Was it one of those that dinged his phone when someone came to the door, like at the town house? If so, he just saw her try to break in. He was probably on the phone with Charlie right now, giving up her location.

Forget the money. She had to get out of here.

She ran down five flights, out the door, and around the corner to where she'd left Sylvia's Volvo. Looking over her shoulder, she slid into the driver's seat. There was hope. No one had followed her yet. If they did show up, they wouldn't recognize this car, which had New Hampshire plates and was registered to a person they'd never heard of. She could get away clean—if not for one problem.

She had to go back for her cat.

At that hour, the drive to the town house took less than ten minutes. She parked a few blocks away, skulking through the alley on a reconnaissance mission to make sure they weren't lying in wait. The house was dark. The only car parked behind it was her own SUV. She went around, cautiously approaching the front of the house. None of the cars on the block appeared occupied. The people walking dogs in the park were too well-dressed to work for Charlie. It seemed like nobody was watching, which surprised her, since the house was the obvious place to look for her. Did they think she'd be too smart to come back here? Hah, they were wrong.

She went around back and let herself in. All was quiet until the security system started beeping. *Damn*. She purposely didn't arm it when she left, knowing they used it to monitor her comings and goings. The last Kathryn heard, Madison was in DC ratting her out to the feds, but she must've come in and reset it at some point. *Great*. If Kathryn let the alarm trigger, it would make a racket and call the cops. But disarming it would also blow her cover, though not as dramatically. They'd know someone had entered the house, though not necessarily that it was her. Still, Charlie would surely come to check it out. Cursing, she tapped in the code and entered an override to change it to a new code. At least then he wouldn't be able to sneak up on her. And if he tried—well, that's what the gun was for.

Lucy came running. Kathryn picked her up, holding her tight and kissing her silky head, tears in her eyes. But this was no time for an emotional reunion. They had to get out of there fast, and for that, she would need to use the cat carrier, which Lucy despised. A few minutes later, she was in the living room, struggling in the dark to get the cat into the damn thing when the security system started beeping again. It had to be Charlie, trying to break in. He would kill her if she let him. Her hands shook as she put Lucy down. The gun was on the end table beside her. She'd never once fired it—not at a person, not even at the range. Yet she knew in her heart that her aim would be true. She and Charlie had been playing chicken since they were kids. Time to put an end to it.

She held her breath. A figure was advancing toward the front door. She was reaching for the gun when Madison touched the alarm panel, lighting it up in the darkness. Kathryn's fingers brushed cold metal, then pulled back as if shocked. She'd been seconds from shooting. *Jesus, I could have killed the kid.* Even if Madison did betray her to the feds, she didn't want her *dead.* And that made things tricky. Madison was probably wearing a wire. Dealing with her would be a huge risk. But running away and leaving her to face Charlie alone—that was something Kathryn just couldn't do.

———

They were on the highway heading north, with Madison driving, when Kathryn's phone rang. When the name MARIE ALLEN flashed on the screen, her heart clutched. Sylvia knew better than to call from that number. It had to be the neighbor, calling from Sylvia's phone to say she'd passed away.

"*Hello?*"

"Kathy."

She went cold and still.

"Ray."

"Why didn't you tell me? All these years, I could have been with her."

His voice was thick and phlegmy, as if he'd been crying. She didn't give a rip about his feelings.

"I didn't tell you because you would've had her killed."

"That's crazy. You know how I feel about her."

"How can I believe you after everything that's happened? I'm just begging you, don't hurt her."

"Hurt her? She's *dying.* I'm sitting here holding her hand while she drifts in and out."

"Oh no, not again. She was so alert when I left."

Tears started rolling down her cheeks. That was a bad sign.

"I wanted to be there for her when she passed. That's why I took the risk of going there. You followed me, didn't you?"

"Yeah, because I was worried what they would do to you. I watched you get on that bus the other night, thinking you got spooked and ran. I followed you to keep you safe. Like, if Charlie actually came at you, I'd intervene. But then you went to New Hampshire. And I'm thinking, what the hell is she doing there, going to this hospital, visiting this Denise person I never heard of? So I kept my distance, thinking I might catch you meeting with the feds."

"It's not what you think."

"Oh, I know that now. It's worse. Come to find out you've been lying to me for years, and not only about Sylvia. Your daughter is beautiful, Kathy. She looks just like you, with those big eyes, watching all the time."

He had her daughter. She wanted to scream. It was her worst nightmare. All the years of precautions blown out of the water in the panic and sloppiness of the last forty-eight hours.

"Where is she? What have you done with her?"

Madison looked over in alarm.

"Relax, she's sleeping in a chair right here. I brought her to say goodbye to her grandma. That Denise? Nice lady. But—I don't know if she was fed up looking after a kid, or what. She handed Grace over without a lot of questions. You should be more careful who you leave her with."

"I'm begging you, don't hurt her."

"C'mon, this is your Uncle Ray you're talking to. You should be thanking your lucky stars I took her, so she's safe. Denise would've given her to *Charlie*."

"What do you want? Anything. Name your price."

"I see I'm not getting through to you. So let me lay the cards on the table. I want to be with Sylvia. That's what I want. It didn't happen in this life. Now I'm focused on the next, and that's right around the corner. I got cancer. It's in my lungs, and it's spreading. I don't have too long."

She'd thought the last few times she saw him that he looked worse than ever, his complexion like spoiled milk, his hands perpetually shaking. She'd put it down to booze.

But Ray was dying.

Kathryn believed that, and her rage began to dissipate.

"I'm sorry to hear that, Uncle Ray," she said, and was surprised to realize that she meant it, even now.

"Thank you, honey. I'm not sorry myself, not if it means I can be with her. But I realized, for that to happen, your mother and I need to wind up in the same place. If I don't atone for my sins and make amends, Saint Peter's gonna take one look at me and send me downstairs."

She didn't say anything. Because she couldn't argue with that.

"I have an idea for how to get my house in order. You're a big part of it."

"I'm listening."

"Not now. I'll hold up the phone so you can say goodbye. And I hope you don't mind, but I'm gonna sing her to the next life. When she's gone, then you and I will talk."

Part Five

End Game

''''''''''''''''''''

37

Madison called Brooke Lee the next morning from the parking lot of a Bickford's across the street from the Best Western where they were lying low. The sky was gray and spitting rain, the temperature rapidly falling. She stood under an overhang, warm in the enormous puffer coat, watching her breath go up in clouds.

"What is this phone number you're calling from?" Brooke said. "The tech guy can't ping it."

"I don't know. It belongs to Judge Conroy. She took my phone and destroyed it because she thought it was bugged."

"We warned you she'd suspect you were cooperating."

"You were right."

"Are you safe?"

"For now. Olivia was smart not to send me in wired. The judge searched my backpack, my clothes, everything. I swore up and down I wasn't cooperating, and when she didn't find anything, that backed me up. I think she's still suspicious. But she trusted me enough to send me out for breakfast. She's holed up in the motel room, expecting me back. So let's make it quick."

"The geolocation on the phone is disabled. You need to tell me exactly where you are.

"In Massachusetts, from the license plates. Beyond that, I'm not sure."

"Do you see any landmarks?"

"A Dunkin' Donuts."

"God, there's a million of those. A street name?"

"Not that I can see."

"Can you get the plate number for the car she's driving? Her Nissan is parked in the alley behind her house, so it must be something else. If you get a plate number, we can pull the toll cameras."

"Brooke, I need to hang up. I think I see her."

"No! We need a location, so we can arrest her. Oh, and rescue you," she added as an afterthought.

"If I can get her location, will that be enough to satisfy the cooperation deal, so Danny's charges get dropped?"

"That and a confession. *On tape.*"

"How do you expect me to achieve that when Olivia didn't send me in wired?"

"Well, aren't you glad she didn't? Conroy would've found the wire for sure. You'd be dead by now."

"Olivia was protecting the investigation. Not me."

"She was protecting both. We care about you, Madison. I just lost one witness; I don't need to lose another."

Yeah, because it would look bad, she thought. But no point in bickering with the prosecutor. She had a goal in mind, and not much time to accomplish it.

"Okay, then hurry up and tell me how to record Judge Conroy without the wire, so I can get off the phone."

"I have a way to do it, but if she figures it out, you could be in danger. Is she armed?"

Madison hesitated. She could tell them about the gun. What was one more crime, on top of all the charges Judge Conroy already faced? On the other hand, the FBI had its ways of locating even the cagiest suspects. If they believed the judge was armed and managed to track her down, they'd storm the motel room. Break down the door, use a percussive device, start shooting. The judge might be killed. Madison could be caught in the crossfire. No, she had to defuse this.

"I didn't see a gun."

"Wait a minute, I don't understand. If she didn't take you at gunpoint, why did you go with her?"

"Are you seriously victim-blaming me? You're holding my brother prisoner in exchange for information. I went because you put me up to it."

"Oh," Brooke said, sounding almost surprised. "Okay, I'll tell you how to record her, but I'm warning you: it's risky."

"I'll take any risk for Danny."

"Well, I don't want to be held responsible if things go wrong."

"You've made that perfectly clear."

"Okay, you need to download an app called Spyware Pro to the phone you're using right now. Then give the phone back to her. The spyware hides in the OS, so she shouldn't be able to see it. *Unless* the phone is set up to detect intrusion, which it may well be."

"Understood."

"You're assuming that risk."

"*I get it.*"

"The app will prompt you to enter a phone number. Put in mine. Any calls Conroy makes from that phone will be automatically shared with me. I'll take care of recording them."

"Understood. If I do all this, and provide you with information leading to her arrest—"

"Then Danny's charges will be dropped. You'll get full immunity. Along with any protection you need and the thanks of a grateful nation. You have my word."

"It's a deal. The judge is coming. I've got to run. Bye."

Dropping the call, she went inside. The restaurant was warm and steamy, smelling of coffee and maple syrup. She slid into a booth.

"I ordered you scrambled eggs with wheat toast," Judge Conroy said. "How'd it go?"

"We're on."

———

Later, when they were back in the motel room, the phone with the spyware rang. The screen showed an incoming call from Ray Logue.

Kathryn caught Madison's eyes. The intern nodded.

"Hello."

"Kathy. It's Ray."

"What do *you* want?"

"I have something that belongs to you," he said. "I think you're going to want it back. I'd like to arrange a handover."

"And walk into an ambush? I'm not stupid."

"I would never do that to you."

"You've been doing it for half my life. Any information I gave. Any cases I threw. And yes, I admit I did some of that, but only because you forced me. You and Charlie and Nancy. She put you up to this, didn't she?"

"What?"

"Nancy Duffy, my so-called case manager. She's Charlie's mother, Eddie Wallace's widow. She's been part of your scheme all along, and she put you up to this."

There was a pause on the line.

"What are you doing?" Ray said. "Leave her out of it."

"I'm sorry, I can't."

"She's just an old woman. I'm not down with this. Nancy wasn't part of the deal. I didn't agree to that."

It was true, he hadn't. But Kathryn had scores to settle, whether he was on board or not.

"Nancy gave the order to kill my husband, didn't she?"

"I won't deny she was involved, but give the order—"

Kathryn hung her head. "I knew it. *God.*"

"Kathy, why are we talking about this now?"

"Because. She kept me a virtual prisoner for years. She's the one who murdered Doug Kessler. I know that because I was there. I saw it, and I have a photo to prove it, of her leaving the scene after Doug was shot. You can clearly see her in the driver's seat. She pulled the trigger. Not me. Not Charlie. And now she wants me dead."

"I'm not bringing Nancy into this when the feds got nothing on her. I'm trying to make things right here, not become a snitch in my old age."

"Oh, come on, Ray. You know she'll kill me the second she has a clear shot. So would Charlie."

There was a pause.

"Ray?"

"Well. It's true you and her never were on the same page. I guess she didn't treat you too good."

She scoffed. "That's an understatement."

"But I don't want to take sides."

"I'm not asking you to. At the end of the day, giving up Nancy is on me. You can have a clear conscience, so don't let it prevent us from doing business. Remember, there's something you want more than anything else, right? Eyes on the prize."

His sigh was audible. "You're right. Where should we meet?"

"How about the Mass. Ave. bridge? There's always traffic there. I'll feel comfortable."

"Works for me. Say, ten o'clock tonight?"

"Sure."

"No funny business now."

"You either."

"I swear it on your mother's life."

"I'll see you then. Oh, and I'll be wearing a plaid raincoat."

"Gotcha. And Kathy?"

"Yeah."

"Take care of yourself."

Tears filled her eyes. This was goodbye, and there had been too many of those. When she finally spoke, it was with a catch in her voice.

"You too, Uncle Ray. You too."

38

....

Judge Conroy had an arrangement with a waiter named Theo, who worked at a restaurant that she'd been frequenting for years. She paid him to do things for her that she couldn't do herself, out of fear of being watched. This waiter had arranged for her to park the Volvo behind the restaurant the night before. Theo was willing to pick up the judge's Nissan and drive it to the Best Western, for use in the meeting later tonight.

The judge trusted the waiter, but Madison thought it would be too great a risk.

"Doesn't Wallace have the town house staked out? Or what about the feds? They could follow the car right to us."

"I don't see why the feds would be watching the town house when they know I'm not there. And Ray will call Charlie off. Tell him I'm somewhere else so he goes chasing after ghosts," the judge said.

Judge Conroy had worked out a deal with Raymond Logue. Their safety hinged on him holding up his end of the bargain.

"I still think you're too trusting. The idea that Logue is taking your side against Wallace—don't you think that could be a setup?"

"Ray knows what he took from me, and what he owes. He wants to make amends. I've known him my whole life. I know his heart. Have you ever read *Harry Potter*?"

"Of course. Every kid my age did."

"You know how Snape seems like a bad guy who hates Harry? But in the end, he helps him, out of love for Harry's mother?"

"Yes."

"It's like that."

"You're sure about him? *Really* sure?"

"Enough to bet my life on it. And my daughter's."

And mine, she thought.

The actual handover of the judge's daughter would take place at 9:00 P.M. At that meeting, Logue would also give the judge the password to a bank account he'd set up in her name. At ten, a second meeting would take place, between Logue and Madison, who'd be posing as the judge. That one, the feds knew about, because they'd listened in on the call setting it up. Presumably they'd be surveilling it. God, she hoped they would. Because either meeting could be an ambush. And either woman could wind up dead.

They were sitting in the room at the Best Western with the blinds drawn. It was dark outside, and they hadn't ventured out since breakfast. The judge said they should eat something. They'd need their strength. Madison would need hers, especially. She called down to the desk clerk, who got them takeout sandwiches from the gas station next door. But neither one could eat. They just took a few bites and cast the sandwiches aside, not that they were great anyway. Ten o'clock on the Mass. Ave. bridge was just three hours from now. The time hung over Madison like a threat of death. Which it was. What she'd agreed to do was incredibly dangerous.

Judge Conroy was having doubts on Madison's behalf.

"It's not too late to change your mind," she said. "You don't have to do this for me. You haven't even known me that long."

"I've known you ever since I saw you speak at Career Day. Ten years. That's how long you mattered to me. I want you to have the life you deserve. Anyway, I'm not doing it just for you. I have my own reasons. To help Danny. You know that."

"The risk to you is so great. Is it worth it? For me, if I stay behind, they'll kill me. But for you—"

"They'd kill me, too. And the feds would refuse to let Danny go. Judge, stop trying to talk me out of it. I'll be okay. Not only am I a strong swimmer, but I swim the Charles every year when they do that public access thing. I love it, actually. The water is surprisingly clean. I've experienced the current. I know what to expect."

"But in the cold? At night? In bad weather?"

"The water is warmer than the air at this time of year. Give me a wetsuit and a headlamp, and I'll be fine."

"Theo is bringing those. But you still have to jump. People die doing that."

"The distance isn't far. I can handle it. My college roommate had a cabin in the White Mountains. There was a flooded quarry where we'd dive in and swim. I never had a problem there, and that jump was longer. You go in feet first to break the surface tension, that's all. Really. I know what I'm doing."

"Madison, I'm scared."

"So am I. But we've been over this. It's the only way they'll stop looking for you. The only plan that achieves both our goals."

That ended the discussion. Because she was right.

Time passed. Around eight thirty, Theo texted to say he was outside with the judge's car. Judge Conroy watched from behind the blinds to make certain that he hadn't been followed, then went out to meet him. She returned with the car keys and bags containing everything they'd need. A wetsuit, a headlamp, wigs, and the judge's beautiful plaid raincoat that Madison so admired. Too bad it was going to end up in the river. After switching clothes and

donning the wigs, they stood side by side in the cramped bathroom gazing in the mirror and giggling like kids at how much they
looked like one another.

"For the first time, I actually believe this will work," Judge Conroy said.

Madison agreed, but her stomach was full of butterflies.

In the parking lot, under cover of darkness, they paused to say
goodbye. The woman with long dark hair, wearing an enormous
black puffer coat, was about to get into an old Volvo with New
Hampshire plates and drive off on the first leg of a journey. It was
a hazardous journey to a distant land, and they knew she might not
reach her destination. The second woman had bright auburn hair
and wore a distinctive plaid trench coat. She was highly recogniz-
able, easy to spot, even as a heavy snow started to fall, obscuring
visibility. She was about to do something so dangerous that even
her history as a competitive swimmer hadn't fully prepared her.
She might not survive the next hour, but if she did, she'd free them
both and save her family in the process.

"I can never thank you enough for what you're about to do for
me. And what you've already done. Promise me you'll be careful."

"I will. Be safe, Judge."

"Call me Kathy. *Judge* never felt like it belonged to me. Besides,
I don't think of you as the intern. You're my friend."

They hugged quickly, going their separate ways with tears in their
eyes, knowing that, whatever happened, their goodbye was final.

———

Madison wore a wetsuit under her clothes and carried a water-
proof headlamp in the pocket of the trench coat. But one hazard
she hadn't prepared for was the snow. They'd checked the forecast,

of course, but the flurries that were called for had unexpectedly morphed into a major snowstorm, the first of the season. Heavy, wet flakes came down hard, looking like a flight of moths in the headlights. Traffic was light, but the roads were slick and icy. Even though she was driving well under the speed limit, she had to fight to keep the car from spinning out on turns. She arrived at the Mass. Ave. bridge nearly half an hour late, with white knuckles and sweaty armpits, wondering if the other participants were still in place, or whether the whole plan would be a bust before it started.

At that hour, in that weather, the area around MIT was quiet. She pulled into an open parking space less than a block from the bridge, took a deep breath, and got out of the car. The snow was coming down hard, limiting visibility. That *might* be a good thing. In this weather, from a distance, the FBI would never know that the redhead in the plaid coat was an impostor. On the other hand, they needed to be able to see her leap into the Charles. If they missed that key moment due to poor visibility, she'd be risking her life for nothing.

As she crossed the street to the pedestrian walkway, a figure started toward her from the other side of the bridge—a hulking man in a dark overcoat with thinning white hair. *Raymond Logue.* Her heart thumped in her chest. Judge Conroy had vouched for "Uncle" Ray. But to Madison, he'd always be the dirty lawyer who framed her little brother, and she could never really trust him.

They met in the middle of the span.

"Kathy," he said.

The greeting surprised her. They stood no more than two feet apart. He could clearly see her face and must know that she was masquerading as the judge. Why call her by the wrong name? Maybe he didn't trust her any more than she trusted him, and he was worried she was wired?

But then he winked and smiled, with a flash of Irish charm.

"You're late, kid. I was worried you weren't gonna make it."

"Yeah, this crazy weather," she said, and her voice was unsteady. Now that the moment was upon her, her whole body was shaking.

"Well, it didn't stop your friends from the FBI. We got company. I make at least three surveillance vehicles. You walked right by 'em."

"They saw me?"

"Yes, and they're watching now. So let's make this quick. It's supposed to be a handoff. You got something for me?" he said, opening his jacket and reaching inside.

Madison gasped, reeling back.

"Hey, hey, take it easy," he said, pulling out an envelope. "This is just for show, to make it look like an exchange is happening in front of them. I handed over the kid an hour ago. Didn't Kathy explain?"

"Yes, sorry. I'm just really nervous," she said, her heart starting up again after skipping several beats.

His eyes were bloodshot and rheumy. But not unkind.

"Steady as she goes, it'll be over in no time. Now, you got something for me?"

They exchanged envelopes. The one she gave him contained the judge's cell phone, with a photograph on it that Logue had been concerned about, depicting Nancy the case manager leaving the scene of Doug Kessler's murder. As much as she'd always suspected that Nancy was corrupt, Madison had been shocked to learn that she was actually a killer. Logue took the envelope, ripping open the top and looking inside. He nodded in satisfaction. But what he didn't know was that, before she left the motel, Judge Conroy had sent a copy of that photo to the FBI. Madison didn't enlighten him. Why disrupt the deal or interfere with Nancy being brought to justice?

"We're good," Logue said, nodding.

She turned, glancing nervously toward the railing that ran the length of the pedestrian walkway. Meant to protect people from falling into the swift-moving river below, it was no more than chest-high. All she had to do was lift one leg and then the other, climb over and let herself fall.

She hesitated.

"Is it time? Should I . . . ?"

Her voice trailed off. She'd been so certain she could handle this part. The jump, the cold, the current. But now, with the wind raging and icy flakes strafing her face, she was terrified.

"Wait a minute," Logue said, looking at his watch. "There's been a slight adjustment to the plan. I'm expecting someone else. The snow must've delayed him."

There was only one person he could mean.

"Wallace? No way," Madison said, starting to back away, but Logue grabbed her by the sleeve.

"Please, kid, trust me on this. He needs to see Kathy jump. He would never take my word for it, but he'll believe his own eyes. Otherwise, he won't stop looking for her. As soon as I see his car, you get up on the railing. I'll give the signal. *Then* you jump. Okay?"

The snow was beginning to let up, visibility improving slightly. The area was largely deserted, with no traffic and virtually no pedestrians. But as Madison glanced down the street, she saw six people emerge simultaneously from three different cars. All of them were men, except for one, whom she recognized. Olivia.

"The FBI, *look*," she said.

"You have to jump, or they'll arrest you," he said. "They'll see you're not Kathy. Go, hurry."

He was right. If the feds caught her, the whole charade fell apart. Not only would they go looking for the real Judge Conroy, but Danny would remain in prison, and Madison would join him.

As she took a step toward the railing, a familiar car came barreling into view. It skidded to a stop in the middle of the bridge, fishtailing wildly, the driver's door flying open. Wallace stumbled out, a gun in his hand, his eyes on Madison.

"Kathy, you double-crossed me. You think I'd let you get away with it?" he shouted, coming at her.

The FBI agents were running toward them with weapons drawn.

Pulling out a gun, Logue gave her a push. "*Go.*"

Madison stepped over the railing and jumped, leaping into darkness as shots rang out behind her.

39

....

With its beautiful beaches and low cost of living, the country attracted visitors from around the globe. The Americans were mostly retirees priced out of Scottsdale, Bluffton, Boca—anywhere in the States with halfway decent weather. They'd rent colorful bungalows near the center of town and hit the bars at night, in their white pants and leathery tans, getting drunk on cheap beer, dancing to fake mariachi bands. Then there were the backpackers, vagabonds of many nations, who came to surf the big waves and smoke their nights away. They lived in crowded hostels and cheap hotels and moved on when the rains came. The foreigners who preferred to live up in the mountains, who kept to themselves and visited town only for necessities—they were a different breed. They'd done their research. The country's appeal to them was the lack of an extradition treaty. They'd stay for a while, or maybe not, depending on who was looking for them, how dangerous they were, and how fast they were likely to catch up. The locals tended to avoid those types, if they were smart.

Jenna Allen didn't fit neatly into any category. She was attractive and obviously well-educated, with a small daughter. Too young to be a retiree, too old to be a backpacker. Well-dressed, short dark hair, a pert nose, and unnaturally smooth skin that spoke of plastic surgery, though the job was good enough that one couldn't be sure, and her dark-haired daughter looked exactly like her. She stayed at the best hotel in town, where the desk clerk examined her passport, finding it to be as fresh and trackless as the beach at sunrise.

The mother and daughter took their meals in the hotel's small restaurant, always sitting at the same table, brushing off anyone who approached. Their solitary ways aroused curiosity. But after a couple of weeks, she struck up a friendship with the hotel manager, a smart, down-to-earth woman named Alejandra. Jenna confided in Alejandra that she *was* on the run—from a bad marriage. Her wealthy, abusive husband had come close to killing her. She was forced to flee with her daughter, but the husband hadn't stopped looking. Her lawyers were working out the terms of the divorce. She expected a substantial settlement and custody of the child. To keep her baby safe, Jenna wanted to stay as far away from her ex-husband as possible. She felt comfortable in the charming resort town, so far from home. She wanted to put down roots, buy a small property, and raise her daughter quietly.

Alejandra had a cousin in the real estate business, who helped Jenna find the perfect place to start her life over. It was a whitewashed stucco house with a red tile roof, behind a tall gate, situated on a small rise on the outskirts of the town, with a beautiful view of the mountains. It had a shady courtyard with a burbling fountain, and grounds lush with fruit trees and birds of paradise. The moment she stepped into the tiled hall, with its carved wooden ceilings and turmeric-colored walls, she felt like she'd come home.

Jenna bought it, taking up residence with her daughter. And while they still kept to themselves, the local people now understood, and felt sympathy. They had nothing but contempt for a man who'd mistreat his wife. Without being asked, and by tacit agreement among themselves, they kept a wary eye out for any Americans asking nosy questions. Jenna and her little girl, Grace, could live life in peace.

40

....

The sun broke through the clouds over Harvard Yard, lighting the last bright leaves that clung to the ancient trees. It was the Wednesday before Thanksgiving, and Danny was coming home that night. In a couple of hours, Madison would go to South Station to meet his bus. Mom had returned from New York, bringing Aunt Nilda with her. They were at Mom's apartment right now, cooking like maniacs. Turkey with all the trimmings, lechón with black beans and rice, two pies, and arroz con dulce. Exams were over, and she'd passed by the skin of her teeth. If future employers questioned her uncharacteristically weak performance that semester, she would point to the shocking death of her professor and mentor, Kathryn Conroy, who'd leaped into the Charles River under fire from the FBI. The final exam for Judge Conroy's Fourth Amendment seminar had been canceled, with every student receiving a pass and an offer of counseling.

She ought to be celebrating. No charges would be brought against her. Danny's charges had been not only dropped but expunged. He was a free man with a clean record, as he should be. Wallace and Logue were dead, killed in the crossfire on the bridge.

Nancy was under arrest. Yet as she hurried toward the law school, late for a meeting, Madison's stomach was in knots. She hadn't slept soundly since leaping from that bridge. The judge was constantly on her mind. She couldn't stand not knowing her fate. And that wasn't the only thing making her nervous. She'd received a strange email asking her to report to the Financial Services Office regarding her financial aid.

She was ushered in immediately to meet with a financial services officer, who sat behind an L-shaped desk, turned sideways in her chair with her eyes on the monitor, not making eye contact. A bad sign.

"We close in twenty minutes," the woman said. "I need to pull up your file right away or there won't be time to complete your paperwork."

"There must be some mistake. I filed my FAFSA last June. My paperwork is complete."

"No mistake. Circumstances have changed. ID number, please."

She recited it from memory. The woman typed. Madison tried to speak, but she held up her hand, peering at the screen.

"Please, you're making me nervous. Changed how?" Madison said.

The woman finally looked at her. "Sorry, I assumed you knew it's good news. You applied for this, right?"

"For what?"

"The Lucy Katz Memorial Award? You were chosen as the recipient."

Lucy Katz. *Lucy Cats*. Kathryn Conroy.

"The— *Oh*. Lucy Katz. Yes. Lucy Katz, of course."

The judge was alive.

She started to cry. The woman pushed a box of Kleenex across the desk toward her.

"It's nice to see happy tears in here for a change. You know it's a full ride, right?"

Shaking her head, Madison struggled to get control of herself. "I didn't know that."

"Well, lucky you. This is one of the best scholarship packages I've ever seen. Full tuition retroactive to the beginning of law school, plus a generous stipend that can be used for living expenses during summer internships and any and all professional development expenses, including but not limited to training courses, bar review, tutoring, and—get this—*wardrobe*."

"Wardrobe?"

"Yeah, you can buy clothes with it. I wouldn't mind a scholarship like that myself."

Madison laughed through her tears. Of course the judge would think of that.

"Now, if we can just get this paperwork filled out, I'll cut your first stipend check. Somebody's going to have a very happy Thanksgiving."

———

The name of the scholarship was an inside joke, but also a reminder of something important left undone.

On the way to meet Danny, Madison stopped at a small grocery store on Newbury Street, a block from the town house. They had delicious breakfast sandwiches, fancy appetizers, and good wine. As she walked up and down the cramped aisles gathering bounty for an appetizer plate, she made sure to grab a can of tuna fish. The cashier let her borrow a can opener.

"You must be hungry," he said, quirking an eyebrow as she opened the can in front of him.

She smiled. "Oh, it's not for me."

As she turned onto the judge's block, feathery snowflakes began to fall. The street looked like a fairyland, decked out for the holidays in wreaths and lights and window candles. The judge's house alone was dark and gloomy. But as Madison walked up to the front steps, she saw a sign of hope. A spot of silver between two bushes, right where she'd left it. Bending down, she picked up the last can of tuna, and saw that it had been licked clean, recently enough to still give off that fishy smell. She set the new can down in its place, waiting. Within minutes, Lucy appeared, slinking elegantly from behind a bush with a familiar yowl and attacking the tuna with a ferocious appetite. When she'd finished eating, Madison scooped her up, and together they went off to meet the bus.

Acknowledgments

....

Writing a book can be a solitary undertaking, especially during a global pandemic. But I am fortunate to work with the best people in publishing, who support me, inspire me, and make even the tough moments feel like fun.

This is my fifth book for my brilliant editor, Jennifer Enderlin, and I'm more grateful than ever for the opportunity to work with her. Jen has an unerring instinct for what a book needs, the vision for how to achieve it, and the patience to let it unfold. I am a better author for working with her, and this is a much better book. I'm also grateful for the talented and dedicated team at St. Martin's Press whose hard work brings the book to readers. Special thanks to Erica Martirano, Brant Janeway, Christina Lopez, Jessica Zimmerman, Kejana Ayala, and Michael McConnell.

I can always count on my dear agents, Meg Ruley and Rebecca Scherer, to be there for me and to have my back. I could not do this work without them, nor would I ever want to. I'm so grateful for their hard work and support, as well as that of Chris Prestia and the rest of the team at Jane Rotrosen Agency, and Josie Freedman at CAA for her work on behalf of my film/TV rights.

Thanks also to Crystal Patriarche, Taylor Brightwell, and the team at BookSparks, who are so talented at publicizing books in the digital age. They have brought my work to the attention of countless new readers and are a pleasure to work with.

Most of all, I thank my husband, the one person who's here every day and has to deal with me while I write. He's a saint, and the best teammate I could ever wish for.